"I was just thinking of you," he said, his voice a low, lion-y growl. "And here you are."

"Here I am," she echoed.

Fritzi, just inches from the lawn, whined plaintively and threw all his eight pounds against the leash. *Let me at that grass.*

"Fancy meeting you here at the crack of dawn."

"I was about to say the same thing," she said, wondering if he could hear the erratic pounding of her heart.

His smile dipped deep, spread up to encompass the corners of his eyes in a friendly crinkle. "Well?" He cocked his head, studied her with steadfast eyes. "What *are* you doing here?"

"The dog needs to do his business," she blurted.

He laughed a cool, smooth laugh, refreshing as peppermint. "That explains the pajamas."

Holy jungle jaguar! She was in her pajamas. And not just any pajamas, but red and white reindeer pajamas.

Her cheeks heated as she ducked her head, hurried Fritzi over to the grass, and fought the urge to run back to the houseboat, slam the door, and never come out again.

By Lori Wilde

THE STARDUST, TEXAS SERIES
LOVE OF THE GAME • RULES OF THE GAME
BACK IN THE GAME

THE CUPID, TEXAS SERIES
MILLION DOLLAR COWBOY
LOVE WITH A PERFECT COWBOY
SOMEBODY TO LOVE • ALL OUT OF LOVE
LOVE AT FIRST SIGHT • ONE TRUE LOVE (a novella)

THE JUBILEE, TEXAS SERIES
A COWBOY FOR CHRISTMAS
THE COWBOY AND THE PRINCESS
THE COWBOY TAKES A BRIDE

THE TWILIGHT, TEXAS SERIES
COWBOY, IT'S COLD OUTSIDE
A WEDDING FOR CHRISTMAS
I'LL BE HOME FOR CHRISTMAS
CHRISTMAS AT TWILIGHT
THE VALENTINE'S DAY DISASTER (a novella)
THE CHRISTMAS COOKIE COLLECTION
THE CHRISTMAS COOKIE CHRONICLES:
CARRIE; RAYLENE; CHRISTINE; GRACE
THE WELCOME HOME GARDEN CLUB
THE FIRST LOVE COOKIE CLUB
THE TRUE LOVE QUILTING CLUB
THE SWEETHEARTS' KNITTING CLUB

AVAILABLE FROM HARLEQUIN
THE STOP THE WEDDING SERIES
CRASH LANDING • SMOOTH SAILING • NIGHT DRIVING

THE UNIFORMLY HOT SERIES
BORN READY • HIGH STAKES SEDUCTION
THE RIGHT STUFF • INTOXICATING • SWEET SURRENDER
HIS FINAL SEDUCTION • ZERO CONTROL

COWBOY,
It's Cold Outside

A TWILIGHT, TEXAS NOVEL

LORI WILDE

AVONBOOKS

An Imprint of HarperCollinsPublishers

This is a work of fiction. Names, characters, places, and incidents are products of the author's imagination or are used fictitiously and are not to be construed as real. Any resemblance to actual events, locales, organizations, or persons, living or dead, is entirely coincidental.

First Avon Books mass market printing: November 2017
First Avon Books hardcover printing: October 2017

Print Edition ISBN: 978-0-06-246823-9
Digital Edition ISBN: 978-0-06-246824-6

Cover and stepback art by Larry Rostant

FIRST EDITION

17 18 19 20 21   QGM   10 9 8 7 6 5 4 3 2 1

For John
Sat Nam

ACKNOWLEDGMENTS

To Leonard Cohen (1934–2016), who died while I was writing this book. His music, lyrics, and golden voice have inspired and kept me company in many wee dark hours of early morning when I write love scenes. Thank you, Leonard, for all the pleasure you've given me over the years. You will be greatly missed.

COWBOY,
It's Cold Outside

PROLOGUE

Virtuoso: A person with notable technical skill in the performance of music.

Christmas Eve, 1997

Nashville, Tennessee

"Always remember . . ." Lorena Colton cupped her ten-year-old son's face in her palms, and stared deeply into his eyes.

She lay propped up in the hospital bed against three hard plastic pillows, and wore a thin white gown with tiny blue squares printed on it. The room smelled of Lysol, wilting flowers, and something darker, uglier. Her skin was spaghetti-squash yellow, and her lips the color of sidewalk chalk. A tube, attached to a bag of liquid, twisted into a vein in her arm like a clear plastic snake.

"Always remember . . ."

Cash hauled in a breath, fisted his hands at his sides, and shifted his gaze to the smiling, paper

Santa Claus taped to the wall above his mother's head, and waited for her words of wisdom.

"*Never* fall in love."

Granny stood at the end of the bed, a deep frown pulling her mouth down, arms folded tight over her chest. Grandpa hovered near the closed door, Stetson cocked back on his head, looking just as stony, but less certain of it.

"Love is a trap," Lorena rasped, her lungs rattling thick and wet. "Don't fall for it. You're special, Cash . . ."

She paused, coughed violently into a tissue. Wheezed. Started again. "You've got talent. So much talent."

A hot shiver ran through Cash, landed hard in his belly. Burst. Bloomed.

"You can be *somebody*." Her voice was low, her lips cracked and dry, eyes glistening with fever. "Don't ever let a pretty face and hot body suck you into giving up your dreams."

"Lorena!" Granny snapped. "That's a horrible thing to tell a child!"

Summoning the last bit of strength in her, Lorena glared at Granny. "Cash is destined for great things, but not if he lets an ordinary life trip him up. He needs to know that."

"He needs love. *Everyone* needs love," Grandpa said, stuffing his long broad hands into the pockets of his faded jeans and hunching his shoulders forward.

"Then let him love Euterpe."

"Who the hell is Euterpe?" Grandpa looked confused.

But Cash knew. His mother had been telling him about the Muses since he was a toddler.

"Euterpe is one of the nine Greek Muses." Lorena's voice grew softer still, losing strength the longer she talked, flickering, fading. "Euterpe . . . is the goddess of music, song, and dance."

"There's no such thing as a Muse." Granny moved to cover Cash's ears with her palms. "Stop filling the boy's head with nonsense or he'll end up just like you."

Cash squirmed away from Granny, perched on the edge of his mother's bed.

"Told ya we shouldn't have sent her to that fancy school," Grandpa mumbled. "It gave her funny ideas."

"You're the one who bought her the guitar," Granny accused.

"Falling heedlessly in love got me here." His mother struggled to sit straight up, her eyes flashing fierce for the first time since his grandparents had brought him into the room. For a moment she was her old self again. "Not education. Not the Muses, and certainly not the guitar. Music is the only decent thing in my life. My only saving grace."

What about me? Cash bit his thumbnail. *Aren't I decent?*

"I passed it on to you, Cash." Lorena collapsed back onto the pillows that crinkled when she landed. "The music. My talent. That's why you can't ever let love lead you astray. You can make it as a musician where I failed." Her voice was thin, evaporating.

He could hardly hear her, and he leaned closer.

"You can be famous, Cash, and rich beyond your

wildest dreams. Just don't let love lead you astray. Not ever."

"This is wrong." Grandpa shook his head like a windmill trembling in a West Texas sandstorm. "Wrong in so many ways."

"Hush." Granny grabbed his elbow and pulled him aside, and said in an angry whisper, "She's dying. Let her say what she needs to say. We can fix it later. We won't fail him the way we failed her."

"Pick it up." Lorena looked at Cash and waved a wispy hand at her guitar propped in the corner. The guitar she had never let him touch.

Cash hesitated, wondering if he'd misunderstood, wondering if it was a trick. Mom could be fickle like that. Tell him to do something, and then get mad when he did.

"Go on," she prodded.

Granny and Grandpa huddled near the door, looking as uncertain as he felt. Granny laid a restraining hand on Grandpa's shoulder, shook her head.

Cash eased toward the guitar, and cautiously picked it up.

"It's yours now," his mother said. "My Christmas gift to you."

His heart caught fire, flamed. She was giving him her Gibson? It felt wonderful and terrible at the same time. Why was she giving him her most beloved possession?

Cash frowned, chewed his bottom lip. He didn't like this. Giving away her guitar made no sense.

No. No. A creepy feeling crawled over the back of his neck.

And yet, and yet . . . he wanted that guitar.

Wanted it with every muscle, cell, and bone in his body. Wanted, yearned, craved.

His mother closed her eyes, her hands flopping to her sides as if they were too heavy for her to hold up, and her chest barely rose when she inhaled.

"Mommy?" Cash called her the name he hadn't said since he was a toddler. These days, he mostly called her Lorena, because she asked him to. She didn't want people thinking she was old enough to have a son his age.

"Play for me, Cashie," she murmured without opening her eyes. "Play 'Stone Free.'"

From the doorway, Grandpa snorted. Granny nudged him in the ribs with her elbow. "Wrong," Grandpa muttered. "So wrong."

Reverently, Cash cradled the Gibson, sat in the chair next to his mother's bed, his fingers strumming the first notes of the Jimi Hendrix anthem to restlessness. His mother's favorite song. The first tune she'd ever taught him to play on the cheap pawnshop guitar she'd given him for his sixth birthday.

He sang the lyrics about freedom and rebellion. Sang as if he would never have the chance to sing again. Sang with all the heart and soul he possessed.

Sang and sang and sang.

Several nurses crowded into the room, watching him with wide eyes and opened mouths. Impressed.

Cash paid them no mind. He was playing for his mother. Giving it his all. Everything. Left nothing on the table.

His fingers flew over the strings, his voice ringing out clear and certain with each guitar lick. He'd never played so masterfully.

He was the music and the music was he.

No separation. No thought. Nothing but experience.

Sound. Vibration. Rhythm.

Jimi Hendrix lived inside him, through him.

As Cash sang the last line, the last words, "bye-bye baby," Lorena—his mother, the woman he'd tried so hard to please but could never seem to make happy—smiled softly, took her last breath, and finally flew free.

CHAPTER 1

Rubato: An important characteristic of the Romantic period. It is a musical style where the strict tempo is temporarily abandoned for a more emotional tone.

December 2, twenty years later

Twilight, Texas

Backstage at the one-hundred-forty-year-old Twilight Playhouse, Paige MacGregor wriggled into her skimpy "Santa Baby" costume, finger-pinched red Lycra leggings up around her waist, flashed her doughy-white belly to the full-length mirror, and quite possibly the ghost of John Wilkes Booth, and swore off Christmas cookies forever.

According to local lore—and open to heated debate—after assassinating Lincoln, Booth escaped, and hid out in Twilight, Texas. He assumed the name John St. Helen and got a job as an actor. On his deathbed, St. Helen, aka Booth, supposedly confessed his true identity.

"Sorry, John," Paige apologized. "But if you don't want to see the sad evidence of my total lack of self-control, you shouldn't haunt theaters."

She was the first of the five Santa's helpers to arrive, and the quiet of the old limestone building offered momentary respite from the extravagant Dickensian hullabaloo ruling the town square. Paige took a deep inhale, exhaled long and slow.

Breathe.

At the narrow oval window overlooking the flat roof of Perk's coffee shop next door, Earl Pringle's pet crow, Poe, pecked at the pane—*tap-tap-tap*—and glowered at her with murderous intent.

Poe was a moody cuss. You couldn't judge Twilightites by him. He was tiny for a crow, barely larger than a female grackle, which might explain his grumpiness. He cocked his shoulders and flared his wings as if trying to convince her that he was a ferocious raven.

Paige pretended to startle because she knew what it was like to be on the short side, and hey, everyone needed an ego boost now and again, even small crows trying to prove themselves worthy of poetic names.

Poe gave a loud "Caw," satisfied that he'd scared her, and flew away to find new folks to terrorize.

She moved to the window clouded with decades of dirt and grime, called, "Go forth and nevermore."

Hey, were those snowflakes?

Her obsessive-compulsive gene wished for window cleaner and a rag, but her curiosity overrode that urge. She undid the rusty latch and, with some effort, shoved open the window for a better view at the street below. The smell of dark roast and yeasty pastries teased her nose, and watered her mouth.

No. No more sweet treats.

Behind the theater and the town square, Lake Twilight stretched sapphire blue, a dazzling jewel in Hood County's crown. If she leaned out the window far enough and craned her neck to the left, she could just make out her uncle Floyd's houseboat where she was crashing for the holidays, and/or until she reglued the fractured shards that were her life back together.

Delicate white flakes coasted silently from the sky, sprinkling trees, roofs, cars, and heads of passersby. Her West Texas heart leaped joyously.

She'd grown up in barren desert surrounded by oil and sand, far away from water and snow. And she was thrilled by the white stuff here in North Central Texas, even though she knew the ground was too warm for it to stick. For this one spectacular moment, Twilight looked like a shaken snow globe.

She took another deep breath, savored the sight for as long as she dared, then reluctantly pulled back inside and shut the window.

With a dreamy sigh, she kicked off her Skechers and plunked down onto the creaky rocking chair. The paint was distressed-dingy white, chipped by advanced age and a vast collection of butts.

Paige zipped up knee-length, black-vinyl, spiked-heeled costume boots. Topped her chestnut, chin-length pageboy with a green elf hat, and examined the results in the mirror.

Turned sideways, sucked in her gut.

"What do you think, John? Give it to me straight.

I know I'm no Eartha Kitt, but put me in a couple of Spanx and I can pull off this hot elf thing. Right?"

She spun around to get a rear view, but her ankle turned in the stiletto boot and she had to grab hold of the mirror to keep from toppling over. "Okay, okay, Spanx and deportment lessons."

It had been years since she'd worn stilettoes. She took a second look, brushed her hair back from her forehead, and reapplied her lipstick. Good enough. Time to clear out. The other assistants would be here soon and they'd need the dressing room.

Carefully, she minced down the stairs, past the stage where the hands were setting up, and went into the auditorium.

The Twilight Playhouse was one of the oldest existing US theaters that still hosted performances, and it was the only building on the town square to have kept its primary function since the town was founded in 1875.

The theater predated the township, having been built the previous year. Next door to what was back then a saloon, but was now a fine dining restaurant nostalgically dubbed 1874.

Not that Paige could afford to eat there.

The playhouse had undergone a historically correct renovation a few years back when Emma and Sam Cheek took over as owners, so while everything looked the way it had almost a century and a half ago, and the exterior was one hundred percent original, the auditorium itself was essentially brand-new.

The theater seated three hundred people, and during the month of December, every performance sold out. This year's Christmas play was *Elf* and on

Saturdays and Sundays they held a two P.M. matinee in addition to the evening performance.

Numerous green wreaths, with red velvet ribbon streamers connecting them, hung from the white limestone walls, festive and inviting. Stacks of programs sat on the apron of the stage, waiting for Santa's helpers to pass them out to theatergoers.

From the slip of light filtering in through the open side doors, the colossal Italian crystal chandelier aggressively created rainbows, dappling the stage and orchestra pit in luminous prisms that twinkled and danced.

Someone had suspended a wedding-bouquet-sized clump of mistletoe from the chandelier's central branch, inviting the audience to indulge in stolen kisses.

Aww, Christmas in Twilight.

Paige picked up an armful of programs, tucked them into her elbow, and tottered over the thick rose-patterned carpet to the theater lobby. No one was at the main reception desk, but rummaging sounds came from the closet on the other side of the room.

"Emma?" Paige called.

"Nope." Colorfully tattooed, multiple-pierced, purple-dreadlocked Jana Gerard popped her head from the closet.

"Oh it's you, Jana."

"Sorry to disappoint. Emma hopped over to Caitlyn's flower shop to replace the blooms." Jana waved at the wilted poinsettias that sat in baskets on the long marble countertop.

From the closet, Jana dragged a life-sized cardboard cutout of an acoustic guitar protected by a sheet of thin clear plastic. The playhouse had used the guitar to adorn the lobby for the summer performance of *Oklahoma*.

"What's that for?" Paige tilted her head.

"Sesty's decorating for the Brazos Music Review fundraiser tomorrow night, and Emma said we could borrow the guitar." Sesty Langtree was a local event coordinator, and one of Jana's two bosses.

A few years back, Jana had moved to conservative Twilight from keep-things-weird Austin, and with her flamboyant appearance, she stood out like a scarlet rose in a planter box of white lilies.

No one knew much about Jana and rumors dogged her heels, which were usually clad in leather motorcycle boots stubbed with metal spikes. The speculations about Jana's past ran the gamut from the absurd—she shot a man for cheating on her—to the sublime—she'd donated a kidney to a sick lover, friend, parent, sibling, child, what have you, but alas, they'd tragically died anyway.

While the truth of Jana's abandonment of the state's capital city for the hinterlands of the close-knit tourist town of Twilight was probably much more mundane, she did nothing to quell the hearsay, and at times actively flamed it. Offering sly smiles and lurid winks.

Paige understood the temptation toward mysteriousness. Even though she had relatives in Twilight, and she was not nearly as exotic as Jana, she, too, had been the topic of whispered speculation.

"Need any help?" Paige asked as Jana hoisted the cardboard guitar onto her back.

Jana eyed her. "You've got your hands full, and I'm not real confident in your ability to walk a straight line in those heels."

"Me either," Paige admitted, but she put down the programs and moved to open the left side exit door.

"Thanks," Jana said.

"Excuse me." Paige raised her voice to the tourists packing the sidewalk. "Woman coming through."

The throng shifted, cutting a narrow path for Jana to join the flow of foot traffic.

And she was off, swallowed up as the crowd closed ranks again. The only visible sign of her was the bobbing cardboard guitar surfing over heads.

Right then, the other four Santa's helpers came bustling in through the door that Jana had just exited, snow-dusted and laughing. They greeted Paige merrily, and trundled off to the dressing room.

All the Santa's helpers had been told to get into costume early so the actors could have the dressing rooms at one-thirty. It was now 12:55. The helpers would work the lobby, greeting guests, passing out programs, manning the cloak room, guiding visitors to their seats, and selling refreshments at the bar.

"You're gonna do great," Paige said, giving herself a first-day-on-the-job pep talk. "Just don't trip and break your neck in the dang boots and you'll be fine."

She spied the droopy poinsettias. A little water and time out from under the heat vents and they would rebound. Taking the initiative, she watered the plants and temporarily relocated them to the closet.

The side door of the theater opened again, this

time ushering in a red-cheeked Emma carrying a giant basket of various white winter flowers. Emma was in her midthirties, and stood a full two inches shorter than Paige's five-foot-two height, possessed flame-red naturally curly hair, peaches-and-cream skin, and an easy smile.

Emma Parks Cheek had once been a Broadway actress, and occasionally starred in a movie or two, but mostly she kept busy running the Twilight Playhouse, and riding herd on her veterinarian husband, Sam, Sam's teenage son, Charlie, from another marriage, and their seven-year-old daughter, Lauren.

Emma stopped short and peered around the basket. "Where did the poinsettias go?"

"I moved them to the closet to make room for the new flowers."

"Why, thank you, Paige. That was considerate." Emma hefted the basket onto the marble counter, moving it this way and that, cocking her head to assess her handiwork, attempting to find the most strategic spot from all angles.

"No problem."

"I should have taken care of the flowers sooner, but when I stopped by the clinic to drop off Sam's lunch, he had a whole different kind of meal in mind." She wriggled her auburn eyebrows. "Word to the wise, a quickie on an exam table is not as sexy as it sounds."

"I . . . um . . . never thought." Paige pressed a palm to the back of her head. "Well . . . um, okay."

"Sorry, was that too much information?" Emma grinned as if she wasn't the least bit sorry. Her husband was one smoking hottie and she didn't mind letting everyone know they had a spicy sex life.

In all honesty, it wasn't Emma's frank talk that gave Paige pause, rather it was the realization that she'd not ever done anything halfway intrepid as a quickie on an exam table.

The bravest thing she'd ever done was to take up residence on a houseboat. And as far as sex went, well, she wasn't exactly a femme fatale, never mind the skimpy Santa Baby costume.

"Now if you want to talk sexy . . ." Emma lowered her voice.

No, no, Paige did not want to talk sexy time with her employer.

"Room nine at the Merry Cherub has a seven-foot jetted tub. Fun!" Emma paused, her face turning dreamy at a spicy memory. "Or try a midnight rendezvous underneath the Sweetheart Tree in Sweetheart Park. But *do* bring a blanket. And you might want to wait for summer."

"Um, doesn't that violate public nudity laws?"

Emma looked like a sly cat that had slurped up all the cream. "It's amazing the things you can do with your clothes on. Plus, sometimes a girl has to let down her hair and take a walk on the wild side."

Wild side, huh? Yeah, well, about that . . . not her strong suit. Paige was more the look-both-ways-ten-times-before-crossing-the-street type. And her hair was cut in a short bob. Nothing to let down.

"But I shouldn't be standing here gabbing about sex," Emma said. "Lots to do."

"How can I help?"

"Guard the doors and do not let anyone in until

one-thirty. The town council has been riding my butt about letting people in early." Emma rolled her eyes as commentary on the meddlesome town council. "You'll only have to monitor the side door. All the rest are locked. Unlock them exactly at one-thirty."

Keep guests out for twenty-five minutes? Sure, she could do that.

Emma stopped on her way into the auditorium. "Oh, and, Paige."

"Yes?"

"You have the most genuine smile I've ever seen. Use it. And often."

"Thanks." Her stomach tingled, fizzed. She smiled a grateful smile, wanting Emma to know just how much she appreciated the job.

Emma disappeared. Leaving Paige more determined than ever to please her new boss.

She marched over to monitor the side door at the exact moment a guy pushed his way in, bringing with him a bracing breath of cool December air.

She was just about to reroute the intruder when their eyes met. *Crash. Bam. Wham.*

Head-on collision.

They both stilled instantly. Gazes fused.

Man. O. Man.

It felt as if the wand of fate had conjured him straight from a fairy tale about stalwart knights and fair damsels.

Snow dusted his thick ebony curls and his broad shoulders were clad in a faded denim jacket over a red plaid flannel shirt. He was average height, five-ten or -eleven, but he had a presence about him that made him seem much larger.

He was lean and narrow-hipped in a pair of well-worn Wranglers. Only the Patek Philippe watch at his left wrist and his handmade James Leddy cowboy boots said he was anything more than an ordinary cowboy.

But his smile!

Dazzling. White. Killer-diller.

Oh, that smile was a dangerous thing! Sprung from full, angular lips that twitched irresistibly as he stared at her—into her—with laser beam focus.

It was a dynamite, TNT, nitroglycerin kind of smile that detonated every nerve ending in Paige's body. Rattling her foundation. Firing off round after round of tingly, breathtaking explosions.

Boom. Boom. Boom.

Euphoric devastation.

A surge of energy, a deep thrill that commenced in her belly, arced up through her heart and lungs, triggered a helpless smile of her own, and scrambled her nervous system. Tempting her to chase the feeling with a kite and key.

"Hello, Santa *Baby*." The last word dripped off his lips like liquid sex and she forgot that she was supposed to say, *Doors don't open until one-thirty.*

Instead, her jaw dropped and her tongue welded to the roof of her mouth, and she made a guttural sound. "Um . . . um . . ."

His smile deepened, moved up to crinkle around his heart-stoppingly gorgeous gray eyes. No doubt about it, he was accustomed to twisting up tongues.

He swaggered nearer, sauntering in an Old West gunslinger gait, the door closing behind him, the sound of his boots reverberating across the polished marble floor.

And still she did not tell him to leave, mainly because she couldn't find her voice. It had gotten tangled in his lasso smile.

The way he moved, smooth and easy, slammed into her chest and kidnapped her breath. She couldn't talk. Couldn't breathe. Couldn't think. She was a fish on a hook. Well and truly caught.

"I'm here for the performance," he said.

Wait outside, she should have said, but her tongue remained glued to the roof of her mouth, peanut butter stuck.

Her first day on the job and she couldn't complete one simple task—tell this red-hot stranger to wait outside with everyone else until the doors officially opened.

Clearly, he was not a man accustomed to following the rules. What applied to regular folk didn't apply to Greek gods in cowboy clothing, did it?

C'mon. Snap out of it. Remember what happened the last time you went gaga over a guy?

"I'm sorry," she said, meaning to sound firm, but somehow her words came out alarmingly shaky. "But we've got a strict schedule to keep and we're not open to the public until one-thirty."

"It's eight minutes after one." He turned his wrist so she could see the face of his expensive watch. Showoff. "Not that early."

"Rules are rules."

"Even in my case?" He gave her a look that said,

Are you kidding me right now? As if she should know who he was. As if he was somebody.

Cocky. He was amazing and he knew it.

His attitude rubbed her the wrong way. He wasn't different than any of the other people lining up waiting to be let in. Peeved and vowing not to be swayed by his lively eyes and knowing grin, she pointed to the sidewalk. "Out, mister."

"But—"

"No excuses."

"I'm—"

"Go." She snapped her fingers, sent him her fiercest scowl, even though her knees were gelatin. He didn't need to know that.

Instead of leaving, he strolled closer.

Paige's heart skipped some beats. Now what?

The stranger studied her with half-lidded eyes and intense interest as if she were the most fascinating creature he'd ever seen. Her. Plain old Paige MacGregor, the most ordinary girl, was being stared at as if she were the most extraordinary thing.

The hair at the nape of her neck tickled. She curled her fingernails into her palms, and gulped.

"No one has to know you let me in early," he whispered. "It'll be our little secret."

He was fully in control. He knew it. She knew it. They both knew she was melted wax in the heat of his sexy stare.

Damn him.

"Leave," she said, and added unsteadily, "Please."

"What do I have to do to get you to bend the rules?" he coaxed, dipped his head, lowered his lips. "Let you kiss me?"

He was teasing, trying to get her goat. She could see it in his eyes, but the joke tumbled into the pit of her anxiety, pinged off her every nerve ending.

Standing here, smelling his stunning scent, feeling the heat from his rock-solid body radiate into her, she wanted more than anything on the face of the earth to turn tail and run.

But she wouldn't.

Couldn't.

For one thing, she'd promised Emma she'd guard the door. For another, if she took off running in the stilettoes she'd certainly fall and bust her ass.

Not. Going. To happen.

He must have seen something on her face, in her body language, because he stepped back. "Only eighteen more minutes now."

"And that's when you can come in." She pointed, surprised by how forceful and commanding her words shot out.

He grinned devilishly, frankly amused, and latched on to her gaze with eyes the color of San Francisco fog. Not that Paige knew firsthand what San Francisco fog looked like. She'd never been out of Texas.

His dusky eyes held the promise of landscapes she yearned for—windswept moors and craggy mountains, foamy ocean waves and rocky deserts, stony castles and petal-strewn gardens.

He'd been around. Seen the world. And his magnificent, experienced eyes left her winded and wondering and wanting.

Wanting so much more than she had a right to claim.

Dear Lord. She clicked the lock on that pitch of

desire. Slammed it shut. Spun the tumbler. Steeled her gaze. Offered him nothing.

His eyes gentled, no longer filled with daring mischief. Nonchalantly, he shifted his attention to the door.

Which she was grateful for because it meant he was going.

Plus, when he turned, she had an unobstructed view of his backside cupped so enticingly in those faded Levi's. A cowboy's butt—firm, muscular, built for endurance—a masculine butt that dared her to touch.

She sucked in a short, shallow breath, and ignored her tingling fingers.

The sleeves of his denim jacket were pushed up enough to reveal tanned wrists roped with strong veins. Long, calloused fingers took hold of the doorknob.

No adornment on those hands. No rings or tattoos. Plain. Durable. Bare. Simple but not simplistic, he was a man of rugged style and surprising grace.

He opened the door.

Going.

Leaving.

Yay!

So why did she want to throw herself onto the marble tile floor, fling her arms around his ankles, and beg him to stay?

"One more thing . . ." He turned back.

Yes? Yes? Yes?

Eyes twinkling like stardust, he studied her a long moment without saying a word. But his mouth, oh his knowing mouth, quirked up at the corners as if to say, *You're as intrigued by me as I am by you.*

She gave him a polite, noncommittal smile in return. He might be interested right now, but he wouldn't be if he knew her.

"What's this sweetheart legend I've been hearing about?" His voice was low and cozy as a fleece blanket in front of a roaring fire on a cold winter evening. There was a lazy lilt to his tone, and his words stretched out slow and sultry.

But there was something steely in there as well. A warning.

It was in the way his tongue hit the back of his teeth hard on the "t" sounds. Determined. Stubborn. A quality and hue that said when this man set his mind to a goal, come hell or high water, he would never, ever give up.

Paige shivered. Just a little.

But he noticed. His eyes darkened and narrowed, taking measure of her.

"Huh?" she said because she was so distracted by his potent sexuality she couldn't remember what he'd just asked.

"The wishing well, the old tree with lovers' names carved in it, the statue of a hugging couple in the park. What's that all about?"

"Uh," she said, and spouted off a condensed version of the town's well-known lore. "Rebekka Nash and Jon Grant, childhood sweethearts from Missouri. They were separated by the Civil War. She was a Southern Belle and he turned Yankee soldier. But they never stopped loving each other. Fifteen years later they met accidentally on the banks of the Brazos River at twilight, and they were reunited."

"Twilight, huh? Hence the name of the town?"

"Indeed."

"Ah." He laughed. A beautiful sound that sent her heart thumping. "There's nothing like a good romantic legend. Bet it stirs tourism."

"You got it."

His stare drilled into her one last time and then he left without another word. Opened the door. Walked out. Disappeared into the crowd.

Gone forever.

Good-bye.

Good riddance.

She was glad he left. Well, not glad, really. Relieved. Yes. Relieved she'd never have to see him again.

Yes, relief. That was the emotion.

Then why did it feel so much like disappointment?

"Paige?"

She turned, spied Emma standing in the doorway between the lobby and the auditorium. "Yes?"

Emma ticked her head to one side in her effervescent way. "I forgot to mention that a VIP will be dropping by."

"Um." A sick feeling washed over her. "What does your VIP look like?"

"Handsome cowboy, stunning gray eyes. Saunters like he owns the world. You can't miss him."

CHAPTER 2

Carol: A song or hymn celebrating Christmas.

Feeling naked without his trademark Stetson, beard, and shaggy shoulder-length locks, Cash Colton moved through the crowd decked out in Dickensian-era costumes.

He'd shed the outlaw image that had been his trademark, and he had to keep reminding himself that clean-cut was his new smokescreen. Without it, he'd be mobbed.

Even so, people were noticing.

Heads turned, especially feminine heads. Although he was used to that. He'd been born with the ability to command female attention. Part of the appeal that had made his music career . . .

. . . and thoroughly crashed it.

Although the square was packed with tourists, the town itself was small. Seven thousand, according to the population sign on Highway 377. He could hide out from the wide world in Twilight, but once people figured out who and where he was, the news would swell like wildfire.

Cash knew about the reality of small towns. He had been born in a place half the size of this one. Tarred and feathered there too. Small towns could look enticing on the surface, but beneath often lurked a dark underbelly of intolerance, ignorance, and harsh judgment.

Been there. Done that. Got the hell out.

So why was he here?

Oh yeah, he was doing a favor for his best friend, Emma Cheek—who he'd met when they were both young and starting their careers—while at the same time keeping a low profile, hiding out from the paparazzi, and searching for his creative mojo.

The last one was damn elusive. He felt as if he'd spent the past year roaming a barren emotional desert, empty, aimless, lost.

On the street, people nodded and smiled at each other in the way of longtime neighbors. Smiles full of acceptance and respect. There was a deep-seated trust here you didn't often find in big cities. Nostalgia washed over him.

Don't fall for it.

He was not going to trip for gorgeous, daydream-hazel eyes, cute freckles sprinkled like cinnamon over a pert little nose, short dark brown hair that curled into question marks at her chin, and a sexy Santa Baby outfit.

Hell, why was he even thinking about the adorable elf who had thrown him out of the theater? She certainly was not his type. She was too girl next door. Not even those do-me stiletto boots could hide that fact.

Not that there was anything wrong with girl next door. She just wasn't for him. All he had to offer was a hot night in his bed, and she was too sweet for that. Still it didn't stop his imagination from unbuttoning her blouse, slipping it off her creamy shoulder, and burying his face against her soft, sweet skin.

McDang, son. He heard his musical career mentor Freddie Frank's voice in his head. *Straighten up and fly right.* If it hadn't been for Freddie, his life could have taken a serious wrong turn, and he respected the man's advice, but his wicked mind kept going.

He liked her refined grit and the way her round chin hardened to stone when she took a stand. Contrast that with her eager grin, acquiescent voice, and optimistic body language. She was a people-pleaser with a determined spine. The spunky kid, tender-hearted, but no pushover.

Something, or someone, had toughened her up.

That bothered him. The idea of someone hurting her didn't set well. What son of a bitch would mistreat a woman with wide Bambi eyes and a dazzling smile that sparked up Texas?

It was all he could do not to walk back into that theater, gather her in his arms, pull her against his chest, and assure her that everything was going to be all right.

Yeah, as if she'd go for that. When he teasingly suggested she kiss him, she looked as if she was going to haul off and slug him in the gut instead.

Not everyone understood his sense of humor. His

ex-girlfriend, Simone, claimed he used teasing as a shield against deeper feelings. Hell, who knew? Maybe she was right.

But he couldn't deny something had passed between him and Miss Spunky Kid.

From the moment their eyes met, he heard chords in his head, his right brain skipping around, playing with sound and images, tickled by the flood of musical fodder rushing in.

Compelling, given that he hadn't heard the music, hadn't written a note, hadn't even picked up a guitar with intent to play, in over a year. His primary guitar, the one he composed on—dubbed "Lorena" because it was his mother's Gibson—had been stolen at the same time all the stuff went down with his ex and the band. The added loss of the guitar had compounded his creative block.

That was one of the reasons he'd gone to Peru. Get his head straight. Get back on track.

Cash was no angel. He'd been with his share of women, but he'd never felt anything quite like that derailing electrical jolt he'd felt when he'd looked into Spunky Kid's eyes. It was as if they'd met before, as if they'd known each other in another life, as if somehow they were fated.

Bizarre idea. He was not the type of guy who believed in anything remotely mythical or mystical, unless you counted the musical Muse.

Euterpe.

The Greek Muse of lyrical poetry and song. Now *her*, he believed in. Hmm. Maybe Spunky Kid was his Euterpe.

That thought took his breath.

If it wasn't for Emma and her charity event, he wouldn't even be playing music. He owed her a big favor, and when she'd called it in, he hadn't hesitated; one, because it was Emma and he would do anything for his best friend, and two, because he owed his record label a new album and the clock was ticking.

And he'd been frozen like a snowman on the Arctic tundra.

But now . . . oh right this minute . . . since looking into Euterpe's eyes, there was a whisper in his ear, a fledgling hope fluttering its wings, a warble of a song rising from the wasteland of his career.

A comeback.

His cell phone vibrated in his back pocket, playing Leonard Cohen's "Nevermind," the song he'd added as his ringtone after his band, The Truthful Desperadoes, split up. Granted, the song was a bit dark, but that's where his mood had been. Maybe it was time for a new ringtone.

The phone buzzed again.

Cash stepped from the foot traffic into a narrow alleyway, fished the cell from his pocket, and peeked at the screen.

It was his manager, Deet Larken, who he'd been dodging for months. He almost didn't take the call, but fell into the suck of guilt, and hit Accept.

"S'up, Deeter?"

"Good mood?" his manager asked as if that was a rare thing.

Which surprised Cash. He'd known Deet for over a decade. Trusted him with his money, his career . . .

hell, with his life. When Deet started his own music industry management company, Cash had been his first client.

"Yeah," Cash said, realizing it was true. He *was* in a good mood. "I am."

"Um. Okay, I'll call you back later."

"Wait . . . what is it?"

"Not now. Don't wanna spoil your good mood."

Air decamped from his lungs. Cash rested his forehead against the cool brick wall of the building he was standing in front of and he caught a vague whiff of garbage from the Dumpster down the way.

"Deet." He injected cement in his voice. "Just tell me."

"It's Sepia," Deet said. "They're making serious noises about dropping you."

Sepia had been The Truthful Desperadoes recording label, and after the group split, Cash had been the only member of the band they'd offered a solo contract. He'd taken the deal more out of inertia than anything else. Deet handled all the legal machinations. His head had been so screwed up, his career and personal life falling in shambles around him.

"That's kind of rash," he mumbled.

"It *has* been a year since you signed that contract." Deet cleared his throat. "Please tell me you've got something I can show them. You know how this business goes. They could drop you for farting in a windstorm."

"Chill, Deet. I haven't been dropped from a contract in years."

"Which means you're due. Plus, you fell off the

end of the earth for a solid year, man. Sepia is nervous. You're looking unstable. Think about it. You had your favorite guitar stolen, lost your band and the love of your life, all at the same time."

"Simone was not the love of my life," Cash disagreed.

"All right, your muse, then."

Cash thought of the girl at the theater, heard a fresh rustle of music sweep through his head. "Simone wasn't my muse either."

"Clearly, or you would have proposed to her like a sane man and kept everything churning along smoothly. If you had proposed, she wouldn't be—" Deet broke off abruptly, tension vibrating through the phone.

The hairs on Cash's forearm rose. He knew Deet well. Something was up. "She wouldn't be what?"

"I didn't want to tell you over the phone." Deet chuffed. "But I suppose it's better to hear it from me than TMZ."

Cash clenched his teeth, braced himself. "Just tell me."

Deet paused. He could be dramatic that way. "Simone and Snake are getting married in Los Angeles on New Year's Eve."

Snake, back when his name was Jake Snider, used to be Cash's good friend. Cash grunted, surprised but not upset. He'd been unable to commit to Simone. How could he blame her for moving on? It would have been nice if she'd broken up with him first before slipping between the sheets with Snake, but hey, it was what it was.

"I thought she and Snake were a short-term thing," he said.

"You know Simone. She's got to have someone to take care of her."

"Well, good for them." Cash nodded as if Deet could see him through the phone, glad they weren't on FaceTime. "I hope they're very happy together."

"You don't sound bitter." Deet seemed amazed.

"That's because I'm not." A man couldn't be bitter when his woman cheated because he couldn't do the whole diamond-ring, overblown-ceremony, I-love-you-forever-and-ever thing. That's not to say it hadn't hurt. It was just that Cash knew the score. If he wanted a high-flying career, he had to avoid anchors and chains.

"That's not the worst of it," Deet went on.

"No?"

"She and Snake also got a sweet recording deal with Apex Records."

Ah, now that explained why Simone was still with Snake. "No kidding," he said mildly, gut churning. "A duet deal."

"You're not the least bit jealous?"

Of a guy named Snake? "No."

"Wow, once upon a time you would have given your left nut for a recording contract with Apex."

He would if he wasn't in such a slump. Right now he was having trouble meeting his contract with Sepia. At this moment, an offer from Apex would be the kiss of death for his career. The Amazon *had* taught him a few things. He wasn't ready. He was still in regroup mode. His time would come. As long as he kept his eye on the prize, and his head in the game and his mind off women, he would achieve his loftiest dreams. No doubt.

He was free after all. No band. No girlfriend. Nothing to hold him back. Stone *freaking* free.

"So I can tell Sepia you have something?" Deet prodded.

Not quite yet, but it was in the works. As of ten minutes ago when he'd looked into a pretty girl's eyes.

"Look, Deet, I'm standing in an alley watching someone dressed like Tiny Tim hobble by. Not the best time for a conversation."

"Tiny what? Who?"

"Never mind," he said. "Any other reason you called besides busting my balls over Sepia, Simone, and Apex?"

Deet made an odd noise. "I'm worried about you, man. First you disappeared to the Amazonian jungle and now to Bumfuzzle, Texas."

"Twilight."

"Twilight, Bumfuzzle, whatever. The deal is you're far away from home, all alone at Christmas, and your ex is marrying your former bandmate."

"Believe me," Cash said, peering from the alley at the steady parade of merry revelers dressed in costume. "The last thing I am is alone."

"Ah, I see." Deet let out a you-naughty-devil laugh. "Some sweet country girl has caught your eye?"

"Nope," he said easily, but thought of the sexy Santa Baby, and a fresh riff of chords played through his head. A song unfurled quickly, hotly, as the best songs often did.

Euterpe.

His muse.

He was unstuck. Thanks to Euterpe and her sweet little smile. She brought rain to his barren soul and watered the roots of his creativity. He had no choice but to bloom.

And he couldn't wait to see her again. Find out for sure if she really was the cause of this tiny flicker of hope. A melody. A chorus. Lyrics. Starting to assemble and gel. It was the end to his miserable creative block.

Cash was already tapping out a beat against his thigh. He glanced at his watch. Saw it was one-thirty. Shifted his phone to the other ear. Left the alley. Wandered around the corner back to the Twilight Playhouse just as Euterpe flung open the doors and let the crowd in.

"Thanks for calling, Deet. I gotta go. You have a Merry Christmas."

"I'll try and stall them, what with it being the holidays and all. It looks like you're in a good place. I'm glad."

"Yeah." Cash smiled as he glanced across the snow-dusted heads of the theatergoers and watched his muse usher people inside. "I think I just might be."

He moved toward her, still smiling.

But she wasn't looking his way, and once folks started flowing in, she turned and headed in the opposite direction.

An elderly woman, smelling of violets, wearing shiny new black patent boots, and holding on to a rolling walker suddenly teetered as the wheels hit the threshold bump between the damp sidewalk and the slick marble floors of the theater.

Instinct—he'd lived with his grandparents long enough to understand the combined hazards of new boots, glassy flooring, and geriatric gaits—and quick reflexes had him jumping to take her elbow to steady her before she tumbled.

"Oh," she gasped. "Oh my! You saved me from a serious spi—" She broke off and stared up at him, her jaw hinging open.

"Ma'am?" he asked. "Are you okay?"

"Liam, Liam." She grasped with trembling fingers, reached over to clutch the forearm of her elderly male companion. "Am I hallucinating or did Cash Colton just save me from breaking a hip?"

"I dunno, Dotty Mae." Liam scratched his chin. "He don't look shaggy enough for Cash Colton."

"He cut his hair and shaved, for heaven's sake. But it's him, I tell you."

Liam studied Cash through thick-lensed glasses. "I dunno . . ."

"I'm telling you it's him. Cash went into hiding since his no-good girlfriend cheated on him and busted up The Truthful Desperadoes, and his creativity shriveled up. I was reading all about it in *Uptown Country* magazine."

Liam looked puzzled. "How can the country be uptown?"

"There was speculation he'd gone to live with some native tribe in the Amazon," Dotty Mae mused. "Shipibo, I believe they're called."

Liam cupped a hand behind his ear. "You shipped what from Amazon? I thought I told you to stop buying so many damn books."

Cash suppressed a grin. Actually, Dotty Mae was

right. He had spent the last ten months ambling through South America trying to figure out what to do with the rest of his life. And he'd come up empty.

"I didn't order any books . . . oh never mind." Dotty Mae waved a hand. "You're missing the point. Cash Colton just saved my life."

"If that's Cash Colton, what's he doing in Twilight?" Liam asked.

"What do you think? Emma Cheek's cowboy music thing."

"I thought you said he was out of the country."

Dotty Mae rolled her eyes. "Well, clearly he's back."

"If it even is Cash Colton," Liam said, "I'm not convinced."

"OMG, y'all!" screamed a teenager in black Lycra yoga pants and pink angora sweater. "It's Cash Colton!"

Cash cringed, braced himself. Fought every urge pushing him to flee as a pack of teenaged girls descended. The last thing he wanted was to be trapped here signing autographs. Emma was expecting him before the curtain went up.

But he'd learned a long time ago, you couldn't always get what you want. Nod to the Rolling Stones for that tidbit of wisdom.

"See, see." Dotty Mae nudged Liam in the ribs with her elbow. "I told you it was him." To the teenagers, she said, "Out of my way girls. I spotted him first," and pushed her walker right through the middle of them.

"Could you sing a few bars of 'Reality Moves Fast'?" begged one of the teenagers.

"Reality Moves Fast" was Cash's most popular, and his least favorite, song.

"Sorry, honey," he apologized with a wink as he signed the back of a grocery store receipt Dotty Mae had pulled from her purse for him to sign. "I have to save my voice for the performance tomorrow night."

"You're performing in Twilight!" squealed the girl in the pink angora sweater as she fanned herself with a theater program. "Lordy, I've died and gone to heaven."

"You ladies have let the cat out of the bag. It was supposed to be a surprise. Emma Cheek is going to announce it before the play starts."

"And may I suggest y'all take your seats so you can hear all about it?" a familiar voice said. "You can see more of Mr. Colton tomorrow night."

Cash looked down into the bright face of his dear friend Emma, who was dressed as an elf for her role as Jovie in the play. Emma took hold of his hand, tugged him through the theater past all the gawkers, and into her private office.

She shut and locked the door behind them. There was a party in her eyes—lights, happiness, celebration—no one did perky like Emma.

They had met years ago, long before he'd hooked up with Simone. They'd been in a production of *Oklahoma* together at a dinner theater in Branson. She'd played Laurey, and he'd been one of the musicians. The producer was coming on to Emma hot and heavy, and Cash had pretended to be her boyfriend to get her off the hook. After that they became fast friends. Nothing romantic ever developed. While they adored each other, Emma was five years older and there had never been a sexual spark between them, but they were closer than most siblings.

"Steal a girl's thunder, will ya?" Emma said playfully, and gave him a hard hug. "This afternoon was supposed to be the big reveal of my surprise coup— Cash Colton, all the way from South America, headlining my favorite charity. And you go and blow it by oozing charm all over the place and getting recognized."

"I tried my best to be incognito. I cut my hair and beard."

"And only managed to make yourself twice as sexy. Why didn't you slip in the side door early like I suggested?"

"I tried. Some determined young woman threw me out before I had a chance to explain."

"Oh." Emma laughed, eyes glistening. "That's Paige. She's got some trust issues, but she's a hard worker and she's loyal as a German shepherd."

"Paige, huh?" Cash couldn't help grinning. Now she had a name. Paige. Not as romantic as Euterpe, but infinitely more practical. He liked it. Paige. Crisp. Efficient. Down-to-earth.

"Oh ho?" Emma's eyes brightened. "What's that sly grin all about?"

"Nothing."

Emma raised a finger. "Don't toy with her, mister. Paige has been through a lot and the last thing she needs is some wandering cowboy musician breaking her heart."

"Been through a lot? Like what?"

"No, no. Stay away. I know how you attract wounded flowers."

"She didn't strike me as the least bit wounded. On the contrary, she seems quite warriorlike."

"Don't let her tough act fool you. She's all soft and squishy on the inside. Which is why you're not going to bother my newest employee." Emma linked her arm through his. "Now come with me. The show must go on."

After Emma introduced Cash onstage and announced he would be headlining the Cowboy Christmas charity fundraising event, the crowd got to their feet in thunderous applause.

Aww, hell. He didn't deserve that kind of fanfare. He was a musician. Not a soldier or a doctor or a fireman or a cop. He wasn't a hero. He was just lucky.

Emma escorted him to the VIP section, and then went backstage to open the play.

Cash found himself seated beside two big-haired, middle-aged women in cowgirl boots and denim jackets. They kept sending him sidelong glances and grinning at each other. Both wore wedding bands and were holding stemless glasses filled with red wine.

"I like him better without all the hair," one of them whispered to the other.

"Not me. The hairier, the better."

Cash ran a hand over his clean-shaven chin. Hairier was easier, but smooth skin was a nice change of pace.

A woman in a sexy Santa Baby outfit escorted a

couple to their seats on the other side of the aisle. His pulse jumped. It wasn't Paige. He swiveled his head, looking for her in the aisles behind him, but the lights dimmed and that was that.

What the hell? He couldn't ever remember being so immediately smitten. Why her? Why now?

He sat through the play, which was really pretty darn good for a small-town production, but he wouldn't have expected any less from Emma. And yet, he couldn't keep his mind on the performances.

His thoughts kept drifting back to Paige and then music would rise in his head again, drowning out the actors on the stage.

Maybe he'd get a chance to see her again once the play was over.

He pinned his hopes on it, but Emma, that force of nature, didn't give him a chance to breathe. She sent her husband, Sam, to collect him while she was changing out of her costume.

Sam Cheek was a tall, dark-haired man with Native American features. He would have been leading-man handsome except for the long scars across one side of his face. Emma had told him Sam had been attacked by a mountain lion when he was an Eagle Scout on a camping trip. Cash had first met Sam when he'd walked Emma down the aisle as a father substitute to give her away at her wedding. Emma's husband held the hand of an adorable red-haired girl.

"Don't tell me this is Lauren." Cash squatted beside her.

"Yep." Lauren offered him a gap-toothed grin and twirled like a ballerina. "I'm me."

"Last time I saw you, you were knee-high to a

grasshopper." Cash held his hand a couple of inches off the floor to show how short she'd been. They'd come to visit him backstage when The Truthful Desperadoes performed at a concert in Dallas not long after Lauren was born.

"Silly." Lauren giggled. "I was never tinier than a grasshopper." She paused, looked up at Sam. "Was I, Daddy?"

"No, sweetheart. Your uncle Cash is given to hyperbole."

Uncle Cash. He liked how Emma encouraged her kids to call him uncle. As if he was part of the family. As if he fit.

It felt nice. Seeing as how he'd never really fit anywhere. Emma understood. She'd had a rough childhood too. Unstable mother. No brothers or sisters either.

"Hyper . . . hyper what?" Lauren crinkled up her nose that was the exact same shape as her mother's.

"He's exaggerating," Sam explained.

"Oh!" Lauren's eyes popped wide. "You mean he tells tall tales like Grampa Cheek?"

"Exactly like that, my bright girl." Sam puffed up his chest with pride.

"Where's Charlie?" Cash straightened.

"He's thirteen, and doesn't like hanging out with the old folks anymore. He's spending the night with his cousins, but he'll be at your concert tomorrow night."

Cash glanced over his shoulder; the audience was thinning out, but a few people were hovering, hoping to speak to him or get an autograph.

"Looking for someone?" Sam asked.

"Huh?" Cash tried to appear cool, but he was embarrassed at having been caught searching for his muse.

"Oh, I get it. You're worried about fans breathing down your neck. Leave it to me." Sam waved at the looky-loos. "Folks, Mr. Colton will be available for autographs after tomorrow night's fundraiser, but right now, he's our guest and we're about to take him out for dinner."

"Sorry," a man apologized.

"Didn't mean to intrude," said someone else.

"Thanks for coming to Twilight," added another.

Cash raised a hand, rewarding his fans with a smile. "See you tomorrow night."

Emma appeared in street clothes and toned-down makeup. "Are we ready to go? I know it's a little early for dinner," she apologized to Cash as they headed toward the front exit. "But I have to be back at six-fifteen to get ready for the seven o'clock performance."

"No worries." Cash patted his stomach. "I'm hungry enough to eat a bear."

Lauren giggled. "There he goes again, hyper . . . hyper . . . telling tall tales."

Emma laughed and pinched her daughter's cheeks. "Daddy's been trying to teach you big words again, hasn't he?" She winked at Sam and slipped her arm around her husband's waist.

Sam leaned down to kiss her.

Not wanting to intrude on their private moment, Cash went ahead of them, stepping into the lobby, just in time to see Paige exiting.

A full musical score galloped through his head—riffs, licks, chords, rhythm, the whole enchilada.

The doors to the theater were solid oak painted cream with windowpane cutouts. She stopped on the sidewalk, turned, glanced back.

Their eyes were two locomotives traveling in opposite directions on the same track, smashing through the windowpanes and into each other.

Smack! Shatter! Train wreck!

And music. So much music shifting through his head like spilled cargo.

Panic widened her eyes and he felt it too—that flutter of fear, the hot thrilling jolt of pure awareness, the absolute knowing that there was something here for him, and the sheer terror that accompanied it.

Quickly, she spun on her heels and sprinted away. Leaving him bedazzled, befuddled, and bewildered.

Call it fate, call it superstition, call it down right crazy, but for the life of him, Cash couldn't shake the nagging notion that somehow this woman and his musical creativity were intricately entwined.

And he had absolutely no idea how or why.

CHAPTER 3

Beat: The unit of musical rhythm.

Paige had enough time to pop home and walk Fritzi, the poodle she was dog-sitting over the holidays, before she had to be back at the theater for the seven o'clock performance. Her next-door neighbor, Sig Gunderson, had gone back to his native Sweden to visit relatives, leaving two days before Thanksgiving and scheduled to return the day after New Year's.

She'd offered to watch Fritzi for free, but Sig had insisted on paying her. Because she was seriously broke, Paige had not refused, even though she loved taking care of the dog. He kept her company.

She stayed in costume. Wriggling in and out of the Lycra leggings was inconvenient, but she threw on an ankle-length woolen duster over the outfit, took off the neck-breaker stilettoes for safety reasons, and slipped into her well-worn Skechers to make the mile-long hike.

Just as the door of the playhouse closed behind her, something caused her to glance back.

And there he was again.

Emma's VIP.

The cowboy who'd tried to persuade her to let him into the theater early.

The snow was back, falling in fat, lazy circles, airy as ballerina pirouettes. A holly wreath hung over the glass panel of the door, creating a circular frame of spry green around him, as a fine mist frosted the pane.

For a quick tick of a second it was a pure Hallmark movie moment. The loner cowboy outlined by a symbol of Christmas. A picture-perfect postcard, mesmerizing and magical.

It felt weighted, monumental, significant in some unfathomable way.

Spellbound, she couldn't move. Couldn't think. Could only stare and stare and stare . . .

He gifted her with his master-of-the-universe smile and broke her thrall.

Paige gulped and whipped her head around so fast she almost got dizzy.

Panic sent her rushing through the crowded square, boots tucked underneath her arm, the sharp stiletto heels poking her in the side. Zigzagging around food and trinket kiosks, dodging kids waiting in line to see Santa, flying past Dickens characters engrossed in playing their parts.

Her heart pounded, and she had no idea why she was running as if hellhounds were nipping at her ankles.

From the moment she'd laid eyes on him it felt as if the sun had come out fresh and shiny after a year of monsoon rains. As if he were the bearer of rainbows and flowers and promises of spring.

And when he smiled . . . oh when he smiled . . . the world sang and lights were brighter and her nerve endings zipped and zinged and her mouth filled with the sweetest taste and . . . God, oh God, this was trouble.

She knew the feeling. Had been deceived by it before. Wanted nothing to do with it.

When she was a kid, not long after her mom took off, and her dad had first gotten sick and she was learning how to take care of him, she had plugged in the breathing machine he needed during one of his respiratory attacks. In her rush, her fingers had brushed against the light socket and a searing electrical jolt zapped her.

A lightning bolt snapped through her hand. A strange you-are-alive-and-don't-you-forget-it thrill that also hurt. A bite. A warning.

Don't take life lightly. You are not safe.

And that's how she felt right now, lit up, alive, and terrified.

She slowed once she got away from the crush of the town square. Caught her breath, headed down the walkway that curved toward the marina. He wasn't coming after her. She had nothing to run from, nothing to fear.

A sweet sadness plucked at her heart.

The ground was slushy. Her head was still buzzy from eye contact with Mr. Hot Stuff, and she wasn't paying much attention to where she was going and nearly ran smack-dab into her cousin Flynn Mac-Gregor Calloway.

Flynn was strolling up from the lake in a red-hooded cloak, a wicker basket of cookies slung over her left arm, looking like a fairy-tale heroine—which was exactly her personality—spunky, perky, wonder-filled. A peaches-and-cream brunette with wild curly brown hair, slender but solidly build. She was kind and caring and had a sprinkling of freckles across the bridge of her nose just like Paige.

Those Scottish MacGregor freckles. Every woman in their family had them except for Flynn's younger sister, Carrie.

"Whoa ho," Flynn said, and put up a restraining hand to prevent Paige from crashing into her.

"Sorry," Paige apologized.

At thirty-five, Flynn was nine years older than Paige. She was married to her high school sweet-heart, Jesse Calloway, who ran a motorcycle shop on the town square. They had two small children, Grace, who was four, and Ian, eighteen months.

Even though they were almost a decade apart in age, Paige and Flynn had a lot in common. They were both caretakers who had put their own needs aside for a chronically ill family member, and they'd both lost a parent.

Paige admired Flynn because she'd achieved her goal of becoming a kindergarten teacher and still managed to be a good wife, mother, sister, daugh-ter, and friend. Flynn gave her hope. If her cousin could go through what she'd been through, and still find happily-ever-after, maybe, just maybe, if

Paige got her act together, her dreams could come true too.

Right now, that felt impossible.

She was broke, living on a borrowed houseboat, and working several low paying jobs to make ends meet. Her friends—the precious few she'd managed to hang on to during those years she was submersed in caring for her father—were either married with children, traveling the world, in grad school, or running their own businesses.

Whereas, she was stuck where they'd all been in high school. Life had passed her by and she'd begun to despair that she would ever catch up.

"Are you okay? You look . . ." Flynn cocked her head, studied Paige with serious eyes. "Dazed."

"I'm fine. Good. Great!" She tacked on an atta-girl smile, fought off the flush heating her neck.

"Didja see him?" Flynn asked. "You must have seen him at the playhouse."

"Who?"

"Why, Cash Colton, of course."

Oh yeah. Paige had seen him. Twice now. Both times, *boom!* But she wasn't about to let on about that to Flynn. "He's a singer, right?"

"Not just a singer." Flynn's voice sailed high like the catamaran gliding past them on the lake. "A musician. He sings, plays, and writes songs. He's the whole package. Not to mention, drop-dead handsome."

That she knew. "What kind of music?"

"Country-and-western."

That explained it. She'd never been much for hokey lyrics and the twang of a steel guitar, and because she'd been so wrapped up in caring for her father, she hadn't had time for lighthearted pursuits.

"Does Jesse know about your crush on Cash Colton?" Paige teased.

"Jesse knows *he's* my one and only." Flynn grinned. "Doesn't mean I can't appreciate Cash's music. He's awesome."

"I'll have to take your word for it." She made a mental note to check out Colton's music later, just to see what all the fuss was about.

"And you know, Cash is a really good guy to boot. Hard to believe someone as famous as he is would bother to get involved in a small-town charity."

"Why *is* he getting involved?"

"You didn't know? He and Emma have been good friends for years."

"Gotta remember, I'm not from Twilight," Paige reminded her. "And with Dad being sick and all." She shrugged. They both knew what the "and all" meant, but neither one of them touched it.

"We've got to get you off that houseboat more often." Flynn nodded as if it was a serious plan she'd already been fretting over.

"I'm good. Really. I don't need to be in on all the local gossip."

"You have been spending too much time alone. You're twenty-six, and you've led a cloistered life. You should be mixing it up. Dating like crazy." Flynn readjusted the hood on her cloak and a look came into her eyes, a matchmaking kind of look that sent fear rocking over Paige's spine.

"I don't want or need a man."

"Honey," Flynn said in an urgent voice. "I know you don't need a man, but you've got to get back on the horse. You can't let one bad spill ruin you on the entire gender."

"Why do people say that?" Paige asked, shivering a little as the breeze blew over the lake.

"It's just a figure of speech."

"Why do you have to get back on the horse? Why can't you stay off the horse? Why can't you stay as far away from horses as possible? If you did that, you'd never again get thrown. Seems like an easy solution to me. Don't. Get. Back. On. The horse."

Flynn blinked at her, an expression of rueful pity. "Why? Because you'd never have the thrill of riding a horse again."

"I can live with that. Plenty of happy, well-adjusted people go their whole lives without riding a horse."

"We're not really talking about horses, Paige."

"I know that."

"Maybe I'll throw a dinner party just to get you out of the house, and I'll invite some of Jesse's single friends—"

"I was out of the house last night at your Christmas cookie club swap," Paige interrupted, desperate not to get fixed up. She talked fast, hoping it would distract her cousin. "Thank you for inviting me by the way. Everyone was really nice."

"Oh, that reminds me. The reason I came down to the houseboat. You forgot your take-home cookies." Flynn extended the wicker basket stuffed with Christmas cookies.

Paige suppressed a groan. She hadn't forgotten

them. She purposefully left them behind so she wouldn't be tempted to eat the delicious goodies left over from the cookie swap. But she didn't want to be rude, especially since Flynn had made a special trip.

Liar, liar, pants on fire.

Careful. Careful. She had to fit into this costume for the next three weeks through the last performance of *Elf* on Christmas Eve, and the Lycra leggings were already pretty darn snug.

Paige gathered every ounce of willpower she could muster, and gazed longingly at the cookie basket. "Why don't you take them home to Grace and Ian?"

"Please take them," Flynn begged. "My house is overflowing with cookies. And my kids on a sugar high is not a pretty sight. Please, please."

What was a cousin to do? Paige caved. "Give 'em here."

"Thank you, thank you." Flynn handed her the basket. "You're a lifesaver."

"If I gain five pounds and outgrow this costume, it's your fault."

"I'll let it out for you."

"You can't sew," Paige pointed out.

"I'll get someone from the True Love Quilting Club to do it."

"You owe me." Paige bit into a perfect caramel apple cookie, crisp on the edges but chewy in the middle. Yum.

"Name it," Flynn said. "Your wish is my command."

"Do not, under any circumstances, try and fix me up."

Flynn made a face. "I can't promise that. You know me. I can't help myself. I love happily-ever-after."

"Don't do it or I'll buy all the pastries at the Twilight Bakery and bring them over to your kids," Paige threatened out of self-preservation. If Flynn turned to full-on matchmaker mode, she was doomed.

Flynn laughed gleefully. "Okay, okay, I'll try to resist."

Snorting, Paige turned, tucked the basket under her arm, and stalked over the wooden decking to the houseboat.

And ate another cookie.

Given the situation, it seemed the only reasonable thing to do.

Never in his life had Cash eaten dinner at four-thirty in the afternoon. Breakfast, yes. Dinner, no.

Apparently Emma and her family did it all the time, as did the silver-haired crowd lining up outside the Funny Farm restaurant for the early-bird seating.

"They don't take reservations," Emma explained, "but Sam called ahead to see if we could get private seating so you won't have to constantly be fending off fans while you eat."

"You have plenty of fans of your own," Cash pointed out.

Emma swatted the air. "Everyone is used to me around here. I'm old hat. You're the big news in town."

A hostess came out on the porch of the restaurant and clanged a wrought iron triangle dinner bell as if calling in hungry farm hands from the field. It was cute, it was quaint, and it was corny, but everyone seemed to love the show.

Waitstaff opened up wide double doors leading into the Funny Farm. Diners streamed inside as the waitstaff passed out laminated cards with color-coded seat assignments.

The hostess crooked a finger at Sam and passed him a card with pictures of black and white Holstein dairy cows on it. "You're at the rooftop."

"Thank you," Emma said, and slipped a twenty-dollar bill into the hostess's palm as she guided them toward an old-fashioned cage elevator in the corner.

Farming equipment and memorabilia were mounted on the walls. An old horse-drawn plow, pitchforks, butter churns, shiny silver milking pails, wooden cutting boards in the shape of barnyard animals. Country music was piped in through the sound system.

Sam had hold of Lauren with his left hand, and reached over with his right to take Emma's as they got into the elevator. Cash felt out of place again. He stuck his hands in the front of his jeans' pockets, hunched his shoulders, and wished for his Stetson to pull down over his eyes.

They stepped off the elevator into a private dining area that was empty of diners. The hostess escorted them to a circular table in the middle of the room underneath a domed ceiling.

The floor tiles were black and white checkerboard, the walls adorned with dairy cow murals—Holsteins, Jerseys, Burlina, Tux. Cash had spent enough time on his grandparents' small ranch to distinguish one breed of cattle from another, and it surprised him to realize he was proud of that knowledge.

Layered on top of the cattle decor were Christmas decorations. Mistletoe hung from the chandeliers, pine-scented candles flickered on the tables. The life-sized, fiberglass Holstein standing beside the door wore a red nose and a Santa hat.

Cute. Quaint. Crazy.

Amber handed them menus before she disappeared back to the hostess stand with a parting, "Enjoy, y'all."

If the place was whimsical, their server was the opposite.

From his head (shaved) to his build (ancient oak tree) to the lurid skull tattoo covering his neck, he gave off a Halloween-might-be-ten-months-away-but-I'm-ever-ready vibe. One arm held a breadbasket covered with a white linen cloth, and in the other, a dish of individually wrapped, tablespoon pats of Irish butter.

His eyes were blank, his face expressionless. Nothing impressed this muscled wall of flesh. "Welcome to the Funny Farm," he intoned, and glanced up.

His gaze settled on Cash. Startled, his eyes flew wide open. He cocked his head, leaned in, and grinned like Forrest Gump. "Flying cats! It's Cash Colton. You're him. I mean, you're you."

"Last time I checked," Cash drawled. The guy shook his head so hard Cash worried it might swivel right off his thick neck.

"Man, you screwed up. How the hell did you let a

hottie like Simone Bishop slip through your fingers? If she were my woman I'd ruin her for any other man." He chortled, winked. "If you get my drift."

"Stanley." Emma cleared her throat, and wiggled a finger at Lauren. "There are seven-year-old ears at the table."

"I didn't catch his drift," Lauren said, sounding ages older than her tender years. "What is his drift?"

"Far away from appropriate dinner conversation," Emma said. "Stanley, how's your mama?"

At the mention of his mother, Stanley wiped the lewd expression off his face, deposited the bread and butter on the table, took their drink orders, and rushed off.

"Sorry for that." Emma gave Cash a plucky smile. "Are you still taking a lot of blowback over Simone?"

"Don't worry about Stanley. I'm used to it. Simone leaving me was the best thing that could have happened." Well, except for the fact it had broken up the band. "I wish her nothing but the best."

"TMZ says she's getting married on New Year's Eve to your former drummer."

"So I heard."

Emma reached over and wrapped a hand around his arm. "How do you feel about that?"

"Just dandy."

"Pinky swear?" She stuck out her pinky.

He wrapped his little finger around hers. "Pinky swear."

They grinned at each other, shook their pinkies. He was lucky to have a friend like Emma. He'd made at least one right call in his life.

"What are you doing for Christmas?" Emma asked, smoothing her napkin on her lap.

"Haven't much thought about it."

"You should stay in Twilight. Spend Christmas with us," Emma said.

"Nah, Sam's got such a big family and you've got so much going on. I'd just get in the way."

"Oh for heaven's sake, you wouldn't be a bit of trouble. And you don't have anywhere else to be. Do you?"

No. No, he did not.

He'd never been much of one to celebrate holidays. He'd not really felt it, the spirit of Christmas everyone carried on about. Just seemed liked a lot of fuss and bother for little payoff.

His main MO for surviving the holidays? Hunker down and gut it out from Thanksgiving to New Year's.

"If I stay in town," he said, "I'll get my own place. I can't intrude on your hospitality."

Emma beamed. "All right."

Cash narrowed his eyes. "Wait a minute. I've seen that look on your face before. You've got something up your sleeve."

"What look?" Emma blinked, rearranged her smile into angelic innocence.

"That matchmaking look," Sam supplied. "Leave the man alone, Emma."

"I just want him to be as happy as we are," she said, leaning into her husband.

Sam kissed the top of her head. "Leave him be."

"Spoilsports." Emma sighed. "But I'll lay off the

matchmaking if you agree to stay in town for the holidays."

"Do you know any vacation rentals available?" Cash asked. He'd blown into town at noon without a reservation, thinking he'd stay a couple of nights with Emma and be gone by Monday, but if he stayed longer, he'd need his own place to work. "I'd like something more homey than a motel."

"Twilight is so popular at Christmas I'm sure the B and Bs are all booked up," Emma said. "But honestly, stay with us."

"Nope. Not for three weeks. It's too much. You know what they say: 'fish and visitors stink after three days.'"

Lauren crinkled her nose. "You don't stink."

Cash grinned at her. "Not yet. It hasn't been three days."

"The owner of one of my patients has a houseboat on the lake," Sam said. "He's in Sweden through the new year. Do you want me to see if he'd be willing to rent it?"

Cash shrugged. Did he really want to spend the next three weeks in happy-happy-joy-joy land? He loved Emma and her family, but there was only so much sappy sentimentality a cynical man could take.

Then again, he had nowhere else to be.

As if the universe was conspiring against him, he caught the strains of a Christmas song through the sound system. It was The Truthful Desperadoes singing their version of "All I Want for Christmas Is You." He could hear Simone's husky voice curling around the words, soft and seductive.

"You're going to be okay," Emma said, reading his mind.

"I know." He smiled and something jagged and ugly coiled in the pit of his stomach.

"You'll get your creativity back. You don't need Simone."

"I know." This afternoon when his eyes had met Paige's and he'd heard the music again for the first time in over a year, he felt a stirring of hope.

And fear.

He dropped Emma's gaze, suddenly breathless. Chest tightening, throat squeezing, pulse pounding. He wanted to sprint back to the Twilight Playhouse, hunt down Paige, tell her what she did to him, and see if this was for real. At the same time he wanted to jump into his Land Rover and zoom away from this town as fast as he could drive.

But mostly, he wanted to believe in the magic of Christmas. That for once in his life he could fully, completely, feel like he belonged somewhere.

And that, friends and neighbors, was where the terror came in.

"Please stay." Emma's voice was slow and low, full of kindness and compassion. "You need this."

Cash took a deep breath, snatched air into his lungs, slowly let it out. Emma was his one true friend. For the third time in the conversation, he murmured, "I know."

CHAPTER 4

Accessible: Music that is easy to listen to and understand.

It was nine-thirty that same evening when Paige left the theater in her street clothes. She'd scrubbed off her makeup and pulled her hair back from her face with a candy-cane barrette.

The crowd in the square had lightened considerably with nightfall, but there was still plenty of activity. People were lined up at Santa's workshop. Guides dressed in period clothing led a group of tourists on a ghost tour. Kids in nightclothes, holding stuffed animals tucked under their arms, were leaving the storytelling pajama party event at Ye Olde Book Nook.

Christmas karaoke spilled out of the wine bar, Fruit of the Vine. Paige snuggled deeper into her duster, bunched her shoulders up around her ears, and hummed along to "Frosty the Snowman."

The song, and kids in pajamas, reminded her of her job at the day care center. She loved children and considered herself lucky to have landed the position even though the pay was barely above minimum wage. Just thinking about the children brought a smile to her face.

The previous day, she and the day care owner, Kiley Bullock, had taken the class on a field trip to the Dinosaur Valley State Park in Glen Rose to see dinosaur footprints and have a picnic. The outing had been the most fun she'd had since . . . well . . . she couldn't remember when she'd had so much fun.

The children's giddy excitement lit her own dormant joy, reminding her of the childhood she'd missed out on. She'd scrambled over the tops of rocks, leaped over river basin puddles, and breathlessly played hide-and-seek among cedar elms, Texas sugarberries, bur oaks, and green ash of the bottomlands where dinosaurs had once frolicked.

Her hamstrings were telling her about it, aching in unusual places, but maybe that was from the stiletto boots. Somehow, she'd managed not to fall and bust her butt in them.

"You did great today." She gave herself a pep talk. "Good job."

She left the merry holiday lights of the town square, headed west down a side street toward Shady Hills Nursing Home. Hurrying to get there before they locked the doors at ten. She passed by a family pulling a wagon decorated like a sleigh and filled with packages and a sleeping toddler.

The older kids were in pajamas. The girl, about six, carried a copy of *The Magic Christmas Cookie* written by a local children's author, who was also a friend of Flynn's. The boy, a year or two younger, toted *The Polar Express*. The whole family was laughing and singing an off-key version of "Santa Claus Is Coming to Town."

Somewhere in the region of her heart, Paige felt a sharp knife of loss. She stopped, pressed a palm to her chest. Exhaled.

The family saw her watching them, smiled, and waved.

Offering up a smile, she waved back and scurried on her way.

She skirted a nativity scene that extended out onto the sidewalk, tiptoeing around a spotlight shining on the baby Jesus swaddled in his cradle. Crunched through fallen leaves in the gutter. Cut across the lawn of the First Baptist Church of Twilight. Walked past the fire-ambulance station on Eton Street, and tried to ignore the hop-skip of her pulse as her memory dragged her into the past.

Paige recalled being two or three years old, her father in his turnout gear, hoisting her onto his shoulders as he took her into the firehouse. She remembered laughter and the deep rumble of men's voices.

They teased her dad, telling him there was no way a girl as pretty as she was could possibly be his child. They let her climb on the fire trucks, and gave her sticks of gum to chew. They smelled of spicy cologne, Lava soap, and smoke.

Then came the shriek of an alarm. Men running. Her mother taking her from her father as he joined his crew and raced off on the screaming red fire engine.

Danger. Excitement. Solid. Strong. That was how she'd thought of her vibrant father.

Until the day came when the combination of his job, heredity, a stint as a rescue worker at Ground Zero in 2001 when the twin towers in New York City were struck by airplanes in a foreign attack on American soil, and a cigar habit formed the perfect storm of chronic obstructive pulmonary disease. The condition robbed him of his health, his livelihood, and finally his life.

Tears pushed at the backs of her eyelids. Quickly, she blinked them away, rushed down the alleyway to the rear entrance to Shady Hills, pushed open the gate, hurried up the stone steps, and rang the back door buzzer.

In the room closest to the back door, the TV was turned up loud on a hockey game. The Dallas Stars versus somebody that had the room's resident, ninety-six-year-old Mr. Gentry, fussing loudly. "Block 'em, block 'em, you sumbitches!"

Paige checked her duster pocket to make sure she had the bag of pigskins she'd promised him.

"Punch him in the throat!" Mr. Gentry howled.

Anyone listening to the murderous sports talk would never guess the elderly man was a former Methodist preacher who'd served in the peace corps in the sixties, donated a kidney to a friend on dialysis, and raised a flock of children—biological, adopted, and foster.

"That's it! That's it. Smack down!" Something about hockey threw the otherwise kindhearted man into bloodlust.

The door opened and Addie Small, one of the nurse's aides, smiled down at Paige.

Addie was a big-boned, red-faced girl of Swedish descent. The top of her head barely missed brushing the doorframe. Her golden, waist-length hair was wound into a braided bun and pinned up, tendrils of flyaway hair illuminated in the yellow-glow of fluorescent hallway light behind her. She wore a blue ruffled pinafore that hit just above ample kneecaps and revealed a small semicolon tattoo on her right knee, and an exclamation point on her left.

She motioned Paige inside with a beefy hand and shut the door behind her. "Cutting it close."

"First day at the playhouse. I had to stay late to vacuum the auditorium."

"Emma doesn't have a cleaning service?"

"Popcorn was everywhere. I didn't want to leave a mess for janitorial."

"People are animals," Addie pronounced. "And you're too nice."

It wasn't the first time Paige had heard that.

"Turn-the-Page!" Mr. Gentry called, laughing like he was the first person to ever use that pun. "Is that you?" His door opened a crack and the skinny nonagenarian poked his head out. The sound of the hockey game blared into the corridor.

"Evening, Mr. G." She fished around for his treat.

"Got my pigskins?" He rubbed his palms together like he was trying to start a fire.

"You can get away with smuggling contraband because you have such an innocent face," Addie said.

Paige startled. "Contraband? He's not supposed to have pigskins?"

"Low sodium diet," Addie said.

"Gimme." He snatched the fried pork rinds from her hand. "Thanky kindly."

"But you're not supposed to have them," Paige protested.

"Too late." He cackled like a cartoon villain. From the TV, the crowd cheered wildly. "Oh shoot! Stevenson got a hat trick. Gotta go catch the replay." He slammed the door.

"Should I try to wrestle them away from him?" Paige gnawed her bottom lip.

"Nah." Addie waved a hand. "He's ninety-six."

"But if he's on a low sodium diet . . . I didn't mean to violate the rules."

"I'd be more worried that he didn't pay you for those illegal pigskins," Addie said.

"He's on a budget."

"And you're not?"

"Like you said, he's ninety-six."

"And you're extraordinarily nice." Addie said it as if that was a bad thing.

"How is she tonight?" Paige asked, shifting the topic away from Mr. Gentry, the pigskins, and her foolish niceness.

"It was a good day." Addie nodded, leading the way down the corridor. "When I asked her who the president was, she said, 'Please don't make me say that name.'"

"She says that because she doesn't remember, and she's hoping you'll think she just doesn't like whoever is in office."

"Still, it was a good day." Addie shrugged. "Besides, who cares what goofball is in office? Nothing ever changes. I work hard every day and I'm still broke."

Paige couldn't argue with that last part. But the fault of her misfortune didn't lie with politicians. Rather, she was the architect of her own bad luck, no one else to blame. She'd made bad choices. Gotten involved with the wrong man.

Boy, had she paid for that mistake.

They stopped outside the door of room number eleven. "The med nurse gave her a sleeping pill at nine," Addie said. "She might already be out."

"If she's having trouble sleeping, hot herbal tea with milk usually does the trick."

Addie shook her head in a slow swish. "We tried that. She wakes up in the middle of the night and keeps trying to get out of bed."

"Oh dear." Paige made a mental note to talk to the doctor.

Addie knocked lightly, and then pushed open the door. "Don't stay long. It's almost ten."

"Thanks for letting me see her this late."

"No prob." Addie went on down the hall and Paige eased into her grandmother's room.

Grammie MacGregor was propped up in bed; the bedside lamp above her head was on, reading glasses riding the end of her nose, an infamous tabloid magazine clutched in her hands. The pages curled from many readings.

Her snow-white hair stuck straight up in the back, the bedcovers dropping catty-cornered. On the bedside table, the Christmas cactus Paige had brought her on Thanksgiving was blooming.

"Well, well." Grammie set the magazine aside,

pushed her reading glasses up on her forehead, and broke into a wide grin. "Look what the cat blew in."

Paige didn't bother to tell her that she was mixing her metaphors. The fact she was even attempting metaphors was a good sign.

"Hey, Grammie." She moved to the bed, bent to kiss her grandmother's forehead, smelled lemon cough drops and Vicks VapoRub.

Grammie reached up to cup Paige's cheek. "You look exhausted, sweet pea."

"Just finished my first day on the job at the Twilight Playhouse."

"And you still came by to see me?" Grammie clicked her tongue, shook her head. "You should be in bed."

"Can't go to sleep without seeing my most favorite person in the whole world." Paige straightened the scrambled covers.

Grammie yawned.

Paige leaned over and eased the reading glasses off her grandmother's forehead.

"Wait," Grammie protested, yawned again. "I wasn't finished reading my paper."

"You can hardly hold your eyes open."

"I gotta find out who is Wayne Newton's secret new love."

Paige picked up the gossip magazine with the headline "Wayne Newton's Secret Mistress." "Grammie, this magazine is a year old."

"Did I ever tell you that I once dated Wayne Newton?"

She had, but Paige didn't interrupt her.

"It was 1965." Grammie's eyes turned dreamy.

"Vegas was in its heyday and I was dancing in the chorus at the Flamingo."

The old photograph on the dressing table featured Grammie draped over a chaise longue wearing sequins and pearls and pink flamingo feathers attached to her costume like wings. She looked both sweet and sultry. Her hair was dyed platinum blond, her fingernails and lipstick the color of bing cherries. When she was a kid, Paige would gaze at the picture and sigh because she knew she'd never be that adventuresome, glamorous, or exotic.

"You were so beautiful," Paige said.

Grammie waved a hand. "Beauty is fleeting, but you don't usually appreciate it when you've got it. I thought my nose was too long and my thighs were too heavy." Grammie whacked her upper thigh with a hand. Laughed. "Look at me now."

"You're still beautiful."

"And you are such a liar, but I love you for it."

"Did you like Vegas?" Paige asked.

Grammie crinkled her nose. "Too hot and dry. Even though I was born and raised in West Texas where the wind blows like crazy more days than not, I never had windburned skin until Vegas. I kept running out of hand lotion."

"I've never been."

"Sin City is an eye-opener. Not a place to raise kids in my opinion. But everybody oughta visit at least once."

Maybe one day, when she was financially solvent, she'd get around to it.

"Anyway, I met Wayne at the Ali–Patterson fight. Man, that was a night." A wistful smile plucked her lips. Her grandmother's short-term memory might be shot, but it was a steel trap when it came to long-ago events.

"Our eyes met across the ring. And we couldn't stop staring at each other. We were missing the fight, but we didn't care. I think my jaw might have dropped open. He winked, and blew me a kiss. When the fight was over, I stayed in my seat and he came over to me. Wayne Newton! I tell you, I thought my heart would stop."

"He was a good looking man."

"In those days, he still had an adorable baby face," she said. "And the sweetest smile! It was one of those chemical things between us. Bam! Boom! Right away we were smitten. He asked me out. Neither one of us were in a relationship, so I thought, why the heck not?"

"What was he like?"

"A complete gentleman. Funny. Smart. Smiled all the time."

"So what happened? Why did things fall apart?" Paige pulled her legs up into the wide-bottomed upholstered chair, sat tailor-style.

"Wayne was a shooting star and I had no illusions about my abilities to keep him. Women threw themselves at him constantly. He was big-time and I was just a girl from Abilene, Texas, who could dance a little." Her eyes twinkled in a way that touched Paige's heart. "But in the meantime, oh my, did we have fun."

"How did it end?"

"We'd been seeing each other for a month and Wayne was wanting more from me."

"You mean sex?" They'd never gotten this far in Grammie's story before.

"Back then girls didn't slip so easily into men's beds. The pill was still fairly new and women didn't have a lot of reproductive options."

"So you didn't . . . ?"

She shook her head. "I couldn't keep him on a string, but I knew if I gave myself to him, I wouldn't be able to leave, so I broke things off."

"Did you regret it?"

"Not sleeping with him? Not at the time, but if it was nowadays, with all the options you girls have, you can bet your sweet Christmas cookies I would have gone to bed with him. But back then?" She shrugged. "We weren't as free."

"Was it difficult?"

"What?"

"Ending things with him."

Grammie clasped both hands to her chest. "It broke my heart into a thousand little pieces, but I knew it was for the best. For both of us."

"I'm so sorry you got your heart broken," Paige said, thinking about her ex, Randy, and how she wished she could have been as smart about men as Grammie. "How sad to lose the love of your life."

"Oh, Wayne wasn't the love of my life." Grammie shook her head. "We had chemistry and lots of fun together and we cared about each other. That month was glamorous and gave me great stories, but the second I met your granddaddy, I knew he was The One. No one in this whole world could ever match my Luke."

Paige reached over to squeeze Grammie's arm. "You were so lucky. Wayne Newton for fun. Grand-daddy for happily-ever-after."

"I know that." Grammie smiled and patted Paige's cheek. "But cheer up. Your true love is out there wait-ing for you."

It was a nice thought. Paige really wanted to be-lieve it, but she'd thought she'd found love before and look how that had turned out.

Grammie yawned again.

"I better scoot and let you get some rest."

"Will you read me that article before you go?" Grammie pointed at the tabloid. "I hate to think Wayne is cheating on his wife. That's not the Wayne I knew."

"Gossip magazines like to make stuff up to sell papers. I'm sure Wayne is true blue."

"Read me the story . . . please."

"All right, but just the one article and then you need to sleep." Paige picked up the magazine and it flopped open to the centerfold.

There was a handsome long-haired, bearded man wearing a Stetson and a devastating hey-there-girl grin. The header read "Country Crooner MIA in Wake of Band Split."

The first paragraph began, "Cash Colton, lead singer for the now defunct band The Truthful Desper-adoes, hasn't been seen in public since his girlfriend, sultry songbird Simone Bishop, threw him over for his best friend and bandmate, Snake Cantrell."

The photograph had been snapped by paparazzi. Late night. After some party or another. Ambush shot. Cash looked startled, peeved, and a little drunk. His arm wrapped around a statuesque, big-breasted blonde in killer high heels.

Simone Bishop.

The woman was stunning, classic Helen-of-Troy-launching-ships-with-her-face beautiful. High cheekbones. Sloe eyes. Head cocked at a coy angle. A knowing smile, as if she'd been the one to alert the paparazzi to their whereabouts, lifted the corners of her full rich lips, a golden goddess who inevitably trailed broken hearts behind her like confetti.

Paige should have remembered where she was, flipped right on past the page, gone looking for that article about Wayne Newton. But her gaze was welded to the photograph of the man with enigmatic eyes.

Specific words floated up at her from the text, almost as if they were bolded, italicized, and glittering hot.

Crushed.

Lost.

Devastated.

Self-destructive.

Disappeared.

He must have loved Simone beyond all measure to be so shattered by their split. Simone had cheated on him with his best friend and bandmate. Not just cheated on him, she'd busted up the band as well. Who wouldn't be wrecked?

Paige knew exactly what it felt like to be betrayed by someone you trusted. Her gut did maniacal push-ups, flipping up and down. She read on.

Colton met Simone at Toby Keith's house during a pool party three years earlier and he'd been quoted as saying, "The minute I saw her in that bikini, I went straight home and wrote 'Like the Night' in forty-five minutes."

"Like the Night," the article went on to explain, was The Truthful Desperadoes' first chart topping hit, and their first song with Simone as lead singer.

Wow.

The minute Paige had seen Cash at the theater all the breath had left *her* body. Something crazy tightened her chest. Something erratic. Something tight that had her digging her heels into the floor and pushing back into the chair cushion as nervous as a newbie rider trying to keep a high-spirited horse from stampeding.

The next paragraph was a quick history lesson.

Cash was born to a single mom in Rankin, Texas. His mom had big dreams of becoming a country-and-western star. He never knew his biological father, but he was rumored to be a musician, one of his mom's many boyfriends. His mother died when he was ten, leaving him to be raised by her parents on a broken-down old ranch that cost more money to run than it made. Until he was fifteen, when he ran away from home seeking fame and fortune as a musician.

She couldn't begin to imagine what life on the streets had been like for a motherless teen.

Aww, damn. Poor kid. This time her stomach did the entire P90X workout.

The article went on to say Cash had gotten a leg

up in the business when famed country-and-western singer Freddie Frank, who was also from Rankin, decided to mentor him.

The reporter speculated about Cash's current whereabouts at the time of the article. Cash had sold his mansion in Nashville and most of his possessions and he'd completely dropped out of sight. His manager had no idea where he'd gone. Simone and Snake Cantrell both stayed mum on the subject. Various friends and associates that the reporter had contacted, including Freddie Frank, were either clueless or stonewalling.

Cash's former housekeeper had said he'd gone to South America and the reporter learned Cash had indeed bought an airplane ticket to Peru and hired a guide to take him up the Ucayali River where intrepid travelers often went on spiritual quests. The reporter speculated that Simone's perfidy had stymied Cash's musical mojo and he was desperate to get it back. Simone had been his inspiration and, without her, his talent had vanished. Cash was, the reporter claimed, in a creative tailspin.

The main question the article posed: Could Cash pull out of the nosedive or was his career over?

"Read it out loud, please," Grammie said.

"Wh-what?" Paige jumped. She'd been so caught up in the article about Cash she'd forgotten where she was and what she was supposed to be doing. Quickly, she leafed through the magazine, found the story on Wayne Newton, and started reading.

"That proves nothing." Grammie snorted when Paige finished the article about a mysterious blonde woman Wayne was supposedly caught canoodling with in a Branson, Missouri, restaurant. "Let me see the picture."

Paige held up the magazine for her grandmother. It was a photograph of Wayne spliced with the shot of a much younger woman.

"Ridiculous. That's clearly Photoshopped."

Paige grinned because Grammie was right and because, tonight at least, she was as sharp as the proverbial tack.

"Gossipmongers," Grammie muttered. "They're just trying to stir up trouble."

"I'd better get going." Paige stood. "Before they send Addie to throw me out on my ear."

"Yes, yes." Grammie worried the covers between her knotty fingers. "I don't like the idea of you walking home alone in the dark."

"I'll be safe. It's Twilight after all, and my cell phone is charged up."

"You never know. Anything could happen. You could fall and twist an ankle." Grammie's forehead wrinkled into a frown.

"I'll pay close attention to where I'm walking."

"Please do. If anything ever happened to you . . ." Grammie's voice choked up and she pressed a hand over her mouth.

"Nothing's going to happen, Grammie. I promise."

Her grandmother looked up at her with wide, vulnerable eyes and her bottom lip trembled. "You promise?"

"Cross my heart." Paige drew an X over the left

side of her chest, then leaned over to kiss Grammie's forehead. "I'll be here for you always."

Grammie's eyes closed. She was already falling asleep.

"Good night," Paige whispered, tucked the covers around her, and tiptoed out.

She waved to Addie, who was pushing a linen cart down the hallway, let herself out the back door, and into the night. The sky was clear. Stars glimmered overhead, and there was a quarter moon. Music still played from the town square. "The First Noel."

A sweet night. A perfect night.

And yet, Paige experienced a pang of loneliness, a bittersweet bite. She couldn't really pinpoint why she was feeling that way. Her heart lay heavy in her chest and her head seemed disconnected from her body.

She drew the collar of her coat up. Took care on her walk back. She'd almost reached the lake when her cell phone buzzed in her pocket.

Even though she didn't recognize the number, it was similar enough to Flynn's that she automatically answered it.

Big mistake.

"Paige MacGregor," snarled a voice on the other end.

She wasn't a liar so she wasn't going to deny who she was. Her instinct yelled at her to just hang up, but that wouldn't solve the problem. Squaring her shoulders, she stopped on the promenade at the marina. "Yes."

"You owe Megabank forty thousand dollars. Pay up, you deadbeat."

"That's not my debt. I've been through this with

Megabank. My identity was stolen. Credit cards taken out in my name—"

"Yeah, right, that's what all you losers say. Who are you to welch on your debt when honest, hard-working people pay what they owe?"

Fury blasted through her. "Listen, buddy, you are not allowed to call me this late on a Saturday night."

"Ah, so you know the debt collection rules. Only someone dodging their bills would be that savvy."

"That's not true—"

"Pay up!" He went on to use ugly, threatening language.

Her chest squeezed and her throat iced up. Even though she had not run up that debt, it had been acquired in her name and she couldn't help but feel responsible. Straightening it out was an ongoing battle.

She hung up.

He called back.

She blocked the number, but she knew from experience he'd call her back from a different one. Maybe not tonight, but he would call. And Megabank wasn't the only credit card company trying to collect from her.

Shaking with anger, she stuffed her cell phone back into her purse, took several long, slow deep breaths.

Calm down. It was okay. She didn't owe that money. Eventually her lawyer would make this all go away. When she could scrape the money together to pay him.

But it had already been six months, and no light at the end of that tunnel. Would she ever again have normal life? Especially when she was having trouble coming up with her lawyer's fees.

Eventually.

Hang in there. Chin up. This, too, shall pass.

Platitudes. She wasn't buying into her own hype because right now, tonight, it felt like the nightmare would never end.

CHAPTER 5

Accelerando: A symbol used in musical notation indicating to gradually quicken tempo.

Fritzi woke her, as he did every morning since she'd been looking after him, by rudely using Paige's bladder as a trampoline.

"Dang it, can't you just lick my face like a normal dog?"

Fritzi gave her a dazzling poodle smile that said, *Nah, I want you to fully get how much I need to pee. Misery loves company, dontcha know.* He did another bounce for good measure and hopped to the floor.

"Okay, okay. I'm up, I'm up." Paige groaned and threw back the covers. Six A.M. and still dark outside. Disturbed by the debt collector's phone call, she hadn't fallen asleep until long after midnight.

Yawning, she headed for the bathroom. Fritzi danced around her feet. "I'm gonna be selfish about this. Me first."

Fritzi whined.

"I'll hurry."

She finished up in the tiny bathroom, hit the power button on the coffeemaker she'd loaded up with fresh coffee the night before, slipped on her coat, jammed her feet into house slippers, stuffed a baggie into her pocket just in case, clipped the leash to Fritzi's collar, and opened the door.

The poodle pranced ahead of her, nostrils sniffing, head held high.

She stepped onto the decking, the houseboat swaying gently under her weight, although she barely noticed the movement now. After two months of living on the water, she was finally getting used to the motion.

White twinkle lights glowed from the marina, cutting through the predawn darkness. Across the lake, lights at Froggy's, her uncle Floyd's restaurant, cut through the morning mist. Froggy's started serving homemade breakfast at six and Paige had a sudden hankering for one of their delicious greasy sausage biscuits.

"Hell, no," she scolded herself. "Not with all the cookies you've been scarfing down. It's a banana for breakfast."

And maybe, whispered the devil on her shoulder, one of Flynn's delicious caramel apple cookies? Bananas and cookies went so well together.

No. No more cookies either.

Fritzi was sniffing the air, eyes blinking, ears laid back, enjoying the breeze. The air smelled of water and fish. Ghostly white-hulled boats bobbed in the quay. Metal moorings clanked. Water lapped softly against the shoreline. A blue jay burred from the cedar copse.

Paige guided the poodle down the houseboat's gangplank and over the wooden walkway that ran between boat slips. The leather leash felt smooth and cool in her palm. Fritzi surged forward, surprisingly strong for such a small dog, tugging her toward the grass on the other side of the marina.

She crested the top step just as a man climbed from the black Land Rover parked at the curb. He was unexpected and enigmatic in the dawn, a raven in a flock of white-winged doves.

She stopped.

He stopped.

They stared at each other.

He grinned.

She grinned.

"I was just thinking of you," he said, his voice a low, lion-y growl. "And here you are."

He'd been thinking about her? Her pulse dashed. Incredible. Impossible. Intoxicating.

"Here I am," she echoed.

Fritzi, just inches from the lawn, whined plaintively and threw all his eight pounds against the leash. *Let me at that grass.*

Cash wore faded Levi's with a hole in the right knee, the same cowboy boots he'd had on the day before, a red flannel shirt, and a brown leather bomber jacket. "Fancy meeting you here at the crack of dawn."

"I was about to say the same thing," she said, wondering if he could hear the erratic pounding of her heart.

His smile dipped deep, spread up to encompass the corners of his eyes in a friendly crinkle. "Well?"

"Well, what?" She pushed a fringe of hair from her eyes, blinded a moment by the intensity of that fantastic smile.

He cocked his head, studied her with steadfast eyes. "What *are* you doing here?"

"The dog needs to do his business," she blurted.

He laughed a cool, smooth laugh, refreshing as peppermint. "That explains the pajamas."

Holy jungle jaguar! She was in her pajamas, and not just any pajamas, but red and white reindeer pajamas.

Her cheeks heated and she ducked her head, hurried Fritzi over to the grass. She quelled the urge to snatch the dog into her arms and run back to the houseboat, slam the door, and never come out again.

He followed her. "It's Paige, right?"

"Huh?" She blinked, and glanced over at him. He knew her name. OMG, he'd bothered to find out her name! Her knees swooned.

He raised both eyebrows. "Your name?"

"Oh," she said, like an idiot. "Yes. It's Paige. That's me. Paige MacGregor. Paige Hyacinth MacGregor." *God, just shut up.*

"Emma told me who you were," he explained. "But not the Hyacinth part."

"Why?" She couldn't figure out why a successful, sexy-as-sin cowboy musician would be interested enough to find out her name.

"Maybe she doesn't know your middle name is Hyacinth."

"Not that 'why.' Why did Emma tell you who I was?"

"Because I asked." He studied her with those amazing gray eyes the color of smoke and fog and mountaintops.

"Why did you ask?"

"You are seriously nosy."

"Not any nosier then you." She stuffed her hands in her pockets. "Asking people's names and stuff."

The crinkles at the corners of his eyes deepened and he looked like a movie version of a romantic outlaw—sexy, handsome, naughty, but not truly bad. "Because it's not often someone throws me out of an establishment."

"Just doing my job." She could hear her defensiveness.

"I'm Cash by the way," he said, and extended his hand. "Cash Henry Colton."

She had no choice but to take his hand. His handshake was as firm and reliable as she'd expected it to be, and it shook her up more than she cared to admit. Warm. Friendly. Easy. She dropped that hand as quickly as she could.

"I know who you are." She pressed her palm against her side. Felt his residual heat leak through her skin. "You're kind of a big deal."

He made a dismissive face. "Hype."

"That's not what I hear."

He ignored that, squatted beside Fritzi, held out the back of his hand for the poodle to sniff. "Hey there, fella."

"So what are you doing here?" she asked, tilting her chin and studying the top of his head, thick with curly black hair that swirled to the right at the crown. "No one gets up this early on Sunday morning around here unless they're going fishing. You don't look like you're going fishing."

"You're right. I'm not fishing."

"Then why are you at the marina at six in the morning?"

"I'm an early riser."

"Uh, that surprises me."

"Why?"

"Musicians are infamous for their late night shenanigans."

"My shenanigan days are behind me." He latched on to her gaze and no matter how hard she tried, Paige could not look away. "But musicians' hours *are* crazy. When the creative spark wakes up, you work."

"And did the creative spark awaken you?"

He stared at her for so long without answering that a nervous tingle shot up her spine. His gaze doubled down, not just looking and observing, but peering into her, through her, down into the depths of her soul.

When he spoke it was a shadow of a whisper, low and filled with mysterious meaning. "The creative spark awakened."

She didn't know what to say to that so she dropped her gaze and jiggled Fritzi's leash, urging him to hurry up.

"Actually," Cash said, "I'm moving in."

Her pulse shot up, teetered on the verge of bring-out-the-defibrillator. Huh? What? "Where are you moving to? There are no houses near here."

Cash got to his feet, sent her a devilish grin that dissolved both her kneecaps and her common sense. "Houseboat."

There were only four houseboats on Lake Twilight and they were all moored on this side of the lake. There was Uncle Floyd's boat where she was living, two more that were the summer homes of Dallasites. And the fourth—the one moored right beside her place—that belonged to Fritzi's owner, the diving instructor.

She had a sinking feeling she knew which one. "Sig Gunderson's houseboat?"

"How did you know?"

She inclined her head toward Fritzi, who was sitting in between them, looking up from Paige to Cash and back again like he was watching a tennis match. "Fritzi belongs to Sig. I'm dog-sitting."

"You live nearby?" he asked.

"Houseboat," she admitted, saying the word as succinctly as he had.

And that damn grin of his exploded all over his handsome face, a ballistic missile of a smile. "No kidding."

She did her best not to match his over-the-top enthusiasm, and he chuckled like someone had whispered in his ear the most sublime joke ever told.

"Something funny?" she asked, painfully aware of the thin material of her pajamas, and not just because it was chilly, but mainly from the way he was staring her. As if he was Superman and amusing himself with his X-ray vision.

Paige crossed her arms over her chest as best she could while still clutching Fritzi's leash.

"I'm sorry," he said, not sounding the least bit apologetic. "I was just thinking that living near you would be a dream come true."

Was this really happening? Was Cash Colton standing here in the purplish light of impending dawn flirting with her? It didn't seem rational. He'd had Simone Bishop. Could have a million Simone Bishops if he wanted them. Why was he coming on to *her*?

Okay. This must be the deal. She was still asleep. In bed. Dreaming. Never mind the dewy mist soaking her house slippers.

Unless she was sleepwalking. Maybe she was sleepwalking.

She had sleepwalked before. When she was ten. After her mother left. Her dad came home from a twenty-four shift to find her hoeing in the garden. Come to think of it, that had been at dawn as well.

"Or a nightmare," she quipped, purely as self-protection. If she wasn't dreaming and he really was flirting, this had disaster written all over it. She'd had her fill of charming, handsome men. Cash Colton had absolute zero chance of sweeping her off her feet. She was unsweepable. Randy had seen to that.

He laughed again as if she was the most amusing woman he'd ever met. The sound plucked a truculent string inside her, tight and irritated, although she wasn't sure why.

Maybe it was because he was so damn good looking.

And irresistible.

And sexy.

And magnetic.

And . . . and . . .

He could absolutely crush her if she allowed it. She was not going to allow it. She had lost almost everything, but the one thing she had going for her was her willpower.

Well, except for when it came to cookies. She had no willpower around cookies. Luckily, he was not a cookie.

Unfortunately, he looked as good as cookies tasted. She tried not to check him out, but c'mon, he was the hottest thing in town, and there were a lot of hot guys in Twilight. In fact, the place—with its proximity to the Dallas/Fort Worth Metroplex, a host of outdoor activities available, and laid-back style—was a hot-guy mecca.

His jeans fit his body as if they'd been tailor-made. Clinging in all the right places to muscular thighs and a tight, firm butt. Michelangelo himself could not have sculpted a finer figure. Hard. Lean. Tanned.

She raised her chin, and wow, he was checking her out too. His gaze traveled from her hips to her chest to her lips, and then he was staring straight into her eyes.

Her breath stumbled, tripped, stopped.

He wasn't breathing either.

The silent communication rippling between them had power and heft. *I like you*, his eyes said. *I want to know you better.*

Her leaping heart answered, *I'm in*. But her troubled brain whispered, *Caution! Danger! Here, there be dragons!* She didn't know why she thought that last part, except she'd been reading a book of that title.

"How . . ." She paused, moistened her lips, not really sure what she was going to say until the words spilled out. "Um, how long are you in town?"

He shrugged slow and casual as if he had all the time in the world. At her feet, Fritzi had given up on her and was busy gnawing on a stick he'd found in the grass.

"For starters, until Sig Gunderson comes home. After that . . ." He shrugged again, one shoulder going slightly higher than the other. "Who knows?"

"You don't have anywhere else to be?"

"Nope." His head rotated at a leisurely pace, matching his languid tone of voice. He could be a hypnotist. He was that mesmerizing. Every cell in her body was drawn to him. It was scary. Damn scary.

"Nothing to do. Nowhere to go. Nothing to get." His eyes and voice were low and sultry, promising long, hot summer right here in December.

"So you might stay in Twilight for a while?"

"Depends." His gaze was a drilling derrick and she was an oil well.

"On what?" Her pulse was a pogo stick, bouncing up and down. Boing. Boing. Boing.

"How long it takes me to decide what to do with the rest of my life."

"I totally get that," she said. "I'm in a transitory phase myself."

"Ah," he said. "Another thing we have in common."

"What's the first thing?"

"Both our middle names start with an H."

"And?"

He held up a key. "We both live on houseboats."

"So we do." She laughed against the tight squeeze of her chest muscles and felt both happy and scared.

"Would you show me the way?"

"What?" She was so starstruck that she was having trouble paying attention. No wonder everyone was infatuated with Cash Colton. What wasn't to love?

"Show me where Sig's houseboat is moored."

"Oh, yes, right, that." Heat spread up her chest to her neck, chin, cheeks. "This way."

Realizing they were finally on the move, Fritzi jumped up and led the way down the metal stairs to the wooden decking between the boat slips. Pastel shades of pink, orange, and purple tinged the eastern sky. Dew dampened her house slippers and she snuggled deeper into her coat, acutely aware that Cash was behind her.

Paige couldn't help wondering if he was staring at her butt, and her face flushed even hotter. She tried not thinking about it.

Failed.

The vapor lamps were still on, casting the morning mist in a fuzzy Monet hue.

A fish flopped nearby, breaking the surface of the water, and leaving behind widening ripples.

They passed Uncle Floyd's houseboat.

"Here's where I live." She waved. "You're in the turquoise houseboat next door."

"Turquoise?" Cash laughed.

"Sig's got a crush on New Mexico."

"So why doesn't he live there?"

"He's a diving instructor, and he's built up a thriving business in Twilight. Besides, I think he likes having New Mexico as his mistress. Moving there would kill the allure."

"Absence makes the heart grow fonder?"

"Something like that."

Cash sank his hands on his hips, looked out across the lake, inhaled deeply. "It's eerie quiet here."

"It's dawn and December. Things really hop on a summer afternoon."

"How long have you lived on the houseboat?" He nodded at her place.

"Since Halloween."

"Then how do you know what summer's like?"

"My uncle, cousins, and grandmother live here. I've spent a lot of summers on this lake."

He cast her an amused look. "Cinnamon."

"What?"

"Your freckles remind me of cinnamon-dusted apple pie. I love apple pie." He paused a beat. "And cinnamon."

She brought her hand up to cover her nose. Peered at him over her fingertips. She felt self-conscious and wished she wasn't in her reindeer pajamas. "I've always hated my freckles."

"That's like Mona Lisa hating her smile," he said. "The smile is what makes the picture."

"You're saying the freckles make me who I am?"

"I'm saying"—he inclined his head in a sexy way—"I find them adorable."

Holy felines! He was totally flirting with her.

"Well, there you are," she mumbled. "Home sweet

home until Sig gets back." Without waiting for a reply, she turned to leave.

He was blocking her way. Not in a threatening manner. He was just there and it was a small space.

"Oops," she said, feeling crazy breathless, and stepped the other way, sending Fritzi dancing in circles.

But Cash moved at the same time.

When she moved again, he waltzed right along with her, and she wondered if he was doing it on purpose to tease her.

"Excuse me," she murmured, and did not meet his eyes.

He made a soft sound of amusement and stepped aside. "Thanks for showing me to the houseboat."

"You're welcome." Her heart was a bongo— *thump, thump, thump, thump.* Fritzi was busy sniffing the leg of his jeans. "Have a good day."

"You too." His voice was rich and smooth and full of promise.

"C'mon, Fritzi."

The dog sat down on Cash's boots, and gave Paige an I-ain't-goin'-nowhere-sister expression.

She tugged lightly on the leash.

The dog balked, dug in.

"Aww, Fritzi, come on," she coaxed, heard the rising anxiety in her voice. Stopped. Took a deep breath. The dog sensed when she was upset.

Fritzi wagged his tail, but didn't move.

She tugged a little firmer. "Come, come, Fritzi. Let's go home."

The poodle didn't budge. Barked, a short, declarative yelp. *I am home.* Technically, he was home, but not for the month of December.

Feeling desperate, she squatted to the dog's level, attempted to bribe him by sticking her fingers into her pocket and pretending to pull out food. "Treat?"

The dog narrowed his eyes and leaned forward, nose twitching to smell if she really did have a treat, discovered she was trying to pull the wool over this eyes, sat back on the toes of Cash's boots, and sent her a scathing look of betrayal.

Impatience tightened her muscles. The dog was small enough for her to pick up and carry him back to the houseboat without his permission, but she didn't want to look pushy in front of Cash.

"You've certainly got a way with animals," he said, sounding thoroughly entertained.

Her impatience turned to irritation, because she was actually pretty good with animals, but then she realized he was joking.

She softened. Stood up. Smiled. Met his bold gaze again. "Yep, that's me. A real Francine of Assisi."

His lively eyes studied her for several long seconds, and his lips parted slightly.

She didn't know what to say or do next.

Full dawn broke.

The peep of sun cast his face in an easy light. She now saw clearly the faint ring of beard stubble at his chiseled jaw, the small but jagged scar at his left temple, and the mesmerizing, pulse-pounding look in his eyes that said, *If there wasn't a dog on my foot I just might kiss you.*

Or maybe she was projecting since she wanted to kiss him.

Projection. That had to be it. Why would this stranger, this famous handsome stranger, want to kiss a rather ordinary girl like her?

Because, said her healthy self-esteem, *you're kind of awesome too.*

And gullible. Don't forget gullible. Look what had happened the last time she kissed a man she thought was out of her league.

That was just it. She had been out of Randy's league and couldn't even see the truth of it because he'd been so good looking and charming.

Just like this guy.

Not that she thought Cash was a con-man identity thief, but she'd been naive before. Randy had taught her a thing or two. Be careful in love. Don't give your heart away too fast.

Love? What in the jackhammer was she thinking?

Was she attracted to him? Oh for sure. Did she want to sleep with him? You bet. Was he the love of her life? Hells to the no.

She took a deep breath. No hurry. No rush. No sweat. Savor the moment.

Which was kind of nice and kind of awkward and full of new beginnings and aching awareness.

Cash gently nudged Fritzi off the toe of his boot. "Go on, boy."

The poodle hopped right to his feet. Paige trolled him toward her with the leash. Fritzi shot a longing glance over his shoulder at Cash.

"Go on." Cash nodded.

Fritzi lowered his head as if he was very sad, but went with Paige.

"What are you? Some kind of dog whisperer?"

"I worked at an animal shelter when I was a kid."
He lowered his lashes. "My first job besides working on my grandparents' ranch. What was your first
job?"

"Besides babysitting?"

"Besides babysitting."

"I worked at a dance studio."

"As an instructor?" He lifted an eyebrow, sent
her a measured expression as if reevaluating her.

"Don't look so impressed. I taught tap dancing
to toddlers. Not much different from babysitting."

"How old were you?"

"Sixteen."

"You must have been pretty damn good to teach
dancing at sixteen."

"Did you miss the part about my students being
toddlers?"

"That sounds way harder than teaching adults,"
he said. "And you've got all those parents breathing
down your neck."

"Oh my gosh, it was." She felt her tongue loosen-
ing. Told herself to shut up. Ignored it. "Especially
with the Toddlers and Tiaras set. Talk about demanding! Those stage parents can be fierce."

"So do you still teach dance when you're not
playing Santa Baby at the theater?"

"No," she said, sounding more curt than she
meant. It was still a touchy topic. "I gave up dancing."

"Why?"

"Long, boring story." She moved her hand. A
wave. Dismissal. Good-bye. She was not going to
get into *that* with him. Randy had ruined her love

of dancing and it was none of Cash's business. Plus, she was still achingly aware she was in her jammies around Mr. Hot Stuff. "But I do work at a day care center Monday through Friday. Seems I can't pull myself away from toddlers."

"I'd like to hear about it sometime."

"Why?" She said it curtly, maybe too curtly, but seriously, why?

That seemed to surprise him, both eyebrows arched up on his forehead like twin question marks. "Well, we are neighbors."

"Are you this chatty to all your neighbors?"

He studied her with an intensity that ripped her breath right out of her lungs, shook it up like a snow globe, and threw it to the wind. "Only the pretty ones with cinnamon freckles over the bridges of their noses."

Her entire body went hot—her face, her chest, her belly, even her feet, which were pretty cold in the dew-dampened slippers.

He was giving her the full court press and she didn't know how to handle it. Not from a guy like him. Before Randy, she would have fallen for that smile. Opened herself wide up. Told him everything. Stayed. Lingered. Pursed her lips. Hoped for a kiss.

But now? After all the crap she'd been through? Not on your life.

"I gotta go." Feeling like an inept tap dancer who'd badly misgauged the stage distance and was dangerously close to falling off the apron into the orchestra pit, she scooped up Fritzi and fled to the houseboat.

CHAPTER 6

Chord progression: A string of chords played in succession.

So much for sleeping in on Sunday morning. Paige was wide awake, every nerve in her body pulsing, tingling, throbbing with fiery energy.

And she did not want to be alone with her thoughts and fantasies about Cash Colton. Not to mention, she was out of milk, and dry Raisin Bran wasn't that appealing. There were the cookies, but no bananas or milk for those either. And shh, she was honestly a little burned out on cookies.

Besides, she had a coupon for a free cappuccino at the Twilight Bakery with any Sunday morning purchase before ten A.M.

She got dressed, and stepped out onto the boat deck, peeked over at the turquoise houseboat next door. The lights were on inside.

Quietly, so as not to draw his attention, she got out her pink bicycle with the white wicker basket hooked on front, walked it off the dock and up the metal stairs.

One of these days she was going to buy a new-to-her car. Losing the cute little yellow Mustang that Dad bought her for high school graduation was still a sore spot. Screw you, Randy.

Various family members had offered to help her out, but none of them were rich, and she didn't want to feel beholden to anyone. She was determined to clean up her own messes.

The sun was an egg yolk. Bright. Golden. Happy.

She thought about riding around the lake to her uncle's restaurant, but the hankering she'd had for a sausage biscuit had been replaced by a craving for a chocolate croissant.

A chocolate croissant? C'mon, Paige, really?

If she wanted to lose those ten pounds she'd put on after her dad died last year and the other whole mess started, she would pedal the two-mile trek to Froggy's and order an egg white omelet with turkey bacon.

She did not go to Froggy's. The bakery was closer and the yeasty smells wafting on the morning air whispered in the husky, rich voice of a chocolate croissant, *Paige, come eat me.*

And she had that coupon for a cappuccino.

Stress eating. Yes, she knew. Cash had thrown her off her game. She needed comfort food to restore her balance.

This early on Sunday morning, there wasn't a line at the counter. A few regulars sat at various tables around the room. She greeted them with a cheery smile, and made small talk while she waited for her order.

She took the croissant and a large cappuccino to a small bistro table with two red metal chairs that sat in front of the large picture window overlooking the square and the big community Christmas tree. She pulled out a chair, and it scraped against the ceramic tile in a friendly squeak.

Inhaling the scent of the croissant, she savored the full experience. Over the past few years, she'd learned to take nothing for granted, to appreciate the small things. The smell of pastries. People-watching. The creamy taste of coffee with steamed milk and frothy foam.

Lucky.

She was so lucky. Things could have been so much worse. She had a roof over her head. And three jobs! Okay, none of them paid much, but she had work. Family and friends who loved her. Honestly, who could ask for more?

She sipped and noshed. Closed her eyes to get the full impact of the chocolate and coffee pairing. Yum.

"May I sit here?" asked a seductive voice that sent goose bumps flying up her arm.

Holy mountain lion. It couldn't be.

She paused midchew, opened one eye. Yep. It was he.

Cash Colton gave her a grin that just about caved in her chest and, without waiting for her permission, plunked down beside her.

She opened her other eye, swallowed hard. Apparently they were going to have a conversation.

"Hey," he said brightly.

"Hey," she answered weakly.

The girl from behind the counter, Amy Jones, came to the table to take his order, which was strange because the bakery was counter service only. Amy was nineteen, blonde, big-busted, and wearing a pink T-shirt that said *Delicious* in blingy rhinestones.

"Hi," Amy said breathlessly, and extended a hand. "I'm Amy."

"Well, hello there, Amy." He winked, and shook her hand. "Nice to meet you."

Paige suppressed an eye roll.

"I just love your music so much," Amy simpered.

Cash smiled. Nodded. "Thank you for listening."

"Oh, it's my pleasure." Amy twittered and flittered and pressed a hand to her chest and blushed red.

Paige couldn't help it. She glanced at the ceiling and snorted. C'mon, she chided herself. Honest self-assessment? She was no better than Amy. The guy was a uterus magnet who turned normal, rational women into blithering idiots.

"Could I have your autograph?" Amy's eyelashes fluttered wildly.

"Sure thing." His smile was so sweet it could put a triathlete into a diabetic coma.

Amy pulled a Sharpie from her pocket, unbuttoned two buttons on her blouse, giggled, and leaned toward him. "Could you sign me?"

He didn't bat an eye and Paige was suddenly certain that this wasn't the first time he'd been asked to autograph a woman's chest. Nor, mostly likely, would it be his last.

Being his girlfriend couldn't be easy. No wonder

Simone dropped him. Then again, Simone probably had more than her share of men asking her to sign their chests too.

Cash autographed the young woman's creamy cleavage with a flourish and handed back her Sharpie as automatically as brushing his teeth. A day in the life of Cash Colton. Get up. Brush your teeth. Go for breakfast. Sign a boob or two.

Amy glanced down at her illustrated breast, sighed dreamily. "I might not ever shower again."

"Won't the customers object?" Cash asked.

"Yeah, I guess." Amy traced a finger over his signature, sighed again.

"Should I sign a piece of paper as well?" he offered.

"I have a better idea." Amy handed Paige her smartphone. "Would you take a pic of us?"

Cash gave Paige a sheepish grin, full of apology and bad-boy charm, but hey, he didn't owe her anything. What did she care?

She snapped the photo. Amy simpered some more and finally made her way back to the counter when an irritated customer loudly cleared his throat.

"Now," Cash said, giving her his full attention. "Where were we?"

"We weren't anywhere. I was eating breakfast. You sat down."

"Exactly." His grin was a firecracker, hot and sparkly.

"Exactly what?"

"That's what I want to know."

Her stomach did a slow roll, flipping all the way

over like a biplane at an airshow. "What do you want to know?"

"Why did you run out on me?"

"I didn't run out on you. I went back home."

"You *ran* back home."

"I moved quickly."

"Same thing."

"I did *not* run."

"Okay, you scurried. It was definitely a scurry."

She *had* scurried. He scared the hell out of her. "I had somewhere to be."

He glanced around. "I can see this was a very urgent appointment."

"A chocolate croissant was calling my name."

"Well," he said. "A chocolate croissant can't be denied. Mystery of the runaway woman solved."

She narrowed her eyes. "Are you stalking me?"

"Not that you're not stalk-worthy, darling," he drawled. "But no. I'm meeting Emma and her family here for breakfast. It's just a happy coincidence."

She didn't know how happy it was, but an exploding, effervescent, Mentos-dropped-in-diet-soda feeling spewed from her stomach to her heart to her throat.

Paige crumpled her napkin and the parchment paper sleeve that the croissant had come in, and dropped it into her empty paper coffee cup. "I gotta go."

"Scurrying off again." His tone was light, bright, and accusatory.

"What do you want from me?" She hitched her purse strap up on her shoulder.

"A date." It was a firm, declarative statement.

Stunned, she simply stared at him as that Mentos-in-diet-soda response went off again inside her. "Huh?"

"Ya know. You. Me. The two of us. Go somewhere together. Laugh. Talk. Have fun."

Her heartbeat slammed against her eardrums. *Bam. Bam. Bam.* Seriously? Was this really happening? A famous country-and-western musician was asking her out?

She folded her arms over her chest, sent him a measured stare. "Why?"

He looked surprised by that, as if no one had ever questioned his motives. Probably they hadn't. When you were that good looking, rich, and talented people fell all over themselves to hang out with you.

"Because you're cute and I really like you and I'm a sucker for those cinnamon freckles."

Her heart was thumping so hard that she could barely hear herself answer. And she felt a hit of pure pleasure that resembled the feeling she got when she bit into that chocolate croissant—warm, happy, fulfilled.

Cash Colton stirred her in a hundred different ways. Stirring up feelings she'd vowed never to feel again. It was sexy and provocative and terrifying. She wasn't ready for this. For the likes of him. She needed a Shetland pony before she got back on the dating horse again, and he was a motherjamming Clydesdale.

"I'm flattered," she said, somehow managing a cool, collected tone. "Truly. But no thank you."

For a split second the expression in his eyes flattened out as he took the hit of her rejection, and in that moment he looked like a vulnerable little boy. But it was just for a breath.

"You don't like men?"

She blinked. "Excuse me?"

"No judgment if you don't like men." He held up his palms. "Just wondering."

Her mouth dropped open. Was his ego that big that he couldn't conceive of the notion that a woman had turned him down for a date?

He nailed her with his stare. "Or do you have something against musicians?"

"I have nothing against musicians."

"So it's me in particular."

"Well, you are being a bit annoying at the moment."

"Coming on too strong?"

"Yes."

"I'm sorry," he said, sounding completely sincere. "But I can't seem to get you out of my head."

She hauled in a deep breath, ignored the part of her that wanted to tell him, *Yes, yes, yes, I'll go out with you*, and said instead, "It's not you."

"Oh." His smiled finally vanished. "You're already in a relationship."

She wanted to lie. It would be easier to lie. But she simply wasn't wired that way. "No."

He paused and they looked into each other's eyes and she could not ignore the zap of electricity or the panicky rush of vertigo.

"I want to press, but I don't want to be *that* guy so I'll let you go," he said.

Whew!

He got up, gave her the sweetest, gentlest smile.

"Since we're going to be neighbors, I hope we can at least be on friendly terms."

"Friends? Yes. I can do that."

"Good enough for me." He turned to go to the counter.

Amy was standing directly in front of him, crowding his personal space. He jumped back, and his hip crashed into Paige's butt just as she was standing up.

Contact.

His pelvis to her backside.

Holy freaking catfish!

Hot tingles shot up and down her body. Her head spun pleasantly. Just friends? There was no way she could be just friends with this guy. Not when it felt as if a nuclear reactor was going off in her pants.

"If she won't go out with you," Amy declared, almost panting, "I certainly will."

McDang, son, you let her put you in the friend zone.

In all his thirty years on the planet the only other woman he'd kept in the friend zone was Emma. But in that case, he and Emma had been on the same page. They liked other—hell, they loved each other—but neither one of them had sexual feelings for the other.

Paige was another matter entirely. She fired all his engines with rocket-boosting intensity, although he wasn't quite sure why. She certainly wasn't his usual type. He wanted to run after her and convince her to give him another shot, but . . .

1) That would look pathetic and he never begged.

2) He had to deal with Amy, who was touching him inappropriately.

3) Emma, Sam, Lauren, and Charlie were walking through the door.

He smiled at Amy, but put a thorn in his tone as he untangled her arms from his neck. "You're a beautiful woman," he said. "But I'm too old for you."

"I'm nineteen, I swear."

"And I'm almost thirty-one."

"I'm a lot more experienced than I look," she wheedled.

"I'm sure of that," he said. "But you need to be wild and free and enjoy your youth. I've been there, done that."

"Oh," she said. The expression in her eyes told him she was hankering for a ticket out of town. Bright lights. Big city. Champagne and cocaine.

He knew that last part because he could see the "champagne" and "cocaine" tattooed along her hairline at her right ear.

"Amy," barked a woman from the kitchen door. "Quit coming on to the customers and get back to work."

Amy rolled her eyes, made sound effects from *The Wizard of Oz* when the Wicked Witch of the West called out her monkeys, and sauntered back to the counter.

Emma touched his shoulder, laughing. "I see you've met Amy."

"I've had the pleasure."

"Pleasure?" An amused eyebrow went up on Emma's forehead. "You really are a nice guy."

"I'm gonna take a wild stab in the dark here and guess that Amy grew up without a father figure in her life."

"Bingo." Emma linked her arm through his and guided him toward a table with Sam, Lauren, and Charlie. "Sit."

"I haven't ordered breakfast yet."

"This is a rescue mission," Emma said. "I'll order for you, so you don't have to converse with Amy."

"I appreciate the save, but I can't let you carry all that back to the table by yourself."

"Don't worry, Charlie's going with me. You can keep Sam and Lauren company." Emma gave Sam a meaningful look that Cash didn't understand.

Charlie pushed back his chair and got up to follow Emma to the counter.

"Hey," Cash called. "You don't even know what I want."

"Fried egg sandwich," she tossed over her shoulder. "Large coffee, black." She knew him too well.

"She's an amazing woman," Cash said.

"Yes, she is." Sam had the look of a man sappy in love who fully trusted that his woman loved him back with equal zeal.

A quick pang of jealousy knifed him. Sam knew what it was like to be well and truly loved and to be so sure of that love. Cash had no reason to be jealous of his friends. He'd made his choices. Sacrificed love for a career. Was generally okay with it.

"Why don't you go help your mother and Charlie?" Sam prompted Lauren.

"'Kay." The second grader hopped up and took off.

Uh-oh. Why was Sam sending his kid away from the table?

"How's the houseboat?" Sam asked, his tone mild but his eyes serious.

"Turquoise."

Sam's mouth tipped up in amusement. "Forgot to mention that. It's not a deal breaker, is it?"

"Not complaining," Cash said. "I'm just happy to have a place to call home for a month."

"Ever thought about settling down for good?"

"Never ran across a town that could anchor me."

"It's not so much the town, as the people. I was born here. Raised here. Plan to die here. Twilight is my home." Sam seemed proud and happy about that. Which was fine. He was a vet, not a musician.

Cash hadn't had a real home since he'd run away from his grandparents' faltering ranch at fifteen, seeking fame and fortune. Oh, he'd had houses, several of them strewn around the country. But he hadn't stayed in any of them more than a few months at time. Even when he was with Simone. She was just like him. They'd always been on the road. It was one of the reasons they'd stayed together for so long. They were both wandering troubadours. Vagabonds. He told himself that's who he was, figured that's probably how it always would be if he was lucky.

"We ran into Paige on the way in," Sam said casually, but there was nothing casual about the way he rested his hands on the table with a solid *thunk*, interlacing them tightly into a joined fist, a gesture of we-need-to-have-a-serious-talk.

The easiness he and Sam normally shared around each other evaporated. He stared at Sam's fisted hands, noticed a dog hair on the sleeve of his jacket. The vet was known for being laid-back, but Cash could feel tension radiating off him like hot coals.

"Yeah?"

"Did you know that Paige is a cousin to Emma's best friend Flynn?"

Huh? That let the air out of his sails. He thought he was Emma's best friend. Then again, it had been over three years since he'd seen her in person. Not since he hooked up with Simone. Emma hadn't approved of her, and so he hadn't reached out to Emma when Simone left him. They'd only reconnected because Emma had written to Deet asking if he knew how to get in touch with him. It had taken three weeks for her letter to reach Cash in the rain forest, but when he'd gotten it, asking him to headline her charity event in Twilight, he'd packed up his things, traveled to Lima, where he'd called her, accepted the gig, and they'd talked for hours.

Of course, he should expect that now Emma's best friend would be another married woman with kids who lived in the same town. He had no right to feel slighted.

But he did. Emma was the one person he'd always been able to count on through thick and thin. Emma and his mentor, Freddie Frank, they had his back, even when he fell off the earth a bit and didn't keep in touch.

"In fact," Sam went on, "Emma and Flynn are close as sisters. We're all family. And by extension, so is Paige."

"She's a lucky woman."

"Paige has a huge heart." Sam's serious expression intensified. "Too big, some might say. She trusts too easily. Or at least she did . . . She's been through a whole lot lately. Last thing she needs is more heartbreak."

That pissed him off. What the hell was Sam eluding?

"Did Emma put you up to this conversation?"

"No," Sam said. "But she stayed up until one this morning baking cookies and muttering about you and Paige. I don't mind you being Emma's friend, but when you keep her awake at night, that's another story."

"Got it," Cash said evenly, kept his tone conciliatory. He didn't want to ripple the waters with his best friend's husband. He might no longer be Emma's best friend, but she was still his.

They both looked off in opposite directions. Sam had done his duty, warned Cash off, and Cash had absorbed the message. Paige was a sweet small-town girl with small-town dreams. No rambling man need apply.

CHAPTER 7

Musette: A Baroque dance with a drone-bass.

After breakfast, Cash walked back to the house-boat, his thoughts on Paige. She wasn't a traditional beauty, but there was something about her that appealed to him more than the classic ideal.

She was cute, and spunky, sassy, fascinating, and . . . oddly mysterious for the girl next door. It was surprising to him that he was falling so hard for someone who was not really his type, had never been his type.

He admired her determination, her loyalty, and the way her smooth dark hair curled like a question mark at her chin. Liked those big hazel eyes that studied him warily from underneath a soft slash of dark eyebrows. Adored the perfect shape of her sweet, pink mouth.

And that body! His hands tingled at the thought of touching her.

On the walk back, he had to stop several times to speak to fans and admirers. He'd be lying if he said he didn't enjoy the attention. But that wasn't why he'd gone into music. He hadn't set out to be famous. Celebrity had a darker side. Whenever he found himself getting too caught up in the trappings of success, he always came back to the bottom line.

Music.

That's what drove him. The unstoppable desire to make music that mattered. Music had saved his life. End of story. Everything else was icing on the cake.

He moved down the dock.

Music cranked up to maximum volume pulsed from Paige's houseboat. Cash recognized the tune immediately. It was his song "Toasted," about a man haunted by the inability to make love stay.

Ironically, he'd written it six months before he learned Snake and Simone were carrying on behind his back. In some far alcove of his mind, had he suspected something? "Toasted" had been The Truthful Desperadoes' last recording.

For a sad topic—lost love—the music had an upbeat, I-will-survive quality. *Rolling Stone* had dubbed it a male breakup anthem, saying it was Kelly Clarkson's "Stronger" for men. At the time, he hadn't cared for the corny comparison, but in the wake of his song's overwhelming success, he'd warmed to it.

So Paige was playing "Toasted." Coincidence? He didn't think so.

And her houseboat was seriously rocking in the slip.

Was she with someone? *If the houseboat is rocking, don't come knocking*. But she'd told him there wasn't anyone special in her life. Ah, but she had said she wasn't in a relationship. She never said she didn't take booty calls. It could be a short-term hookup.

His smile stumbled into a frown as he walked onto the deck of his houseboat, stuck the key in the lock, and turned to push it open. From his peripheral vision, he caught a flash of movement, and swiveled for a better look.

The window blinds were open on the houseboat next door and he could see straight into the main living area.

And there, in pink cotton undies and matching bra, was Paige MacGregor dancing *Risky Business*–style to *his* song.

Not just dancing, but flinging herself wildly around the room in an incredibly graceful ballet of pure joy. The woman had crazy-mad skills. Why wasn't she a dancer or at least a dance instructor? He made a mental note to ask Emma why she had Paige working as a Santa's helper when she should be onstage in dance numbers.

Cash stood mesmerized, stunned by her performance, and . . . let's face it . . . the fact she was in bikini underwear and a push-up bra the color of cotton candy. Her gorgeous full breasts bouncing and jiggling with every twist and turn.

Entranced, he couldn't have looked away if someone had yelled, "Bomb!"

The new song, which had begun writing itself in his head the minute he'd met Paige, started up again, additional chords and new lyrics unfurling as if by magic. He realized he could make it into a second song, or keep it as one song with two distinct parts with changing tempo, pace, and cadence, something along the lines of "Bohemian Rhapsody" perhaps.

Excitement churned his blood. Stirred his soul. Watching her, he felt inspired, gifted, blessed. His imagination sparkled and glowed. Rolled like a boulder down Mount Everest, picking up speed, gathering momentum, rushing gleeful and headlong to the bottom. Swallowing him up in the flow of creativity that had, for the past year, evaded him.

Abruptly, she stopped dancing, turned down the music, and picked up her cell phone.

He should have gone inside. The performance was over, but he didn't move. A gentleman would avert his gaze, but no one had ever called Cash a gentleman.

Okay, it was voyeuristic. Guilty as charged.

He stared. Frankly. Appreciatively. Thank you, God, for your gift to the world that is Paige Mac-Gregor's body.

What a figure! Beautiful bust, just beautiful, ample, but not overwhelming. Curvy waist and hips and a softly rounded belly that was a real turn-on. Generous thighs. Have mercy!

And here she was. A woman with a goddess body, standing right in front of him, talking on the phone in her pink feminine underwear, sweat glistening on her skin. He felt like he'd won the lottery.

Still on the phone, she bent over to pick something up off the floor. Giving him a fantastic view of her gorgeous butt.

More pillowy softness. Full. Lush. Irresistible.

His erection, which had been growing, lengthened and tightened against his zipper. His blood spewed hot as an overheated radiator, and his breath shot out in ragged chugs.

Her fanny wriggled, and he finally noticed she was trying to take something away from Fritzi, but the poodle was intent on playing tug-of-war.

His gaze traced from that sweet rump to the indention where it joined her thighs and tapered down to shapely legs. A backside like that could lead a man straight to hell and make him damn grateful to be there.

His throat constricted. Cash wanted to touch her so badly he had to knot his hands into fists to keep them from quaking.

She got whatever she'd been trying to wrestle away from Fritzi, and tossed it on the table. Straightened, cell phone still pressed to her ear, and glanced up.

Their eyes met.

Deadlocked.

He was busted.

She looked shocked, then mortified, and immediately jumped to the window. Snapped closed the blinds. Shutting him out. Shutting him down.

He should have been ashamed of himself for spying on her. He wasn't. Grinning, he went into the house, happily whistling, "Toasted."

It had been Emma on the phone, asking Paige if she could work the charity fundraiser at the Brazos River Music Review instead of Santa's helper at the playhouse that evening, although she would be wearing the same outfit. With a sellout crowd eager to see Cash Colton, they didn't have enough ushers at the venue.

"You're a lifesaver, you know that?" Emma sighed with relief when Paige agreed to switch work assignments.

Unfortunately, Paige had said yes before she'd caught Cash peeping in her window.

Okay, he wasn't exactly peeping. She'd had the blinds up. Her bad. But a gentleman would have politely gone inside his own fricking houseboat, not stood on the deck staring.

She sank onto the couch, wondering how long he'd been standing there, and how much he'd seen. Had he seen her dancing? Had he heard her playing his music? Had he figured out she'd Googled him, discovered his discography, and ended up downloading several of his recordings because she really did like his sound?

All that evidence, in the hour and a half since she'd seen him at the bakery, suggested she was obsessed with the man.

She glanced down at her nearly naked body.

Oh crap. He'd seen *a lot*.

Groaning, she collapsed onto the couch cushion, covered her face with a pillow. Mortified didn't begin to cover how she felt. Flaming shame was closer. Now, Cash not only knew that she liked him enough to dance to his music, but he also knew exactly what she looked like in pink underwear.

God, why hadn't she thought to close the blinds? She'd opened them before she'd left for breakfast because Fritzi liked looking out the window whenever she was gone.

To top things off, now she was going to have to work the event where Cash was the headliner.

What to do? What to do?

Paige nibbled her bottom lip. Maybe she should call Emma and ask if there was someone she could swap places with and stay at the playhouse tonight instead of heading over to the music venue. Except Emma had so much on her plate coordinating both the theater and charity event, on top of playing Jovie in two productions of *Elf* today. She didn't want to inconvenience her.

One phone call. How inconvenient would that be?

She picked up her phone, debated on whether to punch Emma's number on the speed dial button or not.

C'mon. It was only for a couple of hours. Cash would be onstage. She'd be helping audience members to their seats. He would probably never even know she was there.

As for the embarrassment? Well, it wasn't the first time she'd made a fool of herself and most likely it wouldn't be the last.

Fine. She would do it. Decision made, she put the phone in her purse, went to the bedroom to get dressed.

While secretly, a small part of her—okay a medium-sized part of her—jumped like a gleeful antelope.

She would get to see Cash perform.

The Brazos River Music Review was a large white domed building made of Texas limestone and capped with a shiny tin roof that shielded it against hail season. The Music Review was five miles out of town down Highway 51, which ran from Twilight to the neighboring town of Jubilee.

Emma had lured Cash to town with stories of some of the famous acts that had performed there— Willie Nelson, The Band Perry, the Tejas Brothers, Brent Amaker. She told him that his name would be added to the ring of honor lining the inside of the dome.

He felt kind of weird about that, but if he could bring in money for the charity that helped under-privileged children, he was in.

Cash arrived an hour and a half early, and the parking lot was already jam-packed. Fans were throwing tailgate parties waiting for the program to start, cowboys in Wranglers and Stetsons, cowgirls in stylish boots and tight-fitting jeans. The smell of hamburgers and hot dogs filled the air. Coolers full of iced beer and sodas provided both seating and portable refrigeration. A few people had gui-tars and were picking out tunes for singalongs. Kids played tag on a patch of grass beside the asphalt parking lot.

Cash smiled. This was nice. Real nice.

He parked around back like Emma had instructed and retrieved his guitar case from the backseat of his extended cab pickup truck.

The evening air was cool and crisp, a typical early December day in North Central Texas.

During the scheduled, three-hour afternoon re-hearsal and sound check, he'd met the manager of the Music Review and the band with whom he would be performing. They weren't the slick professionals he was used to, but they were competent enough and eager to please. He had enjoyed riffing with them.

It reminded him of the old days when he'd first started in the business. When all that mattered was the music. It dawned on him that was part of the reason he'd come here. Not just because he couldn't refuse Emma anything. This was an opportunity to get back to his roots. A chance to recapture his youth.

An assistant, hired to wrangle the musical talent, ushered him backstage where the band was tuning up. They greeted him jovially.

"Yo, Cash Register." Kenny Wilson, the string-bean drummer, grinned. He had long blond corn-rows that accentuated his sharp straight nose.

By day Kenny was a welder, and when Cash had asked him during rehearsal how he did his job without his hairstyle getting in the way, Kenny had said, with another rampant grin, "Panty hose, man, panty hose."

"How's it hangin'?" quipped the bass guitarist who was so tall his head almost touched the papier-mâché reindeer dangling from the ceiling. His name was Igor Bunch and he worked as a short-order cook at Froggy's restaurant.

"Looking sharp," the tambourine girl said breath-lessly, and gave him a saucy wink. She was just out of high school and the daughter of one of Sam's friends.

The red-haired keyboardist, nicknamed Rojo, was dressed all in black. He simply nodded and tipped his hat. The strong silent type. Rojo was the only one of the group who eked out a living as a musician, performing at county fairs, honky-tonks, and roadhouses. Cash had been there, done that, knew how hard it was. But damn if a part of him didn't miss it.

He greeted the band members, gathered them together, and gave a rousing pep talk. "I'm going to do another sound check."

"That's the third time," Kenny pointed out with a flip of his head, his braids whacking against each other.

"OCD much?" Igor asked.

Rojo bobbed his head once, a stoic man's *yes*.

"Be right back." Cash pushed through the split in the black curtain, went to the apron of the stage, hopped off into the auditorium, and went in search of the sound engineer.

Even though this was just a small-town charity event, Cash was determined to put on a good show. His biggest fear was disappointing his audience. Call him a control freak, he'd wear the label with pride, but when it came to his music Cash always gave one hundred and ten percent.

Tonight, he had two stumbling blocks. One, the inexperienced band, and two, the fact that he hadn't performed in over a year. Had barely even picked up a guitar since Simone left him for Snake and broke up the band and someone had stolen his favorite guitar, Lorena.

Familiar anxiety crept over him. Jittery stomach. Sweaty palms. The critical voice in his head yelling, *You're gonna screw this up, you're gonna suck!* That was his greatest fear. Sucking onstage.

A side door opened, letting in a glow of outside light, along with a shapely young woman in a sexy Santa Baby costume.

Paige!

His pulse jumped, galloped. A grin stole over his face and he sidled up behind her. "I'm sorry," he said, repeating what she'd said to him the previous afternoon. "But we've got a strict schedule to keep and we're not opening to the public until seven."

Her face dissolved into a helpless grin. "I'm an usher."

He clicked his tongue. "Rules are rules."

"Even in my case?" she asked in a voice so sexy his head buzzed.

Was she enjoying this as much as he was? "Out, lady."

"But—"

"No excuses."

"I'm—"

"Go." He snapped his fingers and sent her his fiercest scowl.

She turned to leave.

"No, wait." He grabbed her elbow. "Come back. I was only kidding."

She faced him again, looked impish. "Gotcha."

God, he liked her. It washed over him, strong and overwhelming. He *really* liked her. He was still holding on to her elbow and enjoying the hell out of it, but he didn't want to appear pushy.

He dropped his hand.

She dropped her gaze.

Her chestnut bangs were brushed back off her forehead and held in place with a candy cane barrette, showing off a bewitching widow's peak. The ends of her hair curled at her chin, framing her face and calling attention to her hazel eyes that were an arresting mix of brown and green.

The Santa Baby costume was as sexy as he remembered. The bodice fit snuggly around her breasts, nipped in at her waist, the short green skirt flared out over sturdy, shapely legs. What would it feel like to run his hands up one of those thighs, feel the heat of her body, the softness of her skin?

"Hey," he said, holding her gaze.

"Hey," she whispered in return.

"Why aren't you at the theater?" he asked.

"Emma said they needed help here."

Good old Emma. She loved to play matchmaker. He should be irritated with her over it. He wasn't.

"I'm glad Emma sent you instead of someone else," he said.

Paige was holding her breath, her eyes going big and round, and she said it so softly that he barely heard her. "Me too."

He thought about saying something about seeing her dancing inside the houseboat, but decided against it. She'd been embarrassed. Let it slide.

"Are you nervous?" she asked. "Do you get stage fright?"

"Every time," he confessed. "But tonight more so than usual."

"How come?"

"This is important to Emma. The charity is a good one. The audience deserves the best performance I can deliver."

"I'm sure you'll come through."

"I'm rusty. I haven't performed since—"

"Simone left."

He winced. "I was going to say the band broke up and my favorite guitar was stolen."

"Her leaving is what broke up the band, right? At least, that's what I've read."

"Been Googling me, have you?" He leaned in closer, heartened that she'd bothered to research him.

She didn't admit anything, but neither did she back away.

He took that as an encouraging sign.

"It's all Christmas songs, right?" she said in a honeyed voice that sent shivery goose bumps singing over his skin. "That should make it easier. Old favorites. Nothing new. Nothing challenging."

She was correct.

"I imagine you know those songs inside out," she went on. "You've got this."

He liked her pep talk. Hell, he liked her, and not just because she'd cracked his creative block. He was into her.

Unfortunately, he couldn't figure out if she was into him or not. She didn't seem to care one whit about his celebrity—which he found refreshing—but he didn't often come across people who were unimpressed by his success. It made him ache to find ways to impress her.

"You boosted my confidence. Thanks," he said.

"That's what friends are for." Her smile was innocent, a baby lamb of a smile.

Oh yeah. He was still in the friend zone. He cocked his head, sent her a measured look, trying to decide what it would take to get into the lover zone. At least for the month.

"I think it's sweet," she said.

"What?"

"That you care enough about a small-town charity event to be nervous. A lot of people would just go through the motions."

"I always bring my A game."

"I know. I read that about you."

"On Wikipedia?"

She gave a half smile that said, *You got me.*

Ha. She wasn't as impervious to his charm as she wanted him to believe.

She tilted up her chin in that perky way she had, as if she was an inquisitive bird, curious but ready to fly away the instant danger reared its head. The look in her eyes, the position of her body, the color of those gorgeous lips, shot a bolt of desire straight down the center of his body.

He wanted her. Right now. Right here. It was crazy how much he wanted her. Scary too.

"Well," she said. "We both have jobs to do. Break a leg . . ." She paused, put a finger to her lips. "No, wait. Do they say break a leg in music or is that only in acting?"

"It works for any performance artist."

"Oh good. Then do that. Break both legs."

"I admire your enthusiasm." He wished he could stay and talk to her all night but the door opened and the sound engineer appeared, reminding him where he was and why he was here.

"Listen," he said. "You wanna grab a pizza or something after this shindig?" He saw the word "no" forming on her lips and quickly added, "Strictly as friends, of course."

"Emma's throwing a party for you at her house after," she said. "Remember?"

That's right. He'd forgotten. "You'll be at the party?"

"No. I've got to go to work early in the morning. No late night for me."

"You ready?" asked the engineer.

Cash scrambled for something else to say but she was already headed out the door. He shook his head and followed the engineer to do the final sound check. He might have struck out again with Paige, but he wasn't going to strike out with the audience. He vowed to keep his focus where it belonged.

Squarely on the music.

CHAPTER 8

Operetta: A short, light musical drama.

The houselights went down at seven o'clock to a cram-packed auditorium. The band stood ready for his cue. Sweat beaded the back of Cash's neck the way it always did before a performance and his stomach was tight as a drum skin.

The curtains parted.

Cash stared out into the sea of faces, and somehow, in that dark and crowded place, his gaze landed on Paige. She had her back to the wall near the exit door, eyes trained on him.

His heart softened and his stomach settled and the sweat evaporated.

He nodded to the band, hit the first lick of "It's Beginning to Look a Lot Like Christmas" on his guitar, and stepped up to the mike.

And boom . . . they were off.

Cash played with all his heart and soul, putting everything he had into the familiar Christmas song. Played as if he were at Carnegie Hall.

They transitioned into "Rudolph the Red-Nosed Reindeer" which had the kids cheering and singing along. Then it was on to Alan Jackson's "Let It Be Christmas."

Women sighed. Men doffed their hats. Old and young alike applauded.

Wings of joy that he hadn't felt since . . . well, since he'd gotten his first paltry recording deal eleven years ago at Christmastime and found himself living out his mother's deepest dream for herself. The feeling rose up high and true. It came up through his throat and mouth, vibrating out with his breath, his song spilling into the auditorium.

What was this miraculous sensation?

The spirit of Christmas.

He named it, felt lightened and enlightened as it surged and throbbed his muscles, cells, and nerve endings.

For the past year, he thought this feeling was lost to him. The joy. The sheer pleasure he took in music. The buzz of performing live onstage. The sublime exhilaration he got from the audience's reaction. He came alive again.

Was reborn.

He remembered that he'd been put on earth to make music. It was his life's purpose. Even if his mother hadn't preached it to him night and day, he knew in his heart he was a born musician.

Bliss guided his fingers over the guitar strings, plucking swift and familiar.

His eyes found Paige in the darkness again, latched on to her. Held tight. His vision narrowed to Paige and her alone and he sang to her from the basement of his soul, belting out the song's message of hope, peace, and love.

Sappy. Sentimental. Yes. Yes. Yes. He reveled in it. The gush of that idealized moment.

He wanted to change her mind about him. How could he get her to give him half a chance? He needed a romantic gesture. Something big. Something showy.

Paige's body swayed in time to the music. She wanted to dance. He could see it on her. In her. She twitched with rhythm.

An idea hooked him.

The band started into their next tune, "Rockin' Around the Christmas Tree," but instead of singing as planned Cash took the microphone and hollered enthusiastically, "Hello, *Twilight*!"

"Hello, Cash!" the crowd yelled back.

"Y'all like this song?" he asked.

The crowd cheered. Arms waved in the air. Cell phones lit up the darkness. Thunderous applause shook the building.

"It's a great beat to dance to," he murmured into the mike, swiveled his hips Elvis Presley–style for effect.

"Yeah!"

"You said it."

"Sing your heart out, Cash!"

He seduced the audience with the come-hither look he'd perfected for the stage. The extroverted mask his introverted side pulled out when it was time to perform. "In a minute I'm gonna ask you guys to dance your hearts out . . ."

"Woot! Woot!"

The band elongated the intro of the song, confused by what he was up to, but adapting quickly. They might be mostly amateurs, but they wanted to put on a standout performance as much as he did.

"There's a young lady out there who loves to dance . . ." He pinned Paige with his eyes. "She's got some serious moves and I've been admiring her from afar."

Even across the auditorium in the glare of the stage lighting, he could see her face pale. People turned their heads, curious, gawking.

"Let's convince her to get up here onstage and show us exactly what she's got. Give it up for Paige MacGregor!" Cash put the mike back on the stand and started a slow clap.

The audience followed his lead, a steady, measured tempo. *Clap. Clap. Clap.*

Igor broke into a drumbeat that matched the clapping.

Paige dropped his gaze. Shook her head.

Vigorously.

Cash increased the speed, so did the audience and Igor on drums. "C'mon on up, Paige."

"Paige, Paige, Paige!" chanted the crowd.

She raised her hands, kept shaking her head, and looked utterly humiliated.

Ah damn. What had he done? Regret strangled him. What was he thinking? Clearly she did not want to do this, and the last thing he'd wanted was to embarrass her.

"Paige. Paige. Paige."

Clap, clap, clappity-clap.

He wanted to call it off, but didn't know how.

He'd made such a big deal of having her onstage, worked the crowd up into a frenzy, how could he back down now?

Egged on by the idea of a romance playing out before them, the audience went nuts. "Paige! Paige! Paige!"

He held out his hand, crooked a finger at her.

She flattened her back against the wall. Swiveled her head from left to right, right to left.

Igor was Mick Fleetwood-ing the hell out of that drum with a gut-punching tom-tom beat right off the *Tusk* album. Rock on, Igor. *Boom. Boom. Boom.* The cadence matched the pounding of Cash's heart.

No backing down. Only one direction. Full steam ahead.

He hopped off the stage, started down the aisle, going after her. He was putting her on the spot. He knew it. Did it anyway.

The sea of people parted as he swaggered toward her in time to the beat. Seducing her with his voice and his moves the best way he knew how. The idea was to waltz her up onto the stage the way Bruce Springsteen did with Courtney Cox to "Dancing in the Dark."

But when he got to her, Paige balked.

Shook her head like a wet dog. Tucked her hands into her armpits. *No.*

Um, knock-knock, jackass. Courtney had been planted in the audience. Bruce didn't spring it on her unaware.

Paige's mouth was pressed into a firm line. Her eyes seemed haunted, her face flaming red.

Damn, he'd messed up royally. He extended his

head. Sent her a deep apology with his eyes. *Sorry.
Sorry. So sorry.*

"Paige! Paige! Paige!"

The band played the first stanza of "Rockin'
Around the Christmas Tree" over and over and over.
Everyone was waiting for her to get up onstage.

"Please," he whispered. "It's for charity. Don't do
it for me. Do it for the children."

She glowered. Hard. If looks could kill, he'd be
headless.

"Paige! Paige! Paige!" The applause grew louder
and louder, faster and faster.

"You are so dead," Paige muttered, but offered
up an I'm-a-good-sport smile. "So very dead."

Hmm. Intrigued, he upped the heat on his smile.
How did she plan on getting even?

He kept his hand extended. "I figured."

Finally, reluctantly, with a resigned sigh, she sank
her hand in his. Her palm was cool and soft. Refreshing. He interlaced their fingers, pulled her to
his side, and escorted her back up the aisle to enthusiastic cheering.

He helped her onto the stage, realized belatedly
she was in those ankle-breaking, six-inch stilettoes.
God, he was a jerk.

But the band and the audience were completely
into it. Everyone was hopping and jumping and singing. Lively. Heartfelt. Fun. Any musician's dream.

Except he'd shamed the one person he most wanted
to impress.

Stagefright ransacked her lungs. Lurched her stomach. Sent tremors shaking her entire body.

Flashback.

The last time someone had ambushed her publicly, made a grand gesture, well . . . she'd ended up losing her house, her car, and her identity. She stood frozen, throat constricted, feet welded to the floor.

In front of her, Cash danced. Shifting his feet to the beat, snapping his fingers, singing his heart out. Gazing into her as if they were alone in an empty room, his eyes whispering, *Come dance with me.*

He was just trying to put on a good show. Not his fault that she had hang-ups.

Move!

She didn't want to make either of them look like a fool. Goal: get through this with as much grace and good humor as possible.

The swell of bubbly music washed over Paige, and the part of her that missed dancing, the part of her that loved to have fun—the part of herself she'd put in a box and locked down tight—cracked that damn lock and broke free.

Here we go. She gave in, gave up, surrendered. Smiled brilliantly . . .

And danced her ass off.

Danced the way she had not danced since before Dad died, danced with more verve and soul than she'd danced in her panties on the houseboat, danced like no one was watching. Danced as if she were with Bruce Springsteen.

Take that, Courtney Cox.

Joy lit up Cash's face like hot sunshine on an icy morning.

The crowd went insane—cheering, clapping wildly,

calling her name again as they had before. "Paige, Paige, Paige."

She felt powerful, wrestling control back from Cash by going with the flow. Embracing the situation instead of fighting against it.

Oh, she was still plenty mad at him for ambushing her, but she was going to take those sour lemons and make a pitcher of the yummiest lemonade ever tasted.

The faster she danced, the freer she felt. All the grief, regret, and anger she'd been holding on to slipped away, falling like shooting stars across a midnight sky.

She jumped and jiggled, writhed and wriggled, skipped and spun.

It might have started out with Cash her puppet master, but now, she was the one pulling the strings.

She felt great.

She felt exhilarated.

She felt like a goddess.

Something she hadn't felt in very long time. Cash pushed her. He'd coerced her. He'd led her where she had not wanted to go.

And she loved him for that.

Which, of course, scared the stuffing out of her.

The notes of the song slowed. Cash slowed. Paige reluctantly slowed too. Pulse hammering, sweat soaking her clothes, tattered scraps of thoughts fluttering through her mind. Ribbons in the wind.

What does this mean? Where did things go from here? When had he slipped under her skin? How did she stop it? Who was she now?

He took her hand and hauled her to him as the

band played the song to the end, and the audience applauded as if their hands would fall off. Cash pressed his mouth to her ear. "Thank you. You were awesome. I am so sorry I got you into this. It was an impulse and I certainly didn't mean to make you do something against your will. I just wanted to dance with you. Too late I realized I'd blundered, a huge mistake. I feel awful about this. How can I make it up to you?"

To his credit, he looked deeply contrite. "Please," he groveled. "Give me a chance to make this right."

"You want to make it up to me?"

"Name it," he said. "It's yours."

"Please, just leave me alone." With that, she turned and fled the stage.

"You sure you don't want to go to Emma's party?" asked Flynn from the front passenger seat. Her husband, Jesse, was driving the family minivan.

They'd been the ones to give Paige a ride to the Brazos River Music Review, and after they dropped her off at her houseboat, they would head to the party Emma was throwing for Cash.

"No," Paige said, drawing her coat more tightly around her. "I just want to get into bed and forget this night ever happened."

"Why?" Jesse asked, sounding truly confused. "I thought it went well."

"I know you were embarrassed," Flynn said, poking her head over the seat, "but honestly, you did an amazing job. I had no idea you were such a good dancer. I mean, I know Grammie taught all us kids to dance, but some of us were born with two left feet."

"You're a great dancer," Jesse said to Flynn.

"I'm not, but thank you for lying." Flynn reached over to pat her husband's arm.

"I told Cash specifically that I had quit dancing," Paige said, not to be swayed by Flynn's compliments. "Why was he so determined to make me look like a fool?"

"You didn't look like a fool," Jesse said. "You looked like a professional dancer."

"Got a question for you, Jesse." Paige nibbled her bottom lip, stared out the window at the Brazos River rolling under the bridge below them.

"What's that?"

"Why are men such jackasses?"

"Um . . . um . . ." Jesse stuttered, laughed. "Because we're men?"

"Okay," Flynn interrupted. "I'm on your side, Paige. Cash should have never put you on the spot like that, but don't you think you're overreacting a wee bit? Almost any other woman in the auditorium tonight would have killed to be invited up on that stage."

"I would gladly have let them go up there instead," Paige said, wondering why she was so upset when the experience onstage had been so invigorating.

"From the wonderful things Emma has told me about Cash, I don't think he meant to upset you. I bet he thought you would secretly enjoy it."

"Paige," Jesse said in a quiet voice.

"Yes?"

"Why *did* you stop dancing?"

Why? Because Randy had ruined dancing for her,

but tonight, Cash had given her the joy back. She had to admit, he'd shoved her out of her comfort zone, and she hadn't been happy about it, but now? In the aftermath, she realized he'd resurrected the love of dancing in public she believed Randy had killed.

"Shh," Flynn said, and lightly swatted her husband's shoulder.

"Never mind me, Paige." Jesse braked at the traffic light leading into Twilight, cleared his throat. "I'm a jackass too."

"You're not a jackass." Flynn scooted over to nuzzle his neck. "You're just a little clueless sometimes."

Jesse cupped Flynn's face with his palm, said in a husky voice, "What would I ever do without you keeping me on the straight and narrow?"

Paige forced herself not to roll her eyes. After all, Jesse could see her in the rearview mirror. And besides, as sappy as her cousin and her husband were, they were really sweet together. Jesse and Flynn had the kind of closeness she'd always longed for and had given up on having. Some people just weren't cut out for happily-ever-after.

"I think you might be forgetting one thing," Flynn said when the light changed and she sat up from canoodling her husband.

"What's that?" Paige fiddled with the clasp on her purse.

"If Cash has got you this freaked out, it must mean you have feelings for him."

"Yeah," Paige muttered. "Feeling I wished he'd leave me alone."

"Colton likes you." Jesse guided the minivan through the quiet town square. Thank heavens they were almost at the marina.

"Of course he likes her," Flynn said. "Everyone likes Paige."

"I'm not talking about that kind of like." Jesse turned his head to beam at his wife.

"Oh." Flynn giggled. "Are you talking about the way you liked me in high school?"

"I'm talking about the way I've liked you since the first time I laid eyes on you."

Paige coughed. Loudly.

"I think we're getting too mushy for her," Flynn said. "She doesn't believe in fated love."

"You guys could just let me out here," she said at the stop sign in front of the Twilight Playhouse.

"Nothing doing. Twilight is a safe little town, but you're still half a mile from home and in high heels. We're taking you to the marina," Jesse said. "But we'll try to tone down the schmaltz."

"Thank you," Paige said, even though it wasn't the schmaltz that bothered her, rather it was her jealousy of their closeness and she didn't want to be *that* person. Just because she'd been unlucky in love didn't mean that Jesse and Flynn didn't deserve all the happiness in the world.

Apparently it was obvious to everyone that Cash liked her. When a musician pulled a woman up on-stage, he was interested.

Or rather, he wanted to have sex with her.

Secretly, that's what floored her. Why on earth would someone like Cash Colton, who could have his pick of beautiful, sexy women, want *her*? She was as ordinary as it got.

That's where she kept hanging up. That's why she was suspicious.

Why shouldn't he like you? bristled the part of her that had enjoyed dancing onstage.

She might not be a drop-dead beauty, but she was a nice person. After Simone Bishop, maybe he was ready for nice and ordinary.

Um, yeah. Sure. Magical thinking much?

Jesse pulled up to the marina. "Hang on, I'll walk you to the door."

"I'll be fine," Paige said, already bailing out of the minivan. "You can see me from here. Bye. Thanks so much for the lift home. Sorry to make you go out of your way."

"It's no trouble," Flynn said. "You're family. Are you sure you don't want to come to the party with us?"

"I'm good." She forced a smile. "You guys have fun."

She went into the houseboat, changed into jeans, a sweatshirt, and sneakers, and got out her bicycle. It was after nine, but she hadn't seen Grammie today. She had just enough time to slip in and kiss her good-night.

"How is she today?" Paige asked Addie when she let her in the back door of the nursing home.

Addie shook her head. "Rough one."

Paige's chest tightened. "What happened?"

"She was really confused. Kept trying to leave her room. Saying she had to find Wayne Newton and explain why she broke things off. The nurse ended up having to give her something for anxiety."

"Oh dear." Paige put a palm to her mouth. "Is she still awake?"

"Yes. She's pretty agitated. Maybe you can calm her down?"

Paige hurried to Grammie's room. Her grandmother was sitting straight up in bed, worrying the covers with her fingers. Her hair stuck up in all directions and her eyes were wide and wild.

The minute Grammie spied her, relief washed over her face. "There you are, Emaline! Where have you been?"

Emaline was Grammie's best friend when they'd both danced at the Flamingo in the 1960s. The friend had died a decade ago, and Paige had even attended the funeral with Grammie.

She hesitated at the door, not sure if she should correct Grammie and tell her who she was, or simply roll with the delusion. Her emotions crashed on rocky shoals. It killed her to see Grammie like this. Her stomach was a yo-yo swinging from the highs of dancing onstage with Cash to the lows of finding her grandmother in such a state.

"Come here, come here." Grammie motioned her inside with a frantic wave.

Paige shut the door.

"Sit." Grammie patted the mattress beside her.

Paige perched on the bed, slipped her arm around her grandmother's shoulders. "What's wrong?"

"It's Wayne," Grammie whispered.

"Has something happened?"

Grammie reached for Paige's hands. She interlaced her fingers with her grandmother's. "He wants more."

"More?"

Grammie blushed, her cheeks pinking, and lowered her eyelids. In that moment she looked like a shy young woman, and Paige saw in her the beauty she'd once been. That's when she realized Grammie was firmly stuck in 1965.

"You *know*," Grammie said, sounding scandalized. "He wants more than just kisses."

"You mean . . ."

Grammie bobbed her head. "He asked me to spend the night with him."

Paige sucked in a deep breath, not knowing how to tread this terrain. If she continued letting Grammie think that she was Emaline she might find out something about her grandmother she really didn't want to know. But Grammie was so caught up in her delusion, trying to tug her back into reality could worsen her agitation.

"I like him very, very much. In fact, I think I could fall madly in love with him if I let myself . . ."

"But?" Paige couldn't resist asking.

Grammie's eyes met hers. They were the eyes of a woman stuck in a long ago dilemma, a dilemma that had trailed her into old age.

Paige's heart broke for the girl that her grandmother had been and for the elderly woman dogged by dementia. She squeezed Grammie's hands.

"He's so famous. He's got women chasing him right and left. How can I trust that he truly cares for me? How do I know he's not just trying to get me into his bed? What's to say he won't dump me after we sleep together?" Grammie moistened her lips.

Paige had no idea how to answer that. Her mind drifted to Cash. Saw in him a parallel. She understood Grammie's dilemma. Found herself in 1965 and slipping under Emaline's skin. "But what if he loves you back?"

"Maybe that's even worse." Grammie looked frightened. "I want to get married someday and have children. I can't raise kids in his lifestyle. I enjoy dancing, but I can't do it forever. I don't want to do it forever. I can't see Wayne leaving the bright lights of Vegas for me. Not even if he loved me. He will always love performing more."

Paige thought again of Cash, felt a strange twist deep inside her. "What if you just had fun? No expectations. Just enjoy the time you have with him and let it be enough."

"I don't know how to have sex and not fall in love. If I give myself to Wayne, I *will* fall in love with him. I just can't bare the pain of losing him once I love him."

"Then you have your answer," Paige said, placed a palm on her grammie's chest. "It's been in your heart all along. Wayne's not the man for you."

Grammie's face softened and her grip on Paige's hands relaxed. Her eyes lightened. "Yes, yes. You are so right. I have to break things off with him."

"You'll find your true love one day," Paige promised her.

"I have already met someone else," Grammie said.

"You sly girl, stringing along two men at once!"

"No, no." Grammie laughed. "I just met him yesterday. He's working construction at Caesar's Palace. He's smart and funny and he's from Midland, Texas, which is just down the road from Abilene . . ." A dreamy expression came over Grammie face. Then she blinked. "Paige?"

"Yes, Grammie, it's me."

She shook her head, looked confused. "I think I had one of my bubbles."

"It's okay." She patted Grammie's hand. "You're safe."

"When I get those bubbles . . ." Grammie flicked her index finger against her thumb. "Pfftt, I disappear into a cloud."

"That must be scary."

"It is."

"Do you feel like you can relax and go to sleep now?"

Grammie's smile was wan. "As long as you're here."

Paige tucked her grandmother in, sat beside her bed until she fell asleep. By the time she left the nursing home, it was after ten-thirty and she was exhausted mentally, physically, and emotionally.

All she wanted to do was drop into the bed and sleep hard until the alarm went off. But there was still a mile-long bicycle ride back home.

CHAPTER 9

Progression: The movement of chords in succession.

The black Land Rover was parked at the marina when Paige cycled up in the dark. Was Emma's party for Cash over already? It wasn't even eleven yet.

She got off the bike at the metal steps, walked it down to the wooden dock leading to the boat slip. As she reached the houseboat, a shadowy figure stood up from a seated position beside her front door.

Her heart leaped to her throat, adrenaline pumped furiously through her veins, grabbing her breath in a chokehold and holding on with a death grip. Who was this?

Then he stepped forward into the glow of the security lamp.

Cash.

Her heart flopped back down to where it belonged and she started breathing again, but she still felt jacked up and jittery.

"Hello, Paige," he said, his tone as smoky as his eyes.

"What are you doing here? Why aren't you at Emma's party?"

"I left early."

"Why?" Her mouth tasted of spent adrenaline, astringent and electric.

"You." His voice drove the word like a hammer slamming into a nail. Hard. Solid. Righteous.

She locked her knees to keep them from buckling. "What about me?"

"We need to talk."

He was standing on the gangplank between the houseboat and the dock, blocking her from the front door. But she wasn't going to let him intimidate her. She pushed her bike forward.

Cash didn't budge.

She bumped his knee with her front tire. "You're in my way."

He puffed his chest, put a steel rod in his spine, and for a moment she feared he was not going to move. He studied her with serious intent, and then at last he stepped aside, waved with a flourish of his hand, but did not leave the gangplank.

To get to where she was going, she had to brush past him.

Fine. So be it.

She pushed the bike forward, trying to stay as far to the opposite side of the narrow gangplank as she could. Even so, on the way by, her hip scraped against his outer thigh. She felt the blister of contact.

He sucked in an audible gulp of air, sounding utterly vulnerable.

She didn't look at him, kept her gaze trained ahead, kept walking.

He peeled off behind her. Following.

She could feel his energy, his heat. Her pulse spiked, erratic and forceful. She parked her bike next to the house, put down the kickstand, and squatted to chain and lock it to the deck railing.

When she straightened, he was standing directly in front of her.

"Good night," she said crisply.

"I'm coming in," he said in a vigorous pitch that brooked no argument.

"You are not coming in." She was shaking, not so much because she was scared of him, but more because she was scared of herself. She *liked* this alpha, macho crap he was pulling.

He slapped a palm on the side of the houseboat just above her head, leaned in. "We're having this out."

"I asked you to leave me alone," she said, even though a part of her was happy that he'd left the party early and waited outside her door for her to show up. She'd gotten under his skin as surely as he'd gotten under hers.

Heady stuff. Dangerous stuff.

"No, you asked me to leave you alone *if* I wanted to make it up for persuading you onstage. I don't regret doing it. You were amazing."

"Persuaded?" She sank her hands on her hips. Struggled to look mad. "Is that what you call it? Try blackmail. It's more appropriate."

"I did not blackmail you. I coerced you. Big difference." He was leaning in, hand still planted against the wall above her head. Power posing.

"Results were the same. I ended up onstage dancing after I told you I'd quit dancing."

"We both know that's not true." He arched an eyebrow and it gave him a devilish look. "You still dance."

"In private. Not in public and certainly not onstage as the center of attention."

"And that's the end of the world?"

"I didn't want to do it. You disrespected my wishes." She had no idea how she managed to remain controlled on the outside. On the inside she was a gooey mess, going all soft and melty by the proximity of his tantalizing mouth.

He dropped his arm then, stepped back, ran a hand through his hair, shook his head. "Look, I realized trying to coax you onstage was a bad idea halfway into it, but by then the crowd had momentum and I was stuck. What I do regret is making you feel uncomfortable. I know I screwed up. Please forgive me."

"Really?" Paige scrutinized his face. He seemed sincere.

"It was never my attention to embarrass or belittle you."

"No? What was your intention?"

"It was supposed to have been a romantic gesture. I was trying to romance you."

Huh?

"Stop looking at me like I'm a lunatic." He growled, but it was a pleasant sound, more like a tomcat than a tiger.

"How in heaven's name was that romantic?"

"As things turned out, it wasn't. But most women I know would be over the moon to get pulled up onstage—"

"Does it hurt?" she asked.

"Does what hurt?"

"Carrying around such a gigantic ego?"

"Well, when you put it that way, it does make me sound like a jerk." His smile was full of apology and starlight.

"Look," she said. "I know you're used to women falling at your feet, and because I don't, you see it as a challenge. But please believe me when I tell you I'm not impressed."

He leaned in again, the wicked eyebrow going up on his forehead. "Not the tiniest bit?"

"Well, I do like your music, but all that other baloney . . . girls asking you to sign their boobs, people thinking you're a god simply because you sing and play a guitar with some level of talent—"

"*Some* level of talent? I've won a Grammy."

"Big whoop. Awards are just popularity contests. That's the part that *doesn't* impress me the most." She unlocked the door, opened it, and stepped inside.

"Wow." He looked surprised and impressed by her. "Good to know."

"Now, if you'll excuse me, I have to get up early in the morning . . ." She moved to close the door.

He reached out to block her from shutting it in his face. "Paige." Just the one word. Her name. Said commandingly. "I came here to apologize, not make you madder."

She paused. Damn her, why did she pause?

"May I come in? Speak my piece?"

"Will you go away if I do?"

"Yes."

"Five minutes." She spread the fingers on one hand and stepped aside to let him in. "You get five minutes to plead your case."

"Thank you." He pulled his spine up tall and waltzed into the house. Stopped. "Whoa."

"What?" Paige glanced around to see what had arrested his attention.

Three Christmas trees in the tiny living space—small, medium, large. The small one was a blue spruce with gold and silver ornaments. The medium tree was a Douglas fir flocked pink and themed with angels. And the big one, that touched the ceiling, a Leyland cypress adorned in red and white with candy cane ribbons, glittery red garlands, and numerous kitschy ornaments, from Santa flipping an omelet to Rudolph snowplowing on skis. And that didn't include the nativity scene on the counter or the snow village on the kitchen table or the twinkling Christmas lights strung from every corner of the room.

She loved Christmas, so sue her. So had her father. The majority of this stuff she'd inherited from him. It was the one thing Randy hadn't stolen from her.

Cash chuckled, gently poking fun. "It looks like Santa Claus exploded in here."

Paige raised her chin and her fighting spirit. "I like it."

"How do you keep Fritzi out of the trees?"

"He's pretty well mannered," she said. "Although

he kept attacking the rotating Little Deuce Coupe ornament that plays 'Little Saint Nick' I had to move it to a higher branch."

Fritzi himself was dancing his I-gotta-pee dance at the door.

"But right now, he needs to go out." She hooked his leash to his collar.

"I'll go with you," Cash said, and opened the door. "This puts a pin in the five minutes."

"Four minutes," she corrected.

The three of them walked back out into the nippy night air. Fritzi charged for the grass, yanking Paige behind him. Cash had to quicken his stride to catch up. They didn't talk, just huddled in their coats, waiting on Fritzi. Paige let the dog sniff and explore and ten minutes passed before they were back inside the house. The poodle promptly curled up into a ball on his pillow and went to sleep. It was past his bedtime.

Cash walked over to the tree, spun the Little Deuce Coupe, made it sing "Little Saint Nick."

"You're a Beach Boys fan?" he asked.

"My dad," she said quietly, then quickly changed the subject. "Four minutes."

"It must have taken you days to do all this decorating." He stepped to the snow village, studied the intricate details.

"You didn't notice the decorations when you were peeping in my window?"

"I wasn't peeping—" He shook his head, telegraphed her an enigmatic look she couldn't read. "Look, I'm sorry about that too. It was boorish to stare. But I didn't notice the surroundings because I was mesmerized by the floor show."

Her. Dancing. In pink underwear.

A knot of heat balled up in her chest, pushed up her neck to her jaw and skidded to a stop at her cheeks, burned hot and bright. Briefly, she closed her eyes, fought off the blush, opened her eyes again, and found him staring at her with surprising compassion.

"You have nothing to be ashamed of," he said.

"No, but you do, mister."

"About that . . ." He came closer.

She would have backed up, except there was no place to go. The cypress tree was behind her.

The scent of his aftershave wrapped around her, nice and masculine, sage and sandalwood and soap. He smelled so good it was hard to remember why she'd been mad at him. Even though he was average height, he loomed over her. Those shoulders, thick as oak trees, crowded out the light.

"Look," he said. "Here's the bottom line. I was really impressed when I saw you dancing this morning—"

"You mean when you were spying on me."

"You had the blinds up. Not my fault. If you don't want people to look, close the blinds."

He was right. She'd been careless. Had a secret part of her *wanted* him to look? It was an alarming thought.

"Three minutes," she said, holding up three fingers.

"Here's something else." He took another step, eyes narrowed, hips loose. His body radiated so much heat she could feel it through her clothes. "I'm attracted to you and I think you're attracted to me too."

Oh hells to the yeah, she was. But she wasn't about to let him know that. She was too raw, too vulnerable, and he could shatter her into a million little pieces. She thought of Grammie and her feelings for Wayne Newton. Suddenly had a new understanding of her grandmother.

He dipped his head, his nose inches from her.

She sucked in a deep breath. Her chest rose sharply, causing her breasts to graze his arm.

He smiled and, without another word, hooked a finger under her chin, tipped her face up, and sank his mouth down on hers.

Startled, she hitched in another breath without letting go of the first one and her breasts rose even higher, coming into contact with his hard, muscled chest.

"Exhale," he whispered.

She did, slowly letting the air leak out in one long, controlled hiss.

Cash kissed her again. Taking over. Taking charge. Capturing her. Raiding her. It was a blistering kiss, hot and insistent. Inflammatory.

One of his big hands slipped around her back to where her spine curved just above her butt. Every touch of his fingers was liquid fire. Igniting her in a blaze of sensation.

She was aware of everything—the richness of his scent, the roughness of his fingertips, the scratch of his beard stubble, the sight of his mesmerizing gray eyes locked squarely on her.

Hyperaware.

It was as if she had sensory superpowers. Her cells zinged. She sat up and took full notice of this man.

He was every fantasy come true. But that was just it, wasn't it? He was a fantasy, a daydream, an illusion. He couldn't be a serious boyfriend. Not for her. They were too different.

Not to mention that he was on the rebound from Simone Bishop. That's what her mind said. But her body, oh holy kittens, her recalcitrant body . . .

Her body was alive with information: salty-sweet lips that made her think of kettle corn, the firm planes of his abs pressed against her belly, the gentle way he cradled her in his arms and whispered her name like it was a mantra from heaven. "Paige, Paige, Paige."

A small sound slipped from her lips, half gasp, half moan. Oh, she was pathetic. Melting for him like rocky road ice cream in the August heat.

He tasted like a fairy tale, like Prince Charming. She knew it was a trap, but she fell anyway. Surrendering to the moment. Knowing she was treading on risky territory. Knowing she was going down . . .

His pelvis pressed against hers, surging and urgent.

He wanted her. No doubt about that. He was big and hard and hungry. He was way too much for her.

And yet, she wanted him so badly she couldn't think straight, and that's what finally sobered her.

"Stop," she said, pulling her mouth from his, her heart pounding so loudly she thought it was going to leap right out of her chest and run over her.

"What?" he asked, his eyes dazed. He looked as flattened as she felt.

"Your five minutes," she said, trying her best to

keep the quaver from her voice. Pointed at the door. "They're up."

Cash staggered out of Paige's houseboat, drunk on the taste of her lips. *McDang, son, what the hell just happened?*

Was he turning into one of those entitled assholes who thought just because he played a guitar and made some money doing it that he could kiss a woman whenever the urge came over him?

And when he'd kissed her the world had shifted. It was as if he'd been wearing a blindfold all his life and someone had yanked it off to reveal a lush, beautiful garden full of wondrous things.

Her lips had sent his mind spinning, whirling, swirling with music. Filling him with songs and lyrics, harmony and melody, rhythm and cadence. Altering everything he thought he knew about music . . .

. . . and women.

He hadn't gone there to kiss her. It hadn't even been in his mind until he'd been in front of her, those sweet lips of hers pursed, and he'd gone pure Neanderthal. Damn his hide. He'd scared her.

That cut him deep.

Nauseated, he paused on the dock. Rested his forehead on the pole of the vapor lamp. Took several slow, deep breaths. He'd not ever pursued a woman the way he was pursuing her. He didn't have to. Normally, women fell at his feet.

But not this one.

Was that the reason he wanted her so desperately?

Was it because she didn't fall at his feet? If so, that was messed up.

Except for a second there, she'd sunk against him and opened her mouth wider and made a sweet sound of pleasure and . . .

Unless he was deluding himself.

Was he deluding himself? He'd been in South America for almost a year. Had he forgotten how to read the signs where women were concerned? How to play the game of polite society? Honestly, he'd been out of touch for so long, living in the land of the rich and famous, had he forgotten what it was like to be a regular person?

He needed to stay away from her. That's what he needed to do. She'd made it clear she wasn't interested, even if she had kissed him back, however briefly.

It sounded logical. Leave her be. Stay away.

But she was living in the houseboat next door, and the taste of her was branded on his tongue. Seared into his brain.

Didn't matter. He was going to have to find a way to keep his distance and if that meant disappointing Emma and leaving town before Christmas, then so be it.

Emma would forgive him.

If he upset Paige again, Cash wouldn't be able to forgive himself.

A few years back, a tornado had hit Twilight on Valentine's Day. Paige had been in town visiting Grammie during the storm and she vividly recalled the violent winds spinning and churning across the sky as they ran for the storm cellar. The same kind of crazy storm whipped inside Paige all night long. No sleep. Not a wink. Just troubling thoughts.

Cash had kissed her.

And she'd liked it.

A lot.

Cash had liked it too. She'd felt his erection against her body. Felt the tremor in his hands. Tasted desire on his lips. A red-hot desire that matched her own.

But there'd also been an underlying tenderness that delighted and surprised and, frankly, worried her. She could resist his charming cockiness, but tenderness? After the way she'd been treated, tenderness was a huge turn-on.

He moved her.

In ways she'd never before been moved.

She wasn't ready for this emotionally, but oh how her body longed for him. She couldn't reconcile the conflict.

Just after dawn, she'd taken Fritzi out. When she got back, her boss from the day care center, Kiley Bullock, called and asked if she could come in a few minutes early.

Paige's mind jumped to worst-case scenarios. Had Kiley heard about her dancing onstage in a skimpy costume and was calling her on the carpet for behavior unbecoming a preschool teacher?

She left the houseboat, casting a sideways glance over at the turquoise boat next door. The lights were out and Cash's vehicle was in the marina parking lot. He must be sleeping in.

Reaching up, she fingered her lips.

She'd allowed it to happen. Let's be honest, she'd *wanted* it to happen. Now *that* was behavior unbecoming a preschool teacher.

Kiley was sanitizing the communal toy box when Paige got there, but she immediately stowed the antiseptic wipes and plunked down on the corner of a long squat folding table.

"There you are," she said so perkily that Paige relaxed. "Have a seat."

Paige perched on the edge of the table beside her, prayed the flimsy table meant for three-year-olds wouldn't collapse under her weight.

Kiley was in her early thirties with mahogany skin and deep-set dark eyes. She was tall and sporty, an almost carbon copy of her mother, Marva, who'd been the Twilight High School principal for almost two decades. She kept her coal-black hair cut short and lived in athletic wear. She'd been a kindergarten teacher in the Dallas ISD, but got burned out in the big-city rat race and came back home to start her own day care center. She'd given Paige the job almost solely because she was Flynn's cousin. Kiley and Flynn had grown up together, and their mothers had been best friends.

"I was at the benefit concert last night," Kiley said. "Saw you up onstage."

Uh-oh. Paige held her breath. "Listen, I can explain—"

"Clearly, you know Cash Colton."

"Not really." She didn't *know him*, know him, but she had kissed him, so maybe that counted as knowing him?

"Oh come on now." Kiley wagged a finger and

lobbed her a sly expression. "You can't fake chemistry. You two have got it going on."

"There's not—"

Kiley raised her palms. "But hey, if you aren't ready to go public, I understand completely. He's a celebrity. The media would be on it in a heartbeat."

"There's nothing to go public with," Paige protested.

"*Riiiight.*" Kiley winked. "I can keep a secret."

"There's no secret to keep."

"I need a big favor."

Paige hesitated. *I need a favor.* It was the siren's call she couldn't resist. Whenever anyone was in need, she was there. Her altruism had blown up in her face more times than she could count.

"If I can," she said.

"Could you get Cash to come talk to the class for career day?"

"Three-year-olds have a career day?"

"They will if you get Cash to come."

Paige lifted her shoulders. "I don't hold that kind of sway over him."

"C'mon. Women always know how to get their men to do things."

"He's not my man."

"You could give him sex." Kiley touched one index finger with the other. "Or withhold sex." She ticked off her middle finger. "Promise him a blow—"

"Kiley!"

"I'm just saying . . ."

"He's not my boyfriend. We're not dating. I've known him all of two days. He pulled me up on-stage. That's it."

"That's not what Amy from the Twilight Bakery says."

"You're listening to a girl who believes she was abducted by aliens?"

Kiley twisted up her bottom lip. "You've got a point."

"I've had a couple of conversations with him." *And kissed him.* "I had no idea he was going to pull me up onstage."

"But you do live next door to him."

Wow, the gossip had gotten around quickly. "Temporarily."

"So you could ask him, neighbor to neighbor? Please, please, please, please." Kiley clasped her hands together over her heart. "I love his music."

"We're really not that chummy."

Kiley played her trump card. "I gave you a job when no one else would."

Zing. There it was. She owed Kiley. "Okay, okay, stop with the pouty fan girl face. I'll ask."

"Yay!" Kiley clapped like she was thirteen instead of thirty-three. "Thank you, thank you."

"I'm not promising anything."

"He'll do it," Kiley said confidently.

"What makes you say that?"

"What's with you, girl? Even my legally blind granny can see that man's crazy 'bout you."

CHAPTER 10

Rhythm: The element of music pertaining to time, played as a grouping of notes into accented and un-accented beats.

"You're not going to catch anything," Paige said to Cash when she got home from work at four-thirty.

Cash was sitting on a deck chair, fishing off his houseboat, a cane pole in the water, watching the sunset, and nibbling what looked like one of Emma's caramel apple Christmas cookies.

"I thought you were mad at me," he said.

His feet were propped on a blue and white Igloo cooler. He wore cowboy boots, jeans, and a thick blue flannel shirt. His hair was tousled and wind-blown. The tops of his ears and the apples of his cheeks were red, letting her know he'd been out here for a while.

Waiting.

For her? Her heart, the treacherous thing, did a merry little jig.

"Fool's mission." She came closer, but not too close.

"What?" He grinned, spreading happiness like rainbows. "I'm too sexy for you to stay mad at me?"

Paige rolled her eyes. "No. Fishing off the houseboat is the fool's mission."

"Why's that?" He sent her a lazy look that strolled up and down her body, taking in the faded jeans, long-sleeved T-shirt, and thick woolen sweater she'd worn to work.

"One," she explained. "The water's not really deep enough."

"Deep enough to float a boat," he drawled, his gaze hanging on her mouth. It was all she could do not to touch her lips.

"Two," she went on. "The churning of boat engines coming in and out of the marina tends to chase the fish away. Although I suppose you might luck into a small perch or two."

"That'll do. I'm a catch and release fisherman anyway."

"Then what's the point?"

"Get to sit outside and watch the world go by."

"In forty degree weather?"

"I'm not a hothouse orchid." He finished off the cookie, dusted his palms together, crumbs tumbling into the water. Minnows swarmed after the crumbs.

Eyes alight, he met her gaze. No man had ever looked at her in quite that way. Like she was a precious treasure he'd unearthed while digging in his backyard. "And you said there weren't any fish in here."

"So have you been doing this all day?"

"Feeding cookies to the minnows? Yup, pretty much." He cocked his head, studied her a long moment, grinned infuriatingly. "How about you? How was your day?"

"Busy chasing a dozen three-year-olds." She inhaled sharply, drawing in cool air, trying to figure how to pose the question.

Amusement marked the press of his lips. "You're here to ask me a favor."

"Says who?" How had he known?

"You."

"What?"

"It's in the way you hem-haw around. I might have only known you since Saturday, but you don't strike me as a hem-hawer."

"How do you know? I might be a hem-hawer of the highest order."

"Are you?" He picked up his Stetson from the dock, cocked it on his head at a rakish slant.

"No."

"So spit it out." His smile was a wheel turning up the heat brewing inside her. "What do you need? Autograph? Head shot? Autographed head shot?"

"You do know that 'head shot' has a completely different meaning here in Non-Celebrityville."

"And you're imagining taking a head shot at me right now?"

"Don't tempt me."

"I like that about you. Barely sheathed aggression."

"I'm not aggressive, dammit."

"Well, except for the cursing."

"You bring out the worst in me. I hardly ever swear." Out loud anyway.

"Or conversely, I bring out the best in you. We all need to let loose and cuss now and again. You're welcome."

"Look it," she said, restraining herself from stamping her foot. She wasn't about to let him know how much he could irk her. "Be serious for a second."

"I get it. You hate to grovel. It makes you pissy."

"I'm not piss—" Her voice came out too high and loud, proving his point. She lowered her tone and pitch, smiled as if her lips were spun from sugar. "The woman I work for, the woman who gave me a job when no one else would, is a big fan of yours. Lord knows why, but she is."

He did not respond the way she hoped he would, which was, *Sure thing, whatever you need.* Instead, he said, "Why wouldn't anyone else give you a job?"

"We're not talking about me. Kiley—that's her name, Kiley Bullock—wants to know if you can come talk to the kids this week for career day."

"They have career day for three-year-olds?"

"They do now."

"Because of me?" He looked inordinately pleased.

"She's hoping you'll bring your guitar. Play a song or two. Maybe even read them a story."

"Me? Read a book?"

"You do know how, don't you?"

"Cute." He chuckled. "I did get my GED."

"Good for you. So I can put you down for story time?"

"I'll sing. That should be enough."

"I get it. You have to move your lips when you read," she teased.

He chuffed. "What book?"

"I dunno. You're the celebrity. *Everyone Poops*?"

"Ha. Ha. Good one. Creative."

"It's a real book."

He looked startled. "I know that."

"You're lying."

"Okay, I was trying to be cool. How was I supposed to know there was a children's book about pooping?"

"Try trusting someone who works with three-year-olds."

"You have my sympathy."

"You don't like kids?"

"I don't like reading books about poop."

"Will you do it?"

"Read the pooping book? No, I don't think so."

"No." She snorted. "Will you come to the school and talk to the kids and play kid songs for them? I'll take poop books off the table."

"That's a relief. No one wants poop on the table."

"So you'll come?"

He lowered his lashes, lazily pulling in his pole, paused a long time. Oh crap, he wasn't going to do it. Finally, he raised his head, and shot her a sizzling stare. "What's in it for me?"

"Kiley's undying gratitude."

"Well, you see . . ." He paused again, his gaze doing that thing where he looked up and down her body. "Since I don't know who Kiley is, that's really not going to work for me. I need more incentive."

"Then do it for the kids. Think of the fans you'll gain. Not only the little tykes, but their parents."

"From the size of the audience last night, I'd say I already have plenty of fans in this town."

Paige sighed heavily. "What do you want?"

A wicked smiled played at his lips. "You."

"Huh?" She was so shocked by his audacity she assumed she must have heard him wrong.

"Have dinner with me."

She tilted her head back. Looked up at the sky, and spread her arms wide. "Why?"

"Because you're awesome and I want to get to know you better and you need a favor and we both need to eat."

She folded her arms over her chest, a shield, a guard, holding him out. "When do you want this dinner to happen?"

"You name the—"

"Is it when I come in from the day care center at four-thirty, walk Fritzi, and then get ready for the evening performance at the theater?" Okay, she had to get rid of the sarcastic tone or she'd never convince him to come speak to the class.

"How about after you get off work at the theater?"

"I go visit my grandmother in the nursing home from nine to ten every night. We could go after ten, I suppose. But no restaurant in Twilight stays open after ten except for fast food joints. You wanna meet at Whataburger, say ten-fifteen-ish?"

"What about the weekend?"

"Two shows at the theater."

"Saturday morning?"

"I have a third job waiting tables for my uncle Floyd at Froggy's restaurant on Saturday morning in exchange for the rent."

"Sunday morning?"

"Church. You can come to church with me."

"Pass."

"Whataburger is looking like the date." She rubbed her palms together, pretending it was the optimal choice.

He scratched his chin. "When do you have time for yourself?"

"What's that?"

"Time is a commodity."

"Meaning?"

"If there's a will, there's a way. You're the one who needs the favor," he drawled, long and sweet as if he had honey wrapped around his tongue. "I'm telling you the price. Up to you to figure out how you can afford it."

She bit her bottom lip. Thought about it. She should have been peeved, but instead she was beguiled. What was wrong with her? "You've got a bit of the devil in you, Cash Colton."

His grin turned diablo-pepper hot. "So I've been told."

"Dinner, huh?"

"I tell you what, since you're so busy, I'll make dinner for you."

She eyed him suspiciously. "You can cook?"

He thrust out his chest, lifted his chin. "I'm not just a pretty face."

His voice was black velvet caressing her skin,

spreading goose bumps with each syllable. Soft and smooth and dark and elongated. Seductive, hypnotic. A spiderweb of words twining stickily to lure her in. A silky Gordian knot.

Her mind's eye got sneaky and she saw him in a frivolous apron emblazoned with "I'm the Reason Santa Has a Naughty List," deftly chopping vegetables with a chef's knife, happily humming one of the Christmas songs he'd sung last night. It shook her, that sweet, domestic image.

"So you'll come talk to the kids on Thursday?"

"All right. And for you, dinner. Friday night. Give me time to prepare," he said. "Ten o'clock. We can pretend we're in Spain."

"Spain?"

"They eat dinner at ten."

"You've been to Spain?" she asked, hearing the wistful sigh in her tone. She'd always wanted to travel. Never had the chance.

"Several times on tour. We'll have tapas."

She thought at first he said "topless," but that made no sense. She had no idea what tapas were but she wasn't going to ask and look like a rube.

Instead, she said, "My houseboat or yours?"

"Now that's what I'm talking about. C'mon on over to my place." He held out his hand. "Give me your phone."

"What? Why?"

"So I can program my number in and you can give it to your friend to call me about toddler day."

"Oh. Right. Okay." She passed him her phone.

He tapped in his number, eyed her with a gleaming smile, and handed the phone back to her. It was still warm from his body heat. "Feel free to call me anytime."

"You can be annoying. You know that? But I'll overlook it for the sake of the children."

"Big of you." A sprinkling of cookie crumbs dusted the corner of his mouth, and she couldn't help thinking about last night and his kiss and how delicious he had tasted.

Absentmindedly, she reached up to finger her own lips.

His eyes tracked her movements, settled on her mouth. Was he remembering too? Would he try to kiss her again when they had dinner? Maybe she should backtrack. Tell Kiley she tried, but his price was too high?

She dropped her hands to her sides.

His scrutiny deepened. Lingered. Twisted her up inside. That tornado of emotions that had kept her awake all night. His eyes turned wily, wolfish, and she just knew without a shadow of a doubt he was picturing her naked.

He swiped a hand over his mouth, dislodging the sugar. Stood up. The wooden dock creaked from the shift of his weight. His gaze was a lawn mower, sheared right over her. Scalped. Clipped.

Left her raw and vulnerable.

Paige felt as if she *was* naked. Nipples beaded taut. Chill bumps covering every inch of her body.

She'd made her share of mistakes in life, but she wasn't about to make one with him. Not when he had the ability to flamethrower her heart to ashes. "We need some ground rules for this dinner."

"Wait a minute, you didn't say anything about ground rules when you were asking for a favor."

"I'm bringing them up now," she said. "You've demonstrated unpredictable behavior and I want to circumvent any misunderstandings."

"Unpredictable?"

"You called me up onstage. You burst into my house—"

"I didn't burst, I persuaded you to let me in."

"You coerced your way in—"

"To apologize."

"Cards on the table—"

"We're playing poker?" He pushed back the Stetson.

She gave him a chiding glance, even as she secretly reveled in his teasing. It felt as if they'd known each other for a thousand years. His every gesture, every expression, vibrated with familiarity.

"We both know you could have any woman you wanted and you're only chasing me because I'm not after you. I'm a challenge and you love that."

"So, you barely know me, and already you know what I love?" he asked.

Love? God, why had she said that word?

"You love attention."

"Doesn't everyone?"

"Not the way you do."

"You just haven't been receiving the right kind of attention." His voice, his eyes, his mouth. Silk. All of it was smooth, soft silk.

She folded her arms up tight underneath her breasts. "I'll have dinner with you if you promise not to kiss me again."

"What if you kiss me first?" he said.

"I won't."

"But if you did . . ." He dipped his head, leaned in closer.

"I won't." Instead of sounding staunchly adamant as she intended, her voice cracked. Making it seem as if she was easily breakable.

"But if you were to kiss me first, it's okay for me to kiss back?"

"It's. Not. Going. To. Happen."

"But if . . ."

"Fine. If I take complete leave of my senses and fling myself into your arms, you can kiss me back. But I won't."

"Challenge accepted."

"It's not a challenge—" She snorted, rolled her eyes. "Oh never mind."

"Never mind about dinner or coming to the kids' school or—"

"Come to school. I'll come to dinner."

"But we won't come together?" He smirked, clearly trying to get her goat.

And succeeding quite spectacularly. Now all she could think about was him, her, a mattress . . .

She refused to blush. "Now you've got it."

"You know, I'm not as big of a skirt-chaser as you think I am. I know you've been looking me up online, buying into the rumors. But here's the deal, just because women—and a few men too—chase after me doesn't mean I give in."

"Regular choirboy, are you?" She kept her words dry and chalky.

"Now, darlin'," he drawled, whipping out his

country twang honed sharp for the groupies. "I never said I was celibate."

"I get it. You only want what you can't have."

"You sure like putting people in neat little boxes, dontcha?"

Paige startled. Did she? The comment struck a bit close to the bone. "We both know this isn't going anywhere."

"We do?"

"Don't be coy. You're so far out of my league I couldn't reach you with an extension ladder."

His eyes and tone softened. "Aww, honey, you have no idea what rock I crawled out from under. You're the one who's out of *my* league."

She felt flattered and that was awesomely weird. "Yeah, right. Mr. Multimillionaire Country-and-Western Star and the woman who works three jobs and still can't afford to buy her own car."

"I'm not talking about fame and fortune. I'm talking about strength of character. You've got more in your little toe than I've got in my entire body."

Oh God, he was being nice. Why was he being nice? She could handle him so much better when he was wearing his cocky musician persona. This sincerity was harder to guard against.

"Paige," he said, his tone full of kindness and understanding. "I can tell you're struggling with something. I'll stop teasing you. I'll do the kid thing. You don't owe me dinner. You don't owe me anything. If anything, I owe you."

"No, no." She shook her head. "A deal's a deal. I agreed to dinner and I always keep my word. No matter how much I might end up regretting it."

Chapter 11

Parody: A composition based on previous work. A common technique used in medieval and Renaissance music.

It was Thursday the seventh, six days after he'd rolled into town. He hadn't seen Paige much in the past two days since their conversation on his houseboat. He was busy putting the song together that had come over him the day he met her. And she was busy with her multiple jobs. But each morning, he made a point to go jogging when she walked Fritzi before work. He'd wave and jog on by and pretend it was coincidence. He didn't know if she bought it or not.

Give Cash a stadium packed with country-and-western fans and he was in his element. He could perform for hours.

But a roomful of three-year-olds?

Not so much.

Twelve sticky-fingered toddlers sat around him in a semicircle, staring blankly. They weren't impressed.

"Class, this is Cash Colton." Kiley Bullock clasped her hands and interlaced her fingers. The raven-haired preschool owner stood beside him. He'd already given her an autographed head shot at her request and she'd oozed all over him. "He's a musician."

One kid yawned. Another picked his nose. A third bared his teeth at Cash like he was an ankle-biter for real.

Cash gulped, forced a smile. Why the hell had he agreed to this?

Oh yeah, Paige.

Paige stood at the back of the room looking well and truly pleased by his discomfort. She wore dark wash skinny jeans, a long sage-colored cardigan over her blue sweater that played up the green in her hazel eyes, ankle boots, and a let's-see-your-fame-get-you-out-of-this-one grin.

Just the sight of her cheered him up and bolstered his courage. He was falling for her. No doubt about it. Honestly, who wouldn't fall for her? That irresist-ible smile. The curvy body. Her delicious scent that made him think of maple syrup drizzled over hot pancakes.

And then there was the way she took care of people—her grandmother, her boss, these kids. She had an appealing down-to-earth, levelheaded quality that stirred him.

And then there was the way she stoked his cre-ative muse. Hell, *was* his muse. Whenever he was around her, his creative synapses fired on all cylin-ders, revved up and ready to roll.

And of course there was that red-letter kiss . . .

He couldn't stop thinking about the taste of her

lips, the heat of her mouth, and the sound of her soft sigh.

The woman was something special.

If he were smart, he'd pull the plug on the houseboat rental and find somewhere else to hole up and finish writing his song. But would his creativity fail him without her?

Paige motioned toward the children with a jerk of her head and he realized he'd been woolgathering and his audience had grown restless. One little girl pulled the tail of her shirt up over her head. A boy was kicking the rungs of his chair. Another boy was blowing spit bubbles.

He raised a palm. "Hey, kids."

"Hay is for horses," the little girl with the shirt over her face quipped.

Cash shot Paige a desperate glance. *Help! I'm in over my head.*

Paige pantomimed playing a guitar.

Whew. Yeah. Right. That's why he was here. The music. Well, from what he could tell, he was really here because Kiley Bullock had a crush on him. But music had saved him throughout his life. When in doubt, go with what works.

He picked up his guitar, settled it on his knee. It felt comfy, familiar. He plucked a couple of chords.

That got their attention. The kids sat up straighter. The little girl pulled her shirt down.

"Instead of doing a bunch of blabbing. Let me show you what I do for a living. Anyone know 'Old MacDonald Had a Farm'?"

All twelve hands shot in the air.

"Smart kids," he said, and launched into the ditty.

Old MacDonald worked his magic and they were off. Cash singing and playing, the kids joining in making animal noises, clapping their hands, and stomping their feet in time to the music.

"And an oink, oink here, and an oink, oink there. Here an oink. There an oink. Everywhere an oink, oink," Cash sang.

Paige gave him a you-get-a-gold-star smile and he knew he'd pleased her and suddenly everything was easy.

"On your feet boys and girls," he hollered, and stood up. He led them around the room like the Pied Piper. The kids marched and tromped behind him. Kiley and Paige joined their barnyard conga line.

Around and around the room they went.

It was going swell until he sang, "And on this farm he had a goat . . ." Cash paused, stopped, looked around at the children—who all belatedly put on their brakes and ended up smacking into each other. Chain reaction crashes.

Oops.

Cash strummed a few more chords while everyone shook off the body slams. "Anyone know what the goat says?"

"Baa!" hollered the ankle-biter.

"That's right," Cash said. "Baa."

One little girl scowled and crossed her arms over her chest. "A sheep goes 'baa,' not a goat."

"Psstt." Kiley leaned over to whisper in Cash's ear, casually grazing her shoulder against his in the process. "Lily's dad is a goat farmer. She knows her stuff."

"If a goat doesn't say 'baa' what sound does he make?" Cash asked Lily.

The little girl opened her mouth and let loose with a gut-splitting scream that sounded exactly like a grown woman being murdered.

Lily's scream caused another little girl to let out a high-pitched, bloodcurdling, eardrum-piercing cry, the likes of which only three-year-old girls can produce. Then all the girls were screaming, seemingly trying to outdo each other with the pitch and tenor of their shrieks.

The boys clasped their hands over their ears, looked frightened. The ankle-biter vigorously shook his head from side to side, yelled, "Shut up, shut up, shut up."

"Children, children," Kiley cried, and clapped her hands. "Quiet, quiet."

The kids ignored her, ramped up and in a tailspin. Wriggling, jiggling, making all manner of noises.

Paige took a long, slow, deep breath as if centering herself, and an expression of peace came over her face. It was the same kind of body language Cash had seen on the shaman he'd visited when he was in the Amazon. He was amazed and impressed that she could gather that much self-control amid the chaos.

He could almost feel the calm, steady strength radiating from her out into the room.

"Shh, shh," Paige whispered gently, and put her index finger to her lips. "Inside voices."

Immediately, the children calmed.

"Let's all go back to our seats." She led the way,

sitting down on one of the tiny kid's chairs. Like sweet little lambs, the dozen toddlers followed.

Kiley's eyes bugged. "Remind me to give that woman a raise."

"She does have some kind of magic," Cash said, unable to take his gaze off Paige.

Even though his part of the program was over, he stayed for story time. He didn't read *Everyone Poops*, but Paige did. She read like a true storyteller, with dramatic voices and lively facial expressions.

The kids were on the edges of their seats.

Cash was agog.

She turned the page, and before she read the next line, she glanced up.

Their eyes met.

She smiled at him, an angelic, sage, impossibly wise smile, as if she knew the answer to all life's complicated questions.

Boom!

The now-familiar cascade of music and lyrics filled his brain the way it always did whenever he connected with her. Inspiration for another song. She was a muse for a lifetime of music.

After story time, it was lunch. While Kiley herded the kids to the dining area, a cook brought out almond butter and apple jelly sandwiches, banana slices, and juice boxes.

Cash cased his guitar.

"Stay for lunch?" Paige asked.

He couldn't tell if she was teasing or not. "You eat here?"

"Sure." She shrugged. "Job perk. Free food."

He was about to bow out gracefully but then the

children begged him to stay and Paige gave him that soul-melting look of hers and he did something he thought he'd never guessed he'd do in a million years.

Cash folded his knees to his chest, perched on one of those kid-sized chairs, and ate lunch with twelve three-year-olds and the prettiest preschool teacher he'd ever met. They chatted with the kids and exchanged smiles over the table and damn if he didn't end up having a great time.

After lunch, Kiley put the kids down for a nap while Paige walked him out of the building. "Thanks for agreeing to this," she said at the exit door. "The kids loved it."

"Sorry about getting them riled up with 'Old MacDonald.' Who knew it could be such a controversial song?"

Paige chuckled, soft and low, and the sound lit him up like Christmas Eve. "Three-year-olds have a lot of energy. It doesn't take much for them to get rowdy. They'll nap well."

"I gotta say I was dreading today, but I'm glad you conned me into it. It was fun watching you in action. You're good with kids."

"So are you."

"You don't have to be nice."

"I'm not. You're just a big ol' kid yourself. That's why they let loose with you so easily."

He didn't know if that was a compliment or not.

She smiled at him softly.

He smiled back, hoisted his guitar case onto his shoulder. "Don't forget your side of the bargain. Tapas. My place. Tomorrow night. Ten P.M."

Her smile disappeared and he could have kicked himself for reminding her that she owed him.

An awkward silence fell.

"Look," he said. "I can tell you really don't want to come to dinner. I'll let you off the hook. No harm. No foul. You really don't owe me anything."

She shook her head, lowered her lashes. "A bargain is a bargain. I always keep my word. I said I'd come, I'll come."

Geez, she made it sound like a trip to the dentist for six root canals.

"Paige—"

"I gotta go," she interrupted, using her thumb to point over her shoulder. "Get back to the kids."

"Have a good rest of the day," he called.

But she was already gone, disappearing back into the classroom. Leaving him feeling that he'd gained her respect, and then lost it again in some deeply fundamental way.

At ten P.M. on Friday evening, December 8, following her nightly visit with Grammie at the nursing home, Paige brought Fritzi with her as a buffer to Cash's houseboat. Dinner couldn't get too out of hand with a lively dog between them.

Right?

Cash was waiting for her beneath the misty yellow circle of the vapor light. The night sky was thick with clouds. His shoulders leaning against the lamppost, his long legs stretched nonchalantly out in front of him.

His eyes were lowered, a black Stetson tipped

down over his forehead as he watched her walk toward him.

Her heart saltoed, a freewheeling gymnast in her chest.

The northerly breeze was frosty as an iced beer mug, with a spicy chipotle bite from the Mexican restaurant on the promenade pier upwind of them.

She flipped up the collar of her too-thin duster. She couldn't afford a heavier coat, and she'd learned that in North Central Texas, you could usually wait out a cold snap in a couple of days.

Fritzi pulled on the leash, anxious to get to Cash. Paige held the poodle back, felt her pulse pick up.

She wore the same jeans and blue sweater that she'd had on at school, putting the clothes back on after changing from her Santa Baby costume following the evening performance of *Elf*. She nibbled her bottom lip.

Should she have dressed up? Suddenly, she wished she had made more of an effort. Who was she kidding? She didn't own anything remotely worthy of a date with a famous country-and-western star.

It wasn't a date, she reminded herself. Just dinner. On a private houseboat. Just the two of them.

Oh God, what had she gotten herself into?

Cash raised his chin, but never took his eyes off her, staring as if she was still in the slinky Santa Baby outfit and high-heeled boots.

He was motionless. Statue still.

Disturbingly so.

It *was* a date.

Anxiety clasped her in a heavy embrace and it

was all she could do not to turn tail and dash back to her houseboat.

Then his lips curled upward in a slow, sexy, seductive smile.

Smack!

His grin hit her with the impact of a bone-crunching, heart-stopping, head-on collision. A grin that said, *I'm gonna do serious damage, babe, and there's nothing you can do to change your fate.*

She knew it was true. Knew it to the bottom of her soul, but she kept walking toward him, high on adrenaline, buzzed on heat and hormones, hungry, and ready to throw caution to the winter wind.

He was one hundred percent male, one hundred percent in control. She was both happy and inordinately worried about it.

"Hi," she said breathlessly, overwhelmed.

"You brought Fritzi."

"Do you mind? He stays cooped up by himself all day." That was her excuse anyway, and she was sticking to it.

Cash squatted to scratch the eager pooch behind his ears. Fritzi thumped his back leg and gave a soft little moan of pleasure.

"You know," he said. "You don't have to keep popping home during your breaks from your jobs. I can dog-sit anytime. I'm home all day."

"Thanks, but he's my responsibility."

Cash shrugged, a casual lift to his shoulders. "Standing offer."

"I'll keep it in mind."

He straightened, tilted his cowboy hat back on

his head, and swept his hand toward the houseboat. "After you."

She walked the gangplank to the turquoise houseboat. It rocked gently beneath her weight. She'd heard that sex on a houseboat was quite sensual, but she'd never tried it so she couldn't say firsthand. But the easy motion did create a rock-a-bye rhythm that lulled her to sleep every night.

Come to think of it, she hadn't had a lick of trouble falling asleep since she'd been living on the houseboat, until she'd met Cash. Thoughts of him kept her awake at night. Made her restless, and edgy.

"It's beautiful here," he said.

She turned, saw he had stopped on the gangplank and was looking out over the water. The shoreline was peaceful in the darkness. Christmas lights twinkling from numerous docks. An owl hooted nearby and somewhere across the lake another owl answered, asking eerily, "Who, who?"

Paige shivered.

"Cold?" Cash moved to put a palm to the small of her back, used the other hand to open the door.

"A little." She stepped over the threshold fast, moving away from him, from his touch. Fast. "Mostly, I'm nervous."

"Nervous? What of?"

"You."

"You think I'm the Big Bad Wolf luring you to my place so I can make a move on you?"

"We *are* all alone in the marina this time of night, this time of year."

"Give me some credit, will you? Why do you have such a low opinion of me?"

"You did kiss me the other night without my permission." She notched her chin up. "And you forced me to have dinner with you in exchange for coming to the school. What am I supposed to think?"

"Oh no, no, no." He shook his head. "You don't get to do that."

"Do what?"

"Blame me. I gave you an out. I let you off the hook, and yet you're still here. You didn't have to come."

"I'm a woman of my word."

His eyes narrowed, turned flinty gray. "Don't put this all off on me, Paige. Own your needs. You *liked* that kiss as much as I did."

He was right. She had.

"You *want* to be here."

Guilty. She did.

"But for some reason you don't want to admit it."

"I . . . I . . ." She didn't really know how to respond. He was right. She did not want to admit her attraction to him.

He doffed his Stetson and dropped it on her head. A playful gesture that let her know she was safe with him. The hat was so big on her that the brim fell over her eyes and she had to tip it way back in order to see him.

"Listen to me good, woman. I am absolutely *not* going to kiss you again. Got it?"

"All right," she said, disappointment plunking down solidly in her lap. She removed his Stetson from her head and hung it from a hook on the coat-rack near the door.

He paused, shot her a look weighted with meaning. "Not unless you ask me to."

"Thank you for straightening that out. I feel so much more comfortable now."

"Sarcasm really isn't your strong suit." He winked.

She undid Fritzi's leash, let him go inside the house. Thrilled to be home, the poodle immediately went to his favorite spot on the back of the couch and peered out the window. Across from the couch was a small gas stove lit with a festive faux log, emitting toasty heat.

She slipped off her coat, hung it on the coatrack beside his Stetson. Swallowed a couple of deep breaths to calm down.

The galley did smell heavenly. Several covered dishes rested on the sideboard and a small table for two had been set. Red placemats, green plates, napkin rings decorated with faux mistletoe. A potted poinsettia, flanked by white flickering candles, served as a centerpiece.

Sexy. Romantic. A date.

"Have a seat," he said with the sweep of his arm.

She settled at the table, feeling a skosh self-conscious.

"Sangria?" He took a pitcher from the refrigerator. Red wine filled with fresh citrus fruit. He'd gone all out.

"Why not?"

His smile was sunshine and rainbows as he poured two glasses of sangria, handed one to her. Raised his glass. "A toast."

"What are we toasting?" she asked.

"Music," he said. "Because it brought me to this town . . ." He paused a moment, stroked her with his eyes. "To music."

"To music," she said past the lump in her throat. They clinked glasses.

"First course, Tortilla Española," he said, rolling his "r" like a Spaniard and lifting the lid on one of the many pans on the stove.

This was awesome. No man had ever cooked for her, not counting Dad, and she could get used to it.

Tortilla Española turned out to be a dish of potatoes and eggs. He served it in the small omelet pan he'd cooked it in, placing it directly on the table between their plates.

He sat down across from her, settled a napkin in his lap, closed his eyes, and paused a moment as if silently praying.

"Did you want to say grace?" she said.

His smile was simple, honest. "No need for anything formal. But I like to take a moment to appreciate my blessings before I eat."

"Hmm."

"What does that mean?"

"I didn't take you for a religious man," she said.

"Not religious per se, but I do think there's something bigger than us afoot in the universe. I just like to give thanks and acknowledge how lucky I am."

Intrigued, she leaned forward. "Is this from your time in the Amazon? I read that you were on a spiritual quest."

"Don't believe everything you read." He shrugged. "I was just trying to get my head screwed on straight after . . . well, let's not talk about ancient history. Dig in. Tapas are meant to be shared."

She dropped the thread of that conversation, spooned a modest portion of the potatoes and egg dish onto her plate. Took a bite. Brought a hand up to cover a mouth as she moaned, "Omigosh, this is so good!"

His smile turned proud. Of course. Any man who could make magic like this from eggs and potatoes had a right to be smug.

She wolfed down that portion, reached for another, realized he hadn't served himself. Stopped. "Why aren't you eating?"

"I'm getting a kick out of watching you." His tone was light, but she heard an undercurrent running through his words, something much weightier, and more meaningful, as if she'd passed some kind of test she wasn't even aware she was taking.

She set her fork down, far more than a skosh self-conscious now. She took a big drink of the sangria, felt cool warmth slide down her throat.

"You don't get to have much fun, do you?" His tone held a note of pity that had her stiffening her spine.

She hated when people felt sorry for her. "Between three jobs and looking in on my grammie, no. But I take pleasure in the simple things—a beautiful sunset, an earnest smile, a man who can cook . . ."

He inclined his head and his smile. "Why, Paige MacGregor, is that a compliment?"

"Don't let it go to your head."

His eyes met hers full-on. His expression controlled, inscrutable. For a minute she thought she'd offended him. Her pulse did a crazy *rat-tat-tat*. But then his eyes lit up and a lazy, good-ol'-boy smile drifted across his face and just about ripped her chest wide open.

"*You've* gone to my head." His voice was deep and husky, smooth as midnight and twice as sexy.

Her breath evaporated. Sucked right out of her lungs by his smoky eyes.

"Pace yourself," he said, standing up to raise the lids, one by one, of the pots and pans on the stove. "We have six more courses. And for dessert . . . Emma's caramel apple cookies."

"Oh no," Paige moaned, and put a hand to her belly. "Don't tempt me. Those cookies are addicting."

His gaze dropped to her belly and then rolled on down from there, setting her on fire with his hot stare. She liked the way he was looking at her. Wanted more of it.

That's when she realized that Fritzi, who was snoring loudly on the back of the couch, was no buffer at all.

CHAPTER 12

Nocturne: A musical composition that has a romantic or dreamy character with nocturnal associations.

"I think that's just about the best meal I've ever had," Paige declared, a dreamy expression on her face. "You're an excellent cook."

Dirty tapas dishes were stacked around them. She let out a happy sigh, and licked her lips.

Sweet, pink, adorable lips.

Cash wanted her.

Badly.

So badly he had to grip the table to keep from touching her. He'd asked her to dinner because he'd wanted to see her again, to hold her, taste her, smell her, know her . . . *bed* her.

But now that she was here and his goal was imminent, doubt wrapped around his gut and squeezed.

Hard.

Not because he'd changed his mind about taking her to bed. Not at all. In fact, the incessant urge pushed relentlessly at him. Rather, it was the quiet dawning that if he slept with her he was going to fall for her in a major way.

He never felt this way before, didn't know if he was ready. Didn't know if she was. Fun and games was one thing. A serious relationship was something else entirely, and Paige MacGregor wasn't the kind of woman you could walk away from unscathed.

And that, friends and neighbors, was why he picked up dirty dishes and carried them to the sink instead of sweeping Paige off her feet.

She got up to help him without saying a word, and for several minutes they worked side by side, cleaning up. The houseboat didn't have a dishwasher so they did the dishes by hand. Cash washing and Paige drying.

Occasionally, their elbows would bump and they'd grin or giggle and keep right on washing. The silence was easy, companionable, and comfy as a warm sweater and old house slippers.

It felt nice, this domestic scene, and his mind started spinning into the future, imagining more nights like this.

Thin ice.

He was treading on thin ice and he knew it.

Didn't care.

And that right there shocked him enough to fake a yawn and say, "It's eleven-fifteen. How'd it get so late?"

"It's not *that* late." Paige stepped closer, draped the kitchen towel she'd used to dry dishes over the oven door handle.

She plunked down on the couch, reached out to scratch Fritzi's belly.

Cash sauntered over to join her.

"It's cool how he can do that," she said.

"Do what?"

"How can he sleep when I'm rubbing his belly?"

"I don't know," Cash said. "I certainly couldn't."

"I used to be like that." She sighed.

"Slept while someone rubbed your belly?"

"Yeah." She sounded wistful. "When I was a kid. With my dad. When I'd get a tummy ache, he'd lie down beside me and rub my belly. Put me right to sleep."

"Your mother didn't do it?"

"She's not very nurturing. She had all these conditions. Dad, on the other hand, loved me unconditionally."

"Did you have a lot of tummy aches?"

"I used to worry about dad's job. That he was going to die in a fire. I was a shy kid with a lot of anxiety and not too many friends. But I've been gabbing about myself all night. Tell me about you."

"Didn't you read about me in your Google search?"

"I did," she said, a smile in her voice. The kind of smile that made a man understand just how lonely he was. "But I'd like to hear it from you."

"Look," he said, more to distract her than anything else. "It's snowing."

"What? Really?" She let out a delighted squeal, looked over a sleeping Fritzi, and out the window at the dark night.

Giving Cash a terrific view of her bottom encased in a fetching pair of blue jeans.

"So beautiful." She breathed audibly.

"Yes," he said, his gaze trained on her fanny. "Yes, it is."

She turned back, beaming so widely he heard music in his head. Sweet music sparked by her stunning smile. "You know what's missing?"

Nothing. Absolutely nothing. The moment was perfect.

"What?" he asked.

"Decorations." She swept a hand at the houseboat. "I know it's a temporary rental, but there's nothing here that celebrates the season. You need a tree and lights and—"

He shook his head. "I haven't really celebrated Christmas in twenty years."

"At all?" She looked as if that was the saddest thing she'd ever heard.

"I go to parties and attend events."

"Things other people put on."

"Yeah. I don't bother with decorating."

"No home traditions?"

"I'm not a traditional guy."

"What about Simone?"

He wasn't surprised she knew about Simone. Their breakup had been rich tabloid fodder. But it felt weird that Paige already knew so much about his background and he knew nothing of hers. "She wasn't really into all that stuff either."

"Do you think that's part of the reason she left you?"

He laughed. "Because I didn't decorate?"

"Because you didn't have any traditions. Because you keep things on the surface."

Her insight surprised him. "No. Simone is as allergic to tradition as I am, maybe more so. For her, everything needs to be shiny and new and different. Come to think of it, she made me look like Jimmy Stewart in *It's a Wonderful Life*."

"That's one of *my* traditions," Paige said.

"Huh?"

"Watching *It's a Wonderful Life*. Dad and I—" She broke off suddenly, tears misting her eyes. She sniffed, blinked.

Cash's gut sloshed. "You don't watch it with your father anymore?"

Her smile was a soggy affair, wet and halfhearted. "Dad passed away eighteen months ago."

"Ah, Paige." Cash sucked in a deep breath, understood that particular burn of grief. Losing a parent when you were young messed you up for life. "That's rough."

She shrugged, hopped off the couch, twirled around the living area. "You could put a tree here, and string some lights from the ceiling, and—"

"Is it really worth the effort? I'm only going to be here through the end of the month."

"Of course it's worth the effort," she said with such earnestness a mixed-up sensation jiggled his chest. "We're talking about the magic of Christmas."

"You do know there's no such thing as Santa Claus, right?" he teased.

"Just because there's no actual Santa Claus is no reason to pooh-pooh the spirit of Christmas."

"Is that what I'm doing?"

"You're not really a Grinch." Her eyes shone like a torch, clear and bright. "I saw how much you enjoyed playing with the kids at the day care, and how you got into those Christmas songs at the Music Review."

"You were the Grinch on that occasion," he said, mildly surprised by the tenderness in his voice.

"Hey . . ." She winked a natural easy wink. "I eventually got on board."

"Because I didn't give you any other choice." He ran a thumbnail over his chin, slanted a sidelong glance her way.

She bounced back onto the couch cushion, peered out at the snow again. Fritzi opened one eye, gave her a "dream-killer" look, huffed, and rolled over.

"Maybe it'll stick this time," she said. "The ground is cold enough. Fingers crossed it sticks." She crossed the index and middle fingers of both hands.

He chuckled.

She turned to look at him, her features beautifully lit by the gas fireplace. "What?"

"You light up when you talk about snow."

"I grew up west of Abilene. We didn't often get snow. I love the stuff."

"I get it. I was born in Rankin. That's even farther west than Abilene."

"Yeah," she said. "I saw that on your Wiki page. But you lived in Nashville with your mom until you were ten, right? I'm jealous. I bet you got lots of snow every winter."

"Snow is romantic in theory," he said. "Not so much when you have to shovel it to get out of your driveway."

"The only place that ever happens in Texas is in the panhandle. But I'd love to experience that kind of snowfall at least once in my life." She turned to face him, planted her bottom on the cushion.

"You're young," he said. "Give it time. No telling where the future might take you."

A troubled look spread across her face and she glanced away. He'd hit on a sore spot. "What's wrong?" he asked.

"The future's kind of murky. I like to focus on right now."

She hooked him with that. He was intrigued. Most people lived in tomorrow or yesterday. "Why?"

Her lips pressed into a straight line, and she gave a short, hard shake of her head.

"What was his name?" Cash growled.

"Who?"

"The man who hurt you so badly that you can't let any guy get close to you."

A startled eyebrow shot up on her forehead. She was surprised he'd hit so close to the bone. "Who says I don't let any guy get close?"

"You're keeping *me* at arm's length."

She chuffed. Paused. Chuffed again. "You say that as if you're just an ordinary guy, Cash Colton. But you're not. You're rich and famous and—"

"Screw that. I wasn't always rich and famous. It's just an act, a costume. Not who I am inside."

"Who *are* you, then?" she asked, tilting her head in an impossibly adorable way.

He wanted scoop her into his arms, take her to bed, and make love to her until dawn. But he knew what she was doing. Stalling. Shifting things back on him. Trying to distract him from digging deep,

getting answers to the questions that had been pes-
tering him.

"Start with his name," Cash said, keeping his voice
firm and steady, hopefully letting her know she was
safe with him. He slid his arm under her shoulders,
tucked her closer to him. Found it encouraging that
she didn't pull away.

"It doesn't matter." Her voice curled into a tight
ball.

"It does if that man is what's stopping you from
giving me a chance. If this thing is going to work
between us, we have to be honest with each other.
Trust, Freckles, is the name of the game."

She gave him a look that said she never expected
anything to work between them; she was bemused
that things had gotten this far. That look sent a sorrowful ache through his bones. Somewhere, somehow, she'd been drop-kicked through the goal post
of life.

"Well?" he prodded.

Silence settled over them, thick and solid. It lasted
so long Cash figured she'd written him off, written
them off, and that she wasn't going to open up.

Fritzi whimpered in his sleep, his little legs running fast to nowhere. That brought a smile to her
face. "Probably chasing rabbits in his dreams."

Another stretch of silence.

A cell phone buzzed. They both jumped.

"That's me." She dug her phone from her back
pocket. Saw the number. Made a face. Switched off
her phone and set it on the coffee table.

Cash tensed. "Unwanted caller?"

"Probably a wrong number," she said, but she couldn't meet his gaze. She was hiding something.

It was none of his damn business, but he couldn't help nudging her. "Paige," he murmured. "Talk to me . . ." Cash took a deep breath, and because it was Paige, he decided to say something that went against his don't-ever-beg-for-anything policy. "Please."

Another long graveyard silence.

"Never mind," he said, trying to keep the disappointment from his voice. If she wasn't ready to confide in him, she wasn't ready. He wouldn't push.

She hiccupped.

He placed his palm over her hand. "It's okay, really. You don't owe me a thing."

Tears shimmered in the corners of her eyes and she managed to hoist up a tiny smile. "His name was Randy Pennington."

Cash sat there, saying nothing. This was all about her. He would give her the time and space to tell her story the way it needed to unravel.

"Or rather, that's the name I knew him by. Turns out his real name was Ludesko Thig and he was originally from Romania."

"Awful name. I can see why he changed it."

"It's a terrible name, yes, but then again he was a terrible person. He had several aliases."

"Did he have an accent?"

"No, his English was impeccable."

"How did you find out his real name?"

"The cops."

"I don't like how this is sounding," Cash grumbled, knots building a Lego town in his gut. "Not one damn bit."

She reeled in a long breath. Held it for a full thirty seconds, released it in a slow hiss through clenched teeth. "It's such a long story I don't even know where to start."

Reaching up, he toyed with her hair, sliding it through his fingers. He loved the floral smell. The silky feel. Loved the smell and feel of *her*.

"Take your time."

"I hope you're not sleepy, because that long story? You're about to get it." She shifted on the couch, faced him. Tucked her knees to her chin, folded her arms around her knees.

He turned so he was facing her, sat cross-legged. "I've got nowhere else to be and I've only got ears for your sweet voice."

"That came off cheesy." She laughed.

"Cheddar or mozzarella?"

She laughed again, her face alive and hopeful. He felt successful for lightening the mood. Her eyes drilled down, narrowing in on him. There was a lot of depth behind those eyes.

"I've become wary of compliments," she confessed. "They aren't always sincere."

"Paige," he said, putting starch in his voice. "I'm completely serious. You fascinate me."

She ducked her head, looked sweet and shy. What had made her so leery?

He felt a protectiveness rise up in him, hot and fierce. He wanted to slay any and all dragons for her. Dispatch them straight to hell.

"When I was fifteen my mother had an affair with a woman she worked for. She divorced my father, left me behind." Her eyes clouded, the icy color of pain brittle with age. "Moved in with this other woman."

He paused a moment, giving her revelation the time it deserved. "That must have been a blow."

"Mom thinks I hold it against her because she's with a woman," Paige said. "But that doesn't matter to me. I guess I was nursing a bit of a grudge that she fell in love with Pamela when Dad needed her the most. She and Pam live in Aspen now."

"Why didn't your mom take you with her?"

"I wanted to stay with Dad." Paige's voice turned slick and solid, coming faster and heavier. Ice skating over the cracked foundation of her childhood.

"How come your mom hasn't helped you out of your financial difficulties?"

Paige's chin notched up. "She doesn't know the extent of it. Call me proud, but I got myself into this mess. I can get myself out."

"What happened with your dad?"

"The month before my mother left him, my father was diagnosed with advanced chronic obstructive pulmonary disease. He was a fireman, and he was part of a local team that went to Ground Zero after 9–11. He also smoked cigars, which wasn't smart. I'm not defending that, but he didn't deserve to go out the way he did." She pulled her bottom lip up between her teeth, tucked her shoulders inward.

"That sucks," he said vehemently. He knew that particular brand of pain. A parent with a lingering illness, partially brought on by poor life choices. Hated that Paige had suffered through that too.

"It does, but that's life. Shitty things happen to

good people all the time. You have to find a way to rise above it and keep on going."

True enough. He had the same philosophy. His own childhood had been pretty rocky too, but he refused to let it define him. He wasn't a victim.

"Dad was forced to go on disability. Mom relinquished her part of the house in the divorce, so we had a roof over our heads at least, but it was a struggle."

"You became your father's caretaker."

Another shrug. "Not in the beginning. Even though Dad couldn't work, he could still take care of himself. The hard part came in the later stages. I was a daddy's girl. I resented my mother for not putting her life on hold to stay with Dad because he was sick. I came to realize that was unrealistic of me and I've forgiven her. It was tough sledding between us for a while, but we've repaired our relationship. Although I don't get a chance to see Mom as often as I would like. We've got plans to get together in the new year when she and Pam get back from a ski trip in the Alps."

He reached over, touched her arm, briefly, lightly.

She seemed to draw courage from his touch. Raised her head. "Dad lived for ten years after his diagnosis. He wanted me to go to college after high school, but I felt I couldn't leave him alone. Mom's partner offered to pay for a live-in nurse, but neither Dad nor I wanted to be beholden to Pam. I stayed at home and got a job working as a day care assistant. I promised Dad I would go to college after . . . well, you know."

What a tough young woman!

"It was rough at the end. Watching my big strong father waste away. He was the world to me." Her voice caught and her lip trembled.

Cash was sorry he pushed her to talk. Every cell in his body urged him to kiss her and make everything better. But as much as he might wish he could, he couldn't rewrite her history with kisses.

"My Grammie MacGregor, dad's mom, taught me how to dance," she said, a wry smile springing to her face. "Grammie MacGregor danced in a Vegas review when she was in her early twenties. Later, after she married Grampa, she ran a little dance studio in Abilene, taught my dad and Uncle Floyd ballroom dancing. My dad started dancing with me when I was a toddler. I'd stand on his shoes and he'd whirl me around the room."

"No wonder you're so good at it. Dancing is in your DNA." Just like music was in his.

"The happiest moments of my life were when I was dancing with my daddy." Her eyes misted over and she dabbed at them with her fingers.

"And so when he died, you stopped dancing," Cash guessed.

"No," she said. "I threw myself *into* dancing. It was my escape. But that's also how I met Randy. I'd advertised for a dance partner who I could enter competitions with and he answered."

Cash winced. "I'm sorry. I didn't know about your dad. I can be dumbass sometimes. Forgive me."

"If you'll forgive me for getting so upset at you." She moistened her lips. "Turns out that night at the Music Review flipped a switch and after danc-

ing with you I felt like my old self for the first time
since . . ."

"What?"

She gulped, stared down at her hands cradled in
her lap. "Randy ruined dancing for me."

"Ah, that asshat." Instinctively, Cash doubled up
his fist. He didn't know what the jerk had done to
her, but from her skittishness, he knew it was significant.

Paige plucked at the hem of her shirt. "After Dad
died . . . well, his medical bills wiped out any savings
he had, but he'd left me the house free and clear. I
didn't want to spend the rest of my life in Abilene,
especially since my uncle, cousins, and grandmother
were here in Twilight."

"Understandable."

"I put the house on the market about the time
oil and gas were booming in Taylor country and
oilfield workers were desperate for family housing.
I was lucky. It sold quickly for well over market
value. It was more than enough to pay for college
and then some. I put the money in the bank until I
could decide how to invest it, and where I wanted to
go to school, and what I should study or if I should
even go to school, because I was thinking about
opening my own dance studio. I took a temporary
job as a waitress and I was renting an apartment in
town. Just something to tide me over until all my
father's affairs were settled and I could decide what
I wanted out of life."

"Nothing wrong with that."

"But along came Randy." Her entire body tensed,
the muscles at her jaw clenching to visible knots.

Cash's stomach soured. He could put two and two together. She worked three jobs, lived in her uncle's houseboat, and didn't own a car. Paige was dead broke for a reason and it wasn't because she was lazy or a spendthrift.

"When I was interviewing dance partners, I had them meet me at the restaurant where I worked. Randy walked in, sporting a grin bigger than Dallas. He was the most handsome guy I had ever laid eyes on." She bit down on her bottom lip, and a faraway look came into her eyes. "He took me in his arms and we danced the tango, and I fell hook, line, sinker . . ." She crooked an index finger inside her cheek, pantomimed as if she were a fish snagged on a fisherman's hook.

Cash put a hand on her shoulder. Said nothing, just kept his hand there, holding space for her.

"God," she moaned, and sank her face into her upturned hands. "I was so stupid. Such easy pickings. Small-town girl. Sheltered. Clueless."

"You weren't the problem."

"He played me for a fool. He said all the right things. Danced like a dream. Told me how beautiful I was. Courted me proper. Showered me with flowers and gifts. No one had ever done that for me. I thought he liked me, but Randy was out to take me for every last penny. And he did." She stopped, caught her breath. "I was an idiot."

Cash shook his head, wished he could meet this Randy character in a dark alley with a pair of brass knuckles in his pocket. "You weren't. You just wanted to be loved. You were hurting after losing your father. He preyed on your vulnerability."

"Did he ever. I let him move in with me. And things were really good for six weeks. We danced together. Won competitions. I thought I'd found the perfect man." She made a choking noise, drew her knees to her chest again, and smacked her forehead with her palm. "Why couldn't he have just taken the money? Why did he have to pretend I meant something to him? Why did he make me fall in love with a person who didn't even exist?"

"Because obviously he's a sociopath and that's what they do."

"It was as if I had 'MARK' carved into my forehead."

"Sweetheart, you have to understand, guys like him turn everyone they meet into a mark. He's a shark and sharks bite."

"He not only took me for every penny I had, he stole my car and my identity. Opened up credit cards in my name. Maxed 'em out. He even filed my tax return and had the refund sent to him! I came home from work one evening to find him gone and the apartment stripped bare."

God, what a nightmare. Cash was squeezing his fist so tight—wishing for five minutes alone with this Ludesko Thig character—his knuckles turned white and his fingers tingled numbly.

"That call just now?" She pushed the cell phone on coffee table with her toe wrapped in a green Christmas sock with red reindeers on it. "It's from bill collectors who refuse to believe those aren't my debts. They call me three or four times a week, at any hour of the day or night."

"That's illegal."

"I know, but it doesn't stop them."

"Have you reported the collection agency to your congressman?"

"I have a lawyer who's supposed to be handling all that, but I owe him money, so . . ." Paige pulled the sleeves of her sweater down over her hands, looking like a lost teenager.

"Did the police ever catch him?" he asked. "Was this son of a bitch made to pay for what he did?"

"Randy was apprehended," she said. "But he hired a high-priced lawyer. Probably with *my* money, and the charges got thrown out on a technicality."

"So he's still out there. Doing the same thing to other women?"

She nodded. "It's amazing how these identity thieves keep getting away with it. Ruining law-abiding people's lives. My lawyer says it will probably take at least seven years for me to fully dig out of this."

"Do you know where he lives?"

"He's in the wind. Left the country with my quarter-million. The authorities discovered he bought a one-way plane ticket to Buenos Aires the day after he cleaned out my apartment."

"Does he ever try to contact you?"

"No. Why would he? Randy knows he took every penny I had. Nothing left to bilk from me."

"I'm glad he's not living in this country at least." Cash scowled.

"Sometimes"—her voice lowered—"I despair of ever digging out of it. My credit is shot. I've been trying for a year now to get it repaired, and straightening it out is such a rigmarole. Do you know what it's like to go to a store and try to write a check and they look at you like you're a criminal?"

"I'm so sorry this happened to you."

"It also makes it hard to date. When guys find out you have messed-up credit, even though it's not a fault of your own, they take a big step back. I can't blame them. No one wants to step into that black hole."

A thought occurred to him. A way he could help her. He'd contact his lawyer and have her put a stop to the harassing phone calls. Paige didn't need to suffer like this, but he had a feeling if he told her outright what he intended, her pride wouldn't allow her to accept his help. If she wouldn't take money from her own mother . . .

She notched her chin up. "But I'm lucky. My uncle Floyd gave me a place to stay, although I do work for him on Saturday mornings as payment. The people in Twilight are so nice. Neighbors check in on me. I might not have any money in the bank, but I'm rich in the ways that count. I'm strong and healthy. I have nothing to complain about."

"Paige?"

"Yes?"

"Was this creep the first guy you ever . . ." Briefly Cash closed his eyes. Why was he asking this? He really didn't want to know.

"Yes," she said. "Randy took my virginity too."

Ah damn. "And there hasn't been anyone since?"

"No."

Dammit all. Her one and only sexual experience had been with a con man.

Right now, in this moment, he wanted to kiss her

more than he wanted to breathe. The woman had no idea how much self-control it took for him not to whisk her straight to bed, tear her clothes from her body, and sink into her. But it was too soon, and she was too special, and she'd been through too much. He was not going to take advantage of her vulnerability. He was not going to make love with her.

Not now.

Not yet.

If ever.

CHAPTER 13

Serenade: A lighthearted piece, written in several movements, usually as background music for a social function.

From outside the houseboat came the sound of loud music blaring out across the lake. Frank Sinatra's "Christmas Waltz."

"What's that?" Cash asked, getting to his feet, still digesting everything Paige had told him.

"The *Brazos Queen*." She beamed and jumped up. "Returning from a midnight cruise. They have them every Friday and Saturday night in the summer and then again in December, weather permitting."

Through the open curtains over the wide back window, Cash spied a churning paddlewheel lit up with Christmas lights come into view. A breathtaking sight. The illuminated boat glided over dark water while heavy, fast-falling snow dusted everything a cleansing white.

Paige let out a soft sigh.

Cash glanced over to see her entire face shining bright as an angel, her hands clasped at her heart. Sinatra's voice permeating the night. Their eyes met, and his pulse quickened.

"Dance with me," she said abruptly, and held out a hand.

"You want to dance?"

"You've convinced me that I need to have more fun."

Waltzing with her, holding her close, was dangerous. He hesitated. She looked at him, anticipation on her lips, a beguiling smile. The boat would soon pass by. The music would drift away. He'd have her in his arms no more than a couple of minutes.

"Paige," he murmured, "I don't know if that's such a good idea."

She looked so enchanting, those sparkling hazel eyes full of life and joy. Then she whispered the magic word. *"Please."*

Weak man that he was, Cash gave in. Reached out. Took her palm. Wrapped her in his arms.

She was light on her feet. Graceful. Controlled. She knew what she was doing. He led her across the small box of the living area, a neat square suddenly filled with motion and feeling. He hadn't waltzed in a long time.

Paige interlaced her fingers through his hands, leaned her head against his chest as they danced as a unit. His hand was around her shoulder as she clung to him. One-two-three. One-two-three.

They turned, stepping back a bit as they danced like characters from a Hallmark Christmas movie.

Eyes glued to each other. Hands melded. Feet floating in perfect rhythm. The houseboat rocking gently with their movements. Outside the window the snow was a wild flurry now.

It was the most damn romantic thing he'd ever done in his life, and he wanted to keep waltzing forever.

But the paddleboat slid away, the music growing fainter and fainter until they were dancing to nothing but the sound of their comingled breaths.

Cash had to find a way out of this before it was too late. Before he was too far gone.

"I've had a great time," Cash whispered, letting go of her, stepping back. "It's been lots of fun—"

She leaned into him, her smile a fishing lure, hooking him, reeling him back to her. "So much fun."

He pressed his chin to the top of her head, loosened his arms from around her waist. "It's getting late."

"Is there any of that sangria left?" She peered around his shoulder at the kitchen table. "It was delicious."

"I think we killed it . . ." He could see the pitcher from where they were standing. There was a third of it left.

"I don't think we did." Her eyes took on a naughty sheen.

He dropped his hands to his sides, felt like a wooden toy soldier. "You have to get up early . . ."

"I can easily get by on just a few hours of sleep."

"It's well after midnight . . ." He rotated his wrist so she could see the face of his watch.

She turned up the sugar on her smile. "I don't have to be up until six."

"Fritzi needs his beauty rest . . ." His own voice was a desperate climber stuck in the death zone on Mount Everest.

They both turned to stare at the poodle curled into a little ball on the back of the couch, snoring softly.

"Looks like he's getting by," she said.

Cash inched toward the front door. "I'll get your coat and . . ."

Paige went to the window, peered out at the rapidly falling snow. "It's really coming down. The dock will be slick."

He opened the small closet, waved at pair of brown fisherman's boots. "There are rubber boots—"

"The electricity is out. It's pitch-black. I won't be able to see my hands in front of my face."

"I've got a flashlight." He reached for his coat, settled his Stetson on his head. "I'll walk you home—"

"Cowboy, it's cold outside, and the fire is so toasty." She scooted over to the fireplace, warmed her hands in front of the gas flames.

He draped their coats over his arm, put his hand on the doorknob. "This town is full of gossips and—"

"There's no one around. We're out here in the marina all on our own at this time of night on a cold December evening."

"Your reputation is important. You live here. Think about how it would look if someone saw you sneaking out of my houseboat at dawn."

She backed up to the fireplace. "You let me worry about my reputation."

"We've had too much to drink—"

"I'm not drunk and neither are you."

"Are you trying to get me into bed?"

"Do you need a rock to fall on your head?"

"I have no willpower, Paige. It's why I'm trying to get you out the door."

"You don't have to have willpower. That's the point."

"I can't," he said, knowing if he made love to her that he was going to mess up her life. He was not a forever kind of man.

"Sure you can." She said it as if it was so simple, so easy.

"No." He swiveled his head from shoulder to shoulder. "No."

"If you're afraid you're going to hurt me, don't be." She touched his hand. "I know this thing has no future. I know you have a high-flying career and can't get bogged down by small-town girls. I know it, and accept it. Look, both my eyes are wide open." She rounded her eyes in a comical expression. "That doesn't mean we can't have fun now. That's all I want from you. Fun. Believe it."

Wow! Really? She was that quick to write him off. Write *them* off.

"I want you, Cash." Her eyes were earnest, her touch on his arm sincere. "For one glorious night."

God, he was wound up. Tight as a drum. Hot. Horny. Hornier than he'd ever been in his life.

But he kept thinking about what she'd told him. All the shit she'd been through. Caring for her ailing father for years and then losing him. In her grief and innocence getting duped by a slick con man. It hadn't been all that long ago. Whether she realized it or not, she was still raw, still vulnerable.

He didn't want to take advantage of that or make things worse for her.

If he had his wits about him, he would insist she go home. But her eyes were hungry and her heart was on her sleeve and he just couldn't crush her.

Find a way to let her down easy.

Good idea. How? He mucked around in the basement of his brain, came up with nothing.

She wriggled against him, tilted her chin. Wanting a kiss.

He was hard as marble. But he did not dip his head. Did not kiss her. Oh damn, how was he going to stick to his guns?

"Please . . ."

His eyes narrowed, glistened. "Please what?"

She wrapped her arms around his neck, leaned into him, coaxed his head down. He did not resist, but neither did he make a move. *Aww, come on.*

"You want it?" he asked, one eyebrow crawling up his forehead.

"Yes," she said firmly.

"Then you're going to have to ask for it."

"Please," she whispered. "Please kiss me." She twined her arms around his neck and he did not resist. She kissed him.

And damn his hide, he could not leave her hanging. He kissed her back with a fierceness that scared him, and delighted her. She let out a happy giggle and slipped her tongue between his teeth.

Good Lord, he was toast. One sip from her sweet

honeyed mouth, one sniff of her fresh scent, one more soft whisper of "I want you," and he was done for.

He broke his lips from hers. Moved back. Stared into her eyes. "Are you sure?"

"Are the birds certain they have to fly south for the winter?"

"Not all birds migrate."

"Well, I'm talking about the migratory ones. Right now I feel like an eagle and I gotta fly."

Got it. That sounded pretty convincing to him. But he had to make sure. "Have you thought about the consequences?"

"I'm on the pill and I brought condoms."

Condoms? *McDang*, she *was* thinking ahead. "I'm not talking about those kinds of consequences."

"Oh." She blinked. "What do you mean?"

"Emotional consequences." He loomed over her. She looked so tiny all alone in the middle of the floor.

"I'm just looking to have some fun."

He didn't believe her. She wasn't the sex-just-for-fun type.

She came to him, wrapped her arms around his waist, held on tight. "I know you're a rolling stone. Don't worry. You're not going to break my heart."

"What if *you* break mine?"

She laughed at that. Long and loud as if that was the funniest thing she'd ever heard. Like hurting him was an impossibility. But he wasn't joking.

"Are you always this hard to seduce?" she asked.

"You are absolutely certain this is what you want?"

"Yes."

"You can change your mind at any time."

"I won't," she assured him.

"You can. All you have to do is say stop."

"Is that your safe word?"

"It's the universal safe word."

"Got it. Go."

"What?"

"Go. The unsafe word."

"Unsafe word?" God, she was so adorable he couldn't stand it.

"The word I'll use when I want more, more, more. Got it?" Her eyes burned brightly, her expression deadly serious.

"Got it," he said.

She stuck out her hand to him. "Well, then . . . Go."

Fueled by sangria, great food, and slow dancing against Cash's red-hot body, Paige simmered, basking in the sweet glow of the evening, feeling happily aimless and momentarily free from responsibilities.

The perfect storm for memorable mistakes.

She didn't care.

Cash took her hand and led her to the bedroom.

It was a small room. But then again it was a houseboat. All the rooms were small, and it was decorated in Sig Gunderson's taste. Southwestern colors. Native American woven rug. Dream catcher over the queen-sized bed. Georgia O'Keeffe, sexytime, desert-scape print framed on one wall.

When she'd Googled Cash, she'd found pictures online of his house in Nashville that he'd shared with Simone before their breakup. Art Nouveau. Sage greens, browns, mustard, lilacs. Furniture ornate with stylized flowers. Varnished dark hard-wood floors.

But she'd known instinctively that was Simone's taste.

She wondered how Cash would decorate a bed-room. Sparse, she decided. Utilitarian. Minimalist. Stone. Concrete.

Or not.

Now that she was getting to know him better, saw how down to earth he really was, maybe he'd prefer rustic. He was a cowboy at heart after all. Sensible. Practical. Earthy. A farmhouse. Yes. On second thought, definitely rustic.

Her favorite style.

In the corner of the room sat an electric guitar and on a small desk beside it an open college-composition-style notebook filled with musical scores and scribbled lyrics. She wandered over to take a look.

Read the first line.

One look. Her eyes. Her lips. Her soul. I'm gone.

Wow. Her heart keeled over. How romantic!

He stopped in the doorway, watching her.

She felt the strain in him all the way across the room. He didn't want her looking at his work in progress. She was invading his privacy. Paige stepped away from his notebook, dropped her hands by her sides.

"You're working again?" she asked.

"How did you know I ever stopped?"

Their eyes met and in unison they said, "Gossips." Laughed. It felt good. Sounded natural.

"I was stymied for an entire year," he admitted. "Couldn't write a word."

"Because of your breakup with Simone?"

He scraped a hand along his jawline. "Not so much Simone—that was a long time coming. More the breakup of the band. I'd been with those guys from the beginning of my career. We started in Snake's garage when we were teenagers. Plus, someone stole my first guitar. The one my mom gave me for Christmas the year she died. It used to be hers. That was a kick in the gut."

"That must have been really hard for you."

"After the band broke up, I got a solo contract with our original recording label, but I froze. Couldn't produce."

"Considering the circumstances, it's understandable."

"I began to think that the band was the source of my creativity. That without them I couldn't create music."

"The creative block is what sent you to the Amazon?"

He nodded. "I was searching for . . . something . . ."

A beat passed between them, weighted and significant. A silent pause she couldn't quite decipher.

She inclined her head toward the notebook. "Obviously you found your way again. The Amazon worked its magic."

"No." His head ticked back and forth like the black cat clock with a swishing tail counting off the seconds that once hung in Grammie MacGregor's black and white, 1950s-style kitchen.

His gaze caressed her face, tender and searching,

and it shook her in ripples, tiny little earthquakes from the top of her head to the tips of her toes.

"I was still blocked when I came back from the Amazon." His voice was even but it held a riptide of unspoken words drawing her deeper into the mystery of him.

"But now you're not." She waved at the notebook. "What happened?"

His eyes were laser beams, sharp and unerring. "You."

"Me?" she whispered so softly she could barely hear herself. "What do you mean?"

"I came home because Emma asked me to perform for her charity and it was time to try and get back to work, but I stayed in Twilight because of you."

Her jaw loosened and her pulsed quickened, a trot, a cantor . . . What was he saying?

"The second our eyes met, the music . . ." He picked up the notebook. "This song sprang into my head. Full-blown. Ready to pluck and refine."

Seriously? Her heart galloped, a wild mustang roaming her chest.

"I've never in my life experienced anything like it."

"Like what?" Her palms were sweaty and she folded her fingers into fists, her mind whirling, a propeller of spiraling thoughts.

"One look in your eyes and it was as if a dam broke and all this music came flooding into my head. As if you were Euterpe ripping apart my creative blocks with your bare hands."

"Um . . ." Paige scratched her chin, felt slightly intimidated. "Who?"

His smile was filled with the knowledge of a

world she knew nothing of. "One of the Greek Muses. Euterpe inspires musicians and poets."

He thought she was his muse? That was both flattering and bothersome. Was he hanging out with her simply because he believed she'd stoked his creativity?

So what if he was?

She knew this could be nothing more than a fling. Anyway, that's all she wanted. What she needed. She'd never had a wild, reckless affair. Never cut loose and just followed her passion.

"If you think looking into my eyes unlocked your creativity, just wait until we have sex," she blurted, shocking herself with such boldness.

He wasn't offended. Not in the least. "Is that a fact," he drawled, his voice deepening, lengthening.

"Never know until we try."

"Hmm." He raked a hand over his jaw dusted with beard stubble, his smile craggy and dark, his pupils dilated and intense.

There was a wildness to him that sent thrilling, rushing goose bumps over her arms, a delicious shiver tickling every bone in her spine.

"What?" she breathed.

"I'm trying to decide if it's worth the risk."

"What risk?" she squeaked.

"That together we'll be too hot to handle."

"Burn me, baby," she begged. "Burn me."

"Ah, Paige."

"Don't think. Just do. Act. Treat me like one of your instruments. Play me."

"Like this?" He stalked across the room, scooped her into his arms.

She let out a startled squeal.

He hoisted her to his chest. Instinctively, she wrapped her arms around his neck. He was so strong, so brawny.

Cash peered into her eyes, and she felt the connection weld them in a way that yanked all the air from her lungs, left her stunned and shaking.

While she might have unblocked him, he'd also unblocked her. A block she'd denied and avoided, sexual and scary. Her one sexual partner had been a man who'd betrayed her in the biggest way. She'd been too afraid to branch out, try again.

Until now.

Until Cash.

He crushed his mouth against hers, hard and demanding, ravenous with need. But underneath the raw masculine power ran a tremor of tenderness that settled her doubts and fears. He would not hurt her. She felt the truth of it to the very marrow of her bones.

It was crazy. Mad. But a madness born of trust and confidence.

In his mouth, his arms, she found a place she'd forgotten. Safety. Reliability. Strength. Roots. The place that had been torn from her by her parents' divorce and her father's illness and untimely passing.

Home.

When he kissed her it felt as if she was returning home after years of wandering aimlessly through the world, not even knowing she was searching.

And now finding it all the same.

It was not the home of parched, sandy West Texas soil. This home was not a physical place. It was an internal place. A place of time instead of space, where she felt of one piece. Whole. Complete. A place of quiet sustenance. A nurturing place. A sheltering place.

A secret, sacred place of the soul.

In this place, this home, waited buried treasures of wonderment, peace, vision, and freedom. Freedom from demands and responsibilities, worries and noise.

In his kiss, she found this place, this home, but more than that, Paige found . . .

Herself.

Paige Hyacinth MacGregor as she'd never been before. Confident in her sexuality. Fully comfortable in her own skin. Acutely aware of her feminine power.

He removed his mouth from hers, but he continued to hold her tightly in his arms. She could hear the hard thumping of his heart against her body, felt the vibration of his life force flowing into her.

This was what she wanted. Him. Tonight. Fully and completely.

Cash eased her onto the mattress, slipped his arms from around her, stepped back. Looked down at her with such wistfulness it took her breath.

"What is it?" she whispered.

"You are so beautiful," he murmured with the reverence of a faithful man in church.

She had never thought of herself as beautiful, but the expression on his face convinced her that *he* thought so. It touched something deep inside of her. Stirred a need she hadn't known was there.

He kept touching buttons, pushing envelopes, surprising her with the things she discovered about herself through the lenses of his eyes. It was heady and a bit disconcerting.

"Come here." She held out her arms to him.

He shook his head. "Paige, I want you so badly I can't breathe, but I'm not sure you're doing this for the right reason."

Baffled, she sat up on her elbows. "I want to have sex. You're hot. I like you, and you like me. What's wrong with that reason?"

"Are you using me to bury the past?"

Was she? "Maybe. Who knows? Who cares? What does it matter?"

"I just don't want you to do something you'll regret later."

"I'm regretting not ripping your clothes off," she grumbled. "And giving you too much time to talk. That's what I'm regretting."

He laughed, a solid sound that filled her lungs with happiness.

"Are we going to do this thing or not?" she asked, terrified he was going to back out.

He came toward her, head lowered, eyes glistening in the muted light from the bedside lamp. That feral jungle cat again. Lithe. Dangerous. Sexy as ten kinds of sin.

She gulped, thrilled, chilled, delighted. He crawled onto the mattress. She fell back against the pillows, stared up at him.

His jaw tightened. Eyes darkened. Breath slowed. He did not speak.

Her heart skipped a beat. Then two. Three.

"Last chance," he said. "You can still back out—"

She didn't let him finish. Just grabbed the front of his shirt in her fist and pulled him down on top of her.

CHAPTER 14

Romantic: A period in musical history during the eighteenth and early nineteenth centuries where the focus shifted from the neoclassical style to an emotional, expressive, and imaginative style.

Paige wasn't just any woman. She may claim she didn't want anything from him, but she was little more than a virgin. If they slept together it would mean something significant to her. He would only be her second lover.

Who the hell was he kidding? If they slept together it would mean something significant to *him*.

And that wild thought spun the illogical notion through his head. What if he could be her *last* lover?

Whoa! Hold the freaking phone. He'd known her a week. One measly week and this was what popped into his head?

His chest muscles tightened, a vise squeezing the air out of his lungs as she pulled him down.

They were pressed together, pelvis to pelvis. He

peered into those bewitching eyes. *Buzz!* The contact hummed like a high-voltage electrical line.

She lowered her lashes and sent him a foxy grin. His heart twitched strangely as if yanked by marionette strings.

What if, what if, what if she was The One? The One he feared did not exist. The One that stirred feelings he'd spent a lifetime avoiding.

Oh shit.

What if he finally stopped roaming, stopped searching for that unobtainable something missing, and opened himself up to what was standing right in front of him? What if he gave up sacrificing love for the sake of his career? What if there was something more important than music? What if everything he'd ever believed to be true was wrong, wrong, wrong, and there was a whole other way of being?

Wow.

He blinked, blindsided by that avalanche of realization.

Who was he going to be for the rest of his life?

The aloof, brooding stranger who didn't truly belong anywhere or to anyone except the music? Was he forever going to be the guy who let the belief that you couldn't have both a committed relationship and big career success hold him back and keep him from taking a chance on love?

Love?

What was he talking about? He was having a moment. That's all this was. Desire. Passion. And a passing moment of wanting it to be more than that.

Focus on the sex.

Good plan. He dove into the feeling. Wallowed in it. Burning hot passion.

For Paige.

Except, as he stared into her eyes, and he saw his own image reflected in that sweet mirror, the passing moment grew, expanded, prodded, provoked. Kicked his persona like an aluminum can.

Cash Colton.

Everything about him was predicated on his musical talent. Even his name. Lorena had named him for her favorite musician, Johnny Cash. From the time he was born, he'd been carrying a tune, tapping out beats, feeling the rhythm of sound pumping through his blood sure as the oxygen he breathed.

How could he throw away his very identity? Without music, he was nothing. Music was the only thing that sustained him. The only thing he'd ever been able to fully count on.

Well, until last year when the music had stopped. After the band broke up and his Gibson was stolen.

The music had gone silent and he hadn't heard it again until he'd looked into Paige's eyes. She was the catalyst. The thing that had brought him back to himself.

And that's where he was getting strung up. That's why he was confused. Paige and the return of his creativity were intricately linked. He was grateful to her, no doubt. Was he confusing gratitude for love?

That must be it. Had to be it. You couldn't have feelings of love for someone you'd only known a week.

But man, was he lusting after her big-time.

"Cash," she called. "Kiss me."

Who could refuse that plea from those honeyed lips? Not he.

He kissed her, amazing himself by how gently he took her mouth. She wriggled beneath him, wrapped her arms around his waist, pressed him closer.

She reached for the buttons of his shirt, worked them with surprisingly nimble fingers for a woman inexperienced at sex. He laughed at her eagerness, the earnest expression on her face. Once she had his shirt opened, she slipped her hot little palms over his bare torso, and spread out her fingers.

He groaned at her fiery touch, the sound raspy and harsh in the darkened room. She pressed her tongue against his throat and flicked him with a daring lick that stirred every part of his body.

Simultaneously, she pushed the shirt from his shoulders, exposing his skin to the air and leaving him in his jeans and cowboy boots.

"My turn," he said, taking the tail of her shirt in his hands and pulling it over her head.

Giving him a heart-pounding view of her plump breasts encased in a white lace bra.

Angel.

She was angelic. Heavenly. Garden of Eden.

He peeled back to revel in this moment, fully take it in. The pulse at her throat throbbed visibly, quickened under his stare.

Her eyes crinkled at the corners and her lips tipped up into a smile that hit him hard as a blow. It was such a beautiful smile. She was so beautiful. Beautiful and kind.

Cash cupped her breasts cradled by that bra, felt the lush flesh fill his palms. He straddled her, both knees sinking into the mattress at her hips. He lowered his head, pressed a million openmouthed kisses over her forehead, cheeks, nose, mouth. Sliding down her jaw to her chin, throat, collarbones.

His fingers adeptly reached around her back to unhook her bra. Gently, he slipped it down her shoulders.

She stared up at him, breathing hard, hands moving to cover her bare breasts. Seemingly suddenly shy.

"You don't have to do anything you don't want to do," he reassured her. "You can say stop at any time."

"Go," she whispered. "Go."

He went. Kissing her gorgeous breasts. Spending his time there. Nibbling and suckling. Feeling her whimper and wriggle. All he wanted was to give her pleasure. Erase her bad memories. Replace them with light and laughter.

They shared languid kisses, deep and long and sweet. Kisses both innocent and carnal. Like teenagers in the backseat of an old Chevy on some lonely lovers' lane at midnight. They embraced each other in heated hugs, wild with solidarity and sedition.

She thrilled him in a way he had not ever before been thrilled. He loved her with his mouth, his tongue, his teeth. Sliding down her body, over those lovely breasts, lingering at her rounded belly, resting his head, and breathing deep.

When he reached the waistband of her jeans, he paused, checked in to make sure this was what she wanted. She raised her head, met his eye, nodded.

He stripped off her jeans and her panties in one

smooth motion, working the garments over her thighs, knees, ankles, feet, and dropping them to the floor. He stood at the end of the bed, legs splayed, looking down at her.

"Wait," she said. "You get undressed too. I want to see you. All of you."

She crawled toward him, reached the end of the bed, reached for *his* waistband. Drew him to her as she frantically undid the snap of his jeans, worked down the zipper.

Her eagerness spurred him and he shucked his jeans in a twinkling. Whisk. Whoosh. Naked.

They gazed at each other, rapt. Awed.

His feet were rooted on the floor at the foot of the bed. She was on her knees at the end of the mattress. Her curvy body illuminated in the silvered moonlight shining in through the window. She was a goddess. Pristine and powerful.

Breath stalled in his throat, reverent and rousing.

His shaft was stone. Growing harder at the sight of her. He wanted to tell her how incredible she was, but words were meaningless. Incomprehensible sounds. A guttural glop on the back of his tongue.

He took her in his arms.

She melted into him. Liquid and lyrical.

Their mouths met, crashed, crushed. Head-on impact of need and desire. A fire. Stoked and fed. Flaming high and hot. A blister. A blaze.

He was overthrown. Toppled. Ego gone. Dissolved.

Cash wanted one thing and one thing only. Her pleasure. Whatever she wanted, he was her servant. Sent to deliver her happiness above all else. He felt it. Knew it. And, in that moment, utterly believed it.

His identity cracked, shattered. He was laid bare and raw and vulnerable. Cash, the brand. Cash, the musician. Cash, the man. Dispatched.

Gone. Disappeared. Vanished.

In place of that old false sense of self was pure essence. He was flooded by blinding white light shining from every pore. Glowing from his cells. Lifeblood. He was vibrating to a higher frequency, true and real and priceless.

He tried to swallow, couldn't. Couldn't breathe either. Couldn't do anything but absorb her.

The smell of her hair, floral and sweet. The touch of her skin, radiant and silky. The taste of her lips, sugared and certain. The sound of her voice, soft and urgent.

"Please," she whispered. "Please, please, please. Cash, please, please me."

A chant. A mantra. A prayer. A request of the highest order.

He was her knight. He would not fail her.

Love her, sang his heart. *Love her like she's never been loved. Give her your mouth, your tongue, your hands, your fingers.*

Show her.

Lead her.

Cherish her.

Protect her.

A song. It was a new song. Inspired by her trembling beauty. Notes and chords danced in his head. A wizardry of pattern and rhyme. Melody. Harmony. Beats and cadence. A measure.

They were wrapped around each other. In each other.

The song played on, poignant and moving. He loved her with his mouth, kissing every corner and alcove. Finding the spots that made her wriggle and sigh. Touching and fondling. Pulling exquisite sounds from her.

Building. Growing. Expanding. A tower of song.

He shivered. Delighted and bedeviled.

When he headed for the most delicate part of her, she sucked in a deep breath and put a hand on his head, stopping his progress.

"Wait." Her voice came out high and nervous.

He raised his head. "What is it, sweetheart? What's wrong?"

"I . . . no one . . . I'm . . ."

"You've never been pleasured like this?" he guessed. She nodded.

An inordinate joy spread through him, unraveling like a black velvet ribbon inside him, dark and mysterious. He would be her first in one way. So special. Such a gift. He was humbled and that startled him. This pious feeling of gratitude.

"Shh, shh," he soothed. "No worries. You lay back and let me take care of everything."

She nibbled her bottom lip, her insecurity so adorable it socked him squarely in the solar plexus. She wanted to trust him. He could see it on her. But she'd been hurt, burned. This secret place where he wanted to go would expose her fully. She was scared.

"It's okay if you're not ready," he said, pulling back, giving her room, even as her feminine fragrance urged every masculine instinct in him to dive in, dive deep, conquer her. "It's okay."

He curled up next to her, pulled her into his arms, and held her. Just held her until after a while she reached out to stroke his face and whimper, "I want it. I want you. Please go there."

Cash smiled in the dark. He couldn't help it. He wanted to give everything to her. His mouth. His skill. The moon on a string. Anything and everything.

At last she relaxed and let him go where he wanted so badly to go. She dropped her legs, opened her playground to him.

Her noises directed him. He was attuned to her every nuance and sound. She smelled of heaven and earth. Ethereal and light, rich and lush.

She tasted like country-and-western music, lively and honest, real and rooted, ageless and timeless. As he savored her, Cash thought dizzily: *bluegrass, rockabilly, western swing, zydeco, honky-tonk*. The twang of guitars strummed in his head. The fast friction of fiddles. The swing of strings, banjoes and mandolins. He heard harmonicas and washboards, cowbells and tambourines.

In her body he supped the history of song. The Celtic footprints of reels and ballads. The drunken beat of tribal drums. The mournful sigh of bagpipes, and the hopeful wheeze of polka accordions. The haunting wistfulness of a forest dulcimer. The sweet, easygoing autoharp.

Reeds slipped in. The shiny tin of woodwinds. Moist mouths. Hot skin. Flutes and oboes, clarinets and bassoons.

Then the bold blast of brass, the sympathetic vibration of lips. Labrosones, resonated and pitched.

Slides and valves, crooks and keys. He shifted and
changed. Lip tension, air flow. *Embouchure.*

From the seat of his spine to the top of his head, he
buzzed with tempo and note. Passed the hum on to
her through his lips and jaw. The puff of his cheeks,
the gentle blow. The six-holed serpent deep and low.
Saxophone jazz. Didgeridoo. Coronet. Zink. Conch
and lur.

The thump of percussions pounded through him.
Tap and pace. Tension and pressure. Bongos. Conga.
Box drum. Snare drum. Kettle and jug.

He rocked it. The greatest sexual performance of
his life. Rocked her.

Hard.

A rambling, shambling, rocking, knocking concert of love. In his deep dive with Euterpe, he found
the meaning of everything and it was music. The
one constant, through the rise and fall of nations,
that made life worth living.

Music.

And she was his never-ending song.

He could listen to her music to the end of his
days and die happy with a smile on his face.

The symphony unfurled in his head. Rising. Rushing. A garden of tune and verse, expanding and
growing. Reaching for the sky, the stars, the universe.

She busted, burst. Cried out. Grasped his hair in
her fingers. Clutched and groaned.

He tasted her release, organic and awesome.
Rolled in it. Reveled. His heart sang out with his
accomplishment. Proud and cocky.

She whimpered and quivered, shaking and sweaty.

Grinning, Cash lay beside her, hooked her to him with his elbow. Held her close. Peppered her with kisses.

"I was . . . that was . . . you were . . ." she gasped.

"Shh." He squeezed her softly. Pressed his lips to the top of her head. Felt the frantic skip of her galloping pulse begin to slow.

They lay curled together in the middle of the bed. Two spoons snuggled together. Her in front, he behind. His arm around her waist. His face buried in her silky hair.

Precious. This moment was so damn precious. She was precious. The world was precious.

It was a word he never used, and yet, now that's all he could think. Precious. Precious. Precious.

They were connected. Linked. It didn't matter if she was the only one who'd found release. He had taken her there and he could not have been more satisfied. This was a gift of selflessness. The noble feeling of putting her needs ahead of his. Hell, his needs were paltry in the face of hers. Didn't matter one whit.

She was the Alpha and Omega. The beginning and the end.

It was powerful and scary because his feelings were so powerful. But he tightened his grip around her. Held on.

After a while, she'd caught her breath, regained her composure, and whispered, "What were you like as a kid?"

"Huh?" he asked drowsily. He'd almost fallen asleep.

"I'm trying to imagine you as a kid. What were you like? Did you collect things? Like to climb high up on things? Were you the ringleader? The class clown?"

No woman had ever asked him this question and he had to think about it. Mostly, he didn't dwell on the past.

"I lived in my head," he said. "Got called out on daydreaming in school. A lot. Loved to pretend to be superheroes. I was particularly taken with Batman. When I was three Lorena could not keep me out of my Batman costume."

"You called your mother by her first name?"

"She wanted it that way." He felt her tense beneath his arm, wondered why.

"No siblings?"

"Nope."

"Just you and your mom?"

"For the most part," he said vaguely, evasively. Licked the back of her neck, hoping to distract her.

She wriggled. Giggled. Squirmed away.

He drew her back.

She leaned against him. "When did you get interested in music?"

"I guess I was always interested. Loved to bang on pots and pans. Loved to sing. Instead of bedtime stories, I wanted bedtime songs."

"So your transformation into a musician was organic?"

"My mom was an aspiring musician. There were always instruments lying around. Musicians, too, for that matter. Lots of late night jam sessions."

And lots of mornings stepping over whiskey bottles and bongs and people passed out on the floor, but he wasn't going to tell her that. The last thing he wanted was her pity. Pity was not sexy.

"I bet you were an adorable kid." She ducked her head to kiss the back of his hand.

The touch of those lips sent a hot shiver shooting through him. She'd had her release. He was still a loaded gun with a hair trigger.

She turned into his arms, to face him. Cupped his cheeks with her palms. Kissed him long and deep. Then from underneath the pillow, she withdrew a condom, wagged it in his face.

"Where did you get that?"

"Hid it there while you were getting busy down below." In the dim light he could see her blush, and he loved that telltale sign of her inexperience.

"Foxy sly."

"You game?" she asked.

"Gimme that." He reached for the condom.

In under a minute he had the condom on and Paige charged up and ready and calling his name.

It was energizing. His name on her lips, chanted like a song. When she begged him to get inside her, he was already there. Sliding into her warm sweetness like a baseball player sliding home on a steal.

Safe!

He sunk in. She squeezed him with her arms and her inner muscles. Welcoming him. *Hello, big guy.*

He penetrated to the core of things, to the core of her.

And surprisingly, startling, to the core of himself.

A cracking sensation in the center of his chest, felt heat and energy pour out. Flow from him to her and back again.

She made a happy noise, full of punch-drunk jubilation. He felt it bubble in him. The same effervescent glee. He strummed with it. Resonant and lingering as a single guitar string plucked in an empty concert hall.

He planted his face against her neck, breathed her in as their bodies snuggly joined. Their tempo was perfect. Moving as a seamless unit. The two of them gliding on rainbows and moonbeams.

It felt like the most natural thing in the world. As if they'd been waiting all their lives to dance this way. To sway and thrust. Slide and swim.

He was a musician and she was a dancer. The two of them in perfect sync, absolute timing. No missteps. No falters.

It started off as a waltz. Romantic and smooth. A flirtation. Soon slowed into the rumba. Passionate and sensual. A languid flirtation of rolling hips, sways and twists. Seduction. From there things progressed into a steady $^4/_4$ mambo beat. Quick, quick, slow. Rising action. And the foxtrot. Building heat and friction. Headed for the top. Finally, the samba. The height of their joining. Quick beats. Fast movements. Acrobatic feats.

Their bodies shook.

The bed shook.

Hell, the whole damn boat shook. Rock and reeling. Dance and rhythm. It was the most erotic thing Cash had ever experienced.

The blissful, mysterious, crazy alchemy of great sex.

At the crescendo, the completion of this dance to end all dances, another song came to him. Exquisite and full-blown. It pushed at the envelope of his mind. Left him stunned and staggered. Barely able to come down with her.

Once he quieted his breath, he gave her a quick hug, kissed her forehead, slung back the covers, and jumped from the bed.

"Huh?" She sat up, looking dazed and mused. "What's happening? Where are you going?"

"To write all this down before I forget it."

"The sex?"

"No, the music."

"What music?"

He leaned across the bed. Tousled her hair. Kissed her. "Your music."

She sat up in bed, tucked her legs underneath her, pulled the sheet to cover her nakedness. "What does that mean, *my* music?"

"The music that pops into my head whenever I'm with you. It was pretty intense just then." He waved at hand at her, the bed, the sheets.

"Everything was pretty intense just then."

"You heard music too?"

"No, but I'm not a musician. Is it always like that for you? Tunes running amok in your head?"

"Rarely. Usually writing a song, lyrics, melody, it's pretty painstaking. But when I'm with you it's . . ." He shook his head as if some long-held misbelief had shattered.

"What?" she asked, intrigued.

"Free, easy. Like magic."

"So this is how it is? One or two quick ones and it's off to write music?" she teased.

"I wouldn't say they were quick ones," he drawled. "But yeah, kind of."

"Righteous," she said in gleeful booming voice.

"You don't mind?"

"I'm honored." She made shooing motions. "Go write. I'm just gonna snooze."

With a serene smile on her face, she flopped back down onto the mattress, closed her eyes, and promptly fell asleep.

Cash plunked down at the desk, reached for his journal and pen. Drew notes. Flats and sharps. Let the beat flow from his mind down his arm to the pen. He doodled and scratched. Wrote and scribbled, filled page after page.

Half an hour later, he stopped, turned to look at Paige sleeping in the middle of his bed. It would be so easy to abandon his project and crawl up beside her. He was torn between his work and her allure.

He paused, watching her, listening to her slow, even breathing. She lulled him. Cash yawned. Fought off drooping eyelids.

Contemplated just how special it had been.

Unique.

Sex with Paige had been utterly unique, unlike any sexual experience he'd ever had. He had no idea why it was different, just knew that it was. Maybe because it was the first sex he'd had in over a year. Maybe because Paige was so easy to be with. Maybe it was because he liked her.

He really, *really* liked her.

Maybe, and this was the dangerous thought, what he was feeling was much more than just intense like.

How could that be? He didn't even know her. What if she was just like the other women who were attracted to his money and fame and not for who he was?

Didn't matter. He wanted her anyway.

That was messed up.

It still didn't matter.

She was his muse. She lit his fire, his heart, and his creativity.

He wanted her.

What now? Where did he go from here? What did he do with these feelings? The last time he'd felt this inspired—well, let's be honest, he'd never felt this inspired—but the last time he'd even come close was when he'd fallen for Simone, and look how *that* stumbled.

Overthinking, whispered a tiny voice in his brain. *Get out of your head. Feel the experience. Turn it into song. Work.*

So he listened to that voice that never steered him wrong. The voice that often got buried during the hubbub of life. He listened and he wrote, and by morning, Cash has created his opus. A song unlike any other he'd ever written.

And as dawn broke and Paige awakened, Cash went back to bed and made love to her all over again.

CHAPTER 15

Deceptive cadence: A chord progression that seems to lead to resolving itself on the final chord; but does not.

Cash drove Paige to her job at Froggy's the next morning. Even though she was exhausted from their wild and wondrous night, Paige grinned her way through her shift. Cash returned home, and spent the day perfecting the song that had come to him in the midst of their lovemaking. Cemented it. Got it prepped to send it to Sepia.

They were worn out by the end of the long day, and ended up sleeping in their own houseboats, sending good-night texts to each other.

The next morning, Cash called her to tell her he'd booked a band and recording studio in Austin for preproduction and would be gone for a few days. Paige tried not to be disappointed that he was leaving right after they'd had sex, but she knew he was excited about his new songs.

He texted her several times a day while he was

away, keeping her up-to-date on how the recording was going. She lived vicariously through his stories. He sent her gifts. Flowers showed up at the day care. A beautiful winter bouquet of red and white roses, smilax, ranunculus, festival bush, tulips, poppies, astilbe, peonies, and amaryllis.

While the flowers were lovely and she enjoyed them, she couldn't help thinking of all the showy bouquets Randy had sent her when he was trying to woo her. She pushed that worry aside. Cash was not Randy. No comparison.

He sent her a basket with hot chocolate mix, a Christmas mug, gourmet popcorn, a flannel blanket, and a DVD of her favorite Christmas movie, *The Christmas Card*—how had he known?

Emma. He must have asked Emma.

And then, when the temperature dropped into the twenties on the third day he was gone and she was bundling up to ride her bike to work, a knock sounded on her door. It was a car service driver, sent by Cash to chauffeur her around town. The gesture touched her more than any of the other gifts. He'd been thinking of her comfort.

She texted him to thank him and they had a Skype session. It was so good to see his face pop up on her phone screen. He was enlivened. Animated. He looked so happy, and she was happy for him. He would finish the recording sessions on Friday, send the finished product off to his manager, and drive back to Twilight.

They made a date for his return. Friday, December 15, a week after their tryst on the turquoise houseboat. They planned to hook up for drinks at

four-thirty after Paige got off work from the day
care center.

She wrangled the afternoon off from her second
job at the theater—Jana Gerard offered to stand in
for her. Flynn agreed to look after Fritzi, and optimistic that their evening together would lead to
bigger things, Paige had asked her uncle Floyd if
she could work the Sunday morning breakfast shift
instead of Saturday.

That afternoon as she rushed across the square
to meet him, Paige felt fizzy, dizzy, and giddy at
the thought of seeing Cash, and the anticipation of
making love to him again.

The town square was bright and brisk and bustling, Christmas lights blazing from every establishment, bundled shoppers hustling and street venders
hawking food, trinkets, and gift wrapping services.

Paige breathed in the excitement. In recent years,
she'd lost her love of the holidays—following Mom's
new marriage and moving to Colorado, Dad's pro-
longed illness, and then, last Christmas, Randy's
monumental betrayal—but this year it felt different.

Hopeful. A bit surreal. Skating between beguiling
and overwhelming.

Buses of tourists deposited schoolchildren, senior
citizens, and singles on pub crawls, overcrowding
the uneven, cobblestones streets. The clip-clop of
horses pulling carriages, decked out with lights and
wreaths and mistletoe, rang out too loudly, too clear.
The Christmas music blared over the sound system
delivering relentless cheer. The profuse scent of cinnamon and pine and gingerbread spilled from shops
and kiosks.

She wanted to embrace it all, but was still just a little too scared to fully let go. She'd trusted before. Had the rug pulled out from under her one time too many.

But in her heart of hearts, she was an eternal optimist.

Which was why she practically skipped down the sidewalk, an abundant smile sprucing up her lips, her pulse *tap-tap-tappity-tapping*. She'd been thinking about this all week.

He was waiting for her outside Fruit of the Vine. She instantly picked him out of the crowd. He had his hands in the pockets of his leather bomber jacket, and dark sunglasses perched on the end of his nose. He was leaning against the side of the building, looking all mysterious and insouciant.

Her heart stopped. God, he was amazing. How had she gotten so lucky to even have this tiny slice of his life? She inhaled, appreciating the preciousness of the moment.

The second he spotted her, Cash broke into a big grin, pushed off from the wall, and came to take her hand.

Breathless.

His touch left her breathless.

And when he slipped his arm around her waist to escort her inside, she feared she might never breathe again.

Paige had never been inside the wine bar. Fruit on the Vine was a fairly new addition to Twilight. She'd been scrimping and saving to get a car and her own apartment and wine simply wasn't in the budget. Besides, she was far too busy.

The hipster count was high that afternoon due to the artisanal cheese festival in town, but Paige didn't care. He guided her past men with thick bushy beards and short, slicked-back hair, and women in pastel Doc Martens. Both sexes wore an abundance of flannel and suspenders. On the small stage a big man was singing a bad karaoke version of "Total Eclipse of the Heart," egged on by the crowd.

"You know a trend is no longer hip by the time it's popular in Twilight." She giggled as Cash led her up the stairs to the dimmer, alcove seating.

"On the plus side," he said. "Hipsters don't tend to be into country-and-western music. It's why I picked the wine bar. Less chance of running into hard-core fans."

Even though it was early, the place was filling up fast, and they managed to snag the last darkened booth in the far corner of the room. He sat beside her instead of across from her, pressing close, their thighs touching. She liked the intimacy.

A waitress came by, and Paige asked if they had sangria. They did not.

"Do you have ice wine?" Cash asked.

"We do."

"What labels?"

She rattled off several.

"Two of the Cabernet Franc," he said.

"What's ice wine?" Paige whispered once the waitress had left, both fascinated and embarrassed that she was so unsophisticated.

"It's a type of dessert wine made from grapes that have been frozen while still in the vineyard."

"So we're drinking dessert before we've had dinner? It feels decadent."

"It is, and it's very sweet. Just like you," he said, leaning over to capture her lips.

Feeling girlish, she giggled and kissed him back.

The waitress brought two small narrow glasses filled with ice cold wine. Smiled. "It's on the house. The owner is a fan."

Cash raised his glass, smiled like it was the happiest day of his life. That smile curled deep inside her belly, took hold, grew. "To us."

"To us," she echoed, feeling slightly faint, hardly able to believe she was here with him, toasting their couple-ness.

They clinked glasses and took a sip and he kissed her again. The wine was nectar sweet and tasted like a golden sunset on a December evening over the lake. It started out cold, but by the time it reached her stomach she felt rosy warm and tingly.

"This is lovely." She sighed, took another sip, and noticed light from the flickering candle on the table glinted off silver tinsel streamers dangling from the ceiling, and a bunch of tipsy young women at a big table in the middle of the room burst into loud laughter.

"Not as lovely as you," Cash murmured, his arm around her shoulders, his distinctive masculine scent tangled up in her nose.

It was an amazing moment, but her happiness had a slippery feel to it, like an unbelievable fairy tale too good to be true. And when he kissed her again, she wrapped her arms around him and squeezed so tightly she feared he might complain, but he only hugged her back.

He tugged her into his lap, her legs dangling over his. This time his kiss was magnificently fierce, almost too fierce for public consumption. Good thing it was dark and they were in the corner and the drunken young women at the big table were drawing all the attention.

Cash stroked her cheek, twisted a lock of her hair around his finger, used it to tug her gently into another kiss. "You make me dizzy, Paige Hyacinth MacGregor, you know that?"

He studied her and they were so close she could see the starburst of darker gray in the middle of his eyes, the softness at the corners where his tender smile reached. Overcome, her heart clutched.

"Is that a good thing?" she whispered. "Or bad?"

Instead of answering, he kissed her long and deep. A soulful kiss thick with a rich undercurrent of meaning that she didn't possess the ability to decipher. But she could feel the hard, rapid thump of his heart through his shirt that matched her own crazy rhythm.

Sexual tension sizzled and crackled, flaming high as dried logs in a fire pit, full of heat and oxygen, ready to explode into an orange shower of red-hot sparks.

She was afraid, so afraid all this deliciousness was going to blow up in her face. Her experiences with love had been tragic and unstable. She'd not ever felt anything this big, this combustible, and each time she was near him it only seemed to expand, stretching and pushing at the edges of possibilities.

On the first-floor level below where they canoodled in the loft, the front door opened, blowing in dead leaves, cold air, and a pack of young women who'd clearly already been drinking. Amy from the Twilight Bakery was in the group.

"Where is he?" one of the young women howled. "We heard Cash Colton is in the house."

"Ah crap," Cash said, hunched his shoulders and tugged the brim of his hat down over his eyes. "Trapped."

"You don't want to spend the rest of the night signing cleavage?" Paige teased.

"God, no. All I want to do is spend time with you."

"Where is he?" Amy hollered from below. "Cashie, Cashie, come out, come out wherever you are."

"Looks like we're sunk," Cash muttered.

"O ye of little faith," she said. "There's a back exit from the top floor of all the old buildings on the square. Come with me."

He tossed a ten-dollar bill on the table to tip the waitress for the complimentary wine.

Paige took his hand and towed him to where a heavy curtain hid a hallway. Their boots clunked against the old wooden, uneven floor as they slunk past the curtain and down the darkened hall, lit only by one small wall sconce.

Behind them, they heard Amy's voice and footsteps getting louder as she climbed the loft. "Cash Colton, where are you?"

At the end of the long hall was an exit door. She hauled him toward it, worried that Amy was going to push the curtain aside and catch them before they got out the door. His big palm was warm against hers and he squeezed her hand.

She pushed against the door handle, but the wooden door had swollen in the damp weather and was stuck.

"Stand aside," Cash said, and put some muscle into it.

Behind them, Amy's voice was high and quarrelsome as she spoke to the people in the loft. "Any of you bitches seen Cash Colton?"

Paige pressed into Cash's back, trying to hide him from view in case Amy came through the curtain. Silly impulse, seeing as how he was a good eight inches taller than she was. But all she could think was, *Protect him*.

Cash hit the door with his shoulder at the same time he shoved on the handle. The door popped open like a wine cork leaving the bottle and, with Paige at his back, the momentum pushed them both out onto the narrow, rickety iron fire escape circa 1874-ish.

"Whoa!" he said, almost barreling over the rail. He put out a hand to steady her, steady them both. The exit door snapped closed behind them, leaving them peering down at the alley below.

"Let's get out of here," she said, and started climbing down the fire escape.

He hesitated.

She peered up at him. "What is it?"

An embarrassed expression crossed his face and he scratched his chin. "I'm a tiny bit acrophobic."

"It's only two stories." Aww, his fear of heights was endearing. Who would have suspected someone as self-confident as Cash would get nervous over heights?

He eyed the fire escape. "The ladder is so old it doesn't have a hinge or slide that allows it to go all the way to the ground. You have to jump."

"It's a short drop. See?" She made the six-foot drop to the ground. "Bend your knees."

"That fire escape is damn unsteady."

"Okay," she said. "Either come with me or go back the way you came. Of course that means Amy . . . Which do you fear most? Her or heights?"

"Right," he said, and scooted down the fire escape after her. When he got to the last rung, he hesitated.

"Amy," Paige prodded.

"Gotcha." Closing his eyes, he jumped to the ground.

"Yay." Paige applauded. "You did it. Squashed that fear of heights."

He straightened, regained his balance, and grinned at her just as the exit door on the second floor opened and Amy poked her head out. "Cash Colton, are you running away from me?"

"Yep," he called, grabbed Paige's hand and, laughing, they ran away down the alley.

"Where are we going?" Cash asked.

"Wait and see."

Intrigued, Cash allowed her to guide him through the town square.

"Where's the Land Rover?" she asked.

"Parked at the marina. I walked. Why?"

"We need it."

He pulled his vehicle's remote control from his pants' pocket and handed it to her. "You drive."

She looked utterly pleased and stopped long enough to plant a kiss on his cheek. Her lips heated his skin, warming him up straight down to his belly and beyond.

Hand in hand they strolled through the square, past the Twilight Playhouse, down the walkway toward the lake and marina. The air was fresh and smelled of impending snow. Christmas music poured from the outdoor speakers, providing a backdrop for the carolers singing on the corner. It was a snow globe town.

Attractive. Innocent. Untouchable.

Cash saw the appeal. Understood why people could spend their entire lives in a place like this one.

The walk took a leisurely twenty minutes as they took time to stop and exchange kisses in the glow of the security lamps lighting their way in the foggy darkness.

Damn, he'd missed her.

The recording sessions had been a big success. The hired band and sound guys had given him multiple thumbs-up. He'd done Sepia proud. Thanks to Paige and her muse power. Now, he was just waiting for Deet to give the songs a listen and get back to him, but he was confident his manager was going to love the recordings as much as everyone else.

"How was your trip?" she asked as they reached the Land Rover.

"Trippy."

"Meaning?" Her hazel eyes hooked his.

"It's the best thing I've ever done," he said, holding open the driver's side door so she could climb up into the cab. "My first solo effort and it's all due to you."

"No."

"What?"

"I had nothing to do with it."

"You had everything to do with it."

She buckled her seat belt and looked over to where he was still standing outside the Land Rover, his hand on the door. "Are you saying that if you hadn't met me you wouldn't have started writing songs again?"

"I would have cobbled something together but it wouldn't have been phenomenal."

"The songs are that good?"

"Beyond," he said. "Since meeting you I've stretched and grown as a musician in ways I didn't know were possible."

"That's great," she said, but her mouth was tight, her eyes worried, as if it wasn't great at all. She was upset with him on some level and he couldn't figure out why. "C'mon, get in. We're going to get you a tree from my friends, Joe and Gabi Cheek, at their Christmas tree farm."

He slipped into the passenger seat, buckled up. "Any FYIs?"

"About?"

He shrugged. "Your friends. Christmas tree selection . . ."

"Are you anxious about meeting my friends?" She sounded amused.

Yes. "No, of course not." He made a dismissive noise, pushing air out through his pursed lips.

"Joe and Gabi are amazing people," Paige said. "They've never met a stranger. No worries. They'll love you. They love everyone."

As it turned out, Joe and Gabi did not love him.

The Christmas tree farm was bustling. Vehicles pulling in and out. Christmas lights strung everywhere. Kids running to and fro. The rolling land covered with trees stirred in Cash the memory of his grandparents' small dried-up ranch. Bittersweet, those memories. He'd loved the land, loved working with livestock, but his grandparents' small-minded judgment and closed-off hearts had pushed him to run away when he was fifteen.

But in this moment, his love of the land tickled him, soft as a feather. A tiny whisper carried on the rich smell of earth and air.

Home.

He had an urge to dig in the dirt.

"We need a tree!" Paige announced gaily to the lean-hipped man, about Cash's age, who sauntered up to the Land Rover as they got out.

"We?" The man raised an eyebrow.

"Well, it's really for Cash," she said, and slung her arm around his waist. "Joe, this is Cash Colton."

Joe narrowed his eyes, gave Cash a flinty stare. "I know who he is."

A petite pregnant woman joined them. She put her left hand on her belly, extended her right. "Hi, I'm Gabi, Joe's wife—"

"Cash!" A high-pitched feminine voice drew everyone's attention.

He turned and saw a blonde girl who looked to be around ten years old bouncing over.

"Hey," she said. "I'm Casey and your number one fan."

"Hello, Casey," he said, offering up his best public-relationships grin. "Good to meet you."

"The first three letters of our name are exactly the same," she said, sticking her chest out proudly. "We have so much in common."

"Casey's my daughter." Joe gave Cash the stink-eye and slung an arm around Casey's slender shoulders.

Casey squirmed away from her dad, leaned in close to Cash, and whispered, "I love your boots. Cool colors."

At least someone was on his side. He gazed down at his black boots detailed with red accents and stitching. "Thank you," he whispered back as if they were keeping big secrets, and cast a sidelong glance at Paige. She was pulling her bottom lip up between her teeth the way she did when she was nervous.

"How long are you in Twilight?" Joe asked, a frown cutting a crease between his eyebrows.

"Until the end of the year." The vibe he was getting was not friendly. It was unusual not to be welcomed with open arms. Most people loved brushing shoulders with celebrity.

"Is that so?" Joe hooked his thumbs in his belt loops and Cash had the strangest vision of those belt loops as holsters, and Joe fingering the butts of two guns with Wyatt Earp imagery. "Where are you off to after that?"

"Who knows?" Cash shrugged, keeping it casual and examining a Virginia pine. The trees were beautifully shaped and planted in rows like soldier regiments. He'd give Joe props for doing his job well, but he wasn't feeling the Christmas cheer. At least, not where he was concerned.

"LA," Paige said, and it dawned on him she'd kept quiet for a while. "He's going to Los Angeles after he leaves here."

"That's where my recording label is located," Cash explained.

"You used to live there." Joe picked up an axe, balanced it on his shoulder lumberjack-style, showing off the sharp, honed edge. "With Simone Bishop."

"I sold my house in LA," Cash said, well-aware this conversation could blow right up in his face, *ka-blewy.* He spied land mines everywhere.

"After Simone cheated on him," Paige added, her voice even and noncommittal. "And broke up his band."

"That's how it went down." What was going on here? "But things were already going south with Simone . . . and the band for that matter."

"So you were already having trouble making things work." Joe held on to the axe with hands encased in thick leather work gloves.

He met Joe's hard, cold eyes. Hell, the dude looked like he wouldn't mind dismembering Cash with that blade. Chop. Chop.

"Relationships go south on you a lot." Joe grunted. "At least what I can tell from the Internet."

Ahh, now they were getting down to it. Cash offered him up a cheery, gee-ain't-this-swell grin. "The music business is hard on relationships in general."

Gabi tightened her grip around her husband's

waist and sent Cash a smile as false as the one decorating his face. Hmm, so she hated him too.

Arms outstretched, Casey twirled around on a patch of ground, humming one of The Truthful Desperadoes' breakup songs. Come to think of it, The Truthful Desperadoes had a lot of breakup songs.

"I'll bet," Joe said. "Most likely the reason you never married."

"Cash's focus is on his music," Paige said, staying even-keel. "He's got a special gift. He's not like ordinary people who get married and have kids and everything they say and do revolves around that. Cash has won numerous music awards, and he's had two albums go gold. Which, in case you didn't know, is a big deal. He's sharp, he's a dynamo, and he's damn good at what he does. Why does it matter if he's lousy at long-term relationships?"

There was something dismal and terrible in her tone, cocked up and defensive and out of context to the discussion.

Unobtrusively, Cash moved his foot to touch hers. Even through her boots, he could feel the line of tension running through her body, substantial and resolute.

She inhaled sharply, held her breath, and when she exhaled, she dropped her arms that she'd had folded tight across her chest.

"It doesn't matter." Joe let the axe slide easily off his shoulder. "His life, his business."

"Damn straight," Cash said, keeping his voice mild.

"He's a big success at his career." Joe rested the blade on the ground, set his palm on the handle, and balanced the axe beside them. "We admire what he's accomplished. Most people don't have the persistence and discipline it takes. Sacrificing love and family for fame and fortune." Joe smiled nice and gentle at Paige. "Don't you agree?"

"Cash knows what he's doing." Paige jutted her chin in the air. "We want a Leyland cypress."

"Joe didn't even know what he'd been missing, until his grandfather turned the Christmas tree farm over to him." Gabi smiled at Cash frenemies-style. "He didn't realize his true calling until he gave up on pipe dreams."

"Music isn't a pipe dream for Cash." Paige's eyes flashed a warning. "It's *everything*. And that's how it has to be in order to be a star."

Gabi clicked her tongue, and her eyes went melancholy, and even though she didn't say a word, Cash heard, *So sad*. The woman felt sorry for him?

"That's the thing about stars." Joe shifted his jaw into a hard line stance. "Eventually, they fall."

Okey-dokey. Cash knew where he stood with Paige's friends. In the garbage dump.

"Tree," Paige said. "Leyland cypress."

"This way." Gabi motioned them to follow her, treading lightly through the trees, her arm resting on her extended belly, Casey skipping along beside them. Joe picked up the axe, put it in a wheelbarrow, and followed them.

Cash kept an eye on Joe.

"Sorry about this," Paige mumbled, walking close to him. "My friends can be a little overprotective."

"You think?"

She poked him playfully in the ribs. "They mean

well. They just don't want to see me get hurt. I'm
sure your friends would look at me with equal sus-
picion."

"No," he said. "Probably not. No one is particularly protective of me."

"Aww, poor baby." She lagged, letting her friends
get ahead of them.

He slowed, keeping up with her pace, pooched
out his lips in a pretend pout. "I'm so maligned."

"I'm sure stardom makes up for some of that."

"What does everyone around here have against
achieving your dreams?" he grumbled.

"Nothing," she said. "It's just that many people
who love their lives in this town have discovered all
that glitters isn't gold."

"Meaning?" He studied her in the glow of the
Christmas lights strung from the numerous poles.
Her glossy hair glistened, her straight white teeth
shone. *She* sparkled bright as gold.

"There is no there, there."

"Meaning?"

"C'mon," she said, looking truly surprised. "When
you were at the pinnacle of your career you didn't
feel like there was still something missing?"

"Who says I've been at the pinnacle of my career?"
he asked, his chest tightening and his heart fluttering in a wild way. "I'm nowhere near the top."

"Oh," she said, in an "aha" voice, as if a lightbulb
had gone on. As if what he'd said had explained everything.

"How's this one, Paige?" Joe called out. He'd
stopped beside a tree, smaller than the rest of them,
the perfect size for a houseboat.

"It's Cash's tree, ask him."

"Cash?" Joe shot him another one of those don't-mess-with-Paige stares.

"It's brilliant," Cash said, choosing his words carefully.

"Live trees need a lot of attention." Joe shifted his gaze to Paige. "Water frequently. Put it up in a sheltered area, away from a heat source."

"I'll cherish it."

"See that you do." Joe's tone was steely as his axe. "I know the tree is temporary, but that doesn't mean it shouldn't be handled with care."

"Got it."

Joe studied him a long moment and Cash held the other man's gaze. Finally, Joe bent and, in three sharp whacks, felled the tree.

Cash helped him load it in the wheelbarrow. The look Joe sent him held slightly less animosity than it had before. Progress. Score.

They took the tree back and loaded it into the Land Rover. Paige said good-bye to Gabi and Casey and got in on the passenger's side. Leaving him and Joe standing at the rear of the SUV.

"Enjoy the tree," Joe said.

"I will."

"And when you're ready to get rid of your tree, call me. I recycle."

"Will do."

Joe clamped a hand on Cash's shoulder. "She's special."

"The tree?"

"No, dammit, Paige. For some unknown reason, she's crazy about you."

"How do you know that?"

"I've never seen her look at anyone the way she looks at you and I've known her since she was a kid."

That was a lot to absorb. Cash chewed on it.

"You hurt her," Joe said, "and I'll hunt you down and kick your ass."

Paige rolled down the window, stuck her head out, and waved her cell phone in the air. "Cash," she called. "We gotta go. Grammie's gone missing from the nursing home."

CHAPTER 16

Accelerando: A symbol used in musical notation indicating a gradually quickened tempo.

Paige fidgeted all the way into town, fretting about Grammie.

According to Addie, Grammie had gone missing from the TV room where the residents had gathered to watch *A Christmas Story*. Addie had been busy calming one of the other residents who'd gotten charged up about the Red Ryder BB gun and she hadn't noticed Grammie slip out the side door.

They had caught Grammie on the video camera, scuttling away toward the town square, and they'd already sent staff out to look for her, but Paige couldn't help putting herself inside Grammie's head. Dazed and confused.

What would it be like to wander the town you'd once been so familiar with but no longer recognized? How scary would it be to bump against bustling strangers not paying any attention to a lost, elderly woman? How lonely she must feel. How frightened.

"Hurry," she urged Cash. "Hurry, please."

Instead of speeding up, he reached across the seat to squeeze her hand. "It's going to be okay. She's going to be okay."

"You don't know that. You can't know that."

"Take a deep breath," he said. "You're barely breathing."

It irritated her that he'd pointed that out, but he was right. She inhaled deeply, squeezed his hand, exhaled, felt some of her anxiety ebb.

"I'm here with you," he said. "All the way. I'll help you. I'll help her. We will get through this."

We.

As if they were together. As if they were a couple.

It felt nice. Better than nice. It felt grand. But it wasn't a feeling she could get used to, so she shook her head, shook it off.

Or tried to anyway.

Cash was making it pretty difficult, holding her hand and all. They reached the square, but there was no place to park.

"Stop at the corner. I'll get out and start searching." She unbuckled her seat belt.

"No," he said firmly. "Stay put. Do not get out of this car. I'm going with you."

Okay, he was being highhanded, but she kind of liked it, so she obeyed. She kept her eyes peeled for signs of Grammie in the crowd, but there were so many people and—

"Spot! Spot!" she hollered as a Jeep pulled away from the curb.

Cash pulled into the parking space smooth as silk. Her hero!

Once they were parked, she tumbled out of the car. Stood overwhelmed on the sidewalk for a second. Where to go? Where to start?

"This way," Cash said, taking her elbow.

"What? Where?"

He pointed to the white SkyWatch manned mobile surveillance tower in the middle of the town square with "Police" written in black graphics. Paige had been so worked up she hadn't even noticed it. He took her head and guided her over to the device that looked like a deer blind on a hydraulic lift.

"How do we get their attention?" Paige asked.

But Cash was already waving his arms in a crisscross, back and forth, SOS gesture. People looked at him weird, but gave him space.

The SkyWatch cab slowly lowered to the ground and Cash dragged her over.

The door opened and a police officer emerged. Cash told him about Grammie. The officer took a description of Grammie from Paige. They hadn't seen her grandmother, but they would be on the lookout. In addition, they contacted the nursing home for their side of the story and put out a BOLO.

It was seven o'clock by the time she and Cash finished with the authorities and the crowd was at its zenith as people filed in and out of shops, restaurants, and entertainment venues.

Feeling marginally better, Paige thanked Cash for helping.

"We're not done yet," he said. "Not by a long shot."

"What next?"

"We're going to start with that shop on the

corner . . ." He nodded at clothing boutique. "Talk to the employees, search the aisles, and then go to the next shop until we've covered every building on the square."

"That'll take all night."

"So be it."

"What if she's not on the square? What if she's wandered off to the lake? What if she fell in?" She clutched his arm, panic rising inside her. "Cash, what if she drowned?"

"Let's not borrow trouble. The nursing home staff is looking for her. Law enforcement is on the lookout. Someone will find her."

They went into the boutique. Grammie wasn't there and the staff, who actually knew Grammie, hadn't seen her. But the store was mobbed. A little old lady could easily get overlooked in such a throng.

"Thank you," Cash said to the clerks, slipped his arm around Paige's waist, took her to the next store and the next. Same results.

The fourth building on this side of the square was empty, several "For Sale" signs in the windows.

"What used to be here?" Cash asked.

"It was going to be a yoga studio," Paige said, "but just after the studio owner finished renovations, a family tragedy forced her to move back home to Seattle. It's sat empty ever since. The building includes the upstairs apartment. That might be why she's having a hard time selling it. No one wants both."

"Is there any way Grammie could have snuck in there?" Cash cupped his hands to his eyes, peered in through the darkened window.

"Doubtful." Paige joined him, staring into the empty room at the new hardwood floors, track lighting, and sound system hookups.

"You know," Cash said. "It would make a great dance studio. Maybe you should rent it and start teaching dance."

Paige snorted. "As if."

He slid his arm around her shoulders, pulled her close. "C'mon, can't you see it? You could put in bars for ballet and—"

"I can see that we're wasting time on pipe dreams when Grammie's missing."

"Right," he said. "Sometimes I can get caught up in big dreams."

"Consider me an anchor, holding you to the earth."

He grinned and kissed the top of her head, and if she hadn't been so worried about Grammie, it would have been her feet not touching the ground.

"Here we go." He pushed the door open to the quilt shop next door.

They emerged five minutes later. The wind gusted and snow started falling, swirling around them in white puffs that would have been beautiful if Paige wasn't so worried about her grandmother. From what Addie had said, Grammie had been wearing a nightgown, slippers, and a bathrobe. Thin clothing. No decent shoes. No coat. She had to be freezing.

Cash kneaded her neck with his thumb and she felt her muscles loosen. How had he known she was knotted up? He led her into the next shop, Ye Olde Book Nook.

The cowbell over the door clanged gaily as if

everything was normal and Grammie wasn't on the loose. It was Paige's favorite shop on the square, filled with the papery smell of books. The place was packed with families. It was story hour and a melodious voice reading *The Magic Christmas Cookie* came from the next room.

Drawn by the flow of pedestrians in that direction, they pushed past the tapestry curtain into the story area populated by plush couches and upholstered chairs. Kids in pajamas clutched stuffed animals and sat in circle around a woman reading from the book.

It was the author herself, Sarah Collier Walker, known publicly by her nom de plume, Sadie Cool. Paige had known Sarah for years.

Sarah glanced up, met Paige's eyes and, without missing a beat in the story, inclined her head toward the Christmas tree to one side of the room where the comfiest chair in the store sat. The tree branches blocked her view of the chair, but Paige could see a pair of feet, shod in house slippers, sticking out beyond the tree. She recognized those slippers and her heart hopped.

Grammie!

Leaving Cash in the lurch, she dodged around kids, making her way around the Christmas tree.

And there was her grandmother, happily munching a cookie, Wayne Newton's biography in her lap, smiling as if she was having the time of her life.

Relief shoved tears in Paige's eyes and she dropped to her knees in front of her grandmother and wrapped her in a huge hug.

"Why, there you are," Grammie said. "I've been missing you for ages. Where have you been, Emaline?"

"Grammie, it's me, Paige."

The little old lady in the pink bathrobe blinked at her granddaughter. "Who's Paige?"

Cash could feel Paige take the sucker punch from where she knelt on the floor in front of Grammie's chair. Saw her shoulders slump, watched her head drop to her grandmother's lap in despair.

He wanted to go to her, to soothe her, make everything all right. But it wasn't his place. This was her battle and to insert himself into her life right now would be an intrusion. He stepped back, helping her the only way he could think of—using his body to shield her and her grandmother from curious eyes.

"I'm your granddaughter."

Grammie laughed. "Stop teasing me, Emaline. How can I have a granddaughter? I'm only twenty-two. I don't have kids. I'm not even married."

"It's time to go," Paige said. "It's bedtime."

"No!" Grammie shook her head, an intractable expression coming across her wrinkled face. "I'm not leaving."

"Please, Grammie."

"I'm not your grammie. I'm not anybody's grammie. Go away and leave me alone."

Paige wiped at her eyes, brushing away tears.

His heart broke for her and her grandmother. And he felt guilty too. He hadn't been there for his own grandparents at the end. His youthful ego and pride keeping him from admitting he'd been wrong.

Of course, they'd been just as prideful. They hadn't reached out. Hadn't told him they were in failing health. And once, when he'd called, Grandpa had hung up the phone on him without ever saying hello.

Aww, hell, aww, damn.

He felt a stab in the center of his chest. Realized his heartache wasn't just for Paige and her grandmother, but for everything he'd lost as well.

"Wayne!" Grammie exclaimed suddenly.

Cash glanced over his shoulder to see what person she was talking to.

"Wayne Newton, are you just going to stand there and not speak to me?" Grammie's voice turned accusatory, but filled with affection.

Cash turned back. The elderly lady was looking directly at him. He pressed a hand to his chest.

"Yes, you. Get over and give me a kiss." Grammie held her arms open wide.

Um. He hesitated, not knowing what to do.

Paige got to her feet. "She thinks you're Wayne Newton."

"I don't look a thing like Wayne."

"It's not that. She dated him eons ago."

"Really?" Cash was impressed.

"I'm waiting . . ." Grammie's arms stayed in the air.

"Do I play along?" he asked Paige.

"When she's in one of her full-blown episodes, what she calls one of her bubbles, it's best to forget reality and just roll with it. Otherwise, if you try to orient her, she gets upset and contrary."

Okay, then. Apparently kissing Grammie was on the agenda. This was for Paige, he reminded himself.

He moved in.

Grammie reached for him.

Cash braced himself.

Grammie cupped his face in her palms.

He saw in her eyes the girl she'd once been, spirited and full of life, the kind of woman who danced in a Vegas review and dated the likes of Wayne Newton. She'd had her own brand of stardom and it hadn't saved her. She'd ended up in a small town, old and confused.

With a granddaughter who was devoted to her. That's what saved her. Family. Connection.

Grammie leaned forward and kissed Cash chastely on the cheek.

He exhaled. Whew. Kissed her gently on the forehead.

She giggled, blushed, ducked her head. "Oh, Wayne."

Cash glanced over at Paige. She was looking at him as if he'd climbed up into the sky and painted the moon and stars her favorite color. "What's her first name?" he whispered to Paige.

"Edie."

"You know what else I want?" Grammie asked.

"What's that, Edie?"

"Will you sing 'Danke Schoen'?"

"Now?"

Grammie bobbed her head, clapped her hands. "Uh-huh."

"Here?"

"Yes, yes."

The woman reading from the storybook stopped reading. Everyone was watching them. They had an audience. Crap.

"I don't have any music," he said, grasping at straws.

Someone in the room said, "Hold on, I've got Spotify," and they called up the song on their cell phone. Seconds later, "Danke Schoen" leaked into the room.

And he was stuck. No excuses. He couldn't sing as high as a young Wayne Newton, but he was a musician and he gave it his best shot.

Grammie was completely charmed. She clapped and giggled and sang along with him, and by the end, the entire room had joined in.

"Thank you," Paige murmured to him when the song was over. "I can never repay you for this."

He wriggled his eyebrows, murmured back, "I could think of a few ways."

She gave him a knowing smile that wrapped around him like a heated blanket and lit him from the inside out. "You've earned it."

"I'm holding you to it." He winked. "It's been a long week."

Then he swung Paige into his arms and planted a kiss on her lips. Her knees buckled and if he hadn't had a strong grip on her, she would have toppled over.

"Emaline," Grammie scolded. "Stop flirting with my boyfriend."

"Sorry," Paige apologized.

"I'll forgive you this time." Grammie shook a finger at Paige. "But back off."

Paige giggled.

"Edie." Cash turned to Grammie. "Would you like to go home?"

"Oh yes," Grammie said. "Please, Wayne. Please take me home."

"Here we go." He held out his arm to her, helped her out of the deep chair. To Paige he said, "Call the police and the nursing home, let them know she's okay."

Paige seemed happy to have something to do. She got busy making calls.

"Edie," Cash said. "You look especially beautiful tonight."

"Oh, Wayne!" She waved a hand at him, gaily girlish. "You sly flatterer, you."

He steadied her on her feet, slipped an arm around her upper back. "You doing okay?"

She fluttered her eyelashes at him. "Never better now that you're here. Do you still have the Corvette?"

"Afraid not. I traded it in."

"Too bad. I loved to feel the wind through my hair when you had the top down."

"It's too cold to ride with the top down tonight anyway," he said, guiding her from the room, ignoring the stares following them.

"So it is," she said, peering out the window. "My goodness, it's snowing."

"Yes."

"It doesn't snow in Vegas."

Was this an opening? Could he slip in a little reality? "We're not in Vegas, Edie."

"Where are we?"

"Twilight."

"Where's that?"

"Texas."

"Texas?" Her face softened. "I'm a Texan."

"I know."

"Born in Abilene."

"I'm a Texan too," he said.

"Tsk, tsk. Why are you trying to pull the wool over my eyes, Wayne? I know you were born in Norfolk, Virginia."

All right, too much reality too fast.

Paige had finished her phone calls and hurried ahead of them to clear the way to the front door.

"Emaline," Grammie said. "Don't you have somewhere else to be?"

"Nope. I'm right here with you all the way."

Grammie made a face, whispered loudly to Cash, "The girl can't take a hint. Help me get rid of her so we can be alone."

"Emaline needs a ride home," Cash said. "I think we can give that to her, don't you?"

Grammie sighed. "I guess so."

"You want to wait here in the building with Emaline while I go get the car?" he asked.

"No way. Now that I've got you back in my life, I'm not letting you out of my sight ever again, Wayne."

They didn't have any choice but to walk Grammie outside in the snow in her house slippers. Paige held on to one arm, Cash on the other. Curious onlookers stepped out of their way, sent them lingering glances. A snapshot of Alzheimer's. It wasn't a pretty sight.

Walking Grammie to the Land Rover was a humbling experience. They had to stop several times to let her peer into windows.

"I want to go shopping for Christmas presents," she said. "But I've lost my purse."

"You haven't lost it, Gram—er, Edie," Paige said. "It's back at home."

She peered at Paige then, blinked hard, a bewildered expression coming over her face. "You don't know how scary it is, to realize you don't know where you are and you don't have a purse and no way to get home and sometimes . . ." Her voice grew softer, sadder. "You don't even remember your own name."

"It's okay," Paige said. "We're with you. We're not going to let anything happen to you."

"You're a good granddaughter." Grammie patted her cheek. "I love you so much."

Paige met Cash's eyes. "She's back."

Grammie broke loose from Cash's arm to rub a hand over her mouth. "Did I have one of my bubbles?"

"Yes," Paige said gently. "You did."

Grammie looked down at her clothing. "I'm in my nightclothes!"

"We're taking you home." Paige got Grammie moving again toward the Land Rover.

"Who are you?" Grammie frowned at Cash.

"This is Cash," Paige said. "My . . ."

"Neighbor," Cash supplied.

Grammie's expression turned suspicious. "You're not Sig."

"No, ma'am. I'm renting Sig's houseboat while he's in Sweden."

"You trust him?" Grammie asked Paige.

"He helped me look for you," Paige said.

Grammie sized him up and must have decided he was on the level because she nodded. "My feet are cold."

"Here we are." Cash hit the remote to unlock the Land Rover and opened the back door.

"This is your car?" Grammie stuffed her hands into the pockets of her robe.

"Yes, ma'am."

"Fancy," Grammie said in a "la-de-da" voice.

"Cash is a musician," Paige said.

"Like Wayne?"

"Like Wayne," Cash confirmed, and boosted Grammie into the backseat.

Ten minutes later, they were back at the nursing home and escorting Grammie to her room. The staff hovered and apologized. Paige assured them she didn't hold the staff responsible for her grandmother's great escape. She took Grammie into the bathroom and helped her change into dry clothes while Cash signed autographs.

Paige led Grammie to her bed, tucked her in. "There now. Snug as a bug in a rug."

"She's always been the nurturing type." Grammie met Cash's eyes over the top of Paige's head as she leaned over to smooth the covers.

"I'm not surprised." A feeling of tenderness and pride stirred inside him. Paige was special. He'd known it from the very beginning.

"Paige couldn't have been more than four or five years old, but she knew her own mind. Tiny little thing looked me squarely in the eyes and said, 'Grammie, I'm gonna have ten children when I get married. Five boys and five girls.'"

Cash laughed, imagining Paige as a five-year-old, fierce in her convictions.

"I swear I couldn't keep a straight face. She looked so serious." Grammie chuckled.

"Hey," Paige said. "I thought ten kids would be fun. An instant softball team with one to spare."

"Anyway . . ." Grammie's eyes were trained on Cash. "I hope you want lots of kids because Paige loves them. When you two get married, I'm sure she'll want to start working on kids right away—"

"Grammie!" Mortified, Paige curled her fingernails into her palms, felt her cheeks heat, didn't dare look over at Cash to see how he was taking this. "We're not getting married!"

"You can't fool me." Grammie winked at Cash. "I see the way she looks at you. The girl's in love."

"I am not! Hush. Don't say things like that." Paige spoke sharply, the first time he'd ever heard her be anything but gentle with the elderly woman.

Grammie looked startled. Her bottom lip trembled. She pleated the covers with her fingers. "Never mind me. I'm a silly old woman."

"You're not silly. I'm sorry I snapped." Paige sat on the mattress beside her grandmother, drew her into her arms, kissed her forehead.

There was a knock on the door and a big blonde in scrubs stuck her head in the door. "I don't want to rush you, but it's time for her meds. After what happened today, the doctor wants us to up her Alzheimer's drugs."

"Will this stop me from having those bubbles?" Grammie asked.

"It won't stop them," the woman said kindly.

"But hopefully it will keep them from happening as often."

"Bring it." Grammie held out her palm.

"We're gonna go now." Paige kissed her grandmother again. "I'll come see you tomorrow."

Grammie nodded. "You go home and get some sleep."

"You get some rest too."

"Cash," Grammie said.

He straightened, gave her his full attention. "Yes, ma'am?"

"You make sure Paige gets home safely, you hear me?"

"You can count on me," he assured her.

Grammie's eyes narrowed. "Can I?"

"Yes, ma'am."

"All right, then." She yawned. "Y'all go on now."

Paige took his hand and led him out of Grammie's room. "You deserve some kind of service award."

"I didn't do anything special."

"Are you kidding? You helped me search for her, you kissed her, and sang 'Danke Schoen' in front of a roomful of strangers. How many men would do that for her?"

That was just the thing. He hadn't done it for her grandmother. He'd done it for Paige, and as much as she'd given him, it didn't seem like nearly enough in return.

CHAPTER 17

Major: One of the two modes of the tonal system. Music written in major keys have a positive affirming character.

"Do you still feel like decorating the tree?" Paige asked when they climbed back into the Land Rover that smelled pungently of pine.

"Do you? It's after nine."

"I'm game if you are."

"Where are we going to get decorations?"

"Oh," she said, "I've got boxes and boxes of them."

"That you're not already using?"

She laughed. "You've only seen half my stash."

"Where do you keep it all?"

"My cousin Flynn's house. We can pick up Fritzi and the decorations at the same time. Still in?" She had to admit she was a little nervous around him after Grammie boldly told him that Paige loved him, but luckily he seemed to have put that down to the ramblings of a confused old lady.

Thank heavens.

She had big plans for tonight and didn't want to scare him off. But considering everything he'd put up with today—getting chased down a fire escape by a pack of avid fans, Christmas tree hunting with her unwelcoming friends, and helping her track down her escapee grandmother—and he was still here, maybe it was time she recognized that Cash Colton didn't scare easily.

Which was both exciting and disconcerting. Because she knew she had no future with him, no matter how much a small slice of her kept spinning crazy fantasies.

Grammie was right. She was in love with him.

Paige wasn't sure how or when it happened. For sure she'd been attracted to him from the first moment he'd strutted his way into the playhouse.

And the attraction had been building ever since.

To the point that whenever he walked into a room her body lit up and her spirits lifted and her heart swelled until it filled her entire chest. All she wanted was to be around him. To hear him laugh, see him smile, smell his special Cash scent, to touch him, taste him.

Oh, she was in so much trouble, and she knew it. Couldn't do a damn thing about it.

It was ten o'clock when they arrived at the houseboat with the decorations, collected Fritzi, and got the tree placed into a stand. Following Joe's instructions, Cash filled the stand with plenty of water and Paige covered the stand with a tree skirt.

While he opened the boxes of decorations, she

made hot chocolate topped with colored marshmallows she brought over from her house. Fritzi was in play mode, hopping in and out of boxes and rolling ornaments around the room.

"Where do we start?" Cash asked as they sat on the couch sipping hot chocolate and staring at the naked tree.

"Seriously? You don't know how to decorate a Christmas tree?"

He shrugged. "I'm rusty. Haven't done it in years."

"Why not?"

"Christmas is a busy time for musicians. You have to let some things go."

"Like your own holiday traditions?"

"Exactly."

She curled her legs up underneath her. "What about when you were a kid?"

"I'm thinking we start with the lights. Makes the most sense." He shifted on the couch, set down his mug of hot chocolate, avoiding her question.

Paige noticed he deflected her whenever she brought up his past. It felt inequitable, the give and take of secrets and confessions. She'd told him everything about her past and he'd told her next to nothing about his. Most everything she knew about his history came from what she'd gleaned from the Internet.

He slid off the couch to the floor, dug through the box marked "Lights" in neon green Sharpie, and pulled out tangled strands of multicolored twinkle lights.

"You don't have *any* family you spend the holidays with?" she asked.

"Does Emma count?"

"When was the last time you spent the holidays with her?"

He shrugged, started untangling the lights. "Not since before she married Sam."

"So, like, almost a decade."

"Eight years," he said. "They've been married eight years."

"You got something against Sam?"

"What?" He glanced up, looked confused.

"Why haven't you spent time with her at the holidays after she married Sam?"

He went back to untangling the lights. "I didn't want to horn in. They were newlyweds, then new parents, and then I was with Simone. Time flies."

"And you didn't miss spending time with her, spending time with anyone important for the holidays?"

"I had the band."

"And they didn't have families they hung out with?" She joined him on the floor, reached for another stand of lights.

"Look," he said, his tone taking on a sharp edge. "I'm not like you. Christmas was never that important to me. I certainly wouldn't be doing this right now if it wasn't for you."

"Oh." She dropped the lights, tried not to get her feelings hurt. "We don't have to do this. I just thought it would be fun, and you could use a little Christmas cheer, but I don't want to push you to do something you don't want to do."

"Paige . . ." He touched her hand, offered a mild smile rolled up with a wince of old pain he struggled to mask. "I . . . it's not you."

She waited, hoping he'd say more, but when he didn't she said with forced spunk, "Let's plug these suckers in and see if they still work."

He took the plug, and stretched out long across the floor, his shirt riding up, revealing taut, hard abdominal muscles. Paige's heart went pitty-pat. He stuck the plug into an outlet and the room lit up in a twinkle of red, blue, yellow, and green.

Cash sat up and they stared at each other across the circle of lights and boxes and spill of ornaments and tinsel. He gulped, moistened his lips with the tip of this tongue.

A measured moment slipped between them. Paige didn't speak. Didn't budge.

Finally, the words dribbled from him, falling in hesitant sprinkles. "My mother . . . she . . . died . . . on Christmas Eve."

Paige inhaled, but said nothing. Didn't want to interrupt. Colors flashed over his face, a rainbow of sorrow. It took everything she had in her not to reach over and touch him. But if she kept quiet, kept her hands to herself, maybe he would go on. She had a feeling he'd been sitting on the full story since the day his mother had passed away.

He pressed a palm to his mouth, his eyes darkening. Haunted with ghosts and shadows. "Growing up, our life was pretty chaotic. I told you Mom was an aspiring musician, but more honestly, she was a groupie. She dragged me from and to everywhere as she followed bands around the country, hooking up with guys she thought could advance her career. She had talent, but she kept giving away her power to the men in her life."

Drawing her knees to her chest, Paige balanced on her sitz bones, swayed back and forth.

"Lorena was beautiful. Men swarmed around her like bees to honeysuckle." He picked up the lights, moved to start stringing them around the tree. "She loved me the best way she knew how. It might not have been the way most moms loved, but she was all I had."

"She was so young when she died."

"AIDS," he said succinctly, emotionless. "HIV was more of a death sentence back then."

Paige bit her bottom lip. She knew the deep pain of watching a parent die of a lingering illness. Understood the feeling of helplessness and despair.

"Her parents, my grandparents, were, of course, very disapproving of her lifestyle. They were simple country folk. They thought having big dreams was selfish and foolish, and given what happened to my mom, I suppose from their point of view they were right. But if she'd only had a little support. Someone who believed in her talent the way she believed in mine . . ."

His back was to her as he fumbled with the lights. She heard the clog in his voice. Saw the tension draw across his shoulder blades. Felt her heart crack. Hurting for the boy he'd been. Admiring the man he'd become.

Paige got up and reached through the top branch to take hold of the lights as he fed them up to her. She looked down at the same time he looked up through the branches of the tree. And they shared a weighted moment of deep caring and understanding.

"I read on the Internet that you ran away from

home when you were fifteen. Were things that bad with your grandparents?"

"They were harsh. Judgmental. Set about trying to correct the mistakes they'd made with my mother." He threaded more lights to her. "But in retrospect I can see I was a handful. I was used to my mother's relaxed parenting style and resented their rules. I was ten when I went to live with them and already set in my ways."

She stood on a chair from the kitchen, wound the lights to the top of the tree, and when they finished, the tree winked brightly at them. Cash sat up from where he'd been stretched out underneath the tree. He looked different somehow. More relaxed.

"What about your father?" she asked, climbing down off the chair.

"You didn't find out anything about him on the Internet?" One amused eyebrow hopped up on his forehead, teasing her.

"The article I read said no one knows who he was." She took ornaments from the box, started placing them on the tree. Fritzi had to sniff them all.

Cash named a country-and-western musician so famous that Paige felt her jaw drop. "Really? Him?"

"So my mother said. He refused to take a paternity test. I'm guessing partially because he was on wife number six and the marriage was already shaky when I went to him after I ran away. Dear old dad booted me out, told me to never darken his door again. I don't know what the hell would have happened if I hadn't run into Freddie Frank in a pancake house where I was counting my change to pay for my meal and coming up short."

"Freddie Frank? The country crooner?"

"Yep. He's from the same small town I was from. He and my mom knew each other since they ran in the same circles, played some of the same gigs, but they weren't particularly close. Freddie even did some cowhand work for my grandfather but that was long before I was born. At the time I ran into him, Freddie's career had just started to take off, but he was still humble enough to eat at the same old pancake restaurant he'd always gone to. It was two in the morning and he'd just finished a performance."

"And he recognized you after all this time?"

"No, but he recognized my mother's guitar that I had named after her."

"The one that got stolen?"

"Yes. Anyway, Freddie paid for my breakfast and took me home. His wife, Maxi, insisted I move in with them. Freddie mentored me, introduced me to the right people. He made my career."

"Do you still keep in touch with him?"

Cash shrugged. "We had a falling-out."

"Over what?"

"You know. Differences of opinion."

She wanted to ask him for more details, but he hardened his chin and she could tell it wasn't something he wanted to talk about. "So true love wasn't in the cards for either of your parents?"

"It's hard to have a successful career and a stable relationship. Stardom requires so much of you. Takes so much away from the people you love. It's easier not to get too invested in the first place."

"Which is why you don't really do Christmas,"

she said softly. "Christmas is all about family ties and tradition, something you haven't had much of."

He looked startled, ran a hand through his hair. "Maybe you're right. But you've had a raw deal too. Why do you love Christmas so much?"

"Why," she said. "Because it makes me feel happy. It was my father's favorite time of the year. He was a regular Clark Griswold. I mean, look at this." She waved at the ornaments. "These are all from my childhood."

"I guess that's the difference. I don't have many happy memories of Christmas."

"That's sad."

A stoic shrug yoked his shoulder. He added a tiny manger scene to the tree, spun it on the branch with his thumb. "I don't think about it that much."

She bit her bottom lip to keep from telling him that she wanted nothing more than to make all the rest of his Christmases merry and bright. That she could love him until the end of her days if he'd let her.

That thought terrified her.

Because it was true.

She was in love with a man who didn't know the first thing about how to make a long-term relationship work. Not that she was any big expert on that score either.

It didn't matter that she'd only known him for two weeks. She felt what she felt. Her feelings for Cash were huge and glorious and growing every day. Heck, the way he was looking at her, every minute.

But she'd fallen for Randy equally fast. Dangerous territory.

Except this was different.

Her feelings for Randy had been a heady rush of excitement. He showed her off like she was a trophy and that had fed her ego. She'd mistaken the thrill of attention for love. She knew now what love wasn't.

Love wasn't butterflies in the stomach, although Cash gave her plenty of those. That was only chemistry.

Love was not convenient. It could show up when you least expected it or wanted it.

Love was not deceptive. It didn't cheat or lie or steal your identity.

What she felt for Cash was respect and consideration. She was willing to have her life complicated by his needs and struggles without impatience or anger. She didn't care about his money or fame. If it all went away tomorrow, she would still love him.

She loved his kindness and his ready smile. She loved the way he nudged her out of her comfort zone and helped her reclaim her playful side. She loved the silly texts he sent and how he thought of her on a cold morning and sent a driver to pick her up. She loved how he'd understood Joe and Gabi's protectiveness toward her and accepted it. She loved how he'd been so gentle with Grammie and sang to her so sweetly. She loved how he smelled, loved the sound of his voice.

It was a crazy wonderful feeling. And she loved him, even if he never loved her back.

"Paige?" he said.

"Huh?" She blinked. Realized she'd been standing there with a ballerina ornament in her hand, staring off into space.

"Something wrong?"

"Um . . . just searching for the perfect spot for this."

"How about next to the guitar. My favorite thing next to yours." He pointed to an ornament hanging near the top, and knelt to dig more decorations from the box.

She went up on tiptoes to hang the ballerina beside the guitar. Music and dance. The two went together like ice cream and sprinkles. She cast a sideways glance at him. He had his head turned up to watch her, an appreciative expression in his eyes.

He liked her. She knew that. He wanted her. But could he love her?

Unable to answer a question that big, she bent to pick up a long strand of candy cane garland to distract herself.

Fritzi took the slithering garland as an invitation to play and snatched the other end up in his teeth and trotted in the opposite direction. The garland pulled tight across Cash's back as he leaned over the box.

"Fritzi. Come back here." She tugged on the garland.

The little scamp was surprisingly strong. He loved tug-of-war. The poodle dug in, jerked hard.

The garland gave way, snapping in the middle. The momentum knocked Paige off balance and she went tumbling . . .

Right on top of Cash.

Full body contact.

The touch of his skin against hers instantly set her

ablaze. Holy bobcats! What sparks! What power! Chemistry might not be love, but it should not be underestimated. They had something.

Kindling. The makings of a big beautiful bonfire.

"Whoa there. Hey." Cash chuckled and shifted so that she fell off his back and into his arms.

"Are you all right?" She peered up into those enigmatic gray eyes, hitched in a breath.

"Are *you* all right?" His smile was as genuine as a top-grade diamond, full of sparkle and clarity. The dourness that had settled about his mouth when they'd talked about Christmas had vanished.

Her gaze buttoned onto that mouth, those angular lips. She recalled what he tasted like, yearned for another nibble. In the shine of twinkle lights, his gray eyes were magic. Mesmerizing and calm.

"Dandy as candy." Okay, that sounded completely uncool. But who could be cool when the man you were crazy about was looking at you like were the icing on his cake?

"That Fritzi," Cash said. "Gotta watch out for him."

At the sound of his name, Fritzi jumped in between them, licking Cash's chin and wagging his tail in Paige's face.

"Attention hog," Cash accused, and rubbed the poodle's belly.

Paige squirmed out of Cash's lap. "Let's get the project finished. It's almost midnight."

"The *Brazos Queen* should be coming by again." He gently put Fritzi on the floor and hopped up. "Would you consider another dance?"

"Let's get this tree done and we'll see."

They finished draping the garland and Paige found the tree topper angel.

"Pink?" Cash said. "Really?"

"It's the only tree topper I have left. I used the other three on my trees."

"It's an affront to my masculinity," he teased.

"Who's going to see it besides you and me?" She handed him the angel.

"Point taken." He examined the angel. "Hey, look, she's got cinnamon freckles, just like you."

"So now you like her?"

"Changed my mind about the pink. Every time I look at her I'll think about you in your pink underwear—"

"Oh, you!" She swatted him and he tickled her and they both laughed and Fritzi jumped around the room like a mad thing and it was a deadly romantic moment.

He looked into her eyes and the laughter died, replaced by smoldering hot embers of desire just as the *Brazos Queen* sailed by the houseboat blasting "Sleigh Ride" by The Ronettes.

"May I have this dance?" He held out his hand.

"Not exactly a waltz."

"How about a ring-around-the-rosy dance?"

Laughing again, she slapped her hands into his. "Take it away, Colton."

They danced like gleeful first graders, holding hands and dancing in a circle. Fritzi wasn't to be left out. He spun around chasing his tail so fast he ended up staggering sideways like a drunk. Cash and Paige wriggled and jiggled and shook their booties as the *Brazos Queen* serenaded them for the second

Friday night in a row. She could get used to this routine.

Except this wasn't routine. This was special. This was Christmas. Soon the holiday would be over and Cash would be gone.

And she'd be stuck with this big old lump of love she didn't know what to do with.

The song ended and they split apart, breathless and perspiring. She yawned, exaggerated it.

"You ready for bed?" Cash asked.

Grinning, she said, "I thought you'd never ask."

"One of these days we're going to do this somewhere romantic," Cash said once they were naked and in his bed.

"What's more romantic than a houseboat?" She snuggled against his chest.

"A five-star hotel in Paris."

"Okay, I'll give you that." Paige thrilled to the farfetched idea that she could find herself in Paris living it up at a five-star hotel, the stuff of dreams, the kind of dreams that had fooled her about Randy. Cash wasn't Randy. She knew that. But Paige couldn't help wondering if she was simply being a fool of a different color.

"I'm just so damn happy to be here. I missed the hell out of you," he said, and kissed her, and her doubts melted to liquid.

Things started out slowly, a leisurely reintroduction to each other's bodies, but then quickly sped up. They couldn't get enough of each other.

"I don't have to work tomorrow morning," she whispered. "We can stay awake until dawn."

"Challenge accepted." He branded hot kisses down her bare belly, launching them into their carnal adventure of homecoming and renewal. He was back and things were deeper, richer, between them than ever before.

It was a whole new way of saying hello. Paige savored each kiss, every brush of his fingers, the sights and sounds and tastes of his body.

How special their lovemaking was, how beautiful. It was a brilliant journey of discovery and novelty, a landscape of dips and curves, hills and valleys. Soft sighs and guttural moans. Arched backs and writhing hips.

They ebbed and flowed, in union, unison. Two bodies joined as one—mixing, melding, merging.

Last time had been fun, but this time there was a lot more going on. There were nuances and shifts in perceptions. Shadows and lights. Secrets told. Vulnerabilities revealed.

As his body moved inside hers he whispered in her ear. About his fears, of losing his talent, of failing to live up to his potential, of what he might be if he was no longer a musician.

Touched that he could open up at such an intimate time, she confessed to her own doubts and insecurities. How gullible she'd been to trust Randy. How she doubted her own ability to make wise choices, her fear of making similar mistakes. The pride that kept her from accepting help from people, afraid that it would make her even more vulnerable.

With each confession, each secret unfolded, they delved deeper and deeper into each other. Falling into a warm cocoon of acceptance.

They made love for hours, coming and going, rising and drifting.

He took her to places that stole her breath and warmed her heart. He carried her to the pinnacle and together they flew, free as eagles. He smashed her previous notions of the world and what was possible.

Leaving her splintered, and intensely baffled, but at the exact moment brimming with an ecstatic glimpse of heaven on earth. It was as if she'd shed an old skin and emerged shiny and new.

The past dissolved. All troubles washed away. The future shone with promise. But the now, oh this sweet now, was the crest of some great miracle.

It was as if all the challenges of her old way of being had been nothing but a vehicle, bringing her here, to this point in time, to this man who embodied goodness and light.

And when their release came, they soared together, clinging to each other and crying out, twin phoenixes rising from the ashes of their old selves.

A blossoming. A blooming. A budding.

Flowering. She was a flower opening to gentle spring rains.

She thought of the students she'd once taught to dance. How their faces lit up when she put on music and showed them how to twirl and dance in time to the music. How they threw their entire beings into the process. Whirling and spinning with heart and energy, new and awkward and not caring in the least.

Paige felt like that now, still in touch with her inner child, not yet trampled by life and other people's expectations. Not skinned and scarred and scared to try, but daring and trusting and free. Utterly free.

She wept because he had not been her first lover, because she'd wasted her virginity on a con man.

He brushed the tear from her cheek with his thumb, concern etched into his forehead. "What is it, Paige? Have I hurt you? What's wrong?"

"It was . . . you were . . . we were . . ." She hiccupped.

"What?" He stroked her back.

"There are no words."

"And that's good?" He looked uncertain. Surprising since he was such a great lover.

"That's very good." She laughed through the tears leaking from her eyes.

"Happy tears?"

"Happy tears."

He gathered her close and kissed her with passionate tenderness, an avalanche of kisses. Short and long. Hot and cool. Peppered and languid. Eyelids and nose. Ears and chin. Forehead and jaw and the hollow space at her neck.

There in his arms, she knew without a doubt that she was in love with this man. She felt it in every part of her.

Love so solid and sure. Far beyond those four simple letters. L-O-V-E.

Her love was dense as summer foliage, wild and willful. Poetry. A book of verse. A romantic ode. A mile of sun-drenched, white sand beach. Ocean waves quiet and timeless. A mountain majestic and unmovable.

It was all that and so very much more.

He was her beloved.

But was she his? Did he feel it too? Was she alone in this feeling? Did she dare tell him how she felt? Should she be the first to say it? Was it smarter to stay silent, keep hidden this light wave of love pulsing through every cell, oozing from every pore?

He had trouble with relationships. He'd admitted as much. His career was his mistress, his soul mate, his true love.

How could she compete with that?

She couldn't. Nor could she control how he felt. All she knew was that she loved him and it didn't matter if he loved her back with the same intensity. Her love was unconditional. Unconditional love was not a loan that needed repayment. It was a gift. A blessing. And she gave it freely.

She accepted him for who he was. She couldn't change him. She loved him anyway. She expected nothing from him. She was just overjoyed that he was in the world.

That didn't mean that she would give her power over to him. That she would surrender control of her life. Randy had taught her those valuable lessons.

She had to love herself first before she could love anyone else, and that meant healthy boundaries.

Knowing all that, fully understanding it, she dove with him again, to the bottom of the deep ocean of physical love. Enjoying what she had while she had it. She would not analyze or philosophize or speculate. That stuff was of the mind, noisy and disruptive. Chatter. Clutter.

Fully, completely, she slipped into her body.

Let go of everything. Thoughts. Hopes. Dreams. Let go and just experienced being with him in this way. Rolled with it. Flowed.

And in his embrace she found a perfect peace.

CHAPTER 18

Minor: The minor mode of the tonal system can be identified by the dark, melancholic mood.

"What's your opinion on late-night snacks?" Cash asked sometime later.

"You mean early-morning snacks?"

"That too."

"I'm pro on both."

"What's your position on bringing the snacks into the bedroom?"

"Right on."

He winked. "I knew I could trust you."

"Trustworthy guys eat crackers in bed?"

"Oh, we're not having crackers. I've got leftover pizza in the fridge. I picked it up for lunch while I was waiting on you to get off work."

"From Pasta Pappa's?"

"None other."

"Yay." She clapped. "Pepperoni?"

"With black olives."

"Yum. Go get it."

"I'll take Fritzi out first."

"I love you!" she blurted, and immediately slapped a palm over her mouth. She could feel the weight of her words drop through the air like an anvil.

Cash froze halfway to the door.

"I mean for taking the dog out," she babbled. "I appreciate you taking the dog out. It's so kind of you to take the dog out. I didn't mean I *love* you, love you. It's just an expression."

Oh dear God, shut the hell up, Paige Hyacinth MacGregor.

Fritzi, apparently hearing his name, pushed open the door with his nose and popped into the room, dragging his leash and wagging his tail.

"Be right back," Cash said, clipped the leash to Fritzi's collar, and practically sprinted from the room.

Wow.

Had Paige just told him she loved him?

Cash shoved a hand through his hair as Fritzi towed him toward the front door. He paused to jam his feet into deck shoes, and then stepped out onto the deck into the bracing slap of cold wind.

Nah. She'd said it was just a turn of phrase. She didn't mean she *loved* him, loved him. Did she?

Did she love him?

Cash realized he was smiling. Not just smiling, but grinning as if he were a freaking loon, drunken and dizzy with it.

Could Paige be in love with him?

Fritzi trotted in front of him, headed toward that small patch of grass at the top of the metal stairs.

What should he do? Bring it up? Let it lie? Wait and see what she would do? Burst back into the houseboat and tell her that he was falling in love with her too?

But what if she wasn't falling in love with him? What if she had truly meant that she loved the fact he was taking the dog for a walk? That would be egg on his face if he told her he had feelings for her and she had to tell him she didn't feel the same way.

He was used to women falling in love with him. It happened all the time. What he was not accustomed to was being the first one to fall. Let's be honest, he'd not ever felt like this before. This feeling was new and startling, a major revelation. And he finally understood what everyone carried on about when they talked about love.

But he'd not ever said the words out loud before to a woman. Hell, he didn't even throw it around casually the way some people did. *I love pizza. I love houseboats. I love girls with cinnamon freckles on the bridges of their noses.*

How did he start to wrap his tongue around those three little words? *I love you.* Why did his chest ice up and his throat spasm at the thought of it?

Someone moved in the darkness near where his Land Rover was parked.

Fritzi barked, quick and frantic.

Figuring it was paparazzi after a picture or a stalker fan after an autograph, Cash picked up the dog, cradled him in the crook of his arm, leash dangling over his hand, and demanded, "Who's there?"

A woman stepped from the shadows, the security lamp showcasing her glimmering beauty.

Simone.

"Hello, Cash," she whispered in what *Rolling Stone* had dubbed her "black velvet" voice.

Cash gritted his teeth. As far as he was concerned, listening to her was like getting sucked down in quicksand.

Fritzi growled. He stroked the dog's head, soothing him. "What are you doing here?"

"I . . . had to see you."

"How did you get here?"

"I parachuted in," she said, familiar sarcasm curling her voice. "What do you think, nimrod? I rented a car." She jerked a thumb over her shoulder and he spied a black sedan parked behind the Land Rover.

"Alone?"

"This is private."

"At four in the morning?"

"Flying under the radar," she said. "Last thing I want is for someone to snap a photo of us and it end up a twisted lie on TMZ."

"Well, if you hadn't shown up under cover of darkness at four A.M., this might not look like something they could twist into a lie."

"The idea is not to get photographed with you in the first place," she said.

"Here's a thought, leave me the hell alone."

"I had to see you." She moistened her lips. "Before I got married."

"Does Snake know you're here?"

"No." She shook her head. "He wouldn't understand."

"That makes two of us, because I don't understand what you're doing here either."

"How was South America?"

"You weren't there, so it was great. Fantastic."

"Don't be bitter."

"I'm not bitter. I'm feeling bushwhacked. How did you know where to find me?"

"Deet."

Cash made a mental note to give his manager hell for telling her where he was. "What do you want from me, Simone?"

"To make amends."

"For Snake or busting up the band?"

Her nostrils flared and she looked as if she were struggling to hold on to her temper. Which was progress. In the past she would have just launched into him, convinced she had a right to express her anger whenever and however it suited her. "I'm not sorry I went with Snake. You couldn't commit. What was I supposed to do? Wait around on you forever?"

"You could have left me *before* you crawled into his bed." It was a circuitous argument. He didn't know what he was getting into again. "But never mind. Who cares? That was a year ago. Question is, why are you here now? Why are we having this conversation at four A.M. on an empty dock in the middle of nowhere in forty degree weather?"

"Aren't you listening? I already told you, to avoid the paparazzi by doing the unexpected."

"Mission accomplished. What do you want?"

"One," she said. "I wanted to invite you to the wedding."

"Most people fill out those little white cards and mail them . . . what are they called? Oh yeah, wedding invitations."

"Smart-ass as always, I see. Peru didn't knock that out of you."

"Leopards. Spots." He shrugged.

"So you'll come to the wedding?" She looked hopeful.

Cash snorted. Hard.

"Should I mark you down as a maybe?" She raised a perfectly arched eyebrow.

"Ha. Good one. What else do you want?"

"Two, there's some old history we need to clear up before I can move forward with the wedding."

"No, we don't."

"Look, do we have to do this out here in the cold? Could you invite me in, please?"

He glanced over his shoulder to look at the houseboat, saw Christmas lights twinkling through the window. Thought of Paige in bed waiting for him to return with Fritzi and the pizza. "Now's not a good time."

Simone shifted her gaze from him to the houseboat. "Oh," she said. "You have company."

"I do."

"Can I meet her?"

"No, you may not."

"Her dog?" Simone nodded at Fritzi.

"Not exactly."

"Don't tell me you finally got a pet. The man who could not commit to anyone or anything has a dog?"

"It's not my dog."

Fritzi growled at Simone again.

A light came on behind them and Cash knew without turning around again that it was Paige. A door hinge creaked in the night, followed by a tentative, "Cash?"

"Ooh," Simone said, straightening and fluffing her hair. "The girlfriend. Do I get to meet her?"

"I already said no. Be on your way." He moved to block her from heading toward the houseboat, still holding on to Fritzi, who was eyeing Simone as if he wouldn't mind taking a chunk out of her.

The sound of footsteps vibrated up the wooden dock. "Cash?"

He sighed, turned to see Paige standing behind him, wearing one of his T-shirts emblazoned with "The Truthful Desperadoes," and her denim jacket thrown over it, cowboy boots, and nothing else. Her hair was mused, her mascara smeared, and she was shivering.

"What are you . . . ?" Paige stopped. Her brow furrowed and she tilted her head.

Cash stepped aside so she could see Simone standing there.

"Oh . . . uh . . . well." Paige slid her palms down her sides, embarrassment and insecurity flaring in her eyes. "You have company. I didn't know."

Damn Simone for putting him in this position. Cash hated that he was the cause of Paige feeling anything but strong and brave and self-confident. "She was just leaving."

Simone breezed past him, a perfectly manicured hand outstretched. "Hi," she said. "I'm Simone, and you are . . ."

Paige looked thunderstruck, took Simone's hand, and pumped it like she was trying to siphon lotion from a dispensing bottle. "I'm Paige."

Simone fluttered her eyes at Cash. "She's ador-able. Where on earth did you find her? One of those wholesome 1950s sitcoms?"

Paige dropped Simone's hand, yanked her spine up tall, and jutted out her chin. "What's wrong with wholesome?"

"Nothing." Simone smiled her aren't-I-beautiful smile. "Nothing at all. It's just that Cash has never much gone in for wholesome."

"Well," Paige said tartly. "First time for every-thing."

He watched her eyes dart as if adding up compli-cated calculations in her head. Was she about to tell Simone to shove it where the sun didn't shine? He wouldn't blame her if she did.

"I'm freezing." Paige folded her arms over her chest. "And I imagine you are too. Cash, why don't you give Fritzi to me, and you take Simone inside to finish your conversation?"

"Yes," Simone said, her tone dry as vermouth. "Why don't you take me inside, Cash?"

Cradling Fritzi in her arms, Paige turned and clomped off. She was pretty damn adorable wearing those boots. Cash's heart turned to mush watching that fanny walk away. But she did not head in the direction of his houseboat.

"Hey," he called. "Where are you going?"

"Home," she said. "I'll leave you and your friend to it."

"Gotta tell you," Simone said as he escorted her up the gangplank. "I thought she'd never leave."

Cash scowled and closed the door behind them.

He craned his head to peer out the window at Paige's houseboat. A light was on in the living room, but she had the window blinds tightly drawn.

"Quit dwelling on Pollyanna for half a second. Eyes on me, please."

He sighed. "Why are you really here, Simone?"

"Don't get me wrong. I like her, very girl next door, and spunky too. I get why it's playtime for Cash, but do you think it's fair?"

"Do I think what is fair?" He forked his fingers through his hair, wondering how quickly he could get Simone out of here so he could go check on Paige.

"The way you're leading her on."

"Who says I'm leading her on?"

Simone gave him "the look." The one she whipped out whenever she was pissed off at him. The look that said he was a total idiot. "She's sweet and traditional. A real Suzy Homemaker. And you, my friend, are allergic to commitment."

"This isn't serious. We're just having fun."

"*You* might be just having fun, but that girl is smitten."

"How do you know?" he asked.

"*Pull-ease.* Should I buy you a Seeing Eye dog?"

Suddenly, the image of Paige sitting in the middle of the bed, eyes shining happily as she declared, "I love you," popped into his head.

Simone had a point.

"Kindest thing to do is break it off now before she's in over her head."

Hell, he was in pretty deep too. But Cash didn't want to think about that too hard. Not right now. Not with Simone. "Just tell me what you want."

"I have something for you." She fiddled with the button on her coat.

"If you take off that coat, and you're naked underneath, I'm throwing you out on your ear."

"Good grief, the ego! No wonder I left. I'm not trying to seduce you. I'm marrying Snake in just a few weeks."

"You cheated on me with him. You're not above trying to cheat on him with me."

"Believe it or not," Simone said, "I came here to make amends."

"Or not," he said.

"Don't be flippant. I'll be right back." She went outside and returned a few minutes later carrying a brand-new guitar case.

"You're giving me a guitar? Why are you giving me a guitar? I have six of them."

"Open the case and find out."

He sank down on the couch, set the guitar case on the floor, leaned over to flip open the clasp. Opened the lid.

Caught his breath.

There lay Lorena, the Gibson his mother had given him when she died on Christmas Eve. The guitar he'd named after her. The guitar he'd believed had been stolen from a recording session. The same session where'd he caught Snake and Simone kissing in the hallway and he'd stormed off.

He slipped the Gibson from the case, settled it on his lap, stroked a few chords, felt a strange sadness slide over him.

Heat pushed into his body, followed by an icy coldness. He looked over at Simone. "You took Lorena?"

She shrugged, squirmed a little under the glare of his stare. "I brought her back."

"You let me think someone had stolen her."

"I'm not proud of myself."

"You cheated on me and broke up the band. Why did you have to take Lorena too?" He clutched the neck of the guitar, saw in his mind's eye his mother playing this guitar, smiling, her body moving in time to the music, eyes closed. She'd looked happy when she played. Free. It was the only time she was at peace.

Simone flipped one shoulder forward, trying to look casual, nonchalant, but she didn't quite pull it off. Tension plucked at the corners of her mouth and she kept brushing back hair that had not fallen into her face. "I took Lorena because I wanted something to remember you by."

"Be honest. You just wanted to twist the knife. You were angry because I wouldn't ask you to marry me."

"Maybe I was."

"We weren't good for each other."

"I know that now." She chuffed, sounded defensive, and rubbed her palms over her upper arms.

"My God, woman, do you know what losing this guitar did to me? You killed my creativity for an entire year."

"It's just a guitar, Cash. It doesn't have magical powers to grant musical talent or success."

"It was my mother's guitar."

"Who, by the way, never had a drop of success in her life," she said.

"Because of me," he said staunchly, feeling his

jaw tighten. "If my mother hadn't fallen in love with my father and gotten pregnant trying to hang on to him, she could have been a huge star."

"Could she have?" Simone challenged. "Really?"

"Are you trash talking my dead mother?"

"I'm saying she twisted your head up right good. You believe what she told you about not being able to have love and a big successful music career. That's something she made up in her head and you bought into."

He plucked the guitar strings, eking out the first few notes of "Stone Free." Simone's words burned the corners of his mind, singeing the memory of his mother.

"It's probably a good thing you didn't try to hang on to me," Simone said. "It broke my heart at the time, but in retrospect, we weren't a good fit."

He paused, stopped strumming, and met her eyes. "I cared about you, Sim."

"But you never loved me, did you?"

Cash thought of his feelings for Simone. Compared them to how he felt about Paige. It was the difference between monochrome and Technicolor. Between a minor fall and a major lift. Between a lone ukulele strummed on a street corner and the New York symphony.

"I'm sorry," he said.

"No need to apologize." Regret filled her tissue-paper smile. "I knew it all along." She bit her bottom lip, shook her head as if waking from a dream. "Anyway, I had to get Lorena back to you before I could fully move on. I hope she brings you all the success in the world, Cash. I truly do."

"Thank you, Simone." He set the Gibson down on the sofa, stood up.

"We had some good times, didn't we?"

"We did."

"You're not coming to the wedding, are you?"

He shook his head. "It's for the best if I stay away."

"I guess this is good-bye, then."

He crossed the room, gave her a hug. "I wish you and Snake a rich and happy life."

"Well." She laughed. "This is very adult of us."

"Be well, Sim."

She opened the door, stepped out to the deck, stood underneath the light looking vulnerable.

He followed, trying to decide if he should offer to walk her to her vehicle, when she turned, wrapped her arms around his neck, pulled his head down, and kissed him.

He did not kiss her back. Gently he untangled her arms. "Sorry, Sim. It really is over."

"I know," she said. "I just thought one last kiss for old times' sake."

"That's all?"

"That's all. I'll go now. Need to return the rental to DFW airport for my eight A.M. flight back to LA."

"You really didn't come with the expectation of spending the night?"

"I did not." She opened her smartphone, showed him the bar code of her boarding pass. "See for yourself. Quick, round-trip red-eye to get the guitar back to you and hide from the paparazzi."

He smiled at her, proud of how far they'd both come. "Go. Be happy with Snake. And thanks again for bringing Lorena home."

She turned and walked away. Stopped. Gave him one last parting glance over her shoulder. "I hope you find what it is you're looking for, Cash . . . before it's too late."

With that, she pushed him inside. "Don't watch me walk away," she said. "It's too sad." Then she closed the door in his face and Cash never saw her leave.

Simone *Freaking* Bishop.

Paige was standing in the middle of her houseboat with Simone *Freaking* Bishop, and the woman was beautiful enough to stop clocks. Beside her, Paige felt like a bag lady.

After running inside, she'd given up all hope of sleeping and decided to wrap Christmas presents. She'd been sitting on the floor surrounded by brightly colored foil paper, ribbons, and bows, trying not to think about what was going on in the houseboat next door, when Simone knocked on her door.

Simone Bishop looked like a 1940s film-noir, silver-screen siren. She towered a good five inches above Paige, and had a slender neck long enough to make a giraffe jealous. The lights from the three Christmas trees shimmered off her wavy golden tresses and sky-high cheekbones and reflected back the sheen of her black lamé blouse.

Her eyes were the color of emeralds, slightly almond shaped and fringed by lashes so long they had to be false. A faint dusting of lavender shadow over her eyelids, and her spectacular mouth, full and marshmallowy, was painted a vibrant fire engine red. Her coltish legs were swathed in black skinny jeans and her busty bosom pushed insistently against her buttons, as if begging, *Let us out*. And she smelled like Chanel.

Absentmindedly, Paige pressed a palm to her heart. This incredible creature had been alone with Cash in the houseboat for a good thirty minutes. What had been going on over there? Had they reconciled? Was Simone here to gloat? *Nah, nah, I've reclaimed my man.*

She let Simone in, and it felt as if a stone settled in her stomach as her hands went numb. "What . . ." Paige cleared her throat, started again. "What can I do for you?"

"Be careful." Simone's eyes narrowed.

Paige bristled. Sank her hands on her hips. Okay, the woman might be a goddess to end all goddesses but this was *her* home, dammit. She wasn't going to let her march in here and threaten her. "Are you trying to start a fight? Because I gotta warn you, lady, while I might be small, I'm feisty."

At that, Simone laughed like it was the funniest joke she'd ever heard in her life. She hooted. Guffawed. Kept laughing. Pressed a hand to her side. Laughed some more.

Hey, hey. Paige scowled. What was so damn funny? Did the glamorous giraffe doubt that she could hold her own in a tussle? She knotted her hands into fists, but that only sent Simone into fresh peals of laughter.

"Oh, doll baby," Simone said. "You are so precious. And you really do look like a nice kid. Honest, I didn't come here to threaten you. I came to warn you."

Paige folded her arms under her breasts, deepened her glower. "What's the difference?"

"You think I want him back?"

"Don't you?"

"No, no, no, no." Simone shook her head like she was a wet dog shaking off water.

"Then why did you come to see him in the middle of the night even though you're marrying his best friend on New Year's Eve?"

"To return the guitar I stole from him."

"I see," Paige said, even though she didn't believe Simone that she wasn't still hung up on Cash.

"He's a good guy, and he's handsome as the day is long, and he's damn easy to love, but he's never going to commit."

"I know that." Paige squeezed her rib cage, hugging herself tight.

"Do you?" Her voice held a superior I've-been-there-you-haven't tone.

"I'm fully aware of who he is," Paige said. "I want nothing from him."

Simone clicked her tongue. "You sure?"

Did she want Cash to tell her he loved her? Yes, yes, she did. Wanted it with every cell, every breath, in her body. But did she expect it? No.

"I hope you're not falling in love with him."

"Of course not." Paige scoffed, but it came out sounding lame and lean.

"Everyone loves him, you know. Friends. Fans. Women . . ." Simone paused. "They love him at first. And then they realize the love is one-sided. He can't return the love. It's not his fault, poor pet. I blame his mother. She screwed him up royally. So Cash and I were doomed from the start. *Anyone* who gets with him is doomed from the start."

"The fact that you cheated on him with his best friend didn't have anything to do with the doomedness?" Paige asked dryly.

"Hey, that's not fair. I wanted to marry him. I wanted him to say he'd be there for me forever. But he wouldn't. Or he couldn't. And I fell in love with someone else. He didn't fight that hard to keep me. So I'm not saying this to be a bitter bitch, but because I'm worried about you. I'm afraid he's going to break your heart. He can't help himself."

She took the bait. She couldn't help *herself*. "How so?"

"When he was ten years old, his mother told him that falling in love would kill his success. On her deathbed no less. On Christmas Eve. She told him that the only thing he was allowed to love was Euterpe."

Euterpe.

That stopped her heart. The nickname he'd given her. His muse.

"Do you know who Euterpe is?" Simone asked.

"I'm not an idiot," Paige snapped, although she hadn't known who Euterpe was until Cash told her. Then an awful, stomach-churning thought struck. What if he'd given Simone the same nickname?

"Did he ever call you that?" Paige ventured, wondering why she was torturing herself.

"What?" Simone asked. "Euterpe?"

Paige nodded.

"He calls you Euterpe?"

Should she admit it? Find out he called all his lovers that? She bit her bottom lip, barely nodded.

"Oh shit." Simone slapped a palm over her mouth. "You're in more trouble than I thought."

"What does that mean?"

"Here." Simone fished around in her clutch purse for a business card. "Here's my number. Feel free to call me when you hit rock bottom, and you will hit rock bottom. Call me and we'll commiserate."

Paige took the card Simone pressed into her palm. She had no intention of calling the woman. Ever. No matter what happened with Cash, but it seemed rude not to take the card.

"Good luck," Simone said.

And then she was gone. Leaving a waft of Chanel in her wake.

CHAPTER 19

Expressionism: Atonal and violent style used as a means of evoking heightened emotions and states of mind.

Simone *Freaking* Bishop left without explaining what she meant by her parting comment. Leaving Paige flabbergasted and more than a tad nervous. The look on the beautiful woman's face before she walked out the door had been one of absolutely pity.

And she was worried about that Freudian slip she'd had at Cash's houseboat. One of the last things she'd said to him was "I love you" and he'd not reciprocated. Had not even acknowledged she'd said it.

Hey, maybe he believed her when she'd said she didn't mean she *loved* him, loved him, and he'd completely forgotten about it.

She could hope, right? They could just ignore this and go right on as if she'd not uttered a word. Still have fun. Still enjoy each other's company. Still keep things light. No strings attached.

Yeah, about that. Her feelings for Cash lashed her down like Gulliver in Lilliput. Chained by her emotions, stings all over the damn place.

They were going to have to talk about it eventually; no matter how much she might not want to, she knew ignoring things only worked for a little while.

Paige thought about her first car. A used clunker that she'd neglected to take in for service. It rattled and knocked, but it still kept driving, so she'd ignored the noise. Until the day the engine blew up when she was driving home from high school, leaving her stranded on the side of the road in a thunderstorm. Smoke steaming from the hood, lightning crashing all around her, cell phone battery dead, and no way to charge it. Later, the mechanic told her if she'd just brought the car in for service, she could have avoided a cracked block, and the car wouldn't have been totaled because it cost more to fix it than it was worth.

Yep. In the long run, ignorance was definitely not bliss.

Ah crap.

She turned off the lights on the Christmas tree, stumbled into the bedroom just as the sky was lightening, preparing for dawn, and face-planted into the mattress beside a sleeping Fritzi.

She'd no more dropped down than a fierce knock sounded on the front door. Seriously? Who was smashing the hell out of her door at six A.M.?

Sighing, she got out of bed, padded to the door, peeked out the window to see Cash standing on the deck. He looked so damn gorgeous, his hair mussed as if he'd been raking his fingers through it. Wearing a leather jacket, red western shirt, and Levi's as if he were up for the day.

Heart thumping, she drew back from the door. She wasn't prepared to talk to him. Not now. Not until she'd sorted out the night's events.

He knocked again. "Paige," he called. "You awake? We need to talk."

Fear played her spine like a glockenspiel, tingling up and down, going faster, higher, until her lungs seized up. She couldn't talk to him. She was still too thrashed by what Simone had said to her. By what she'd told Cash. *I love you.*

Remember that blown-up engine?

She put her hand on the doorknob, but did not turn it. If she opened the door, she knew without a doubt that she would take him into her bed and show him with her body exactly how much she loved him. She couldn't help herself.

Not when it came to Cash.

Because this wasn't the car all over again—with the car, she'd ignored a short-term problem that turned into a permanent issue. Everything with Cash was short term. She'd known that all along.

How could there be a permanent issue when they would not have a relationship past New Year's? Why couldn't she ignore it? Why *did* they have to talk about it?

Slowly, Paige backed away from the door. Stood staring at it. Waiting for Cash to knock again—to coax, to wheedle, to cajole.

He did none of that. Footsteps echoed on the wooden deck as he walked away.

Her spirits curled up into a ball and rolled right down her stomach to her thighs, knees, and settled with a hard, solid *plunk* into the soles of her feet. He'd given up mighty easily. Leaving her to assume he wasn't all that keen on talking it out either.

She went back to bed and tried to sleep, but all she could hear was the sound of her old car engine knocking out a warning, *Do something before it's too late.*

But in her heart, she knew it had been too late from the moment she'd slept with him.

She was madly in love with a man who had no idea how to love her back.

Stuffing his hands into the pockets of his leather jacket, Cash hunched his shoulders against the cold and headed for the Land Rover. He was too keyed up to go back to bed, and disappointed that Paige had not answered her door.

He was ready to tell her that he loved her too.

But he hadn't wanted to keep knocking and wake her if she'd managed to fall asleep. Their talk could wait until she'd gotten some rest. In the meantime, he would head for breakfast, and as soon as the stores opened he'd look for a Christmas gift for Paige to show her what he couldn't find the words to say.

You mean so much to me.

He drove to the town square, parked, and went into Perks coffee shop, which was already buzzing with activity. There were Christmas trees in every corner, and over the sound system, Alan Jackson was singing, "Let It Be Christmas."

At this hour of the morning, the majority of the clientele were locals—farmers and ranchers in Stetsons and jeans talking cattle futures, horses, and the weather.

The sight tugged at his memory and he remembered the country diner near his grandparents' ranch. How they took him to breakfast at the diner every Saturday morning. He recalled the sense of community. How he'd been welcomed and doted upon.

He had liked it. Working the land. Riding horses. Tending cattle. Forgotten exactly how much he *had* liked the land. Those days on the ranch had seeped into his music. Many of his songs were about a rambling cowboy unlucky in love, and sorrowful over what he'd lost.

And until this very moment, he had no idea how much he missed the ranch and his grandparents. Hadn't realized *he* was that rambling cowboy searching for where he belonged.

It struck him as he walked to a lone table in the corner—every eye in the place tracking his movements, voices lowered in murmured gossip, his name on tongues—the full impact of what he'd lost out on by running away from home.

At fifteen, he'd viewed his grandparents' strict rules as an obstacle to his music career, instead of what it really was. Loving discipline to keep him safe.

His grandparents must have gone through immeasurable pain when he'd followed in his mother's footsteps. Blowing off their advice, clinging to Lorena's vision for his future, no matter the cost.

They hadn't lived long enough to see him succeed. His grandfather had died of cancer four years after Cash ran away, and his grandmother passed away a few months after, some say of a broken heart from losing everyone she loved.

The memories were knives, sharp and brutal, stabbing him from every direction.

How selfish he'd been. Concerned only about making it big in the music world. Not thinking twice how his leaving had devastated his grandparents.

His appetite vanished in the wake of this gut-punching revelation. He'd been such a wizard at burying his feelings, he was just now truly feeling the impact of his mistakes and all he'd lost.

"Hey there, handsome," flirted the cute waitress whose name tag identified her as Jill. "What'll you have? Coffee, tea, or me?"

"Coffee," he said, not the least bit interested in flirting back.

"I love 'Toasted,'" she said. "It's my favorite song *ever.*"

"Thanks," he mumbled, picked up the menu from the wire stand on the table, stared at it hard to keep from looking at her. He could feel her ogling him. *McDang*, sometimes celebrity was a real pain in the ass.

"I've been following your music since I was a little girl."

"That's nice. Eggs. I'll have two eggs over easy and a side of bacon."

"Okay," she said, sounding disappointed, but she didn't move away from the table.

Finally, Cash glanced up to see what she wanted. "Yes?"

"You know," the waitress said. "I've admired you for years . . . until now."

He affixed his trademark smile to the woman hoping to disarm her. "Look, I didn't get much sleep. I'm not my usual self."

"I'm not talking about that," she said. "I'm talking about the way you're cheating on Paige with Simone Bishop."

What? Huh?

"I knew you were a player," she went on. "But I didn't think you were a two-timer. You ought to know better since Simone cheated on you with Snake and you know how bad that feels. For shame."

"How do you know about me and Paige?"

She just rolled her eyes, gave a snort. "Don't even."

"Jill," interrupted a cowboy from the next table. "Can I have a refill?"

Jill leveled Cash a look. "Let's just say you've lost a fan."

What the truck? He scratched his head. His cell phone buzzed, letting him know he had a text. It was from Emma.

EMMA: WTF!!!
CASH: ???
EMMA: U haven't seen the video?
CASH: What video?

A minute passed, and then a video clip appeared in a text bubble. Someone had filmed him sing-

ing "Danke Schoen" to Grammie and then kissing
Paige in Ye Olde Book Nook, and uploaded it on
YouTube.

EMMA: 500k hits since upload at 10 P.M. last night.

It was just now seven o'clock in the morning. How
had the video gotten that many hits in the middle of
the night?

CASH: No kidding? Why?
EMMA: This.

And there it was, a photograph of Simone kissing
him in the doorway of his houseboat. Now it was
all making sense why Jill had been upset with him.
His stomach sank. How long before Paige saw this?
Had she already seen it?

CASH: Not what it looks like.
EMMA: I hope not. I'll kill U if U hurt Paige.
CASH: Simone kissed me.
EMMA: Why is she in Twilight?
CASH: Story too long to text.
EMMA: U got a mess on UR hands.
CASH: It'll blow over.
EMMA: Good for your career?
CASH: Bad for me & Paige.
EMMA: What is going on with U and Paige?
CASH: I don't know.
EMMA: Twitter is blowing up.
#CashColtonOnNaughtyList

He opened the Twitter app on his phone, discovered indeed half the world seemed to be weighing in on his character. God, didn't people have anything better to do than stick their noses and opinions in other folks' business?

Then he saw what the Internet trolls were saying about Paige and his blood boiled. Calling her ugly and fat and undeserving of his attention. Cruel vicious tweets that made him want to track down the culprits and smash their heads in. God, he prayed Paige did not get on Twitter.

His cell phone rang, and Deet's number flashed onto the screen.

CASH: Getting a call. Talk later.
EMMA: K.

He hit Accept on Deet just as Jill set down his coffee. He gave her a brief smile, but she tossed her head and tipped up her nose and pivoted away with a "Hmph." He supposed he would be getting a lot of that today.

"Hey, Deet," he greeted his manager, moved his chair around so he was sitting with his back to the wall and could see both entrance and exit into the coffee shop.

"What the hell have you been up to, buddy? You're trending on Twitter. 'Danke Schoen'? For real?" Deet chuckled.

His manager's laugh was a lively sound that pissed Cash off. He was still mad over those tacky tweets about Paige. "People are assholes."

"Hey, there's no such thing as bad publicity."

"Have you listened to those recordings I sent you?" Cash asked, cutting off any more discussion of the social media fiasco.

"Actually, that's why I'm calling."

"Well . . ." Cash held his breath. He *knew* the songs were the best work he'd ever done.

"I listened to them when you sent the recordings on Thursday afternoon, listened numerous times, and I loved every single song."

Yes! Cash pumped his fist. All right!

"But . . ." Deet's voice came out rough and prickly as tire spikes. Roadblock.

Cash's gut twisted. He knew that tone. It wasn't good. "Tell me."

"I sent it over to Sepia on Friday morning, and opened my email with their feedback . . ."

The hairs on the back of Cash's neck rippled. "They don't like it."

"They liked the music itself," Deet said. "What they didn't like is that it's not your brand."

"Huh?"

"You're known for your Southern soul, breakup, loose-footed rambler sound. Jazzy Hank Williams with a millennial mind-set is how they pictured selling your solo career."

"That piece of marketing crap is an insult to me and Hank," Cash snarked.

"What you turned in is some kind of lovey-dovey male version of Faith Hill. And it's not just the lyrics. The sound is a complete one-eighty from what you produced with The Truthful Desperadoes."

Cash recited a string of well-chosen curse words.

"Not my words," Deet said. "Straight quote from the horse's mouth."

"Horse's ass is more like it."

Jill put his breakfast in front of him, narrowed her eyes at him, and walked away. Cash glanced around to see that most everyone in the place was watching him as if he was the most interesting thing that had ever crawled into Perks.

"The execs think you've fallen in love. They want love-adverse Cash. That's why they gave you a solo contract. They were hoping for post-Simone, your-cheatin'-heart kind of songs."

He cursed again.

"Tough break," Deet said.

"You know those songs are the best thing I've ever written."

"They are."

"But they'd rather have some derivative, recycled crap from The Truthful Desperadoes than the best work I can produce?"

"It's all about sales and marketing, Cash. You know that. Money talks, everything else walks."

"So where does this leave me with the contract?" Cash asked.

"Nowhere." Deet grunted. "They're dropping you."

Deet's words hit him like a blow. Cash's worst fear was upon him. Being without a contract.

"There's nothing you can do?"

"Personally, I think Sepia is in financial trouble, and that's the real reason they're not willing to take a risk on your new direction. Think of it as a golden opportunity to explore options. This is your open window."

Cash took the news. Inhaled. Exhaled. Fumed. "Okay. Great. Fine. We're done with Sepia. Let's go wide. Send it to everyone."

Deet hesitated.

"What?"

"Another recording label is going to have the same problem with the songs that Sepia has. They'll have to rebrand you. Start from scratch building a new audience for this sound. And that means they're going to want you to take an offer far inferior to what you're used to getting. If you're good with a seventy-five percent pay cut, okay."

"These people have no creative vision."

"Of course not. They're suits and bean counters."

"So what are my options?"

"Bottom line? Create something that matches your current brand, or go indie with the current project. You already produced a demo. Put it up yourself."

"Are you trying to tell me you're not interested in representing me if I go with this new sound?"

"Let's not jump the gun," Deet said. "My best advice if you want to stay on top? Dance with the one who brung you."

Cash read between those lines. Deet would indeed drop him as a client if he went indie. Unbelievable. They'd worked together for over a decade. It was a cutthroat business, he knew that, but he couldn't help feeling gut-kicked.

"You think I'm a has-been."

"I didn't say that."

"Thanks for letting me know." Cash gritted his

teeth. He needed to get off the phone before he said something he couldn't take back.

"I know this is a blow, but if you stick with your original sound you'll come out of this smelling like money."

Without eating a bite of his breakfast or waiting for the check, Cash left a twenty on the table. He started for the front door. Several people moved toward him, beaming and breathless, pens and scraps of paper and napkins clutched in their hands.

Autograph seekers.

It never ended.

He grunted, pivoted on his heels, and left them hanging. Walked out the back exit of Perks and into the alley that ran behind the old buildings on the square. Pausing, he glanced over his shoulder to see if anyone was rude enough to come after him.

No one followed.

Thank God for small favors.

He rubbed his eyes. The coffee hadn't done much to chase off the ragged feeling of sleep deprivation—it has been an insane twenty-four hours—but the caffeine had left him edgy and buzzing.

Even in the cold air, he felt overheated and rolled up the sleeves of his jacket. He walked down the alley, grateful for the anonymity it provided. No one else back here. No fans. No paparazzi. Just a curious little crow who sat on a wooden fence that ran the length of the alley, studying him with dark yellow eyes.

"What are you looking at?" he asked the crow in a surly tone.

The crow gave a curt caw, flapped his wings, and flew over Cash's head, bombing him with droppings as he went past.

"Son of a biscuit eater." He muttered his grandfather's favorite curse words and a sweet, horrible sense of longing washed over him. He missed his grandparents more than he thought possible. Why were all these old emotions coming out? Why now?

Grunting, he picked up a dried leaf from the ground and used it to scrape the crow poop off his shoulder, and thought of the book Paige had read to her preschool class.

Everyone Poops.

Apparently, it seemed, on him.

Sepia was dumping him. Even though every musician with a recording contract knew they were always at the whim of executives and they could be gone in a breath, he still couldn't believe they'd actually dropped him. Not for those songs.

He clenched his jaw, cracked his knuckles. Jackasses.

How could they not want the music he'd written after meeting Paige? Those heartfelt songs that surged up from the root of his soul and had practically written themselves. He'd stepped out of his own way, let the music come through, and he was certain they were the best songs he'd ever created. Might ever create.

If Deet and Sepia couldn't see that, and support him in his change of direction, then *Adiós, amigo.*

Fresh start might be a good thing. Get rid of everyone and everything in his old life. The thought both exhilarated and terrified him.

But what if he went on that limb, took the gamble, and he failed? What if following his heart, following the song magic that flowed effortlessly from him whenever he was with Paige, killed his career?

What then?

Lorena's dying words whispered in his head. *Don't let love lead you astray. Not ever.* Was that what he'd done? Allowed love to lead him astray?

What should he do? Trust his heart or listen to his manager and Sepia and stick with what worked? Avoiding love had served him well for thirty-one years. Why mess with what worked?

But had embodying the role of lone, rambling cowboy musician *really* served him well?

On the career front, maybe, but when it came to relationships? He'd messed up every relationship he'd ever been in.

A deep ache rocked him to the core. He'd missed out on so much.

He scraped a hand over his chin, scratchy with stubble. Maybe he should grow his beard back. Maybe then he would feel more like his old self.

But did he want that?

He had a hard choice to make.

Gulping, Cash crossed the street, turned right on the square, and kept walking. A handful of people were on the streets, going about their early Saturday morning business, but no one seemed to notice him dodge into the alley again.

He wished he had something to cover his face, a hat and sunglasses. He'd left both in the Land Rover parked in front of Perks.

He passed the buildings he and Paige had gone

into the night before looking for her grammie. Despite the circumstances, he'd had fun. Had a feeling he could always have fun with her.

What was he going to do about his rapidly expanding feelings for Paige? And what could he get her for Christmas that showed her just how much she meant to him? Gifts were much more his style than words.

What gift said *I love you but I'm not ready to say it yet*?

Jewelry? Perfume? Food?

Too general. He needed something special. Something fitting. Something just for her.

He thought of her and the things she loved. Pepperoni pizza. The color pink. Books. Christmas. Children. Dancing.

He stopped in the middle of the alley, and realized he was standing in front of the building that was supposed to have been a yoga studio. On this backside of the building, underneath a big For Sale banner, someone had spray-painted in pink neon a giant heart and block lettering . . .

LOVE IS THE ANSWER TO EVERYTHING.

In a flash of inspiration, Cash understood what he must do.

CHAPTER 20

Dissonance: Harsh, discordant, and lack of harmony. Also a chord that sounds incomplete until it resolves itself on a harmonious chord.

At noon Fritzi nosed Paige awake with the urgent message, *Gotta pee, lady, get out of bed.*

Rats, she'd overslept. She had to be at the theater in an hour to get ready for the Saturday matinee.

Groggily, she pushed herself up off the bed, and the memory of the previous night swept over her like a West Texas windstorm—Grammie going missing, making love to Cash, Simone's appearance and dire warning.

"Hang on, hang on," she said, pulling on jeans underneath Cash's T-shirt she was still wearing sans bra, and throwing on a coat to cover it up. "Here we go."

She clipped the leash to the dog's collar, slipped into her shoes, and headed outside.

The minute she opened the door, half a dozen voices, all taking at once, pelted her.

"Ms. MacGregor, what's your relationship to Cash Colton?"

"What kind of kisser is Cash?"

"Who is the elderly lady in the 'Danke Schoen' video?"

"Is it true you were robbed of your life's saving by a con man?"

"How long have you and Mr. Colton been an item?"

"Are you and Cash having a three-way with Simone Bishop?"

Six people with cell phones surged toward her, recording and snapping photos of her mouth hanging open. Fritzi barked furiously.

Shocked at the influx, Paige backed up, yanking Fritzi along with her, and slammed the door shut. Locked it.

Holy snow leopard! What was that?

She plastered a palm over her chest, felt her rapidly pounding heart. What was going on? And how had those people known about all those things? And what the frack was that about a three-way?

Fritzi hopped on the back of the couch, stared out the window at the people gathered on her deck and, with a quivering upper lip, growled low in his throat.

"Yeah," she said. "I don't much like them either."

Fritzi hopped down, whined, did his I-gotta-pee dance.

Yeah, and she had to go to work. No hiding out. She was going to have to face those annoying gnats clustered at her door. She didn't know what had happened to cause them to gather, but she knew the source.

Cash Colton.

"You ready to run the gauntlet?" she asked the poodle.

He barked.

"No? Me either. But what choice do we have?" It's not as if she could slip out a back door, unless she wanted to end up in Lake Twilight.

"Here goes." She picked Fritzi up, looped his leash around her arm. Hitched her purse on her shoulder. Braced herself. Opened the door. Ignored the onslaught. Locked the door. Straightened. Turned.

Saw she was surrounded. Fritzi trembled in her arms.

"Out of my way," she said, her tone clear, succinct, brooking no argument.

"How long have you been seeing Cash Colton?" asked a whip-thin woman with intense eyebrows. She stood so close that she was almost touching Paige. A Shakespeare quote blitzed through Paige's head: *lean and hungry look.*

"Back off," she growled.

The woman stood her ground, recorder thrust into Paige's face. Around them, the others crowded in. Had to be paparazzi. No legitimate media here.

Was this related to Simone Bishop's wee hours of the morning visit?

Ugh.

"What are you people doing here?" she asked, then immediately regretted engaging them in conversation.

"You haven't seen the YouTube video?" asked Ms. Lean and Hungry.

Paige shook her head.

A twenty-something guy wearing a *Life in Hell* T-shirt called up the video on his cell phone, stuck it in her face, volume cranked.

It was the scene from Ye Olde Book Nook from the night before where Cash was singing to Grammie, and then kissing Paige.

"It's going viral," *Life in Hell* Dude explained. "Cash Colton kissed you and now you're a star."

Not hardly, and if this was what it was like to be a star, give her anonymity any day of the week. She cradled Fritzi against her side, sank her fingers into his fur, and drew comfort from his warmth.

"If you haven't seen the video, you probably haven't seen this either." Another guy, this one older, and more down-at-the-heels, held up his phone.

It was a still shot from a long distance away in the dark. But she could clearly make out the deck of the turquoise houseboat. And underneath the porch light were Cash and Simone Bishop. Caught in an embrace.

Kissing.

Betrayal shattered Paige like a silver hammer rapping against fragile crystal as her brain translated what she was seeing.

Not long after he'd been making love to Paige, Cash had been kissing Simone.

The YouTube video of Cash singing "Danke Schoen" to Grammie and kissing Paige in the middle of Ye Olde Book Nook created a sensation, not just in

Twilight, but in the bigger world beyond. Spurred by technology and social media, *everyone* knew about it.

Paige thought her humiliation over Randy had been seismic. Ha! In comparison, that was a mere blip on the Richter scale. No one other than her family, friends, credit card companies, and law enforcement had known of her silly shame.

This case, however, was an epic, earth-shattering 8.9.

It seemed the entire world rubbed their hands with glee at her flaws and faux pas. Complete strangers had an opinion and felt free to comment on her life. On Twitter, people called her fat and stupid and ugly. Others were on her side and vilified Simone Bishop instead. Some loved that Cash had been caught kissing two women in one night. Others dubbed him a tool, a douchebag, and other, less savory nouns.

After Paige escaped the paparazzi on her doorstep, she'd fled to the loft at the Twilight Playhouse, taking refuge in the dressing room with the ghost of John Wilkes Booth and Fritzi. She didn't know what to do with the poodle since she wasn't about to take him back to the houseboat with those jokers hanging around.

She took her cell phone from her purse. It had been pinging nonstop with texts. The last text bubble on the screen was from Kiley Bullock.

Traitor, the text said, followed by a good-natured smiling emoji. **Cash was supposed 2B all mine.**

That made her smile, but she was in no mood to wade through all those texts, plus she had to get into costume. She was about to power off her phone when it rang.

It was Flynn.

Hoping to convince her cousin to come get Fritzi, Paige answered. "Hello."

"Caught on camera!" Flynn gloated. "Not only is Cash sweet as pie singing to Grammie, but clearly he's sweet on *you*."

"Uh, did you miss the part where he was also kissing Simone Bishop?"

"What!" Flynn exclaimed.

Paige filled her in.

"That dirty rat!"

"Don't jump to conclusions." It was what she'd been telling herself. "I don't know his side of the story. The photo might even be Photoshopped."

"Oh, Paige, I'm so sorry you're going through this, especially after . . . well, you know. Is there anything I can do?"

"Actually, there is. Could you drop by the theater and pick up Fritzi and keep him until I get off work?"

"Sure. No prob. The kids will love having him. I'll send Jesse over to pick him up."

"Thank you."

"If you need anything else, you let me know. Love you, cuz."

"Love you too."

"This will blow over."

"I know," Paige said. "But we've lived through enough West Texas tornadoes to know that even though they eventually blow over, they can leave a big mess behind."

Jesse, whose motorcycle shop was on the other side of the square, arrived not long after she hung up with Flynn. He took Fritzi, and jokingly offered to beat up Cash for her.

"Thanks," she told him. "But I need to fight my own battles."

Jesse gave her a pat on the back and told her to hang in there.

After he left, she changed into her Santa Baby costume. Remembered her first day on the job. The first day she'd met Cash. It seemed like a decade ago instead of a few weeks.

She'd just gotten dressed when there was a knock on the dressing room door.

"Paige?" Emma called. "You in there?"

Paige opened the door. "Hey."

Glee lit up Emma's face. "I'm so happy for you."

"Huh?" Paige wrinkled her nose.

"You and Cash. An item!"

Before Paige could explain that she and Cash were *not* an item, Emma kept chattering.

"I credit the matchmaker cookies for this auspicious turn of events." Emma clasped her hands together and nestled them under the left side of her jaw and her face turned sappy and sentimental.

"Matchmaker cookies?"

Emma ducked her head, and sent Paige a coy glance that was an embodiment of the character Jovie she was playing in *Elf*. "The caramel apple cookies Flynn and I baked for the cookie swap. The same cookies I baked for Cash when he made dinner for you. They were meant to make you guys fall in love."

"Excuse me?" Had Emma gone off the deep end? "What on earth are you talking about?"

"Come with me." Emma took Paige by the hand, dragged her down the stairs, through the auditorium to her office.

From the bookcase, Emma pulled down a copy of *The First Love Cookie Club Cookbook*. It was the baking guide bible for the local cookie club. Emma flipped the cookbook open to a dog-eared page, and passed it to Paige.

MATCHMAKER COOKIES: Warning! Matchmaker Cookies are serious business. Baking them is not to be undertaken lightly. They can have a powerful impact on the lives of those who consume them. Matchmaker Cookies may cause people to fall hopelessly in love with the object of their deepest desires.

Paige was not superstitious, but the hairs on her forearm lifted, and her stomach flipped over. Twice. An icy coldness pushed up from her feet. She didn't believe pastries could make two people fall in love, but the fact that Emma and Flynn had baked cookies for her and Cash with that intention in mind rattled her.

Good grief. Did they think she was that desperate? "You and Flynn baked cookies hoping they would help me fall in love with Cash?"

"Well, not per se." Emma giggled as if it were a fun lark. "You were lonely and we thought you could use a little holiday magic. Our aim was to fix you up with any appropriate male. And then Sam thought of asking Sig to rent the houseboat to Cash . . ."

"So you thought, why not me and Cash?"

"Exactly. You get it," Emma said, clueless to Paige's upset. "Cash needs someone solid and grounded like you. And let's face it, you could use more fun in your life. So we baked the cookies, and look!"

Feeling violated and betrayed for the second time that day, Paige snapped the cookbook closed. She sank her hands on her hips. "Surely you don't believe cookies can cause people to fall in love."

"Well, no. Not really, truly. They *are* just baked goods." Emma's laugh jiggled like Jell-O, unsettled and wiggly. "But it's fun to pretend, and hey, you guys *did* get together."

"We're not together," Paige said, keeping her voice tightly controlled to keep from reading Emma the riot act for meddling in her life.

"What?" Emma's eyes sprung wide, and her mouth dropped round as a full moon. "But . . . but . . . he kissed you. In public. Cash wouldn't do something like that unless he was invested."

"Look," Paige said. "We had fun together, but that's all it was."

"Was?" Emma blinked. "It's over?"

"He's a great guy, but how could it be anything more? He's filet mignon and I'm applesauce." Plus, he'd kissed Simone Bishop last night too. *Not so invested in me after all.*

"You can't lie to me," Emma countered. "I've seen the way you look at him. What you've got going on is more than just fun and games."

"No." Paige hardened her chin, wondered if she was going to have to quit her job. She didn't want to, but she resented being manipulated. "We like each other, but it can't ever be anything more than that."

"Why not?" Emma settled her hands on her hips.

"For one thing, I can't be deal with this." Paige waved a hand.

"With what?"

"The phone ringing constantly. Paparazzi camped on my houseboat. It might seem normal to you and Cash, but to me it's an invasion of privacy. I don't like everyone knowing my business. It's one of the reasons I'm not on Facebook."

"It's a novelty. It'll die down as soon as someone else does something interesting." Emma dismissed the celebrity madhouse with a wave of her hand.

"For another thing," Paige went on. "Cash is not a long-term kind of man and you know that."

"Maybe he hasn't been in the past, but he's never been in love before. Love changes a man."

Paige's heart bumped hard against her chest. Hope, that damnable emotion, knocking. *What if?* "He's not in love with me."

Emma pressed her lips together in a firm line as if to keep from saying something she'd regret later. Paige wished she'd exercised that same decorum before the conversation ever began.

"He's not," Paige assured her.

"How do you know?" Emma challenged.

"Because," Paige said. "Last night, thirty minutes after leaving our bed, he was kissing Simone Bishop."

Somehow, Paige managed to make it through the matinee.

Dozens of people came up to her, offering their

comments and advice on her love life. Paige forced a smile and tried not to lose it. If this was what it would be like to be Cash's girlfriend, no thank you. She didn't have the stamina for it.

After the performance, the other Santa's helpers asked if she'd like to go to Fruit of the Vine with them to hang out and sing karaoke until the next show, but she declined. She wouldn't be good company. She offered to lock up and waved to them as they bundled into their coats and headed out in their costumes.

She locked the doors and turned her phone back on. If something happened to Grammie, the nursing home needed to be able to get hold of her. She leafed through numerous texts, and saw at least a dozen of them were from Cash.

Where RU?

Call me.

Freaking paparazzi.

Don't jump to conclusions.

It's not what it seems.

How is Fritzi?

How RU?

Please call.

I hate this.

We need to talk. It's important.

Text me.

Let me know U got this.

Paige? Sweetheart?

There were voice mails from him too. Four of them. She did not listen. Heart beating crazy fast, she stuffed her phone back into her purse.

She wasn't ready to talk to him. Not yet. Her feelings were still too raw and she didn't know if she could hide them from him. She wanted to go home and lie down until it was time to come back for the second performance, but she couldn't bear the thought of wading through those ghouls on her doorstep again.

But where could she go? The square was packed with people and no matter where she went she was bound to run into someone she knew. It was too cold to sneak off to Sweetheart Park.

The actors were hanging out in the loft dressing rooms and she didn't want to run into Emma again. Grammie.

She'd go see her grandmother. She could use the alleys and go in through the back door of the nursing home. She'd only have to deal with the nursing home staff, and for the most part, she trusted they would leave her in peace.

Paige slipped into her coat and out the rear entrance. She wished she could change out of her stiletto boots, but she'd left her Skechers upstairs in the dressing room and she wasn't going after them.

The alley was empty save for an orange tabby sitting on a Dumpster flicking his tail. Her breath puffed frosty in the cold, and she rubbed her palms together, wishing she'd remembered to bring gloves, but she'd been so discombobulated by the paparazzi at her houseboat she'd left them lying on the kitchen table.

Carefully picking her way down the uneven pavers of the alleyway, she startled the tabby. He dove into the bushes. "Sorry, cat."

The air smelled joyful—pine and cinnamon, coffee from Perks, roasted meats, and popcorn. Paige's mouth watered and she realized she hadn't eaten a thing all day.

Maybe she'd slip into the back door of Perks and get a pastry.

But did she really want to risk running into people who'd ask questions she didn't want to answer?

No, no, she did not. Maybe a hot dog at a kiosk on the square?

She was debating whether going for food was worth the hassle when a man appeared in the alley in front of her, blocking her way.

Cash.

Her pulse thumped, bumped, and if she hadn't been wearing those damn stilettoes, she would have turned and run.

He looked haggard, jaw thick with beard stubble, eyes bleary, hair mussed, clothing rumpled.

But when he spotted her his face brightened like

a light coming on, and every ounce of resentment she'd felt toward him melted. It didn't matter if she was angry with him. She loved him and nothing on earth could change that.

And when he smiled, oh when he smiled, the gray clouds parted and the sun came out and it was full-blown summer, hot and sweet and beautiful.

"My Euterpe." He breathed like she was oxygen. "Here you are."

It hit her then, with the stunning shock of bolt lightning, breaking up with this man was going to be the hardest thing she'd ever had to do.

CHAPTER 21

Grave: Indication that a movement or entire composition is to be played very slowly and seriously.

"I was worried about you," Cash told her as they stood staring each other down in the alleyway. Not the most romantic place in the world, but this is where he'd found her. "Why didn't you call me back?"

"Are you kidding me right now?" Her tone was prickly barbed wire.

An invisible lasso landed around his gut, dallied up. "Is this about Simone, because I can explain—"

"It's not about Simone. I can tell from the photograph that she kissed you."

"Even so, we still need to talk."

"I don't have much time." She glanced at her wrist as if she were wearing a watch. "I have to be back at the theater at six-fifteen."

"It's four-thirty, plenty of time to figure things out. Land Rover is parked on the street." He jerked his thumb over his shoulder. "Let's take a drive."

She nodded curtly.

He moved to take her arm, but she shook him off. She was mad. He respected that. But it killed him that he was the one responsible for upsetting her.

Cash jammed his hands in his pockets, hunched his shoulders, and led the way to his SUV. He opened the passenger's side door for her. Paige did not meet his gaze as she climbed inside.

Okay, he was going to have to work hard to earn her forgiveness. He was prepared. He got behind the wheel, started the Land Rover, navigated through the crowded square, and drove aimlessly around the lake. Not sure where to go. The paparazzi were still hanging around the marina. He'd gone to check earlier, looking for Paige, after he didn't find her at the theater. How long would it take the vultures to get bored and go away?

Finally, he spotted an empty boat ramp on the far side of the lake where the Brazos River fed into it. He pulled up to the edge of the water and put on the parking brake. He switched off the engine, but kept the vehicle in accessory mode so he could run the heater. That duster she wore was too damn thin.

They sat in silence for a moment, staring out at the lake, listening to their breathing fogging up the windows. He rested his fists on his thighs, and peered over at her.

"I've got several things to tell you," he said, making sure his tone stayed even, calm. "But first we need to clear the air. I know you're angry with me—"

"Wrong. I'm not mad. I'm overwhelmed. Reality finally sunk in."

Cash frowned, disturbed by the flatness in her tone. "What do you mean?"

"This morning I got a big dose of what it's really like to be with you. Amy and your ultrafans in Twilight aside, I honestly didn't get what your world was all about. We've been living in a protected little bubble in this town. Where, for the most part, people have respected your privacy."

"It's not always like this," Cash said, and then stopped. Celebrity did carry a price and she had every right to voice her opinion without him interrupting. He shut up.

Their gazes connected, sewn together by an invisible thread.

"You might crave this kind of attention, but I don't."

He started to protest, stopped. She was right. He liked the attention his music brought him. It was validation that he had worth in the world.

"I'm not complicated, Cash. I like a simple life. Friends. Family. A roof over my head. Enough food to eat. Work that keeps me busy."

"Your work might keep you busy, Paige, but are you satisfied? Are you living up to your full potential?"

For the length of a heartbeat, her eyes stayed steady and clear, locked on his. A pucker jerked the corners of her lips, as if she'd eaten something sour and couldn't get the taste out of her mouth. Then her expression shifted and he saw a combination of old hurts and vulnerabilities that jerked his heartstrings and his protective instincts.

"Everyone can't be some big-shot star," she said in a voice so tight and small he knew he'd wounded her.

"That's not what I meant, Paige."

"Not all of us are wildly talented."

"You . . ." He pointed a finger at her. "Are a very talented dancer and it's a shame you're not putting your skills to good use."

"We can't all live pipe dreams." Her eyes turned brittle as ice, cold and sharp. "Some of us find it impossible to turn our backs on our families for the sake of our own careers."

Zing. Jab. Slap.

Cash thought of his grandparents, pulled a palm down his face. "I suppose I deserved that."

"I didn't say it to be mean. There are two sides to every argument. You think your way works best, I think my way does." She shrugged as if it was no big deal, but her eyes were shadowed and sad.

"Well, apparently, I'm not the big star everyone seems to think." He cringed. That sounded pathetic. He wasn't trying to make her feel sorry for him. He was still wrestling the demons that Deet's news about Sepia had dredged up.

That story had yet to break, but when the news got out, it would only feed the social media frenzy and the Internet trolls' schadenfreude. He'd been down this road before when Simone cheated and broke up The Truthful Desperadoes.

Paige canted her head. "What are you talking about?"

"The songs I wrote since I met you . . . the best damn thing I ever wrote *because* I met you . . . Sepia dropped me over them."

Her mouth formed a wide O and her eyes softened with pity. That was *not* what he'd been angling for.

"Oh, Cash," she whispered in a sound as soft as a caress. "That's awful news. A real blow."

"It's the first time I've been out of contract in ten years," he said. "I know I'm lucky on that score. I've had a great run . . ."

"But why did Sepia drop you? They are lovely songs."

He told her about Deet's phone call, why Sepia had dropped him, related the whole story. Opened up. Took a risk. Held nothing back. Confessed his fears that he wouldn't get another contract, that if he stuck with this new direction he'd have no choice but to go indie.

"I am so sorry." She shook her head, eyes brimming with compassion. "I know how much those songs meant to you."

"They mean so much to me because *you* inspired them." He reached across the seat, took her hand. "All my life I wrote and played what was commercial. My only goal was to get to the top and that meant creating the kind of music the majority of people want to listen to. And that was fine. I was happy enough . . . or so I thought."

He paused, rubbed his thumb over the knuckles of her hand. "And then came you."

"Cash . . ." She was breathing only from the top part of her chest. The sound of his name dropped fragile and winded from her lips.

"You changed everything. You changed *me*." He took both her hands in his, looked squarely into her sweet hazel eyes.

She hitched in an audible breath. Her hands were trembling. She must be cold. He folded her fingers into her palms, wrapped his hands around her small fists, trying to warm her up.

"These past few weeks have been the happiest of my life."

"Cash," she said again, and he heard something heavy and atonal rushing up from her throat, something urgent and insistent, as if she were desperate to stop him from saying what he was going to say next.

Nothing could stop him. Cash was on a roll. He'd worked up the courage to say the words he would not use lightly and he was going to say them. "Paige Hyacinth MacGregor—"

"Don't!" she cried.

But his tongue already unfurled them, too late to stop. "I love you."

I love you.

The words Paige had longed to hear him say. The words she did not trust. And not just because Randy had said them to her when he hadn't meant them.

She didn't trust that Cash understood what he was saying. She didn't think he was outright lying. He probably believed that he was in love with her.

That's what she didn't trust.

Cash's beliefs. The way he saw the world.

"I know it's probably too soon. I know you have your doubts about long-term possibilities with me. I'm not expecting you to say it back. I caught you off guard. You're already overwhelmed by what's happened today, but I had to tell you how I felt. I couldn't wait any longer."

The silence in the SUV was a time bomb. Tick. Tick. Tick.

"Have you ever been in love before?" she finally asked.

"No," he said. "You're the first woman I've ever said that to."

Hope grabbed hold of her. That sweet part that wanted to believe that girls like her could end up with guys like him, but she knew better. She might be able to fool herself for a while, pretend it could be true, but then someone would inevitably snap their picture together and ask why a glorious peacock like him was with a plain mouse like her. Or someone like Simone would try to seduce him away from her and the illusion would shatter.

"I'm sure you believe you love me," she said, surprised at how calm and certain she managed to sound. Slowly, she tugged her hands away.

He didn't want to let her go, his fingers hooked around her wrists. "Muse," he said, his voice was kind, but stern. "Look at me."

She did not look at him. Kept her chin tucked to her chest. "I am not your muse. You can't put that kind of pressure on me."

"You *are* my muse." He crooked a finger under her chin, lifted it. "When I see your face the world fills with music."

Her eyes met his, steeled herself for the impact, and absorbed the wild surge of adrenaline like a blow. "And that's why you love me?"

"It is." His smile was sweeter than the best dessert, more earnest than a puppy, and it cleaved straight through the center of her. Broke her into two separate pieces.

One piece wanted to melt into his arms and tell him that she loved him too, and to claim her happily-ever-after. The other piece of her, the piece that had been burned and hurt and betrayed, that part of her wasn't about to trust in fairy tales. That side of her *knew* better.

"Wrong answer," she mumbled, swallowing back her tears, tasting the salt, riding the queasiness that slid up her throat.

He looked as if he wanted to kiss her, but she drew back. If he kissed her, she didn't stand a chance. "Paige . . ."

"What happens when the music stops?" she asked.

"It won't." His eyes drilled into her, searching her face.

"The muse is fickle." The hopeless romantic in her wanted to bind and gag her sensible side with Gorilla Tape and throw it to the bottom of a closet, never to be seen again. "Everyone knows that."

"This isn't going away. Not the musical inspiration you stir in me. Not my feelings for you." He wrapped his arms around her, tugged her toward him, and kissed her.

How she wished she could get swept away by his kisses. Pretend it didn't matter that he loved her because he believed she somehow granted him special creative powers. She forced herself not to kiss him back.

He let her go, the pulse at the hollow of his throat beating hard against his skin. "I apologize for the paparazzi, for Simone, but we can find a way to work through this. I know we can. When two people love each other—"

"You don't love me, not really."

"Yes, I do." He clenched his jaw.

"You just think you do—"

"Hey, lady, saying I love you . . ." His Adam's apple bobbed. "You have no idea how monumental it is for me. You're special, Paige. So very special."

She shook her head.

"No?"

"I've thought about this a lot today. You love the idea of me." She took a deep breath, plowed ahead. Best to get it over with. A clear break so she could start to mend. "You love me for what I bring to the table. In that regard, you're no different than Randy the con man." The truth hurt so badly. It was as if her heart would collapse under the weight of her suffering.

Cash jerked back as if she'd slapped him. His pupils constricted and he looked impossibly hurt. "I can't believe you just said that to me."

"It's not your fault. From what Simone told me about your mother, Lorena set you up to lose at love. Insinuating that if you dared to love anyone it would kill your career. Declaring all that nonsense on her deathbed was a double whammy. She transferred her fears and twisted beliefs onto you. How could you *not* be emotionally crippled?"

"Wow. Emotionally crippled? Really? That's how you see me?"

"It's an observation, I'm not judging."

"Aren't you?" His voice was a harsh rasp, bruised and bleeding.

"No."

"Sure as hell feels like it."

"To make things even more complicated, your mother told you that if you had to fall in love, the only person you could love was Euterpe. That's why you cast me in that role, Cash. It's not because I have some special powers to juice your creativity. It's because you had feelings for me and the only way you could justify them to yourself was to turn me into your muse."

His jaw tightened, but he did not speak. His gray eyes darkened to charred coals.

"Seeing me as your muse gave you permission to create a different kind of music and you soared. You took a chance because if I was Euterpe I was safe to love."

"Is that right?" His tone was dry as peeling paint.

"But here comes this new wrinkle. Sepia rejects you over this new musical direction. With the rejection, you have two choices. You can agree that your mother was right, give up on love, go back to making the music you were making before, and keep your career on track . . ."

"Or?"

"Embrace your new creative direction by falling head over heels in love with your muse. That's what you're doing, Cash."

"You're a regular Carla Jung, huh?"

"Here's the kicker. If you pick the second route, give up the tried and true, the safe method that's worked for you so far . . . and submerge yourself in this new musical venture and it fails, you'll see it as my fault and it will end us before we ever really started."

He inhaled sharply, stared at her as if she'd hit at the very core of him.

Paige explored his face, trying to decrypt his feelings.

A subtle change came over him. His shoulders tugged straight, as if yanked by an invisible string, stretching him up tall. Lifting his head, tucking his chin back, ironing his mouth closed. The light in his eyes going out, his face shuttered, unreadable. Raising the facade. Bolstering the barricade. Cool Cash. Nothing and no one got to him, a little tin soldier like the one dangling from her Christmas tree, forlorn and frozen. Forever isolated and on alert.

"I can't be responsible for that," she added.

"So that's it. You're breaking things off?"

"It's for the best," she said, marveling that she found the strength. Suffering through her relationship with Randy had been worth the hard lessons. Forged by fire. She could take the heat and survive.

He was tough too. His face gave away nothing. They were two scarred warriors damaged by the battlefield of love.

"Now could you take me back to the theater, please?" she asked softly. "I need to get to work."

CHAPTER 22

Klangfarbenmelodie: The technique of altering the tone color of a single note or musical line by changing from one instrument to another in the middle of a note or line.

Was Paige right? Was he in love with her only because of the way she made him feel? Was he emotionally crippled? Simone had told him as much after he caught her messing around on him with Snake, but he hadn't listened.

Maybe he *was* just as bad as the con man who'd swindled Paige. Taking advantage of her sweet nature and giving heart. The notion was a hard, cold bullet straight to the center of his chest.

Cash watched Paige disappear into the side entrance of the Twilight Playhouse where he'd let her out of the Land Rover, felt his world crack and shatter. He'd lost his career and the love of his life all in one day.

Poisonous emotions spread, filled his blood, a

toxic stew of self-loathing, disappointment, shame, and hurt.

He'd taken a risk, worked up his courage, and told her he loved her and she'd shot him down like a pheasant in the sky. He hadn't felt this kind of pain since . . .

Well, since that Christmas Eve in the hospital twenty years ago when his mother had asked him to play "Stone Free."

That's what he was now. Stone Free. Nothing and no one to hold him back. Nothing and no one to worry about. Sweet freedom.

Except Kristofferson's words from "Me and Bobby McGee" kept running through his head. Freedom *was* just another word for nothing left to lose. He had nothing. No one.

His hands were cold on the steering wheel, icy as a dead man's.

He was weary with himself and the same old issues he'd been battling. The same stupid-ass flaws that had kept him from connecting fully with others. A slick smile. A charming voice. A knack for lyrics. It was all a cover-up for his insecurities. For years, he'd been chewing on them like a toothless old bulldog with a beastly leg bone.

It was way past time he let go of this shit.

Except what would he do without that faded, tattered history to hide behind? What would he do now that he was naked and free and had nothing to cover himself with? Where would he go? Who would he be?

Yeah. Serious question. He did not have an answer to that one.

And Paige? What did he do about her? Did he stay and fight? Try to change her mind? Or did he do the right thing and walk away. Get out of her life before he tainted her.

Because his way of life had already dirtied hers like muddy footprints on a new white sheet. He thought of the paparazzi camped out on her houseboat, ambushing her, plaguing her. Those awful comments on Twitter.

She did not deserve that. He loved her too much to let that continue.

Only one honorable option. Determined to do what needed to be done, Cash turned the Land Rover toward the marina.

It was full dark by the time he arrived.

Most of the paparazzi had scattered, but there were a couple of lowlifes huddled in their cars on the boat ramp, cameras with wide-angle lenses focused on the houseboats.

Cash maneuvered the Land Rover so that it blocked both cars. He got out, slammed the door.

The two men shot out of their cars. One had watermelon-seed eyes, long black hair that looked as if he hadn't washed it in months spilling down his skinny shoulders. A Canon camera on a thick strap around his neck and a skull tattoo peeping from the V-neck of his T-shirt branded with the words "Bad Ass." The other guy was a chubby redheaded hipster with adult acne and Green Lantern suspenders.

They must have thought Cash meant them harm, because Bad Ass swung his camera around on the strap so that it was facing behind him and he doubled up his fists and took on a boxer stance. Ginger raised his arms in the air, white flag gesture. *Don't shoot.*

"Evening, boys," he drawled.

"We're not trespassing," Ginger said. "This is a public boat ramp."

"I'm not here to bust your balls, although I'm sure in your line of work that happens quite often."

Bad Ass shifted his camera back around to the front. "Can we have a picture, Cash?"

"Sure," he said. "If you boys will promise to do me a favor."

Ginger and Bad Ass exchanged nervous glances.

"What's that?" Bad Ass raised his chin, grunted.

"Will you please make it known that Paige Mac-Gregor is not my girlfriend?" he asked.

"What is she, then?" Ginger asked.

"Nothing." Cash shook his head. "She's my neighbor, and her grandmother, who has Alzheimer's, went missing and she asked me to help find her."

"Oh." Ginger looked disappointed. "A good Samaritan story isn't as fun, but I can work with that."

"But you kissed her," Bad Ass said. "It's on video."

"Hey." Cash held his hands wide. "Chicks ask me to kiss them all the time. What's a guy gonna do?"

"So no threesome between you and Paige Mac-Gregor and Simone Bishop?" Ginger's mouth dipped glum.

"Sorry to disappoint, but no."

"I knew he couldn't have been with her." Bad Ass nudged Ginger in the ribs with his elbow. "I mean, come on, look at him. The little chick is plain as white bread."

That pissed Cash off. How dare this scumbag

insult a wonderful woman like Paige? But he held on to his temper. He was trying to accomplish something here. "I'm glad you see why I came to you. I can't have people believing I was with her."

"Gotcha." Bad Ass bobbed his head like a yo-yo.

Cash imagined punching him in his slimy face, and that brought a bit of satisfaction.

"What about Simone?" Ginger said. "That kiss was real, yeah?"

Unlike Paige, Simone courted media attention, and hey, she had kissed him. She knew how to handle herself around the paparazzi.

"Simone and I . . ." Cash nodded, letting the jerks draw their own conclusions. "Well . . . you know."

The two men sniggered like horny teenagers.

"Simone's gone back to California," Cash said. "I'm not seeing Paige, so there's really no reason for you guys to hang around once I let you get a photograph."

"He's got a point," Ginger said.

"What if he's just trying to throw us off track?" Bad Ass fiddled with his camera, removing the telephoto lens.

"To prove I'm on the up-and-up, I'll let you boys have an exclusive before some big news breaks."

Cash turned up the heat on his charmer smile to a roaring boil.

Bad Ass's already tiny eyes narrowed to slits, but he leaned in, clearly hooked. "Why would you do that?"

"I want to leak the news myself instead of leaving it in Sepia's hands," Cash said, reeling him in. "They screwed me over, and I want to get even."

Ginger's eyes popped wide. "Sepia dropped you?"

"They did."

Instantly Ginger and Bad Ass grabbed their phones.

Cash smiled. Mission accomplished. Once these two goofballs got the word out that he'd been ditched by Sepia and Paige was not his love interest, the paparazzi would leave her be. Of course that meant they would be swarming around him for details, still clogging the marina and getting in the way of Paige's life.

That meant he had to get out of the houseboat. ASAP.

Hell, get clean out of Twilight. There was nothing for him here. Sure, he had Emma, but she had her own family, her own life.

He turned to go to the turquoise houseboat, his thoughts on packing up.

"Hey," Bad Ass called.

Cash stopped, turned back. "What?"

Bad Ass and Ginger simultaneously snapped his picture, blinding him in a flash of light.

It was ten-thirty by the time Paige got home from visiting Grammie following the evening performance at the theater.

The Land Rover was not parked in its usual spot and the turquoise houseboat was dark. She'd braced herself to run the gauntlet of paparazzi, but no one was there. Apparently, they'd followed Cash to wherever he'd disappeared. She was old news.

Paige should have been relieved by that; instead, a sense of inexplicable loss dog-piled on top of the other emotions that had been gnawing on her all night—regret, sorrow, hurt. She felt wretched, tense, yearning, and vulnerable.

Once inside her houseboat, she called to Fritzi. When he didn't come running, fear and anxiety seized her. But then she remembered Jesse had taken the dog. She sank down at the kitchen table, turned her phone back on.

Saw three separate text bubbles from Flynn.

The first one read: **Kids R loving dog. Don't worry about picking him up until tomorrow.**

Right after that: **RU OK?**

Around seven P.M. the third message from her cousin had come through: **Check Twitter #Cash-ColtonOnNaughtyList**

Knowing she was going to regret it, Paige checked Twitter, quickly ascertained that yes, the Internet was a dastardly place, where any and everyone's humiliation could become fodder for public ridicule. Perhaps future generations would look back on history and view the dawn of social media as barbaric as the Roman Colosseum and human bloodletting for sport.

In the meantime, Paige found something in that blitzkrieg of voices and opinions that kidnapped her breath.

#CashColtonOnNaughtyList from horse's mouth:
Paige MacGregor nobody to Cash Colton.

The tweet had come from someone with the handle BadAssNewsie. Attached to the post was a photograph of Cash standing on the marina dock.

There was another tweet from BadAssNewsie about Sepia dumping Cash.

Paige's kneejerk reaction was dismay and hurt. She'd broken up with Cash, so he'd lashed out, telling the paparazzi she was nobody to him. But as soon as the thought formed in her head, she knew it wasn't true. Cash was not a vindictive man.

Her heart softened and her breathing eased as she realized Cash had told BadAssNewsie that she was nobody and offered up the Sepia news to shift the attention off her and onto him. That explained why the paparazzi had decamped.

He'd freed her.

A tear slid down her cheek. How she loved that man!

She checked her phone to see if he'd tried to contact her. There were tons of other texts and voice mails. Paige searched through them, looking for anything from Cash. Nothing but the old messages he'd sent before she'd broken up with him.

Fresh sadness washed over her, an ocean of sorrow.

She turned on the Christmas trees to cheer herself up, but they only served to deepen her grief. She watched the lights, ensnared in a melancholy trance as she studied the details of the tree, the lights, the ornaments, the cranking sound of the mechanism that operated a twirling gold star, the sharp, earthy scent of pine and bark, the shine of a red light glinting off silver tinsel. Marinating mindfully in the moment, fully aware that she was orchestrator of her own life. For better or worse, she had created this experience.

How tiny her world had been, how narrow her perspective. Until Cash had come into her life, she'd known little beyond small-town Texas. It occurred to her she was scared of that larger perspective, that expanded worldview he'd opened up to her.

Was that secretly part of the reason she'd broken up with him? Because she lacked the knowledge about the complexities of that bigger life beyond her comfortable borders? Because she was afraid to grab hold of a wilder, bolder happening and run with it? Because, ultimately, she had trouble accepting help? That she believed she had to do everything on her own?

What if she called him? Told him she'd made a mistake? Asked his forgiveness? Told him she loved him too?

Her pulse quickened. *What if, what if, what if?*

Racked with qualms, she turned her attention back to her phone, picked it up with trembling hands.

Let him go to his destiny or call him back?

She was struck with the awful feeling that no matter what she did, it would be wrong. Paige hung on the horns of uncertainty and hope, fingers poised over his speed dial number on the screen.

What to do, what to do? Give me a sign!

Something fell from the back of her phone case, and fluttered to the floor. She leaned over to see what it was.

Simone Bishop's business card.

Paige heaved in a heavy breath. She'd asked for a sign and here it was, and she knew without a shadow of a doubt, no matter how much it hurt, what she had to do next.

* * *

Cash woke the next morning in Emma's spare room. He'd come to her place to crash until he could get his act together and decide where to go from here.

It was almost noon and there was an empty pint bottle of Wild Turkey 101 on the bedside table, confirming what his throbbing headache already told him. Yep, he killed it last night and in a desperate attempt to bury the pain Paige had ripped through him.

Hadn't worked.

He could not stop thinking about her. The image of her face, when she'd told him that he couldn't really be in love with her because he'd idealized her, was embedded deeply in his brain. Her hazel eyes, sensual lips, those damn adorable cinnamon freckles, haunted him. Planted firmly in his cerebral cortex, growing bigger, wilder, and more impractical each passing minute. No expunging that picture.

Or her.

She was imprinted upon him forever.

Cash sat up on the side of the bed, dropping his face into his palms as he waited for the dizziness to pass. How had he managed to screw up the one precious thing he'd ever held in his hands?

His cell phone rang.

The noise blasted through him. He winced, cradled his head.

The phone rang again.

He reached for it, contemplated flinging it against the wall. But what if it was Paige? He cracked open one eye, stared at the screen.

Simone.

He groaned and came within inches of throwing it at the wall, but Emma was a good friend to him. She didn't deserve a hole in her Sheetrock.

Viciously, he punched the ACCEPT button and snarled, "What do you want?"

"Good morning to you too," Simone chirped, cheery as a damn robin.

"Simone, I don't have the—"

"Sympathies over Sepia."

"Did you call to gloat? If so, I'm hanging up right now."

"Don't hang up, Cash."

"Why not?"

"Good news."

"What's that?" he asked suspiciously.

"You have been invited to Apex's Christmas Eve party."

He grunted. "Why?"

"Don't look a gift horse in the mouth. If you want access to the Apex execs, get your ass on a plane to Los Angeles."

Cash hesitated. One part of him was already plotting quick-footed networking, but another part of him whispered, *You really want jump back into the frying pan?*

"Deet pulled strings?"

"No," she said in a crisp, matter-of-fact voice. "I did."

"Why?"

"Do you want this or not?"

"What does Snake think about it?"

"He's on board."

"Even after that little social media flurry?"

"He knows that's bullshit."

"Did he see that picture of you kissing me?"

"Honey, that was *all* publicity." She laughed, a self-assured sound that she knew how to use as a weapon.

"You knew paparazzi were following you?"

"Duh. You didn't really think I was trying to start something up with you again?"

Well, yeah, kinda. "No."

"I'm glad since you didn't kiss me back. How embarrassing would that have been?"

"You enjoy messing with people's heads, don't you, Sim?"

"Listen, come to the party, or don't come. Who cares? I'm hanging up now."

The connection clicked off in his ear.

Now he had a purpose. He might not even want to go with Apex, but it wouldn't hurt to go to the party and schmooze. More importantly, it would keep him from moping around here, pining over Paige.

He got dressed and went into the kitchen where he found Emma baking cookies with Lauren.

"Look who finally decided to roll out of bed," Emma greeted him.

"Is there coffee?" He grunted.

Emma nodded at the single-serving coffeemaker on the far corner of the counter. "We're not big coffee drinkers, especially at noon. Help yourself."

Cash got a mug down from the cupboard, shambled to the coffeemaker.

"You wanna cookie, Unca Cash?" Lauren asked.

He cringed at the high-pitch of her little-girl voice. The last thing he wanted was anything to eat, much less a cookie. The Wild Turkey hangover was telling him food was *not* a good idea.

"I'm good, sweetheart."

"I know you're good." Lauren giggled. She crawled off the stepstool she'd been standing on and came over to hold a cookie up at him. "But I baked it myself, just for you."

He shot a glance at Emma, who raised her eyebrows at him, giving no sympathy at all. "What kind are they?"

Lauren stuck her tongue through the gap where she'd recently lost a tooth, gave him the most beguiling grin. "Your favorite." She stuck the caramel apple cookie up to his mouth and he had no choice but to take a bite. "Matchmaking cookies."

"Matchmaking cookies?" Cash mumbled around a mouthful of cookie. "What are matchmaking cookies?"

"Cookies that make you fall in love, silly." Lauren laughed.

Huh?

Emma looked away, busying herself with measuring flour, but she didn't fool Cash.

He stepped to the cookbook she had open on the counter and sure enough there was a recipe for matchmaker cookies. "What the hell, Em?"

"Ahmm." Lauren slapped a palm over her mouth. "You said a bad word."

"Honey." Emma put a hand to her daughter's back. "Could you go get me apples from the pantry in the garage?"

"Sure, Mommy." Lauren took off after apples.

Cash waggled the half-eaten cookie at her. "You've been feeding me matchmaker cookies? Trying to fix me up with Paige?"

Emma made a face. "Just a bit of fun."

"So you're the cause of my broken heart?" he growled. He didn't really blame Emma, of course, but it felt good to take her to task for her failed attempt at playing matchmaker.

"You two are so good together," Emma said, her shoulders sagging. "I just didn't want to see you mess it up."

"Too late. I already did."

"I know." She sighed. Folded her arms over her chest, leaned her butt against the counter, and faced him.

"Look, Emma, thanks for the room and all, but I just decided I'm going to California as soon as I can get on a plane."

"What? Why?"

"Simone wrangled me an invitation to Apex's Christmas Eve party."

"Oh, Cash, do you think that's a good idea? Is this about Apex or about Simone?" She looked alarmed.

"Simone's not trying to get me back."

"You sure?"

"Pretty sure. She and Snake seem tight."

Emma sighed again, stronger and longer this time. "But Christmas is only five days away."

"There's nothing for me here, Em. After Paige . . ." He shrugged, unable to say anything more on that topic. "If I don't go and make a pitch to Apex, I won't even have my career."

Emma sank her hands on her hips, nostrils flaring. "I have just one thing to say to you right now."

"What's that?"

"If you don't go make things right with Paige before you leave, Cash Henry Colton, you're a damn fool." Then she threw a matchmaker cookie at him and stalked out of the room.

CHAPTER 23

Key: System of notes or tones based on and named after the key note.

Call him a damn fool, but he was in California on Christmas Eve, walking into the swanky Beverly Hills Hotel.

He arrived in the Ferrari that Simone and Snake had rented for him. It had been waiting for him at LAX. And though, no lying, the sports car was fun to drive, for some crazy reason he kept thinking about his first vehicle, an old farm truck given to him by his grandfather as a reward for helping bring in the hay harvest.

Security stopped him before he reached the ballroom where the party was being held, and asked for his credentials. He half expected to be turned back. *Ha-ha joke's on you*, courtesy of Simone.

But no, he was on the list. *This way, Mr. Colton. Welcome to the Beverly Hills Hotel.*

As a musician he'd been to more than his fair share of all kinds of parties, but this had to be one

of the fancier shindigs he'd attended. Simone had
texted him two words about that.

Tux, dude.

He was prepared. He fit right in. Glitterati to the
left of him, glitterati to the right. He was in the big
middle of it all. Shiny. Pretty. Lights. Colors. Open
bar. Ice sculptures. Chocolate fountains. Sports fig-
ures. Actors. Artists. The "in" crowd. Sexy Santa,
ripped physique, only in Hollywood. Live band
onstage. Hottest act currently burning up the pop
charts.

Top of the world. Stuff of teenage wet dreams.
Fantasies come true.

A hundred different conversations. Humming.
Buzzing. Talking, talking, talking. Everyone talking
and no one listening. Lips moving. Teeth flashing.
I. Me. My. Mine.

This was the pinnacle of success?

Glossy.

Slick.

Glib.

Superficial.

He stood in the middle of the room, in an expensive tuxedo, surrounded by the rich and famous, the
hungry and desperate. People everywhere, crowded
in on each other, all vying for top billing. So many
people would give their eyeteeth to change places
with him.

And he'd never in his life felt this degree of lonely.

None of it meant a damn thing without Paige.

"Cash!" Simone's voice cut through the noise. "There you are."

He turned. Relieved to see her in the sea of faces, Snake at her side.

They took one look at each other. Snake held out his arms. Hesitating for only a beat, Cash brought it in, clapped his old buddy and bandmate into a masculine embrace that quickly dissolved into shoulder pounding and feigned fisticuffs.

In that snap of a moment, all was forgiven between them, the past swept away by a friendship that spanned more than a decade.

Cash turned to Simone. "Hey, thank you for wrangling me an invitation to the party. That was nice of you."

"I didn't do it for you." Simone shot him a pitying look that sent his stomach crashing sideways and he had no idea why.

Cash cocked his head, puzzled and sizing her up. "What did you do it for?"

"Several reasons." She offered one of those enigmatic smiles that drove him bonkers. "One, so the three of us could finally mend fences . . ."

Snake nodded. He was on board.

"Two," Simone went on. "I did it for Paige."

"Paige?" Huh? "I don't get it."

Simone shrugged, casual, not really invested. "She asked me to."

"Paige asked you to get me invited to the party?" It still wasn't sinking in.

"She asked me if I could find a way to help your career and the party leaped to mind."

Cash's head whirled. "Why?"

"Why did she ask or why did I agree?"

"Both."

"I agreed because I felt sorry for her. I know what it's like to want your attention and not get it."

"But why did Paige ask you to lure me to LA? Especially if she wants my attention? You'd think the last thing she'd want is for me to go to a party with my ex."

"Who knows? Maybe she's desperately in love with you and she's doing that whole if-you-love-something-set-it-free thing to see if you'll fly back to her of your own accord. Maybe she gets that she can never have you because of that insane belief of yours that love kills creativity. Maybe she wants you as far away from her as she can get so she can start healing. Or hey . . ." Simone lifted her shoulders and her hands. "Maybe the girl just be cray-cray. Wouldn't be the first time you drove a woman nuts."

His stomach, which had already crashed sideways, fell off an embankment and hit the ground with a hard, smashing jolt.

"As to why I agreed to finagle you an invitation? Well, now, champagne is in order," Simone announced, and flagged down a passing waiter. Held up four fingers.

"What are we celebrating?" Cash asked.

"This . . ." Simone motioned for someone in the crowd to come over as the waiter dispensed flutes of champagne.

Deet Sutton joined them, grinning from ear to ear. It felt like old home week as Cash and Deet embraced. It had been more than a year since the four of them had been in the same room together.

"Simone tell you yet?" Deet asked.

Cash looked from Deet to Simone to Snake. They were wearing best-night-of-my-life smiles.

"In the wake of that viral video of you singing 'Danke Schoen' to the old lady . . . how many hits he got now, Sim?" Deet asked Simone.

Simone looked like a cat licking cream off her face. "Ten million in six days."

"Apex sat up and took notice. They've made an offer. *If* you agree to team up with Snake and Simone." Deet went on to name a monetary figure so high Cash blinked.

"What kind of sound are they wanting?" Cash asked.

Deet shifted his weight, but not his smile. "The sound that made you a star in the first place."

That's what Cash figured, more of the same old, same old.

"And they'd like it if you'd grow the hair and beard back."

"You're kidding."

"All right, that last bit's not a deal breaker, just a suggestion. But for the music: stick with what works," Deet said, his voice taking on the quality of steel-toed boots. He repeated Apex's extravagant offer. "Money talks . . ."

"Here we go." Simone raised her champagne flute. "To success!"

Snake and Deet both raised their glasses, looked at Cash expectantly.

Cash held his champagne flute between two fingers, did not lift it. "I need time to think about this."

"What's there to think about?" Simone asked. "It doesn't get any bigger than this, Cash. You've arrived. This is everything you ever wanted. A seven-figure deal with the recording house of your dreams."

With two major strings attached. He had to keep making the same kind of music and he had to work with Simone and Snake.

Been there. Done that.

Did he really want to stagnate?

What would he do if he didn't take the offer? Paige had chopped off their relationship, and he had no idea if his new creative direction, which had come alive because of her, was viable without her.

Forget that. Bigger question. Was *he* viable without her?

But what did he have to offer her? He knew nothing about maintaining long-term relationships. He'd spent his life avoiding them. His entire focus from the time he was ten years old had been music and his career. Who was he without that?

The thoughts that had been plaguing him since Paige told him it was over circled like voracious buzzards.

The ballad of his life's story didn't make sense to him anymore. He thought he was following the script laid out by his mother. *Forsake love and you'll be rewarded with musical success beyond your wildest hopes and dreams.* But lately he kept finding himself plunged into verse and rhyme that he didn't understand. Music of a different genre. Off-beat tempo. Out-of-step rhythm. Ideas that challenged everything he believed were true about the world.

He put the champagne down on a vacant table, shook his head.

"Seriously?" Simone stared at him as if he'd lost his mind, and maybe he had. "You're saying no?"

"I'm saying I need some air."

"I told you he'd flake," Snake mumbled to Simone. "The man talks a good game but he can't run it into the end zone."

"What the hell, Colton?" Deet snorted. "I flew to LA to put this deal together."

Cash walked away. Stalked out of the room. Almost ran down the hall, past security, to the lobby. His heart was a hammer in his chest, pounding with a righteous beat.

"Cash! Cash Colton, is that you?"

At the sound of the familiar voice, Cash stopped in his tracks.

There stood Freddie Frank, a living legend in the business. On his arm was Maxi, his wife of forty years.

After Cash's first big hit, they'd had a falling-out over Cash's rootless lifestyle and partying ways. Freddie feared he would end up like Lorena. Cash's feelings had been hurt and he'd told him off. Later, Freddie had reached out to him to mend fences, but Cash, busy with his burgeoning career, hadn't bothered to call him back. When Cash got over his upset and was ready to apologize for lashing out, too much time had slipped by, so he'd just let the relationship go.

Freddie held his arms wide, and Cash, feeling

warmed by the smile of a man who wanted absolutely nothing from him, walked into his embrace.

"I'll just go powder my nose," Maxi said, slipping away from her husband. "Give you two boys a chance to catch up without the old ball and chain horning in."

Freddie pulled Maxi in for a long, romantic kiss before letting her go. As she walked away, Freddie's gaze lit on her. "Forty years," he said. "And she's just as beautiful to me as the day I spied her on the city bus in Nashville."

An image of Paige in her Santa Baby costume popped into his head, and Cash found himself grinning as wide as Freddie.

"Damn, I've missed you," Freddie said.

"I've missed you too." Cash swallowed hard. "I'm so sorry I—"

"Pah." Freddie waved a congenial hand. "Water under the bridge. I get it. No worries. I don't hold grudges. Life's too short."

"Thank you," Cash said, his heart filling with gratitude for Freddie's acceptance. "Thank you."

"So what's shaking?" Freddie asked, clasping Cash on the shoulder and guiding him to a sofa in the lobby. "Rumor had it you were in South America."

"I was. Peru. Been back almost a month."

"You got rid of all the hair," Freddie noted.

Cash shrugged. "I needed a radical change."

"Sorry about Simone and the band."

"Don't be. It was for the best."

"Life generally works out for the best on its own if we can get out of the way and let it happen."

He couldn't believe he'd run into Freddie Frank of all people at the Apex Christmas Eve party. Freddie and Maxi were more homebodies than gala-goers.

"Why are you here?" Cash asked. "Aren't you usually with your kids on Christmas Eve?"

"We are," Freddie said. "But the kids are here, all six of them. And they aren't kids anymore. There's even three grandbabies too. They're already inside. Maxi and I were running late. We were . . ." A naughty expression crossed his face. "Never mind about that."

"What's the occasion?"

Freddie waved a dismissive hand. "I'm getting some kind of old fart award. I don't care about the damn thing, but the kids insisted, so here we are. I'm glad too. Otherwise I wouldn't have gotten to see you. So tell me, Cash, what's going on in your world?"

Looking into the face of his old friend, Cash found himself telling Freddie everything. Opening up completely. About Paige. The ups and downs in his career. The regrets he felt over the way he treated his grandparents as a rebellious teen, and his regret over not returning Freddie's phone calls.

When he finished, Freddie chuckled.

"What's funny?" Cash asked, slightly miffed that Freddie laughed. Hell, he'd just spilled his guts.

"Well, for one, rest assured that your grandparents forgave you completely. They loved you, Cash. They understood."

"You think so?"

"I know so. Your granddaddy and I had a long talk about it. Why do you think I took you under my wing in the first place? I promised Hank I'd look out for you. Folks from small towns do that for each other. It's why they call it a community."

"Why didn't you say anything before?"

"I did try to tell you, but you never listened. Or you couldn't hear it," Freddie said sagely. "Your grandparents would have been so proud of you. I hope you know that."

"Thanks for telling me." Cash stroked his chin. "That makes me feel better."

"As for the talent thing . . . look at me. Do you think I'm any more talented than you are?"

"What? You're Freddie Frank," Cash said.

"But I'm no more talented than you. It could be argued I'm even less talented than you are. I only had the one sound, but it was *my* sound, and people seemed to love it. I was always true to myself."

"If I stay true to myself . . ." Cash leaned forward as if by getting closer to Freddie he could soak up his wisdom. "I'm walking away from the deal of a lifetime."

"A lucrative deal with the devil is still a deal with the devil."

"Are you saying Apex is the devil?"

"I'm not being literal. I'm asking if a deal involving Simone and Snake will come back to devil you?" Freddie paused, letting that sink in. "Only you can answer that question."

"But I'd be walking away from millions."

Freddie shrugged as if money was inconsequential. "C'mon, Cash. You've done well for yourself. How much money do you need? How many cars can you drive? How big does a house really need to be? Once you have a roof over your head, clothes on your back, and food in your belly, all you really need to be successful is gratitude."

This was precisely what he needed to hear. "And what about Paige? How can I hold on to her and still have a career?"

Maxi came over and Freddie drew her onto his lap. She wrapped her arms around her husband's neck. He gazed at his wife with adoring eyes. "The proof is in the pudding. Maxi and I have loved each other for forty years. Do you think that held back my career any?"

"Hey, I made your career, buddy." Maxi giggled.

"You are my muse." Freddie nuzzled her neck.

"Okay, okay, enough with the elder love." Cash held up his palms in surrender.

"Look at that, sweetie." Maxi pulled Freddie in for a long, deep kiss. "The poor boy is jealous."

He *was* jealous! Cash wanted this. Wanted what Freddie and Maxi had, a love that would last a lifetime. He hopped up off the couch.

"Where you going?" Freddie asked. "Aren't you going to stick around and watch me get that silly old fart award?"

"Sorry," Cash said. "There's a woman in Texas who doesn't even know she's waiting on me."

Maxi and Freddie gave him simultaneous thumbs-up, and said in unison, "Go get her!"

CHAPTER 24

Finale: Movement or passage that concludes the musical composition.

Enthusiastic, but off-key, carolers sang at the top of their lungs, clutching songbooks and beaming at the residents gathered in the nursing home cafeteria.

It was four P.M. on Christmas Day. A week after Paige broke up with Cash.

The MacGregor clan had spent the day at Flynn and Jesse's house. A day filled with fun, food, and family. But Grammie had wanted to get back to her home for the Christmas program. And Paige, since she had neither children nor a significant other, had volunteered to take her.

Paige sat beside Grammie, who was clapping her hands in time to the music, and tried not to think about Cash.

Failed.

Even with her eyes open, she kept seeing his handsome face. He was carved deep into her memory, deep into her heart. She missed him more than she ever thought possible. Missed the sound of his voice. Missed the touch of his hands. Missed the heat of his mouth on hers.

Many times over the course of the past week she'd almost called or texted him. Told him she loved him too. Asked him to come home.

Home.

Twilight wasn't his home. He had no home. He was a rolling stone. And that was part of the problem, wasn't it? He didn't know how to be still, settled, satisfied.

Sending him on his way had been the right thing. The smart thing. The mature thing. The thing that hurt the most.

She sighed.

Grammie reached over and patted her hand, whispered, "It's going to be okay."

"What is?"

"Love always wins," she said. "Sometimes it doesn't look or feel like we think it should, but it *always* wins."

"Thanks, Grammie," she said, hoping that was true. Maybe one day she would get her happily-ever-after, although right now the odds weren't looking too good.

"Shh." Grammie giggled. "Wanna know the real reason I wanted to come back to the home early?"

"Why's that?"

"Wayne Newton. He's coming to see me." Grammie swiveled in her chair, looked toward the door.

Oh boy, here we go again. "Grammie, are you getting one of your bubbles?"

"No." Grammie frowned. "I'm telling you, Wayne

called me last night and told me he would be here this afternoon."

"Grammie, don't get your hopes up. Wayne's pretty busy this time of—"

"There he is!" Grammie waved.

Paige turned.

Cash Colton walked through the door singing, "Danke Schoen."

"Wayne! Yoo-hoo, over here!" Grammie stood up.

The carolers onstage looked confused. They glanced at each other, and then looked back at Cash, who was walking up the middle of the make-shift aisle formed by folding metal chairs and wheelchairs.

The lead singer gave an if-you-can't-beat-'em-join-'em shrug, nodded at the other singers, who broke into "Danke Schoen."

Paige stood up, feeling both hot and cold at the same time. What was he doing here?

Cash came toward them, his gaze locked on hers, thanking her in German.

Her heart was a butterfly, fluttering, flittering. He was ten steps away from where she was standing beside Grammie. Nine. Eight. The closer he got, the higher her heart flew.

Seven. Six. Five.

Cash stopped, standing right in front of her, still singing. His eyes glued to hers.

"Go to him," Grammie whispered urgently.

"He came to see you," Paige muttered from the corner of her mouth.

Grammie nudged her in the butt with her cane. "No, he didn't. He's *your* Wayne."

"Paige," he said. "I have a Christmas present for you."

"You came back to Twilight to give me a Christmas present."

"Among other reasons." He pulled an envelope from his pocket, handed it to her.

She opened the letter. Read what was inside. It was from the owner of the building on the square that was for sale, accepting Cash's cash offer and agreeing to put the title in Paige's name.

"What's this?" she asked, her knees bobbling. She grasped the back of a nearby chair to keep from toppling over.

"I want you to be a dancer. To teach dancing. Do what you love. I'm giving you the building. Whether you take me back or not. The building is yours. I decided to buy it for you last week, before . . . well . . . I want you to have it."

"But I can't accept this, it's too much."

"Paige," he chided. "Letting people help you is not a sign of weakness."

"I—"

"Have too much pride. It's okay to accept help. When you let someone help you, you're actually giving them the gift of showing you love them when they don't know how else to show it."

"I haven't earned it. I . . . ." Her throat was so clotted with emotion she could barely speak.

"You deserve something good in your life."

It was too overwhelming. She couldn't take it all in.

Cash knelt in front of her.

Holy cheetah! Paige's heart took the express elevator to heaven.

The carolers stopped singing. The room fell silent. Everyone—the carolers, the elderly residents, and staff members—all leaned in closer.

"What are you doing?" Paige asked, slightly horrified that he was doing this in front of an audience.

"Groveling." He looked up at her, took her trembling hand. "Paige, I'm begging you, please give me another chance."

"Please get up," she said, tugging on his hands.

Instead of pulling him up, he ended up dragging her to her knees in front of him.

"I'm embarrassed," she hissed.

"I know."

"Is that why you're doing this? To embarrass me?"

"Not at all. I'm doing it so I have witnesses."

"Witnesses?" She gulped.

"Paige Hyacinth MacGregor, I love you."

"You told me this before."

"I'm telling you again," he chided softly.

"Do we have to go over this a second time?" She didn't think she had the courage to send him away again.

"We do, because clearly you did not hear me the first time." His hands were hot on her skin. "Paige, I love you. I love you more than I love myself. I would give up my very life for you and that includes my creative life. If having you means I could never play music again, so be it. I choose *you*. All the time. Every time. No exception."

"Why would you have to choose?"

"To prove it's *you* I love. It's not just because I hear music whenever I'm around you. It's not just for the way I feel when I'm around you. It's you, Paige. You're my world. My beloved. My everything."

"How do you know?" she whispered, hardly daring to believe this was true. That he really did love her fully, completely, unconditionally, the same way she loved him.

"I love the way you dance with total abandon when you think no one is watching. I love how you put your heart and soul into everything you do. I love those cinnamon freckles on the bridge of your nose. With you, I've found the home I never knew I'd been searching for."

Paige was so focused on Cash and his dear sweet face she forgot about the people surrounding them, forgot about everything but the look in his eyes. Love poured from him, vibrated off him.

"But what about your career?"

"Apex offered me a huge contract if I'd team up with Simone and Snake and keep playing the same old music that I've always played and I turned them down."

"Wh-why?"

"Because I want to move forward with my life. I've changed and grown and I want my career to reflect it."

"But . . ." She bit her bottom lip. What if he'd done this all for her and his career tanked? She couldn't be responsible for that. "What if your indie career doesn't take off?"

"Then maybe you'd rent out the top part of your building to me and I could teach music. It would be a good combo. Song and dance."

"Are you sure this is what you truly want?"

"I've never been more certain of anything in my life. There is one important thing missing." He gulped and she noticed for the first time his hands were trembling too.

"What's that?"

"I love you like crazy, Paige. But do *you* love *me*?"

"Oh, Cash." She breathed. "You silly man. You had me at 'Santa Baby.' I love you so hard I ache."

"I know that feeling." He wriggled his eyebrows. "Wanna get out of here and do something about soothing that ache?"

"You sure took your time getting around to that."

He laughed, scooped her into his arms, cradled her against him, and got to his feet as wild applause erupted around them. They went back to her houseboat, where they made love long and slow as they shared the merriest Christmas ever.

And in the morning when Cash went to walk Fritzi, he found a basket of caramel apple cookies wrapped in big bow sitting beside the front door, with a note that said, *Welcome home.*

Epilogue

Coda: Closing section of a movement.

December 1, one year later

"I told you cookies would work." Emma smiled at Flynn. "As long as you follow the rules, the matchmaker cookies never fail."

"You were so right." Flynn sighed happily as she watched Cash and Paige glide across the floor in their first dance as Mr. and Mrs. Colton. "They are freaking adorable together."

"I admit it was touch and go there for a while," Emma said. "When Paige found out what we'd been up to with the cookies."

Flynn nodded. "We almost blew it."

"Lesson learned," Emma said. "*Never* be forthcoming about matchmaking."

"So should we mix up another batch of matchmaker cookies this Christmas?" Emma grinned wickedly.

"I thought you'd never ask." Flynn raised her champagne glass. "To love."

Emma clinked her glass with Flynn's. "To love. Who shall we bake the cookies for this time?"

"My little brother Joel is heartbroken after his girlfriend chose her career over him." Flynn took a worn copy of *The First Love Cookie Club Cookbook* from her purse, turned to the dog-eared page. "But the rules state to only serve the cookies after all other methods have been exhausted. Joel might not be ready for matchmaker cookies just yet."

"You know who's been single for years and has been looking mighty lonely lately?" Emma said.

"Who?"

Emma leaned over and whispered in Flynn's ear.

Flynn's eyes brightened. "Oh, Emma, you're so right, and I know who would be absolutely perfect for her. Let's head to the liquor store for a bottle of cinnamon bourbon and get started right away. With any luck, this time next year there will be another wedding in Twilight."

FROM THE RECIPE BOOK OF
THE FIRST LOVE COOKIE CLUB

Contributed by Sarah Collier Walker
from the reclaimed files of Gramma Mia

MATCHMAKER COOKIES

Warning! Matchmaker Cookies are serious business. Baking them is not to be undertaken lightly. They can have a powerful impact on the lives of those who consume them. Matchmaker Cookies may cause people to fall hopelessly in love with the object of their deepest desires.

Important!

Rules for the baking, use, and consumption of Matchmaker Cookies should be followed to the letter.

The Rules

These are Matchmaker Cookies. You're the matchmaker helping others find their way on the path to love. Don't make them for yourself. If you need help in the love department, get a friend to bake for you.

Set an intention when mixing and baking these cookies. For example: if the person you're helping is frustrated by the pace of love, bake a batch with the intention that their true love will find them in a timely manner.

These cookies are potent. Keep them out of the reach of children and serve them only to individuals who are not already in a romantic relationship.

Try not to meddle too much. Serve Matchmaker Cookies when all other methods have failed, then get out of the way and let love take its course.

Be very careful to whom you serve Matchmaker Cookies. The lovers' future is in your hands.

INGREDIENTS
1 cup unsalted butter, softened
1 cup light brown sugar
$\frac{1}{2}$ cup granulated sugar
1 egg and 1 egg yolk, room temperature
2 tsp cinnamon bourbon (May substitute vanilla extract, but if vanilla is used forgo an intention because cookies will no longer have matchmaking qualities. At this point, they may safely be consumed for yumminess purposes by anyone, including children and married couples.)
$\frac{1}{2}$ tsp salt
$\frac{1}{2}$ tsp baking powder
$\frac{1}{2}$ tsp baking soda
3 $\frac{1}{4}$ cups cake flour
$\frac{1}{2}$ cup thinly slivered almonds
$\frac{1}{2}$ cup dried apples, diced fine
$\frac{1}{2}$ cup caramel bits for baking

INSTRUCTIONS
In the bowl of a stand mixer fitted with a paddle attachment, beat the sugar and butter until light and fluffy.

Add the eggs one at a time, and beat after each

addition. Add bourbon (or vanilla extract) and beat to incorporate.

In another bowl, whisk together the dry ingredients.

With the mixer on Slow, add the dry ingredients into batter. Scrape down the bowl as needed and mix thoroughly.

Fold in slivered almonds, diced apples, and caramel bits.

Allow the dough to cool in the refrigerator for at least an hour.

Preheat oven to 350 degrees.

With a tablespoon, round mounds of dough on a cookie sheet lined with parchment paper.

Bake for 11–14 minutes until the bottoms look lightly browned (edges should not brown). Serve immediately to the lovelorn in your vicinity. Prepare for fireworks.